Storm Constantine's Wra

Scatterstones

A Story of the Gimrah Tribe

Fiona Lane

IMMANION
PRESS
Stafford, England

Storm Constantine's Wraeththu Mythos

Scatterstones

Contents

The History of Wraeththu
A Newcomer's Guide

Storm Constantine

I want all novels set within the Wraeththu Mythos to be accessible to everyone, whether or not they have read any of the preceding books and stories. This introduction gives readers new to the Mythos an overview of the Wraeththu world and how it's evolved, and I hope it will also be of interest to long-standing fans. (A glossary is also provided at the end of the book listing Wraeththu terms used in this novel.)

The world of Wraeththu first appeared in print in 1987, with the publication of *The Enchantments of Flesh and Spirit*, which was the initial volume in the trilogy *The Wraeththu Chronicles*, but I'd written stories about these beings since I was a teenager. The book – when published – was described as 'groundbreaking' because of genre taboos it challenged. The book opened up new territory for genre fiction. *Enchantments* was followed by the final two installments of the trilogy: *The Bewitchments of Love and Hate* (1988) and *The Fulfilments of Fate and Desire* (1989). The books were published by Macdonald in the UK and TOR in America.

Wraeththu sprung from the ruins of human civilisation after humankind all but destroyed its own environment. Wraeththu (known as hara) are androgynous – having both male and female physical aspects. Their sexuality is a source of power, an ability to transcend mundane reality as well as being an extremely spiritual practice.

While androgynes had been seen in science fiction and – more rarely – fantasy before, they had never been explored in such a way as I sought to explore them. Hara have a deep connection with what we term magic and are more powerful in many respects than humans. Warriors and sorcerers, farmers and diplomats; familiar roles perhaps, but robed in very different forms.

Initially, hara were created through a mutation; Wraeththu blood could transform a human into a har. Once they became established, they were able to breed, (in fact had to learn how to do so), and a new generation of 'pure born' rather than incepted hara was created.

Other aspects that set the books apart from typical fantasy was that their environment was influenced heavily by the alternative music scene of the 1980s and 90s, as well as by paganism, which was becoming more acceptable in mainstream society as an alternative spirituality. Hara were flamboyant peacocks and fierce urban shamans, evolving from feral tribes of the disaffected young of humankind. When the books were first published, these were not characters typically found in fantasy fiction.

In the initial trilogy, I explored the questions that interested me: were Wraeththu the world's revenge on its savage, selfish children, or were they perhaps the outcome of a scientific experiment, designed to save the human race, that had gone wrong?

From the very start, something within Wraeththu – perhaps my own love of that world and its inhabitants – captured the hearts of many fans, who remained loyal to it, even when for over fifteen years I didn't write any new Wraeththu stories. Fans kept it alive through fan fiction – creating their own stories set within the Mythos.

Throughout the 90s and 2000s, Wraeththu's fandom continued to grow and thrive. I returned to writing within the Mythos with the publication of *The Wraiths of Will and Pleasure* in 2003, (the first of *The Wraeththu Histories*), followed by *The Shades of Time and Memory* (2004) and *The Ghosts of Blood and Innocence* (2005). I've since written a third trilogy – the Alba Sulh sequence, which comprises *The Hienama*, (2005) *Student of Kyme* (2008) and *The Moonshawl* (2014), a stand-alone triptych of novellas entitled *Blood, the Phoenix and a Rose* (2016) and two collections of short stories *A Raven Bound with Lilies* (2017) and *Songs to Earth and Sky: Stories of the Seasons* (2017), the latter written with several other Mythos writers.

The first Wraeththu shared world novel was *Breeding Discontent*, by Wendy Darling and Bridgette Parker (2003). This was followed by five other books, written by Victoria Copus, Maria J Leel and E.S. Wynn. Immanion Press has also published several short story anthologies edited by Wendy Darling and me. Details of all Mythos titles can be found at the end of this book.

I feel it's important nowadays to mention that within the Wraeththu Mythos, hara are referred to as 'he', since back in the 1980s when I first started writing within the mythos, this pronoun seemed to me less gender specific than 'she'. A lot has changed in both culture and language since then, but to glue a new pronoun over all the stories would feel at best clunky and contrived. I ask readers to look beyond the loaded meaning of the male pronoun, and to read it as non-gender specific.

'*Scatterstones*' is the latest Wraeththu Mythos novel, set in a country visited fairly briefly by a few of my characters in *The Fulfilments of Fate and Desire*. Gimrah is part of Jaddayoth, a collection of provinces in what was once north-eastern Europe and beyond. Gimrah is also the tribal name of the hara who live there. The story in this book takes place in the area that was once the inland border of Romania and Bulgaria, with the Carpathian Mountains to the north. The Gimrah are known as the Horse Hara, renowned for the magnificent horses they breed. Their farms and settlements, known as *estembles*, are scattered throughout the Steppeland, although the harish population is far lower than the human population of the past. There are swathes of wild, remote land, where only horses and other animals roam.

At the *estemble* named Scatterstones, a foal is born, and Hanu, one of the *eskevi* who care for the horses, knows it's different to any other. Simultaneously, the hara of Scatterstones undergo a tragedy – but what was its cause? The story that follows solves the mystery and reveals an unimaginable threat.

Scatterstones is a tale spiced with excitement and danger. But at its heart is Hanu and the horse he names Tezuk. It is the story of their growth as har and horse, and their relationship as outsiders within their own kind.

Fiona Lane has written several stories for the 'Para' Wraeththu mythos anthologies and brings as usual her deft touch to this novel. There is humour and wry observation of life, but also warmth and thoughtfulness about how we all struggle to 'become', to find our place in the world and comfort within our own skins.

Chapter I
Hanu

Hanu was in a hurry that morning, so he did not stop to have his customary conversation with the Aghama. Instead, he hurried past clutching an awkward assortment of his belongings, with a bread roll clamped between his teeth in lieu of breakfast, and a determined look on his face: he promised that he would be back later to pay his respects.

The Aghama did not reply, which was not unusual, but merely stood as he had always done, rearing up on his hind legs, his mane and tail flowing in the imaginary wind and his forelegs pawing the air triumphantly.

The statue of the Aghama stood in the centre of the Eithak, the central meeting hall of the community of Scatterstones which had been Hanu's home for the whole of his short life. It was cast in bronze and was perfect in every detail, recreating in dark, gleaming metal each line and contour of the most magnificent horse imaginable. Hanu could not remember a time when its commanding presence had not presided over Scatterstones, promising health and fertility to the horses born there, and security and protection to its hara. The statue had been a gift from a renowned Ferike sculptor in gratitude for the skills of the Gimranish horse-hara of Scatterstones who had saved the life of his favourite mare when she'd been struck down by a mystery ailment.

It had become a custom among hara to touch the back-left hoof of the statue to invite good fortune upon themselves. Repeated contact with these superstitious fingers had left the metal on this particular spot bright and shiny, in contrast with the dark hue of the rest of the statue. Hanu was no exception to this ritual – if anything he was more dedicated to it than most, visiting the statue every morning to rub the golden hoof. He would conduct, in his head, an imaginary conversation with the Aghama, in which the First Wraeththu congratulated him on his knowledge of horse-lore and skills in the management of the horses in the breeding stables, and advised him on the best course of action to improve his prospects further.

It was normally the first thing Hanu did every day before commencing his work – even before Nirzhen had a chance to give him his list of tasks for the day, and deploy the rather pained expression he kept especially for lazy hara when Hanu confessed to all the assignments left uncompleted from the day before – and the fact that he had abandoned his morning ritual for once could only mean that something even more important was on his mind. That something was Ishin, one of the mares in the breeding stables, who was due to foal quite shortly.

Hanu was a horse-har of the Gimrah, one of the twelve tribes who occupied the lands east of Almagabra. Each tribe pursued their own unique way of life – the Ferike in the lands to the west of Gimrah were scholars and artists living in their high castles among the green forests, the Elhmen and Sahale pursued a strange, mystical existence based on the principles of fire and water, and the Maudrah, who occupied the neighbouring lands on the eastern border of Gimrah, lived a rule-bound and ascetic life under a religious elite. But the Gimrah were the horse-hara.

Not for the Gimrah the great cities and palaces built by other tribes, with their imposing houses and clean, well-planned streets, and by-laws and conventions and all the suffocating, soul-destroying imprisonment that city life represented. The Gimrah lived in small villages, called estembles, built on the open plains. These were collections of low, modest buildings fashioned in harmony with the natural landscape, where hara could live their lives dedicated to their one true passion – horses.

Horses were important to Wraeththu civilisation. They provided transport and power, from the lowliest estembles and farms and villages across Jaddayoth, all the way to mighty Immanion itself, the great city of the Gelaming in Almagabra, and far-off Megalithica. In return for this gift of service, the Gimrah dedicated themselves to nurturing and protecting all horses. Through carefully supervised breeding programs they produced horses of the finest quality, free from flaws or weaknesses.

Gimranish horses were much sought after by other Wraeththu tribes, and the Gimrah took great pride in the horses they sold. Competition between estembles was fierce; each one's reputation rested on the quality of the horses produced by the breeding stables; therefore competition was equally fierce amongst the hara to be chosen to work in the stables.

It was, of course, no shame for a har to be employed in any of the other areas of work – the managing of livestock, the growing of crops, the manufacture of goods – which were necessary to keep the estemble running and keep the hara who lived there clothed and fed. Hanu had enormous respect for each and every one of these hara, (especially at dinner time), but since he had been a small harling he'd wanted nothing more than to work in the breeding stables and to spend his days tending to the magnificent creatures there. He had studied horse-lore, learned to ride, and to be one with the horse. He had learned about saddles and harnesses and grooming and cleaning and horse-ailments and remedies and horse psychology and everything under the sun pertaining to horses, and shortly after his feybraiha his dedication had been rewarded when he was chosen to serve as an undergroom – an *eskev* – to Nirzhen.

This was the lowliest position in the stables. The eskevi were under the supervision of the anskevi – the overgrooms – of which Nirzhen was one, who in turn reported directly to the Tirtha, the leader of the community. But Hanu did not care. He was a horse-har, and that was all that mattered.

After working in the stables for three seasons, Hanu had at last been given responsibility to supervise a foaling. Ishin was the first mare he'd worked with in that respect and he was taking the responsibility very seriously, determined to show that he was equal to the task. He had decided he would move his sleeping quarters into the stables next to Ishin for the next few days or weeks, or however long it took for the foal to arrive. Now, he was why hauling his bundle of bedding, clothes and personal effects from his small room in the eskevi lodgings to the hayloft directly over Ishin's stall, which he had determined would be the perfect place to keep a constant eye on her.

As he headed towards the stables, he was so intent upon this scheme that he completely failed to notice the other har who waved to him in greeting and shouted his name. Hanu trundled straight past him without any acknowledgement of his presence whatsoever. The har stood with his hands on his hips for a few seconds, shaking his head with disbelief, then he raced after the speedily retreating Hanu to catch up.

Intent upon managing his bundle and thinking about Ishin, Hanu did not notice the har until he felt a tap on his shoulder and a poke in his ribs. He looked round, annoyed, and barely caught the last part of the har's indignant question.

"...this time in the morning?"

"What?" Hanu disentangled himself from his preoccupied thoughts and with some difficulty focussed his attention on his assailant.

"I *said*," the har said, moving ahead of him and turning to face him, so that he was performing a sort of awkward backwards jog, "where are you going in such a rush at this time in the morning? I was expecting you to be in the Eithak. Have you had breakfast yet? I haven't. I'm starving!"

The har came to a stop – requiring Hanu to do likewise – and rested his hands on his knees breathing out theatrically, as if he was breathless from his modest exertions. He grinned at Hanu. "Has Ishin had her foal yet? Is that why you're sprinting off to the stables?"

"I'm not sprinting, and no, she hasn't, but I need to be there in case anything happens."

The har waved his hand dismissively. "Oh Hanu! You worry too much! She'll be fine. She's had two foals already; she knows what she's doing."

Which is more than I do, Hanu thought gloomily, but he gave a half-smile anyway. Tiski was not a har overly beset with worries. While Hanu might rehearse in his head all the potential disasters that might befall a har or a horse during the course of the day, Tiski's default outlook assumed that everything good that could possibly happen *would* happen, and, annoyingly, he was more often proved right than wrong.

Even Nirzhen's grumbles could not dent Tiski's optimism. Hanu sometimes wished he could be blessed with the same degree of careless certainty that all would be well, but apparently it was his lot in life to be the one who always prepared for the worst.

"Just because everything went OK the last time doesn't mean it will this time. You know what Nirzhen says."

Tiski pulled a face of mock-horror at the mention of Nirzhen's famously doomy predictions, and Hanu tried not to laugh.

"Anyway," he continued, "I'm going to move into the stables until the foal is born. In the hayloft, above Ishin's stall."

"The hayloft!" Tiski shuddered. "Rather you than me! There are spiders up there, you know. Great big ones!" He made suggestive wriggling movements with all his fingers to illustrate the horrors of the spiders in the hayloft.

"No there aren't, and spiders are harmless anyway."

"You won't be saying that when one drops into your mouth while you're asleep," Tiski told him smugly, as if that settled the argument in his favour.

Hanu rolled his eyes but said nothing.

"Well, if you'd rather have breakfast with the spiders than me, that's fine," Tiski said, with a melodramatic sigh. "I'm not disappointed or feeling rejected or anything. Not at all. I'll just go and eat my way through an enormous pile of griddle cakes all by myself. Not that I'm trying to make you feel guilty or anything. Although, if you do, you could always meet me for lunch, and I might forgive you. See you then! Give my love to the spiders!"

Tiski laughed and loped off back down the path, waving to Hanu as he went, his long tail of hair flicking vigorously behind him as if it possessed a life of its own.

Hanu sighed and shook his head, but he could not suppress a smile. He and Tiski had both started work as eskevi at the same time and had formed the natural alliance of newcomers. Hanu found the other har's cheerful personality a useful antidote for his own rather more pessimistic nature, especially when it came to the frequent doubts he harboured about whether he was truly good enough to be an eskev.

Hanu arrived at the stables where, despite the early hour, the morning activity had already begun. A few eskevi were fetching water and hay and mucking out stables and cleaning harnesses until the brass decorations on them gleamed as bright as the Aghama's golden hoof. Nirzhen was nowhere to be seen, so Hanu made directly for hayloft above the stall where Ishin was currently housed. It was one of the foaling stalls, larger than an ordinary stall in order to allow a mare to lie down while giving birth, and to accommodate her offspring afterwards, so there was plenty of room for both the hay and Hanu and his belongings in the loft above.

He hauled all his stuff up the ladder, dropping a few things once or twice and having to climb all the way down again to fetch them, muttering a few improper profanities under his breath as he did so. But finally his possessions were all relocated and the hay-bales rearranged to form a snug den where he arranged his belongings; a bedroll and a couple of cushions, some spare clothing, a hair-brush, some perfumed salve for skin rendered dry and cracked by the constant gripping of leather reins, and an extra blanket, because the nights were still cold despite the fact that Bloomtide was fast approaching.

Hidden among the jumble of clothing was a small circlet of rainbow-coloured ribbons, with an embossed medallion bearing the image of a horse's head in the centre. The metal was slightly tarnished, and the ribbons a little creased, but Hanu would not be parted from it. It was the prize for coming first in The Ride – a race at Scatterstones in which young hara and their horses competed to complete a circuit of the whole estemble, including the growing fields and meadows at the far side. Winning this race had ensured that Hanu could become an eskev, as that honour was always offered to the winner.

Hanu's desire to work in the stables had only ever been equalled by his fear that many – or, perhaps, all – of the young hara his age were more qualified than him. More adept at riding, smarter, stronger, quicker to learn – just *better*. No matter how often his father and hostling had assured him that he was every bit as good as any other young har, the doubt had nagged at him. He had done everything he could to try to outperform the others, worked as hard as he could, and when that had failed, he had sought divine intervention.

He had prayed to the Goddess, the Great Mare herself, but this had seemed disrespectful, to ask the Spirit of All Things to turn her attention, even momentarily, from the mighty task of overseeing the fate of the entire universe towards the affairs of one rather insignificant har. So he had prayed to the Aghama, which had seemed less impolite – for had not the Aghama himself once been a har of flesh and blood, and would thus know something of the passions and desires which burned within mortal hearts?

Apparently he did, for as Hanu had stood in front of the statue in the Eithak and asked the Aghama for advice, the Aghama had reminded him of The Ride, for which Hanu had thanked him, and Hanu continued to thank him daily after the race had been won, in acknowledgement of his debt.

Satisfied that his new lodgings were in order, he began his descent back down the ladder, but halfway down a familiar voice caused him to freeze.

"Hanu. There you are. I've been looking for you. You do realise what time it is? Get down here. I need to talk to you."

Hanu slunk guiltily down the rest of the ladder. It was scarcely a heartbeat past his official starting time – the sun was not even over the horizon yet – but Nirzhen expected his eskevi to perform their duties to the utmost of their abilities and took a dim view of latecomers.

Hanu did not actually mind this. He loved working in the stables and would spend even more time there if he could; it was the prospect of facing Nirzhen's disapproval that he didn't enjoy.

He jumped down the last two rungs of the ladder and stood in front of Nirzhen, looking and feeling sheepish. Nirzhen stood with his arms folded across his chest, inspecting Hanu intently, as if all his inner flaws were revealed in his outer appearance

Nirzhen's own outer appearance was of a har of smallish stature, with his dark, curly hair imprisoned in strict braids down his back. A few tendrils of this hair always managed to escape and frame his round moon-face with soft ringlets, giving him a mild and unthreatening appearance. This countenance bespoke of Nirzhen's character in the same way that the delicate, dew-glistening flowers of the carnivorous plants which grew in the nearby bogs lied to the doomed insects which flew into their sticky embrace.

"Where have you been?" Nirzhen demanded. "You haven't cleaned out Ishin's stall yet, and Miran's water bucket is almost empty. And where is Tiski? I haven't seen him yet today."

"Oh, I saw him earlier," Hanu said, hoping that Nirzhen's unerring instinct for detecting lies didn't extend to mere evasion.

Faint hope. Nirzhen tapped his foot. "Not in the stables, though? No, I thought not. Well, send him to see me when he does show up eventually. We've got a lot to do today. The Tirtha is coming for a formal inspection tomorrow, and I want everything to be perfect. In fact, I want it to be *better* than perfect, by some considerable margin. Do you understand?"

Hanu nodded his head vigorously, hoping that Nirzhen would interpret this as both his boundless enthusiasm for and prodigious capability in the job of scrubbing every last atom of horse excrement from the stables. The Tirtha could be found in and around the stables most days, and a bit of dung never seemed to bother him – he was a Gimrah har, after all – but Hanu was not going to argue with Nirzhen.

Nirzhen gave a curt nod in return and swiftly continued on his way to cross-examine the next luckless eskev on his list. Hanu let out his breath, which he realised he had been holding. He supposed that he really could not blame Nirzhen for being anxious about the Tirtha's inspection, as Merac, the Tirtha, was Nirzhen's superior in the same way that Nirzhen was Hanu's, although Hanu doubted that Nirzhen had ever stood fumbling in front of Merac trying to explain his shortcomings in the way that Hanu constantly found himself doing with Nirzhen. Merac was not that sort of Tirtha. And Nirzhen was not that sort of anskev.

As Tirtha, Merac was the ruler and leader of the community of Scatterstones. The title and position had been bequeathed to him by his hostling, and before that his high-hostling and in due course his younger son, Ren would also become Tirtha upon Merac's death. Merac had an older son, too, Velisan, but to honour the Goddess, the title of Tirtha passed down through the hostling line, and Velisan's pearl had been hosted by Merac's consort, Nithevan. Hanu liked Velisan – he was an exuberant har, with impressive riding skills, and had graciously answered Hanu's shy questions on horse-handling on many occasions. His brother, Ren, was quieter and more introverted, and Hanu had never quite felt comfortable enough to approach him with his trivial queries.

All the other Gimrah estembles had their own Tirtha too – there was no single, overall tribal leader, and every Tirtha was the equal of the rest, yet it was unofficially acknowledged that some Tirthas were more equal than others. Merac was held in the highest esteem, not only by the other Tirthas, but by the leaders of the other tribes – the Ferike, the Maudrah, the Kalamah, and – most importantly – the Gelaming. His knowledge of horses and horse-lore was unsurpassed in Jaddayoth and beyond, and his dedication to the care and well-being of his animals was unquestionable. Merac would refuse to sell a horse to a har he considered unsuitable, however wealthy or high-ranking that har might be. Stories were told of a time when he had once travelled to the far reaches of Garridan to reclaim some mares from a local Phylarch, because news had reached him they were being ill-treated, much to that worthy's displeasure.

Hanu was proud that his estemble and its Tirtha held such a

notable position among the Gimrah, and if scrubbing the stables from top to bottom would earn him Merac's approval then he was more than happy to do it. He grabbed a bucket and broom and pushed open the half-door into Ishin's stall, calling out a greeting to the mare as he did so.

Ishin turned round to see him, carelessly dropping a mouthful of hay on the floor of the stall. She nickered in friendly recognition, and Hanu could feel her thoughts – pleasure at seeing him, anticipation of treats and grooming to come, coupled with her discomfort in the late stage of pregnancy and a desire for the foal within her to be born.

"Soon, Ishin, soon." Hanu smiled and patted the mare's neck. Ishin lowered her head, and he dutifully scratched behind her ears, knowing that was a spot where she particularly enjoyed attention.

He ran her hands along her flanks, and over her now huge, swollen belly. Only a few weeks ago, he had been able to make out the occasional shape of a tiny hoof or hock moving underneath Ishin's skin as the foal twisted and turned within its watery enclosure, but now it was too large to move around much, although he could still feel its outline if he prodded and poked. Careful assessment by Nirzhen had assured him that the foal was in the correct position to be born now, and that everything should go smoothly, but the thought of what was to come still made him anxious.

Ishin, named for the west wind, was a sweet-tempered mare and a favourite of Hanu's. This would be her third foal. Hanu had been with her when she was mated to the stallion Torem late last spring, and he had watched over her carefully for the past year as her belly grew in size.

Ishin's last foal had sold for an exceptionally large sum of money to one of the leaders of the Hadassah tribe, who occupied the lands to the north east of Gimrah. This was not surprising – Ishin's pedigree, as kept written in the Great Ledger of the Tirtha, was flawless. It detailed her sire and dam, and her grandsires and grand-dams, and many more generations of horses bred by the Gimrah to be the very best of their kind. Torem, too, could trace his bloodline back through generations of faultless mares and stallions, so it seemed only natural to Hanu that her soon-to-be-born foal would be special. A magnificent creature destined to fetch a dazzling price at one of the major horse fairs from one of

Jaddayoth's highest-ranking hara, and to spread the fame of Scatterstones and its horses far and wide.

Hanu knew that he would devote himself equally to any foal under his care, regardless of its prospects. It was his duty as a horse-har, and he could do no less, but he felt a strong connection to Ishin's unborn foal and he felt impelled to keep a close eye on her, despite the fact that the foal was not due for a while yet. Mares usually gave birth during the dark hours of the night – a throwback to their wild ancestors who had to conceal themselves and their vulnerable young from predators. All the mares in the Tirtha's stables were, of course, entirely safe from such threats, but sometimes the birth was not straightforward – the foal was in the wrong position, or stuck, or there was bleeding – and assistance was required from the hara present

Hanu had yet to see a mare die during the birthing process, but Nirzhen had related to him – with a little too much relish, or so it appeared to Hanu – gruesome tales of terrible events he had witnessed, the better to educate his young apprentice in the less pleasant aspects of his calling. These stories had left an impression on Hanu, as he suspected they were meant to, and he found himself becoming more and more anxious as the date for Ishin's delivery drew nearer, arriving at the stables earlier each morning and returning later in the evening to check on her. Ishin herself remained calm and imperturbable, even as Hanu grew more agitated, and her soft brown eyes would regard him with patient amusement as he poked and prodded her swollen flanks, and consulted both books and auguries trying to determine if the foal was ready to be born.

With a sigh, Hanu took his broom and began sweeping out Ishin's stall, while Ishin herself looked on with interest. He worked hard all morning, and by the time Nirzhen reluctantly allowed the eskevi a break for lunch; the stables were positively gleaming. Hanu bolted down his food, as he was eager to get on to the next part of his day. This was the favourite part of his duties – leading a small group of young horses out for exercise. None of them were old enough to be ridden yet, so Hanu would ride one of the older horses who could be relied upon to chaperone the youthful colts and fillies.

Kavel was a steady brown gelding, now in his elder years, who had never had much of a turn of speed to him even in his youth, but Hanu didn't mind. A horse was a horse, and there was nothing a Gimrah har loved more than to be astride a horse and riding, with the wind in his hair.

Riding along with him was Tiski, with his own band of unruly youngsters to herd. For this run, Tiski was riding on Nuviak, an elegant bay mare named for the first light of the day, with a glossy coat and sweeping black mane and tail, who picked up her dainty hooves high with each stride as if to announce her beauty to the world. Nuviak probably thought it was beneath her to be shepherding two-year olds about, but she obviously enjoyed the attention she was getting, from horses and hara alike.

The same could be said for her rider. Hanu did not know how Tiski had managed to claim Nuviak as his mount for the day – the eskevi were supposed to take whatever horse was given to them when working – but suspected it had something to do with subterfuge, bribery and possibly outright blackmail. If so, he could only salute Tiski's ingenuity when it came to securing a sneaky ride on a more elegant and frisky mount

Tiski rode up to him, Nuviak tossing her mane and prancing like the equine prima donna she was.

Hanu grinned. "I thought you were going to ride Bozim," he said. Bozim was a grumpy piebald gelding whose only talent was for stealing other horses' food, and whose ever-widening girth was testament to this.

Tiski wrinkled his perfect nose. "Bozim is out of sorts," he said. "He ate too many green apples. The aftermath was disgusting, and Nirzhen doesn't want him making any more mess, just when we've got the stables cleaned, so he's in confinement for now."

"You were late this morning," Hanu said, "And Nirzhen noticed."

"Nirzhen notices *everything,*" Tiski said with a sigh, and Hanu nodded in sympathetic agreement.

"Did you get a lecture?" Hanu asked, even though that was a foregone conclusion.

"Yes," said Tiski. "But I explained to him that my highfather had detained me with an errand, and I pouted a bit, and I was let off with a *stern stare.*" He grinned, and shook back his long tail of hair, rather as Nuviak was in the habit of doing.

"Don't you ever worry that you'll get found out if you lie?"

19

Hanu enquired, slightly troubled by Tiski's offhand dismissal of the morning's events.

Tiski was having none of it though. "I never worry about anything!" he declared "What Nirzhen doesn't know won't harm him."

"Nirzhen says that the Aghama sees everything."

"The Aghama must be bored out of his mind then – most hara aren't doing anything worth seeing at all. Unless you count that particularly *unusual* type of aruna that got Shalmik into trouble last Smoketide – I'm sure even the Aghama would have enjoyed that!"

"Tiski!"

Tiski laughed uproariously. "Don't worry, Hanu. If the Aghama ever confronts me with my sins, I'll just pout a bit and look pretty, and I'm sure he'll forgive me. Everyhar else does – even you!"

Tiski gave Hanu his most winsome smile, and Hanu found he had to agree with his friend's assessment, in spite of himself. Hanu wished he had Tiski's way with words, and his easy charm, instead of his own inarticulate stutterings and clumsy comments. It seemed unfair that Tiski had all of these gifts and more, and Hanu had so little.

"Perhaps," said Tiski, leaning back in the saddle dreamily, "I will meet the Aghama in the form of a beautiful young har, running through the grain fields at Cuttingtide, and he will be entranced by my loveliness and grant me all my wishes. Or maybe just three. I don't mind. Three would do. I'm not greedy. Or perhaps he will be the white horse of winter and ensure my fertility. If I can see him, of course – white is good camouflage against the snow. Wily Aghama! But as the dark horse of summer – ah, that is his best form, don't you think, Hanu?"

"That's why we have that statue of him in the Eithak." Hanu said, distantly, looking out across the empty fields and imagining them filled with new foals in the summer. "Nirzhen says he takes the form of the dark horse to protect us."

"Protect us from what?" Tiski asked, giving Nuviak a slight tug on the reins to prevent her from straying off towards a particularly delectable-looking clump of wild garlic. "A horde of marauding Mojags bent on pillaging and singing vulgar songs about it afterwards? The Kalamah sneering at our aesthetic choices?"

"From ourselves, I think."

"Or spiders." Tiski leaned over towards Hanu and gave him a disapproving look. "Are you sure you're not reconsidering your plan to sleep in the stables, Hanu? Won't you be thinking of your lovely warm bed in the lodgings tonight?"

"No," said Hanu stoutly, "The beds in the lodgings are hard, and the stable will be warm enough."

Tiski shrugged. "You do like to make things hard for yourself Hanu," he said. "Come on, let's get this lot back to the stables – the *lovely, warm* stables – it looks like it's going to rain. Or worse. And I don't think Nuvie will like getting wet."

The dark clouds on the horizon confirmed Tiski's words. Hanu and Tiski directed the young horses back toward the stables. Not all of them were eager to go, but a swift nip on the rump from Nuviak, who knew what the darkening skies meant, was enough to persuade them to follow. By the time they reached the stable yard, fat drops of icy cold rain were starting to fall, and there was a rush to get all the horses inside. When they were done, Hanu stood there dripping and shivering, much to the amusement of Tiski who had somehow managed to escape the downpour, and stood there looking as immaculate as ever, laughing at Hanu.

"Oh Hanu! What a state you're in! Here..." Tiski threw Hanu an old towel used for rubbing down the horses.

Hanu sniffed but took it anyway and rubbed his hair fiercely to dry it, making it stand up on end.

"Best start getting used to roughing it. No luxuries for you, Hanu! I intend to have a nice hot bath this evening, in preparation for the Tirtha's inspection tomorrow. I will be scented and delightful, and he will be drawn to my allure. As I stand there among the rest of the exceptionally un-alluring eskevi, our eyes will meet and he will draw me forward and say 'Tiski, this is no place for a har of your quality, let me take you away from all this and make you an anskev and give you a beautiful Faraldienne of your very own to ride'!"

Hanu threw the towel back at Tiski with a grimace. "Tiski, you are so full of horse-shit it would take an entire army of eskevi a month to dispose of it all."

Tiski giggled and clutched at his chest in mock anguish. "Ooh, I am wounded, Hanu! You are so cruel to me!"

"It's for your own good, you know that."

"Nonsense, you just enjoy it! Now don't forget to fetch more straw from the long barn. Nirzhen will not be pleased if we don't have it ready and waiting first thing tomorrow.

At the mention of Nirzhen's name, Hanu made a face. "I'll see if I can fit it in with the hundred and one other things he's got planned for me," he said, sighing in resignation.

"Splendid! Well, if I don't see you later, have a good night. Give my love to the spiders!"

After Tiski had gone, Hanu set about the rest of his tasks, hoping that he could get most of them finished before the end of the day. By the time dusk fell, he was aching all over, but pleased with his efforts. Before retiring for the night, he paid one last visit to Ishin, who was still standing patiently in her stall. He stroked her soft nose, and blew up her nostrils, which she liked, said goodnight to her, then climbed up the ladder to his makeshift bedroom in the hayloft.

It was dark up there, and he only had one small lantern, so could barely see anything, but he arranged his blankets and cushions as best he could, and snuggled down beneath them. Outside, he could hear hail rattling on the shingles of the roof, but his little nest was quite cosy. Despite the dark, and the strange shadows cast by the lantern, he did not feel afraid. He was not alone. Down below, Ishin dozed in her stall, and all around were the sounds of the other horses – the stamping and shuffling of hooves, the occasional snort, the smell of their warm bodies rising up to envelop him in a feeling of security.

He turned to extinguish his lantern, and from the darkness of the roof above, a small, black spider abseiled down in front of his nose. Hanu watched the tiny creature in fascination for a few moments, intrigued by its alienness, and its abundance of legs. Then with a smile he caught its silken lifeline on his finger and transferred it to safety on the other side of his bed.

Within a very short space of time he was asleep. He dreamt of a dark horse galloping, long spindly legs, and black birds flying overhead. In his dreams he thought it must be an omen, of sorts, but of what he did not know.

Chapter 2
Tezuk

The next morning Hanu awoke early, to the sounds of activity already going on in the stables below. He crawled from his bedding, found a clean shirt among his pile of clothes and pulled it over his head. Then he slid quickly down the ladder to see what was going on.

The morning was chilly, and Hanu soon wished he had brought some warmer clothes with him. He made a mental note to return to his room in the lodgings later that day, after the inspection was done, to collect something thick and woolly. Before all that, his first business of the day was to check on Ishin.

He unlatched the door to Ishin's stall and entered. As he did so, his heart seemed to squeeze to a stop within his chest, because Ishin was not standing quietly at the back of the stall as was her habit, but was lying down on the straw, her head towards Hanu. He immediately thought the worst, but his fear lasted only a second as the mare scrambled easily to her feet, and there was a rush of something wet, and something solid, and as Hanu stood there transfixed she turned around to reveal a foal standing behind her.

Standing.

Hanu could not believe it. The foal was just born, of that he was sure. The straw was wet with amniotic fluid and the birth membranes still clung to the foal. It was important that a newborn stand as soon as possible after birth – in the wild, it would need to follow its mother and follow the herd and be able to walk and run almost from the moment of birth – but it usually took about an hour before the newborn was on its feet. A shorter time, perhaps, if it was a strong foal, but Hanu had never heard of one standing within seconds of its birth.

He moved slowly toward the foal, not wanting to alarm Ishin. Mares could be unpredictable with a new foal to protect, and even the most placid could turn uncharacteristically aggressive. But Ishin merely stood there quietly, watching Hanu with her calm brown eyes as if nothing out of the ordinary had occurred.

Hanu stretched out his hand slowly toward the foal, half expecting it to back away, but it stood steady, its long legs planted firmly, neither trembling nor looking as if they might give way at any moment, which was often the case with newborn foals. Very cautiously, Hanu eased past the unperturbed Ishin, who was now nibbling daintily at a few strands of sweet hay, until he could get a good look at the foal.

It was a colt; he could see that. Dark all over. It was impossible to tell at the moment the exact colour of the coat, damp as it still was, but there were no markings or variations of colour. The short mane and tail matched the coat in hue. Dark. A dark horse for summer.

Hanu could only marvel at the perfection of the new creature before him. He had seen newborn foals before – often they were almost comical-looking with their too-long, spindly legs and uncoordinated movements. Sometimes they were thin and weak and exhausted from the trauma of being born. But this one – there was something about him that Hanu had never seen in a newborn foal before. An air of confidence. Strength.

The foal took a step forward – his first – and did not stumble or falter. Hanu watched as the muscles and bones and joints moved under the dark coat in perfect co-ordination, as if the foal had done this many times before. The lines of the colt's body reminded him of the statue in the Eithak – an immaculate representation of a horse, without flaw or fault.

Surely, Hanu thought, *if the Aghama were to take on the form of horse in the earthly realm, it would be a foal like this. Perhaps even this very foal.* And immediately he felt guilty for even thinking such a thing, but the blasphemous thought would not be stilled. He thought again of the statue that the foal so resembled. How could it be co-incidence? The spirit of the Aghama was in every horse, and sometimes that spirit became tangible, corporeal. Why not here? Why not now? If there was a need for protection from some as yet unheralded danger, then surely the First Wraeththu, the protector of all harakind, would know of this and offer his guardianship

A rustle behind him alerted him to the fact that Ishin had now decided to take an interest in her offspring, and he moved judiciously to one side of the stall, allowing the mare to begin the cleaning process, licking to remove the birthing fluids and membranes. The foal began nuzzling at Ishin's flanks, searching for the warm milk he instinctively knew would be there. As he did so, his hind quarters turned towards Hanu and Hanu noticed for the first time that he was not completely dark. Not quite. Above his left hind hoof there was the thinnest line of white hair, and the hoof itself…

For a moment, Hanu's heart seemed to stop beating, just has it had when he had entered the stall and seen Ishin lying on the straw, but this time there was no sudden release of tension, no instant relief. Instead a cold wave seemed to run down his entire body, from the top of his head, his face, his heart and stomach, his legs, and then out through his feet, which seemed glued to the stable floor. Because the foal had three perfect little black hooves, but the back left was a pale, golden brown.

Hanu forced himself to breathe, as it appeared he had forgotten that he was supposed to do so. It seemed impossible, but there it was. A single, golden hoof. Just like the statue. It was not unheard of for a horse to have one hoof of a different shade to the rest, but for it to appear in exactly this form was almost unbelievable.

An omen. Hanu remembered his dream, and now ascribed to it more meaning than he had previously thought.

While he was still struggling to process this new discovery, noises came from outside the stall, and then the door swung open. Two hara entered, chatting amiably to each other, in the way that hara who have known each other for a lifetime do. It was Nirzhen, and with him Merac, the Tirtha. Following slightly behind them was Merac's son, Ren.

Hanu was so stunned by the events of the past few minutes, and now by the unexpected appearance of both Nirzhen and the Tirtha, that he could say nothing at all. Fortunately for him, Nirzhen seemed not to notice his discomfiture. He took in the scene in the foaling stall – Ishin, the new foal and Hanu hovering closely by – and a rare smile appeared on his face.

"Well done, Hanu," he said, clapping Hanu on the back in a congratulatory fashion, as if it had been Hanu himself who had given birth to the foal. Hanu still found himself floundering without words. It was obvious that Nirzhen thought that he had played a significant part in the delivery of the foal, rather than just walking in at an opportune moment. While he felt slightly awkward at receiving unearned praise, now did not seem an appropriate time to fully disclose the circumstances of the foal's birth, not with the Tirtha himself standing there, looking on approvingly.

"Ishin has had her foal," Nirzhen announced proudly, if unnecessarily, to Merac. "She wasn't due for a week or so yet, but you know mares, they give birth when they're ready to do so."

"As they should," Merac said, edging past Nirzhen to get a better look at the new arrival. As he did so, Ishin gave a brief whinny of recognition, and Merac smiled and stroked the mare's nose.

"Well done, Ishin," he said. "Another fine foal. I chose well for you, didn't I? Only the best for the finest mare in the estemble."

Ishin nuzzled his hand and blew gently through her nostrils. Merac rubbed her nose affectionately.

"I rode your great-great grandsire for many years," he told the mare. "He was a fine stallion, and we went to many places and did many things together. I still miss him, my old friend, but his sons and daughters, and their sons and daughters, too, have brought great good fortune to Scatterstones. And now you have given us this new wonder." Merac turned to look at the foal, who was eyeing him warily. The Tirtha reached out a hand to stroke the foal as he had his dam, but the foal's head jerked back and his nostrils flared. His small hooves stamped the straw beneath them. The Tirtha laughed.

"He has spirit, this one. He will be a great asset to Scatterstones." Merac lowered his hand and regarded the foal with a practised eye. "And what, I wonder, are we to call you, little one?"

He turned to look at Hanu, and Hanu felt the colour rising in his cheeks. He was not used to being addressed directly by the Tirtha. He was only an eskev and the Tirtha was the most important har in the estemble. The Tirtha's word was law. He settled disputes between hara, issued decrees and edicts to facilitate the smooth running of the estemble and collaborated with the Tirthas of the other estembles to ensure the safety and well-being of the whole Gimrah tribe. More importantly still, it was the Tirtha who kept the records of each horse's pedigree in the Great Ledger, who knew each horse individually, who decided which stallion would mate with which mare, and who decided which ones would *not* pass their genes on to a new generation.

Merac regarded Hanu solemnly. He was tall, for a Gimrah har, with dark hair into which was woven long strands of horsehair, such that it was not possible to tell where his own hair left off and the horsehair began; it was braided up intricately above his head, giving him the appearance of possessing even greater height.

"You were the first to see him," Merac told Hanu, "You must name him." He looked directly at Hanu as he said these words, to emphasise their importance. Like all hara, Merac bore no signs of physical age upon his face, but to look upon him was to know that there was a lifetime of experience and knowledge contained within.

Hanu swallowed hard but could only manage a nod. He knew it was his duty. A horse was given its name by the first har to see it born into the light, and naming a horse was no small responsibility. Names were important, for horse as much as har, for they carried the symbolism not only of what the bearer was, but what they would become. It was important to find a horse's true name, and not burden them with something which did not match their temperament or inner nature.

Some horses were named for the day in which they were born – the brightness of the sun, or the gentle rain. Some were named for the plants which grew all around in the season of their birth. Some were named for the sounds of the landscape – the whisper of the wind, the running of water across stones. Some were named for an intangible quality, which only the har bestowing the name could see.

Hanu had never named a horse before. He had seen foals born, but the naming of them had always fallen to the anskev present, either Nirzhen or one of the others. Only now did he realise what a difficult thing it was. Both Merac and Nirzhen looked at him expectantly, the Tirtha's dark eyes seeming to bore into him without mercy. Even Ishin seemed to be waiting impatiently for his announcement.

His throat became dry, and his mind was a blank, except for one thing. But he knew he could not give that name; it was not his to give.

He looked again at the foal, with his dark coat and strong legs, and his one, golden hoof, and when he spoke at last, he was relieved that his voice did not break, but sounded calm and clear. "I name him Tezuk," he said. "For his strength."

For he did not dare say the word that was in his head.

Merac nodded in approval, as did Nirzhen, and Hanu was relieved that he had not embarrassed himself with his choice.

"A fine name for a fine colt. It will be written in the Great Ledger by myself today. You will have charge of this colt, Hanu, and raise him. You will teach him what it means to be a har, and he will teach you what it means to be a horse. The har and the horse. The horse and the har. Together. Always be kind. Always be patient. You cannot train a horse through fear or pain. It is a sacred duty for a Gimrah har to care for a horse and to be *his* har. Never abuse this trust. You will forge a bond that will last for both your lifetimes, wherever your paths take you, together or apart, even though the horse's life will be shorter than yours. You were with him when he drew his first breath, and you will be with him in spirit till his last, and he with you. I have all faith and confidence in you, Hanu, that you will be the best har for this horse."

Merac smiled gently at him, and for a moment Hanu could not speak. He felt his eyes swimming with tears that threatened to betray him, but he conquered his emotion and managed to stammer a reply to Merac. "Thank you. I will not let you down, Tiahaar. You, or Tezuk."

"And your first duty to your new charge is to clean up this mess," Nirzhen said, indicating the soiled straw on the floor of the stall, and for once Hanu was glad of his brusque manner; it made everything feel normal and safe again.

Merac turned to his son, who was standing behind him taking only a cursory interest in the proceedings.

"Ren, perhaps you could arrange to have the feeding schedule amended to ensure that Ishin is getting the correct nutrition?"

Ren looked surprised at being spoken to. He was a hesitant har who didn't share Merac's air of calm authority; there seemed something lacking about him. "I did that last week," he said, sounding defensive.

"Yes, but now Ishin has foaled she will need a different diet. Mares who are producing milk need extra nutrients. You should have let Sarun know in advance so that he could have had the extra feed brought in for her."

Ren scowled and kicked at a lump of straw on the floor peevishly. "How was I supposed to know she'd have the foal early?"

"You need to be prepared for these things. Mares don't always give birth on schedule."

"Well if you don't like the way I do things, perhaps you should just do them yourself!"

Hanu was shocked to hear Ren say this. A har should not speak to the Tirtha this way, even if the Tirtha was his hostling. In fact, a har should not speak to his hostling this way, even if he wasn't the Tirtha! Hanu glanced worriedly at Nirzhen to see if he would say anything – the anskev famously took a dim view of disrespect – but Nirzhen's face remained impassive, and he merely stood with his hands clasped behind his back, waiting.

Merac sighed patiently. "I'm sure you'll manage perfectly well, Ren. Now, come along, we've got the rest of the west stables to inspect before noon, and I want you to see how the two-year olds are getting on. Nirzhen?"

Merac favoured Hanu with one last, brief smile and left the stall, followed by Nirzhen and Ren, leaving Hanu alone with Tezuk and Ishin, who by now seemed thoroughly bored with the whole proceedings. Hanu still felt slightly uncomfortable at Ren's outburst, but then he became aware of the soft touch of Ishin's thoughts, indicating that she would like some of the sweet roots he habitually kept about him. She deserved a reward for producing such a handsome foal. A smile crept over Hanu's face as he reached into his pocket to grant her wish, enjoying the mare's pleasure vicariously and dismissing the earlier unpleasantness from his mind.

Ishin had licked the foal dry, and his coat was now rough and shaggy, though Hanu knew that in a few months' time he would be as sleek as his dam. It was not possible to say exactly what colour he would be until the fuzzy outer coat was shed, but a foal who was dark at birth usually stayed dark.

Hanu cautiously reached out his hand to the foal. "Tezuk," he said. "You are Tezuk."

Tezuk did not stretch his nose inquisitively towards the hand, like most foals would. Instead, he eyed Hanu suspiciously and flicked his short tail.

"Who are you, then? If you are not Tezuk?" Hanu whispered to him. But there was no response from the foal, no creeping, inveigling mind touch sending out its tendrils to make contact with Hanu, telling him what he wanted to know.

Sighing, Hanu set about clearing up the stall, disposing of the evidence of the birthing process, the membranes and the remains of the bloody placenta. He knew he had been lucky with this, his first foaling. Birth and death could often be inseparable twins. The Goddess gave life, but she could take it away too, as if there were some cosmic scale that needed balancing, as if there were only so much life available, and a gain somewhere meant a loss somewhere else.

Tezuk ignored him and began butting Ishin's sides vigorously, demanding milk. Hanu was pleased to see this, as it was a good sign the foal was normal. Some foals were reluctant to nurse, and had to be given milk from a bucket, which was a messy process. Ishin was patient with the foal's first, fumbling attempts. She had the calm demeanour of a mare experienced with the process of giving birth and raising a foal, and Hanu found her steadiness reassuring

"We'll take good care of him, you and me, won't we?" he said, stroking Ishin affectionately. He moved a little too close to the mare's rear quarters and was rewarded by a strong kick from one sharp, bright little hoof belonging to the foal.

"Ow!" he complained, rubbing his knee, then laughed. Not an hour old, and the foal was already living up to his name.

"You need to learn not to do that," Hanu told him, "If you are going to grow up to be the best horse in Scatterstones."

The foal paid no attention to his lecture, so Hanu picked up his bucket and left Tezuk and Ishin in the stall getting know each other, while he searched for Tiski outside to tell him the good news.

Tezuk grew strong and fast. At a week old, he could already follow Ishin all the way down to the lower paddock and back without tiring. At two months old, he could leap skittishly over the small pile of logs in the corner of the field that were used to train the two-year olds to jump. At six months, he could outrun the other foals born that spring. As a yearling, he was taller and broader than all the other colts, and as two-year old he was a magnificent, handsome stallion in the making, dark as a starless sky, coat like oiled silk, his hooves hard and shiny – three black, and one golden brown.

He was also headstrong and fierce and would bite and kick without hesitation. Hanu took the brunt of this in his early months, when the foal's teeth and hooves were not quite so damaging, but as he grew older, and the bruises got larger, Hanu learned to anticipate the horse's actions and step aside at the crucial moment.

The same was not true for the other eskevi, who soon learned to avoid Tezuk altogether. Hanu did not mind this, as it meant he spent more time with Tezuk himself, and besides, he was sure that with careful handling from just the one, sympathetic eskev, the colt would gradually become more even-tempered.

In response to complaints about Tezuk's behaviour, Hanu would point out his extraordinary resemblance to the statue in the Eithak, more as a way of distracting attention from his aggressive actions than anything else. The other eskevi agreed that Tezuk was a highly unusual horse. They did not make it sound like a compliment.

In private, Hanu consoled himself with the thought that, if indeed the Aghama were to take the form of a horse, he *would* be a highly unusual horse – it would be ridiculous to think otherwise. There must be a reason for such behaviour, since ordinary horses neither looked nor behaved like Tezuk.

On one occasion, Tezuk aimed a kick at Merac, and only missed because a lifetime's experience with horses of all temperaments alerted the Tirtha to the impending attack. Hanu did not know whether to be mortified or relieved. At any rate, he felt somewhat comforted by the fact that Tezuk did not discriminate between the highest and the lowest when it came to expressing his dissatisfaction.

Nirzhen did not interfere in Hanu's handling of Tezuk – he simply told Hanu to be careful and offered advice on how to approach a nervous or aggressive horse, for which Hanu was grateful. He noticed that Nirzhen allowed him more time with Tezuk than he did the other eskevi with their colts and did not rush him to complete the stall-cleaning and move on to some other work immediately.

Hanu was fiercely proud of the young horse, but sometimes he wished that he could have been given a less headstrong colt to raise. He watched as the other eskevi worked with their charges and felt the occasional twinge of envy when their colts and fillies would come when called, tails high, eager to greet their harish friends. Tezuk would not come when called. Hanu was not sure that he even knew his name, for all the solemnity with which Hanu had chosen it for him.

He consoled himself with the thought that he had been given a unique challenge, and an opportunity to better his skills as a horse-har. He daydreamed that, after years of hard work and intense effort on his part, he would succeed in training Tezuk to be the most intelligent and well-schooled horse in the whole of Gimrah. His fame as a horse trainer would spread across the whole of Jaddayoth, and he and Tezuk would travel the lands together, using his knowledge and skills to magically transform difficult horses into well-disciplined steeds. Hanu would be bountifully rewarded for this by grateful Archons and Phylarchs everywhere.

More often than not, these pleasant reveries were interrupted by an attempted kick or bite from Tezuk, as if the horse were cautioning him not to let his fantasies get the upper hand, and with a sigh Hanu would return to the task in hand, leaving the glowing future he had conjured to reside only in his imagination.

Chapter 3
Savax

Compared with most of Jaddayoth, life in Scatterstones was peaceful. It was situated in the west of Gimrah, close to the mountains that formed the border with Ferike, and the Ferike were a serene and philosophical tribe, who were uninterested in conquest or invasion. The same could not be said of a number of the other Jaddayothian tribes.

There were twelve tribes who inhabited the Jaddayoth region. Some, like the Gimrah, lived in open and equitable societies, welcoming anyhar who was prepared to work for his living. Others like the Elhmen lived strange and secret lives, full of mystery and magic, barely interacting at all with their neighbours, and being the subject of much rumour and conjecture. To the north-east the Gimranish territory was surrounded on three sides by the Elhmen, the Hadassah and the Maudrah. Disputes between these tribes were not uncommon and often spilled messily across their neighbours' borders.

In other parts of Jaddayoth, hostilities were more direct. The Maudrah and the Natawni tribes maintained a mutual loathing of one another, and away to the east, the fearsome Mojags seemed intent upon extending their own territory at the expense of every other tribe in the area. A sensible har feared the Mojag, but feared the Garridan even more, as their methods, though less direct than the Mojag's, were just as deadly in the long run, if not more so. The names of their cities – *Nightshade, Hemlock* – gave a clue to their area of expertise, and a prudent har would *very politely* refuse to partake of any food or drink offered by a member of that tribe. To bring some semblance of order to this chaotic situation, the Gelaming had intervened and set fixed borders between the tribal lands. They had established the Confederation of Tribes, bringing together all the tribes of Jaddayoth under one banner and promoting peaceful relations between them. The outcome of this was to successfully unite the tribes in their mistrust and dislike of the Gelaming.

The Gelaming were Wraeththu's most powerful tribe, both in

military strength and in the psychic abilities that defined Wraeththukind. Among their ranks were many high caste hara – Nahir-Nuri and beyond – and their ability to work with and channel energies through their will meant that there was little the tribes of Jaddayoth could do but accept the situation. This was done with more enthusiasm by some than others, as many suspected, not without cause, that Gelaming rule would put an end to some of their more *interesting* tribal customs.

Despite the grumblings, the initiation of the Confederation of Tribes was generally a good thing for most ordinary hara of Jaddayoth, bringing a degree of stability to the area, which had been sorely lacking before.

The Gimrah, for their part, could see the benefit of inter-tribal cooperation in Jaddayoth bringing peace and security. They were not a warlike or expansionist tribe themselves, preferring to devote their lives to the breeding of horses, and like every other tribe, the Gelaming had a need for good quality horses. So the relationship between both tribes was mutually beneficial, even if a few of the Tirthas grumbled that the Gelaming, as always, had the better part of the bargain.

The Gelaming occupied the lands to the west of Jaddayoth, beyond even Ferike, known as Almagabra. Few hara from Jaddayoth had ever travelled that far, and fewer still had ever reached the fabled city of Immanion, for the Gelaming protected their homeland jealously. They claimed that this was a purely altruistic measure, as too close contact with a more advanced society might interfere with those tribes' natural development. The tribes whose natural development was the subject of such touching concern claimed a number of other things, not all of which reflected well upon the Gelaming. Nevertheless, stories of the magnificence of that city abounded from those who claimed to have seen it – reports of soaring towers and exotic hanging gardens, and jewel-encrusted palaces in the sky. How much of this was actually true was open to debate, but the rumours persisted.

For his part, Hanu could not imagine living in such a place. In the heart of a city, you would have to breathe the same air as countless other hara. The buildings would rise so high they'd blot out the sun, and the ground beneath your feet would be cold marble rather than soft grass and warm earth. It seemed utterly foreign to him, and the creatures who inhabited it even more so.

Hanu was familiar with at least one of these unearthly beings, because there was a particular Gelaming who was a regular visitor to Scatterstones. His name was Gavax har Gelaming, and he was an emissary appointed by the Gelaming administration to oversee the implementation of their plans regarding the Confederation of Tribes.

Gavax apparently found it expedient to maintain his presence in Jaddayoth under the auspices of the Gimrah, rather than risk too close contact with some of the less welcoming tribes, and it was considered an honour that he chose to do so. If he was aware of the dark mutterings from some that this was a gift the Gimrah were powerless to refuse, then he ignored these calumnies with the graciousness for which his tribe was famed.

Gavax was a striking figure. Effortlessly elegant and beautiful, his hair was the golden hue of the corn fields at the moment of perfect ripeness. His clothing was made of a lustrous fabric, almost translucent in its fineness. He was tall, compared to the average Gimranish har, and he strolled around the rough cobbled roads of Scatterstones as if he were floating through the marble halls of Immanion itself. It was impossible to be unaware of his presence.

Hanu was working in the stable yard that morning, grooming Lohish, an attractive and high-spirited three-year old, named for the waves on the water's edge, which was a fitting name for him as he liked nothing better than lying down in the mud on the banks of the river and rolling in it until his bright chestnut coat was completely hidden beneath a layer of dirt. Hanu had been given the task of cleaning him up, and the more mud he washed off Lohish, the more seemed to attach itself to Hanu.

Lohish was feeling particularly pleased with himself – he enjoyed the vigorous grooming sessions which followed a successful roll in the mud almost as much as he enjoyed the mud bath itself – and he performed a skittish little dance as Hanu tugged at his matted tail, knocking over a bucket full of dirty water in the process.

Hanu called Lohish a name which the horse fortunately did not understand, and as he bent to pick up the bucket he saw two figures ride into the stable yard.

It was as if the skies had suddenly parted and a beam of light streamed down into the yard, bearing with it the mounted outriders of the heavenly host. A fanfare of trumpets would not have been inappropriate at that point. Or at least, that was how it seemed to Hanu, scrabbling around on the yard floor, wet and muddy, trying to retrieve the now-empty bucket.

In reality, the arrivals were Ren, Merac's son, and Gavax har Gelaming. Gavax, as always, looked composed and immaculate. No stray hair or disarranged item of clothing suggested recent involvement in any sort of physical activity; no unchecked emotion was displayed upon his faultless features. He looked the very embodiment of the mystical perfection that his tribe strove for. Ren, in contrast, had the rather dishevelled look of a har who had spent quite some time in the saddle, possibly during some rather inclement weather, but if he could not quite match his companion's splendour and presence, his horse at least made up for anything lacking, for the horse Ren was mounted on was a Faraldienne.

Hanu pretended to continue to scrub the mud off Lohish's hind quarters, but he could not help but peer around the horse's haunches and stare at Ren's mount. It wasn't that he had never seen the Faraldienne before – Ren rode Ishfar quite regularly around the Estemble – but it was impossible not to look at the horse.

Faraldiennes were a gift to the Gimrah from the Gelaming, to cement relationships between the tribes. The Gimrah cared little for land or money or political power, or even luxury goods. What they loved best was horses, and so the Gelaming had given them horses. But these were no ordinary equines. They were delicate-looking creatures, almost doe-like with their soft, dark eyes fringed with long lashes, dark muzzles and long, sweeping manes and tails. But despite their ethereal looks, they were fast and strong, could leap over the highest fences with ease and travel miles without tiring. A small herd of them was maintained by one of the other estembles, and only on very rare occasions would the Gimrah sell one of these fabulous creatures to another tribe.

Hanu had tried to dislike them, on principle. They were not proper Gimranish horses, he told himself. They were some sort of Gelaming freaks. They had no proper pedigree recorded in the Great Ledger. With their arched necks, snow-white coats and high-stepping, dainty hooves, they looked like a harling's imaginary dream horse brought to life. But one look into those dark eyes and no Gimranish har could remain unmoved, and Hanu had to admit that the Faraldiennes were a delight. They could never be as magnificent as Tezuk, of course. Tezuk was a true Gimranish horse, the end product of years of striving towards physical perfection. The Faraldiennes were simply a fantasy made real.

Although he admired Ishfar, Hanu was troubled by the fact that Ren had chosen the Faraldienne as his personal mount. He felt strongly that Ren, as Merac's heir and Tirtha-in-waiting, should ride a Scatterstones horse. It was true that some of the other Tirthas rode Faraldiennes, but that was because their estembles specialised in breeding horses that were used for purposes other than riding. Magnificent as the great dray horses of Tail-and-Tether were, their Tirtha could hardly ride one daily about Gimrah. The racehorses of Wind's Edge were too highly strung for that purpose too. It was quite acceptable in that case, in Hanu's opinion, for the Tirthas to ride a Faraldienne.

But here, at Scatterstones, it was different. Ren had the pick of the finest riding horses in all Gimrah. It would have given the ordinary hara a sense of pride to see Ren riding one of their own horses, as his hostling always had.

Merac himself had never offered criticism of his son's choice of mount, but when he was near the animal there was something in his expression, something in the tone of his voice and the set of his mouth that told Hanu the Tirtha was disappointed. Whether Ren noticed this too, or not, he continued to ride Ishfar, ensuring that he made a striking vision, especially when he accompanied Gavax har Gelaming.

Gavax also rode a white horse. A horse that could have been Ishfar's twin. This was a gleaming white steed with muscles like steel and a luxurious cascading mane and tail, whose silver shimmer echoed the golden lustre of Gavax's own hair. A creature invoking the very embodiment of equine perfection, and yet Hanu knew this was no horse.

Hanu knew horses. He had grown up with them, as a har in a tribe dedicated to their veneration and well-being. He knew their smell, their feel, their thoughts and their aura. He knew their ways and their wiles, their habits and their moods and he knew, with every molecule of his body and every particle of his soul, that the creature upon whose back Gavax har Gelaming rode was not a horse.

Sedim, the Gelaming called them. Hanu had heard of their ability to travel through the Otherlanes, covering great distances in short times by moving through other dimensions. He had no idea how this was possible, or even what these mysterious Otherlanes actually were – it was yet more of the strangeness surrounding the Gelaming which set them apart from the other tribes. He accepted that travelling in this manner could probably be a useful ability at times, as could the disguising of a creature that was not-a-horse as something most hara would find unthreatening. Other hara, other tribes, might be fooled by their appearance into thinking that they were the horses they pretended to be, but not a Gimranish har. Not Hanu.

The creature Gavax har Gelaming rode had no true name, had no dam or sire, no lineage or pedigree and no essence of horse within its chosen form. Hanu conceded that its outward appearance was utterly splendid, and if taking the form of a horse was good enough for the Aghama, then it was not hard to see why these *sedim* should choose that also. And yet, wild wolves could not have dragged Hanu onto that creature's back, to sit or ride there, feeling its alienness – its *unhorseness*.

To Hanu's mind, no har in possession of his senses would ride such a thing as that, through the cold emptiness of nowhere, when he could be astride a real horse, living, breathing, galloping across the steppelands, blood racing through their veins and hearts pounding

As if it realised he was staring at it, the *sedu* turned its head towards Hanu, slowly, carefully, in a manner which was somehow *unhorselike*. Hanu felt the hairs on the back of his neck stand to attention, much as the hackles would rise on Pek, the dog belonging to his high-hostling, when strangers approached.

To his relief, neither Ren nor Gavax took any notice of him whatsoever. In truth, they could hardly be expected to acknowledge a small, mud-covered eskev standing behind a dirty horse as they dismounted. Ren led Ishfar towards the side of the stables where the Faraldienne had his own luxurious stall, calling on one of the other eskevi to unsaddle the horse.

Hanu watched with interest as Gavax removed the saddle and bridle from his mount himself. He didn't strike Hanu as a har who was used to doing menial chores, but he surmised that the strange nature of the *sedu* required that Gavax keep other hara at a distance from it.

What happened next was even more surprising. Relieved of its saddle and bridle, the *sedu* turned and trotted casually towards the stable yard exit, apparently without any direction from Gavax. For a single pace, it broke into a loping canter, and before Hanu could shout out that it was escaping, there was a sudden cold judder in the air, a brief moment of pressure in his ears, and then the *sedu* was... gone.

Hanu almost dropped the bucket again. Beside him, Lohish snorted uneasily, and Hanu automatically put a hand on the horse's shoulder to reassure him, but he continued to stare at the now-empty space where the *sedu* had been only moments before. It was exactly the same stable yard it had always been, nothing unusual about it. When, after a long minute, absolutely nothing else unusual happened, he decided that the *sedu* was not going to reappear. He returned, dazed, to the task of transferring the mud from Lohish to himself, determined not to think too hard about what he had just witnessed.

Another motion at the entrance to the stable yard made him jump, unnerved as he was, but it was not the *sedu* magically reappearing, it was Merac. The Tirtha strode purposefully towards Gavax and Ren, dressed in rather more formal clothing than was usual for him. He spotted Hanu and gave him a brief smile, and Hanu jumped, realising that he was not as invisible as he felt. Merac then transferred his attention to Gavax and Ren.

"There you are," he said to Ren, "I've been looking for you. I'd like you to get changed and accompany me to the Eithak. Peridu from Long Ride is paying us a visit and I would like to go over the records for the past three seasons with him. You can help me entertain him while we sort things out."

"Why do I have to get changed for that?" Ren asked sulkily, "Peri has been here lots of times before, it's hardly a great event."

"We should always show respect to our fellow Tirthas whenever we can," Merac told him, "And they will do so for us, in turn. It may seem unimportant to you, but small acts of courtesy are both the knots that tie us together and the oil that lubricates our relationships."

"So we have to ingratiate ourselves to other Tirthas so we can get fawned over in return?" Ren said, scuffing his boot against one of the cobbles on the ground and scowling.

"That's not what I meant, and you know it." Merac's weary expression suggested that this was a conversation he had had many times before, "Now, please just do as I ask. It's not exactly an onerous request. One day, you will be Tirtha yourself, and there will be many other things you will have to do that you won't particularly enjoy, but that is how life is, I'm afraid."

Without giving Ren the chance to argue further, Merac marched from the stable yard, leaving Ren to heave a dramatic sigh, after he was sure his hostling was out of earshot.

"The responsibilities of command are not as easy as they look, are they?" Gavax sympathised. "Many hara do not understand this. They see only the privilege that comes with the position, and never the burdens."

"There are so many petty little rules and regulations that I'm supposed to waste my life following," Ren grumbled. "I'm sure Merac enjoys making them up. What is the point of it all?"

"Each leader has his own idea of how to run things and how best to achieve the results he desires." Gavax said, apparently attempting to mollify the young har. "As Merac said, one day you will be Tirtha, and then you can decide what is important and what is not, and you can do things differently, if you choose." He smoothed away a non-existent crease from his clothing. "If it's any consolation, the Gimrah are not alone in having to deal with bureaucracy. I should not perhaps say this, but the internal politics of the Gelaming administration can sometimes feel equally restrictive. It is simply the nature of things, I suppose – no tribe is immune from the disease, but a good leader can always find a way to do what needs to be done and not get bogged down by petty details. Remember that when you are Tirtha."

"I will," said Ren, "but I will not be Tirtha for uncountable seasons yet, so in the meantime I will just have to put up with Merac's nit-picking, I suppose."

Gavax smiled and laid one elegantly manicured hand on Ren's arm. "The time may pass sooner than you think. Now – if Merac wishes you to make a good impression on this other Tirtha, sartorially speaking, it just so happens that I have some of Immanion's latest fashions with me. Let's go to my residence and see what we can find for you. That jacket you have on is covered in horsehair, it won't do – here, take it off, give it to that eskev over there to look after. Come with me, and we'll soon have you looking every inch the Tirtha-to-be and both Merac and his guest will be dazzled!"

Gavax beckoned to Hanu, who had been carefully scrubbing away at Lohish, pretending not to overhear any of this conversation, but intrigued enough to keep one ear tuned in their direction. Hanu hurried over at Gavax's behest and took Ren's riding jacket, which looked to him like a perfectly serviceable and well-made item of clothing, with hardly any horsehair on it at all. It seemed to be in more danger of soiling from contact with Hanu than from Ren having worn it for riding, but neither Ren nor Gavax seemed to notice Hanu's mud-spattered appearance. They left him clutching the jacket, uncertain what to do with it, as they headed off together in the direction of Gavax's residence.

Hanu was not sure whether he felt sorry for Ren having to spend the afternoon making awkward small talk with a visiting dignitary, or whether he envied him his mud-free duties. It was as Merac had said – there were things in life that a har had to do whether he enjoyed them or not, and that applied equally to a Tirtha as to an eskev. Unless you happened to be Velisan, of course. It seemed to Hanu that Merac's elder son had managed to end up with the best of both worlds – he enjoyed the respect that came with being the son of the Tirtha, without having to shoulder the responsibilities or tedious duties that came with it. At the same time, he would never have to scrub mud off an exasperating horse or shovel mountains of dung. Unless he wanted to, of course. To be fair to Velisan, he probably wouldn't mind doing such things – he had helped out clearing up with everyhar else last year when heavy rain had flooded the west stables, and the resultant muddy mess had made Lohish's current condition look spotless in comparison.

Hanu wondered if Ren resented his brother's relative freedom to choose his own path. In Gimrah, the position of Tirtha always remained within the same family, passing to the previous Tirtha's eldest hosted son. On the whole, this seemed to work quite well, as the young Tirtha-to-be grew up with the knowledge that he would one day assume the responsibility, and spent his youthful years learning everything he would need to know to be a successful Tirtha from his hostling. Dynastic succession of this kind was practiced by quite a number of Wraeththu tribes. Others were reputed to be less patient when it came to waiting for nature to take its course in order to facilitate a change of leadership, but at least the new leaders could say that they had truly volunteered themselves for the position.

Entertaining this thought made Hanu feel a little guilty. Whatever the drawbacks of the Gimranish method of succession, it was certainly preferable to murder and assassination. The Gelaming obviously thought so too, and had made it known that they expected the transfer of leadership in tribes to be conducted peacefully, in whatever method was considered best for that particular tribe. Whether their expectations were being met or not was a subject for debate.

Hanu looked at the riding jacket he held in his hand, then at Lohish, who was now amusing himself by snuffling wetly in the refilled bucket, occasionally lifting his head to give a small, surprised sneeze before resuming his game. Shaking his head, Hanu crossed the yard over to the stable block and once inside, carefully hung the jacket on a hook next to Ishfar's stall. The Faraldienne stood watching him with interest, head hanging over the low door. The horse's dark eyes regarded him solemnly, full of unspoken wisdom. Hanu could not resist stroking its soft, dark muzzle, feeling the warm breath issuing from its nostrils, all life and vitality. Ishfar allowed this contact graciously, as if he were a high caste har and Hanu merely a lowly servant. At least one of these things was true, Hanu thought. Perhaps they both were.

It occurred to him that the gift of the Faraldiennes was in many ways typical of the Gelaming themselves; thoughtful, appropriate, virtuous, correct and beautiful. And somehow, in some small, regrettable, undeliberate way, simply wrong.

Ishfar must have caught Hanu's thought, for he flicked his ears questioningly at him. Hanu gave a gentle tug on his luxurious forelock to apologise for thinking even slightly badly of him, even for a second, and the horse nodded his head, satisfied. Hanu could only smile to himself. Gelaming to the core, even their horses did not bear grudges.

Leaving Ishfar with a parting handful of hay to placate him, Hanu made his way over to the other side of the stable where a horse who unfortunately *did* hold grudges was waiting. Tezuk had been out for exercise early that morning, but had disgraced himself yet again by kicking Ruta, one of the other eskevi, rendering the har unfit for work for the rest of the day. Despite Hanu's impassioned defence that this was because Ruta had laughed at Tezuk the previous day, and had made fun of his inability to trot peacefully in line with all the other three-year olds, Tezuk had been separated out from the group again. He'd been given exercise on a long lunge rein round the paddock instead of a wild gallop across the open grasslands which the horses so looked forward to. This restricted exercise had not gone particularly well either, and Tezuk had ended up confined to his stable.

Hanu had thought this very unfair, but there was nothing he could do about it. Nirzhen's stern expression and his irritation at being one eskev down for the day told Hanu not to argue with him.

Tezuk seemed somewhat calmer now he had spent some time in his stall. He let Hanu enter without creating too much fuss and flicked his tail in the manner which Hanu knew meant that contact between horse and har would be acceptable. Nirzhen had warned him not to go into Tezuk's stall without another har close by, in case he should require assistance, but Hanu knew the horse's moods well enough know when it was safe to approach him and when not. And besides, if Tezuk really wanted to hurt him, the presence of another har would not be enough to stop him.

"You weren't exactly on your best behaviour this morning, were you?" he told Tezuk, who ignored him in favour of rubbing his hind quarters against the back of the stall to relieve an itch.

"Don't worry, you'll get out again tomorrow. They don't mean any harm; they just don't understand you. They think you're just an ordinary horse. They don't know how special you are. But I do. I know you're worth a hundred Faraldiennes. If Ren had any sense, he'd choose you as his mount. But you know what? I'm glad he didn't. I don't want you to be anyhar else's horse. Is that wrong of me?"

As usual, Tezuk failed to respond in any way which might be interpreted as a response to Hanu's questions. Hanu sighed, but he did not really mind. It was enough for him just to be able to voice his thoughts; his doubts and fears and questions. Things that he might previously have revealed to the statue in the Eithak he now found himself confessing to the flesh and blood horse. It somehow felt right to him, as if the cold metal had been a barrier which had now melted away.

He pulled a few strands of Tezuk's mane through his fingers, enjoying its coarse yet silky texture.

"At least you're not stupid enough to go rolling in the mud," he told Tezuk, who gave a snort, which Hanu interpreted as agreement. "I suppose I'd better get back outside and finish up with Lohish. I'll take you out for extra exercise tomorrow, but you've got to promise to behave."

Giving Tezuk a final pat on the neck, Hanu left the stall and returned to the stable yard outside, where he found that Lohish had knocked over the bucket again, and had also broken a large pot full of plants and earth, trampling the whole lot under his hooves into a muddy slop. Lohish whinnied a cheerful greeting to Hanu as he approached, pleased that the grooming session was about to recommence. Hanu merely shook his head, picked up the bucket and went to refill it with water yet again.

Later that day, after he had finished work, Hanu went to his parents' house for his evening meal. Normally he would eat the food provided for the eskevi in their communal lodgings close to the stables, but he enjoyed visiting his father Nalleshu, and Kam, his hostling, quite regularly, both for the pleasure of seeing them and because they were both excellent cooks, a fact which he had not appreciated fully until he had moved into lodgings.

Some other members of his family were also present, including his younger suri, with whom he had always got on well, so it was a convivial evening full of good food and drink and catching up on family matters.

Pek the dog greeted him rapturously on his arrival, leaping up and licking his face and playfully biting his ear. Hanu noticed that there was a framed picture of Pek on the wall, a new addition since he had last visited, done by his father who enjoyed painting and drawing and was skilled at both. Hanu thought that perhaps he might ask his father to come to the stables and do a drawing of Tezuk – it would be a fine thing to hang on the wall of his own small room at the lodgings.

Over dinner, Hanu recounted the events of the afternoon with Lohish, making the entire experience sound rather more entertaining than it actually had been. Reska, his suri, was more interested in hearing about the Faraldienne, and made Hanu describe Ishfar in great detail. He squealed with excitement when Hanu revealed that he had actually patted the horse.

"And Ren was with Gavax again?" Kam asked, through a mouthful of food. "The Gelaming seems to spend quite some time with him. I wonder why that is?"

Hanu shrugged. "I don't know. Perhaps he enjoys Ren's company." He pretended not to notice the brief eyeroll that this suggestion elicited from his hostling.

"Well that can only be a good thing, can't it?" his father said, scraping at one of the empty dishes on the table with a spoon in the hope of finding a few more scraps. "Having an association with one of the Gelaming will benefit not only our own estemble, but the whole Gimrah tribe."

"A tribe should be able to maintain its independence," Kam said. "That's why the different tribes exist, after all. We all have different paths we wish to pursue and attempting to make every tribe follow the rules laid down by the Gelaming can only cause trouble. Not..." he smiled impishly and raised his hand to stave off Nalle's expected retort "...that the Gelaming's ways are not a most excellent and civilising influence – if you happen to be Gelaming. We're not, we're Gimranish, and I'd like to stay that way!"

"Funnily enough," Nalle replied, abandoning his quest for further leftovers, "the Mojags feel exactly the same way as you about maintaining their tribal traditions. Only in their case, those traditions involve wiping out other tribes. I doubt you'd refuse the Gelaming's assistance if a horde of Mojags came calling, or if the Maudrans decided that everyhar in the neighbouring lands had to follow all their bizarre decrees."

"I think I'll go outside and stretch my legs for a few minutes," said Hanu, rising from his seat. He had sat through this argument between his parents before and didn't want to listen to it again.

Kam smiled understandingly at him. "Sounds like a good idea. Don't be too long, I'm just about to serve dessert."

Outside the air felt clear and cool after the warmth of the kitchen. It was dark, but there was still a glow in the western sky where the sun had taken its leave for the day. In the distance, Hanu could hear owls making their strange night-time sounds. He heard another sound he recognised, coming from the fence next to the house and saw a familiar shape moving in the gloom.

Smiling, he approached the fence and reached out a hand to stroke the shaggy head of the elderly pony drooping companionably over the fence.

It was Beyra, who had been Hanu's first horse as a harling. Now too old for work, he was enjoying a peaceful retirement and spent his time dozing or giving the occasional ride around the paddock to some tiny, excited, newly-hatched harling, his slow pace ensuring the small rider would be perfectly safe.

"Hello there," he greeted Beyra, rubbing the horse's nose gently. Beyra whuffed his approval, and Hanu could feel his pleasure at seeing his harish friend once again. There was no hint of recrimination at the fact that Hanu had not been around much lately, just a quiet contentment and an appreciation of the chance to be happy in that moment. Hanu felt humbled by the fact that an old horse could still have things to teach him about life. He sometimes felt that his trips home were as much to see Beyra, Pek and the other animals as to see his parents. And at least Beyra didn't have any opinion on the Gelaming tribe and their influence in Scatterstones, which was a blessing.

Mercifully, both Nalle and Kam avoided that topic during dessert, and the conversation meandered peacefully from discussions as to which stallion would be mated to which mare next season to whether or not the next meeting of the Tirthas would actually reach an agreement on the long-standing dispute as to whether to move the official start of the breeding season from two days before Rosatide to two days afterwards. As this had been an ongoing discussion since before Hanu was hatched, nohar had any great hopes that it would be resolved any time soon. As this situation made no practical difference to anyhar, other than those who kept the records for each season, there did not seem to be any great urgency to settle the issue, and besides, as Kam pointed out, it gave them something to do and stopped them making mischief elsewhere.

It was late by the time Hanu got back to his lodgings. All was dark and quiet; the eskevi started work early in the morning and most were fast asleep well before midnight. But as Hanu passed Tiski's room he thought he heard a muffled giggling, and the sound of more than one voice. Hanu sighed. It would be just like Tiski to stay up late entertaining some alluring har who had caught his attention, and then be too tired to do his work tomorrow.

Although, as Hanu reflected ruefully to himself, he too was up late, but had no companion with whom to share the night. With that rather self-pitying thought, he undressed and crept into his little bed in solitary silence and was soon fast asleep.

Chapter 4
Spinnersholm

Flor was an autumn foal. Too young for one year, too old for the next, she had spent the first six months of her life indoors in the safety of the stables with her mother, never seeing the lush green grass or the tiny white flowers for which she was named; never feeling the sun on her back or the wind at her heels.

Most foals were born in the spring, when the vigorous shoots of new grass provided the nourishment for the mares to make their rich milk on which their foals would grow strong. That was the way of nature, and also the way of the Gimrah, who mated the mares in the spring of one year to have them give birth in the spring of the next.

It was not always the way of certain mares, however. Flor's dam had conceived and borne her foal in the autumn without the assistance of either nature or the Gimrah. The only assistance she had certainly received had been from a willing stallion, although *which* stallion was unclear. Hanu had an idea, though.

Nirzhen said that mares did not care which stallion they bred with. When the heat of mating was upon them, and they desired to be got in foal, they would take any stallion who could do the job. Hanu did not quite believe this – he had seen mares in the full grip of heat point blank refuse to allow a particular stallion to mount, biting and kicking at him angrily, only to stand solidly for the next one the frustrated Merac had been required to pick from his list. And he had seen Flor's dam, Rashal, flick her tail saucily at Dirdun, a handsome if rather wayward bay stallion, and toss her head coquettishly whenever she spied him.

Whatever the truth of the matter, a year after her secret autumn tryst, Rashal had given birth to a filly foal, small by the standards of Gimrah horses, but pretty with her golden coat and silver mane and tail. Unfortunately, Flor's inauspicious start in life and her lack of authenticated pedigree meant that she would never be sold to one of the eager bidders from other tribes – the Gimrah only offered their best for sale – and her small stature meant that she would neither be capable of heavy work or speed at the gallop, none of which bothered Tiski in the slightest.

Tiski was Flor's eskev, and he was as proud of the little filly as if he had given birth to her himself. Tiski saw none of her faults – neither her too-short neck or her knock-knees or her small size – but would talk endlessly to anyhar who would listen about her sweet temperament and her intelligence, and her dainty manners, and praise her pretty silver-and-gold colouring as if there had never been another horse born with this particular appearance.

Hanu listened patiently to Tiski's enthusiastic compliments, nodding seriously when required, and holding his tongue when Tiski's prediction of the filly's future prospects veered a little too far into fantasy – he thought it unwise to contradict Tiski's assertion that Flor would one day win the Grand Jaddayoth Challenge race at the summer horse fair in Ardith – but he found himself in some way moved by Tiski's unwavering devotion to an animal which many of the Gimrah tribe would have considered to be flawed.

Tiski was currently leaning on the wooden fence surrounding the paddock where the two-year olds were gathered. Flor had been put with these, rather than with those a year older for fear that the older colts and fillies would kick and bully her. Horses were not generous when it came to difference among their ranks and would sometimes ostracise a member of the herd who was unusual in any way.

Despite having several months' head start on the rest of the small herd, Flor was smaller than the others, and when the group suddenly took off on a spontaneous gallop around the paddock, stretching their long legs and vying with each other to see who could lead the chase, she was near the back, her awkward gait marking her out as clearly as her colouring.

Tiski pointed her out to Hanu proudly. "Look! She's almost caught up with Biron! He was much faster than her just a month ago!"

He leaned forward over the fence, a rapt smile on his face. "And look at how her coat shines in the sun!"

Hanu had to admit that Flor's golden coat was striking. If that alone were the sole measure of a horse's quality then Flor would be among the top ranks, but unfortunately for her the herd had now outrun her and were galloping with intent down towards the far end of the paddock, leaving the little filly alone except for the one other colt who had not joined in the herd's romp. A dark colt, already noticeably bigger than Flor, despite the difference in their ages, his broad chest and immaculate conformation making the filly look small and skinny in comparison.

Tezuk.

That he had not joined in with the herd's playful racing game was no surprise to Hanu. Tezuk was not like the others. Hanu told himself that Tezuk's unwillingness to run with the herd marked him out as a leader rather than a follower, and yet the herd did not appear to want to be led by him, and Tezuk seemed not to care one way or the other.

Many mares become distressed when their foals are separated from them for weaning, but Ishin, Tezuk's dam, had not stamped or fretted or whinnied after him. Rather, she had seemed to breathe a sigh of relief, for as a foal Tezuk had been demanding and petulant, kicking and biting if his mother sought to discipline him, or had not provided milk quickly enough, until even the long-suffering Ishin's patience was exhausted.

Hanu hoped that once in the company of other young horses his own age Tezuk would become more manageable – horses were sociable animals and being an accepted part of the herd was important to them – but Tezuk seemed not to care if the other horses ignored him. He spent most of his time cantering by himself away from the herd.

Flor, by now abandoned by the main group, yet possessed of a normal horse's innate need for the company of its own kind, pranced cheerfully alongside Tezuk, occasionally stopping to snatch a mouthful of grass or paw industriously at the turf with her hard, little hoof.

"Look!" said Tiski again, "They're friends! Like us!"

To Hanu, Tezuk seemed utterly oblivious to the filly's presence, but he humoured Tiski, as always when it came to Flor. "Yes, I'm sure they are. Come on, you've seen her now, let's get on. We have to deliver that load of flax to Spinnersholm this afternoon, and there'll still be half a dozen stalls to muck out by the time we get back. If we don't get it finished, Nirzhen will be *disappointed in the quality of eskevi today* and we'll be on compost duty for a month."

Tiski laughed at Hanu's dour impersonation of Nirzhen. He put two fingers into his mouth and blew a piercing whistle. Upon hearing this, Flor's head came up and her ears pricked. She galloped over to Tiski, barely stopping in time to avoid running into the fence.

"Hello beautiful," said Tiski affectionately, stroking the filly's nose. "You're looking exceptionally lovely today, but I'm afraid I can't take you out for a run because that slave-driver Nirzhen is making us take a pile of dirty old weeds up to the Spinners, and you're not big enough to pull the cart yet."

Flor snuffled into his hand, ignoring his words and searching for what she knew would be there. With a grin, Tiski took an apple out of his pocket and slipped it onto his palm for the filly to take, which she did gracefully without so much as brushing the skin of his outstretched hand with her strong white teeth.

"There you go. Don't tell the others, they'll all want one, and if I raid Vatha's orchard again I'll be in even more trouble with Nirzhen, if that's even possible!"

Tiski wiped the palm of his hand on his overshirt, even though it didn't need it, and while Flor was distracted by the delicious fruit, crunching and dribbling juice from the corners of her mouth and rolling her eyes in pleasure, the two hara made their way back along the track that joined the main stable buildings with the lower paddock.

When they reached the stables, Hanu went down to the stall at the far end. He led out from it a large brown gelding with a rather sleepy expression, who walked slowly and rather reluctantly behind him to the stable yard, every line of his body indicating that he would much rather have spent the afternoon doing nothing in his pleasant stable than be burdened with the work that was expected of him.

Hanu slapped the gelding's haunches with the flat of his hand to try to speed him up a bit, but if the horse noticed it at all he gave no indication. Hanu sighed. Harcan was strong, but lazy. He needed the exercise, and for a horse his size, pulling the cart with a full load of flax and two hara was no hardship.

Tiski was already out in the yard with the cart, and together they hitched Harcan up between its traces, checking that the buckles were properly fastened and the harnesses in place. Harcan watched them reproachfully, and when they were done, both Hanu and Tiski climbed up onto the driving seat at the front. Hanu grabbed the reins, gave them a flick and shouted "….hup!"

to Harcan, who turned his head, gave both hara a pained look, then slowly began walking towards the stable yard exit, his large hooves making a slow clopping sound on the cobblestone and the cart wheels rumbling.

As they passed out of the yard, Hanu spotted Merac standing at the far side, seemingly engaged in deep discussion with another har, whose aristocratic demeanour marked him out as not being of the Gimrah tribe. It was Gavax har Gelaming.

The discussion currently ongoing between Merac and Gavax seemed anything but friendly. Merac was not a har easily roused to anger or disapproval. As Tirtha he had many years' experience of diplomacy and tact and the art of settling disputes such that each side felt that they had secured a measure of victory. Hanu had never seen him lose his temper, and while he was sure that that was not the case now, he could tell from Merac's stiff posture that he was unhappy about something, and by his curt responses to Gavax's words that he disagreed strongly with whatever the Gelaming had said.

Gavax himself seemed unperturbed, maintaining the aloofness for which his tribe was famed, so Hanu could not really be sure if what he was witnessing could actually be described as an argument, but it seemed odd to him none the less.

He decided to put it out of his mind – it was not his business as a lowly eskev anyway – and concentrate on steering the reluctant Harcan in the direction of the settlement of the Spinners.

It was a beautiful autumn afternoon, the sky a cloudless blue and the sun still warm for the season, as if in denial of the inevitability of the colder days ahead, already heralded by the red and gold leaves still clinging to the branches of the trees. Summers in Gimrah could be fiercely hot, and the harsh winters brought snow and ice in abundance, but at the pivot points of the year, both Bloomtide and Smoketide, everything seemed in balance; both night and day, and warmth and chill. Soon the days would shorten as the year slid precipitously to its end, but for now a har could still enjoy the sun on his back and a ride across the grasslands toward the small settlement on the outskirts of Scatterstones where the Spinners resided.

As far as Hanu was aware, humans lived alongside hara

nowhere else except in Gimrah. There were a number of reasons for this, the most pertinent being that humans were now few in number. After the Devastation and the Days of Change, the human race had declined and withered. Inception had taken some, death and insanity many others. Wraeththu had superseded humanity throughout the entire globe, and yet some individuals had proved resilient; women, who could not be incepted, had come together to form their own communities. They were for the most part tolerated by the Wraeththu tribes, since they posed no threat to them, but only in Gimrah had a mutually beneficial relationship taken root. The Gimrah were fortunate in that their tribal customs were less exacting than some, and, in fact, their veneration of the world spirit in the form of a Goddess found them in harmony with their female neighbours, so it was only natural that the two groups should find that their interests coincided.

Like many of their kind, the women of Scatterstones had returned to the traditional skills of their sex in order to make their living; skills which men had once derided as *women's work*. The men were gone now, but the women and their work lived on – the women of Scatterstones were spinners – *spinsters*. They took the fibrous flax plant, which grew easily and abundantly in the fertile land, and spun it into yarn and thread, which they wove into fine cloth, much prized by hara both in Gimrah and beyond.

Hanu himself had had many an occasion to appreciate the Spinners' work. The clothing of a har who lived life in the saddle (or in the stables) must, of necessity, be hard-wearing, and the leather outer garments favoured by the Gimrah fulfilled this brief admirably, but for comfort underneath, the fine cloth of the Spinners was favoured by all.

The hara of Scatterstones fully appreciated the skill and labour that went into making this fabric, and were supportive of their human neighbours, despite the disapproval it earned them from some other tribes. The flax plant grew well in the fields around Scatterstones, nourished by the rich manure from the stables, and when it was harvested it was sent to the Spinners in its raw form to be transformed by their alchemy into bolts of luxurious fabric, a process which never ceased to amaze Hanu, familiar as he was with the plant in its unprocessed form.

There was another reason for Hanu and Tiski's trip to

Spinnersholm today though – a baby had been born to one of the women, and the hara were to present a gift to the child and also to learn its name for the records.

The birth of a human child was not a common occurrence, and Hanu was curious about the circumstances which had led up to it, although he had not been brave enough to ask Nirzhen the details. No such delicacy troubled Tiski, however, who was currently airing his views quite thoroughly on the matter, oblivious to Hanu's discomfort.

"Have you ever seen one? A human one?" Tiski asked him, grinning salaciously.

Hanu eyed him suspiciously. "A human male? Yes, I saw that one before he was incepted last year."

"No, not a male. A phallus. A human phallus."

"A wha...? No! Of course not! Why would I? Why do you ask such things?!" Hanu shook his head in exasperation, but Tiski would not be discouraged

"I wonder what it's like. Human mating. Is it like horses, do you think? Does the male grab her shoulder with his teeth? Does she kick him if she's not ready? Do they have to keep a spare male handy so they can tell when she's in heat? Is the phallus *looooong* and prehensile?"

"How should I know? Can we change the subject, please?" Hanu scowled at his companion to make his displeasure clear, and to try to hide his embarrassment.

Tiski, however, rather like an untrained horse who had taken the bit between his teeth, was in no mood to be reined back.

"The males have to father another male before they can be incepted," he told Hanu, wagging a forefinger in the way that Nirzhen did when he wanted to instruct the eskevi on an important point. "Otherwise they would all die out. They have to have both males and females to be able to breed successfully."

"Yes, I know."

"I heard," Tiski said, clasping his hands together in a satisfied manner, "about one male who could only sire females. For two years, he mated with all the females, but didn't sire any males. Lots of women babies, but no man babies. Eventually he managed to sire a male, which meant he could be incepted, but it was too late – he died of exhaustion!"

"What? He did not! You fibber! Just stop it – I don't want to think about it! It's disgusting! I… Ugh… No! Just… stop!"

Tiski threw his head back and roared with laughter at Hanu's appalled expression.

"You should see your face," he said "You look as if you've just drunk a whole mug of rancid mare's milk. Oh, that reminds me – do you know how they feed human babies? When they're just born, I mean…?"

Hanu attempted to maintain his expression of prim distaste, but Tiski's affected look of wide-eyed innocence sabotaged his efforts, and he found himself laughing too. It was impossible to remain serious when Tiski was around. Tiski had little time for the niceties of behaviour, which the exasperated Nirzhen repeatedly tried to drum into him. Tiski was prone to what the anskev referred to darkly as *unseemly behaviour,* but Hanu enjoyed Tiski's nose-thumbing of convention, secretly relishing, by proxy, that which he knew he would never have the courage to do or say himself.

"It must be weird, though," Tiski mused, stretching his legs out and leaning back a little in the cart's hard wooden seat, "Humans. Not having aruna. I can't imagine that… whatever they do instead… is any sort of substitute. Can you?"

Tiski looked directly at Hanu as he said this. The same look that Flor's dam had given the stallion Dirdun. Flirtatious. Coquettish. Hanu felt his face grow slightly warmer, and not just from the afternoon sunshine, but he did not look away. No har with any sense would. Tiski had hair the colour of raw flax, the colour of Flor's mane and tail, and he wore it bound in a leather thong as was the custom among the Gimrah, but he wore it high up, so it swished and flicked when he moved his head around, and caught the sunlight, and moved as if it were a living thing. Other hara could not help but stare at it. Tiski knew this and swished and flicked all the more because of it.

Hanu did not wear his hair long, or in a tail. Hanu's hair was short-cropped, dark, and followed the contours of his head closely, save for where it was cut to the shape of a small point at the nape of his neck. The reason Hanu gave for this was that he did not like the work involved in the maintenance of a long, swishing tail of hair, and that in the morning he would rather sleep a little later in his bed than rise early enough to deal with it. And this was true enough – Hanu was not a har who saw much point in giving oneself extra work if it could be avoided – but there was another reason for his short crop, which he did not tell anyhar. He thought that it showed off his long neck and his fine jawline, which he considered to be his best features.

Sometimes he would catch a glimpse of himself in a mirror, and surreptitiously turn his head a little to admire himself, feeling slightly ashamed as he did so, although for what reason he could not say. Vanity was not considered an egregious sin amongst hara, which was probably just as well, considering how widely-spread it was. And if Hanu was a little less given to overt displays of conceit than the average har, then the cosmic balance was more than restored by Tiski's contribution.

Hanu would have been more than happy to ride along in the golden sunshine admiring Tiski and his hair all afternoon, but very soon they caught sight of Spinnersholm, whereupon he directed Harcan into a trot with an encouraging "...hup" and to his surprise the gelding did as he was bid without complaint. The arrived at the forecourt of the main building, in a clatter of hooves and dust, and a number of women ran out to greet them, some of them with small children. Tiski waved enthusiastically as they approached and jumped down from the cart as soon as Hanu brought Harcan to a halt.

"Sofia!" he greeted a tall woman, who was dressed in practical clothing dyed in shades of brown, echoing the current colours of the landscape. She smiled at Tiski, wiping her hands on her trousers before gripping him by the arm in response. Hanu jumped down from the other side of the cart and handed the reins to another of the women. He knew that Harcan would be looked after for the time they were here. In fact, the gelding was already enjoying the attention of several women stroking his nose and offering him some small, sweet roots, which probably accounted for his willingness to break into a trot for the last section of their journey.

"We've brought you more flax!" Tiski said, indicating the laden cart. Already some of the women were unloading it and carrying away the bundled sheaves to the outhouses for storage. "Oh, and here's your bird." Tiski handed her a small wicker cage containing a plump grey pigeon. The women used the birds to send messages to Scatterstones to let them know when fabric was ready for collection, or if more flax was needed.

"That's great, thank you," Sofia said, taking the cage and cooing absently at the bird. "We were just about out. Now we can get started on a new batch. I've got some fabric for you – come into the house and have a drink while we get it ready."

She led the way into the main building behind the forecourt, with Hanu and Tiski following behind.

It was an old structure, unlike most of the buildings at Scatterstones. The greater part of the estemble had been built by the hara who lived there, from wood and stone and clay and earth. The houses, stables, Eithak and public buildings were part of the landscape they came from – some had earth and grass for a roof, others burrowed into the ground or the rocks. Spinnersholm looked different. There was just something about it, not merely its age, which marked it out as human-built.

In Hanu's eyes there was nothing wrong with that – a human building was entirely appropriate for humans. And it was a pleasant space inside its thick walls, furnished with the Spinners' best fabrics, drowsy in the afternoon warmth, with the smell of cooking pervading the rooms.

Hanu settled himself in a comfortable chair, which looked like it had accommodated many backsides in its time and was all the better for it. A large pot of tea arrived and was poured with due ceremony while Sofia instructed her companions on which fabrics were to be sent to Scatterstones in payment for the flax.

"I have a gift for you," Hanu said, rummaging in his satchel, "From the Tirtha. It's for the harling... er... baby. To commemorate its hatching."

Tiski kicked his ankle and smirked at him. "They don't hatch. They..."

"That's very kind of Merac," said Sofia, interrupting Tiski before he could describe how human babies entered the world. "We haven't actually decided on a name yet, but we will let him know as soon as we do. Please tell him he's welcome to come and visit at any time, and all his family too. It gives Lillian a chance to cook a special celebration meal. She loves doing that so he'd be doing her a favour."

"We'll pass your invitation on," Hanu said, feeling sure that Merac would be able to find a space in his busy schedule to enjoy the women of Spinnersholm's hospitality and cooking, both of which were legendary in Scatterstones.

"Would you like to see the baby?" asked Sofia,

Hanu squirmed a bit. He didn't really want to see the child, but he realised it would be impolite to say no. Tiski rescued him from his dilemma.

"Yes, we'd love to. Wouldn't we, Hanu?"

"Yes," said Hanu, with as much enthusiasm as he could muster, which wasn't much, but Sofia appeared not to notice his reluctance, because she smiled and stood up.

"This way, then. He's only a week old, so he'll probably be asleep, but that's OK, he's a little noisy when he's awake."

Hanu wasn't sure he liked the sound of that, but he dutifully followed Sofia through to an adjacent room, where a woman was sitting sewing next to a small wooden cradle.

"Gina, it's Hanu and Tiski from the estemble. They've come to see the baby.

Hanu shyly held out the gift to the sewing woman, whom he correctly determined was the baby's mother, and she took it with a smile. Sofia reached down into the cradle and took out what appeared to be a bundle of rags. She murmured some soft endearments to it, then held it out for Hanu's inspection.

Hanu forced himself to look. It was not as awful as he had imagined, but the child looked… strange. Unformed. Larval. When foals were born, they could stand within an hour of their birth, and run with the herd shortly after. When they emerged from the pearl, harlings were similarly developed enough to walk and talk within days. This thing wrapped in its bundle of rags did not look as if it would be capable of doing either of those things for weeks – if not months!

"It's… lovely." he said, without conviction. He peered down at the child, but he did not experience any of the wonder at the presence of new life that he had felt when Tezuk had been born. All he could think was that this one life was merely a drop in the ocean weighed against the death of humankind. A candle in the dark that could be snuffed out at any moment. It was not an agreeable thought in the face of Gina and Sofia's obvious pleasure in the new baby, so he smiled his most convincing smile and stroked the infant's cheek with his finger, feeling its softness, as cool and smooth as marble.

"He's a boy," the sewing woman said proudly. "A brother for Max."

For the first time, Hanu noticed an older child sitting beside the sewing woman. He was hiding shyly in the folds of his mother's clothing. He looked as if he ought to be able to walk, but Hanu could not tell what age he might be.

"Now Nicolai can be incepted," said Sofia. Hanu did not think she sounded as happy about that as she should have been. Obviously, it was a great thing for Nicolai to become har, and no doubt the women would all be pleased that he would not be condemned to become a man.

Another woman popped her head through the door. "We've got the fabrics all sorted out now. Would you like to come and inspect them?"

Sofia put the baby back into his cradle and they returned to the main room of the house where they had been drinking tea. Here, all the chairs had been covered with bolts of fabric, some plain, some woven into intricate patterns, some dyed in soft yet vibrant colours.

"You are so clever!" said Tiski, stroking a bolt of fabric admiringly. "I can't believe you can turn those dirty weeds into something as lovely as this. I should very much like to have a robe made from this, it's so beautiful. Isn't it beautiful, Hanu?" He turned to Hanu with an appealing look and a very unsubtle fluttering of his long eyelashes.

"I'll put that one in your cart then, shall I?" said Sofia, not even trying to conceal her amusement. She picked up Tiski's bolt of fabric, and another two besides, and took them outside. Hanu followed her lead but found, somewhat to his chagrin, that he could only manage one of the bolts, which were heavier than they looked.

Outside, Sofia passed her bolts easily to one of the other women who was loading up the cart and helped Hanu as he struggled with his burden. Hanu consoled himself with the thought that Sofia must be strong from all the physical work she did. He remembered Nirzhen telling him that women had been considered the weaker of the two human sexes, and he wondered exactly what sort of creatures adult men had been. In his mind, he imagined them to be twice as tall as a har, hairy-faced, thick-necked and heavily muscled, and he shuddered slightly, feeling relieved that there were no more of them in existence.

Sofia herself looked little different from most hara. She was somewhat taller than the average Gimrah har, who tended towards a slightness of frame, the tell-tale contours of her body hidden by both her clothing and a lifetime of hard work. As he stood next to her, however, Hanu could see one difference that marked her out very clearly as not har – her face showed visible signs of her age. Not the deep furrows in the skin that he knew were the sign of a human at the end of her lifetime, but small, subtle lines around her eyes and mouth, and flesh that was coming to an accommodation with gravity regarding its position on the bones that supported it.

Hanu tried not to stare, but he found it fascinating, since no har ever experienced such changes to his appearance due to the passing of time. The oldest hara in Scatterstones looked no different from any young harling just past his feybraiha. Hanu found it very odd that you should be able to tell how many years someone had been alive just by studying the skin on their face. He wondered if the women found it equally odd that it was not possible to do so with a har.

At that moment, another woman, whom Hanu supposed to be not long past childhood, judging by the condition of her skin, ran out of the house to join Sofia.

"Nicolai!" Sofia exclaimed, grabbing the young woman in a fierce, affectionate hug.

"This is my son, Nicolai," she told Hanu, smiling.

Hanu did a swift recalculation, and his brain reset itself with a small jolt. The woman-who-was-not-a-woman did not look any different to the rest of the women. He looked like a har.

"Nicolai is the father of the baby you saw," Sofia told him, and Hanu thought her smile became a little wistful at this point. Behind him, he felt the presence of Tiski staring at Nicolai with unabashed curiosity, and into his mind, via mind-touch, came an unwelcome image involving shoulders and teeth. He banished Tiski's invasion with a stern rebuke, but sensed no contrition from the other har, which didn't surprise him.

"You're the one who's going to be incepted, aren't you?" Tiski asked Nicolai, eyeing him with what Hanu felt was almost a little too much relish.

"Yes," said Nicolai, "at Shadetide. They say it's an auspicious time."

"You will make a most attractive har," said Tiski, with a winning smile.

Nicolai blushed slightly.

"Nicolai," Sofia said, "why don't you go and get some of those reels of thread from Livia – they'll need those for sewing the fabrics."

Nicolai nodded and trotted off in the direction of a small cottage on the other side of the courtyard. Sofia watched him go.

"You must be pleased he's going to be incepted," Hanu said.

"Must I?" Sofia's expression held little to suggest that she was.

"Well… becoming har is better than… what would happen to him if he didn't. Isn't it?" Hanu felt a little perplexed by her apparent lack of enthusiasm.

"For him it is, yes." Sofia glanced over in the direction of the main house. "Gina was hoping for a girl," she said thoughtfully. "A sister for Max."

"Why…"

"We give birth to them and raise them, boys and girls both, but we know we will have to give the boys up eventually. But they are still our children. We love them. But they are not *our* children. Nicolai… once he leaves here and becomes one of you, he will have a new life. He'll forget his old life. Oh, he may come back to visit, once in a while, but the person who returns will not be Nicolai. He will not be my son."

She managed a brief smile in response to Hanu's look of non-comprehension "You don't understand, do you? You don't have children…"

"No," said Hanu, realising he was missing something important here, but not grasping what it was. To him, it was self-evident that to be incepted and become har was a far, far better fate than to slowly change into some hairy-faced, thick-necked monster whose skin would fold and buckle with age.

"Things have changed," Sofia said briskly, as if trying to dispel the melancholy which had threatened to settle on her, "and we must make the best of them, for if we don't it will only be the worse for us! Now, come on, I think you need to be getting back, because the day has changed. It looks like rain is coming."

Sofia was not wrong about that. Dark grey clouds had appeared and covered the sun. A brisk breeze had sprung up, blowing the fallen leaves in the courtyard around in small whirls and eddies, and bringing down more of their companions from the branches of the trees. There was a decided chill in the air, now that the sun's warmth had gone from the day.

"Harcan doesn't like pulling the cart in the rain," Tiski said, patting the gelding who was standing patient and bored in the courtyard.

"Harcan just doesn't like pulling the cart at all. Come on now Harca – back up, round you come..." Hanu took hold of Harcan's harness with the intention of persuading him to turn the cart around, but before he could do anything, Harcan unexpectedly reared up in the traces, moving the cart backwards and snatching the reins from Hanu's hands.

Hanu took a step back in surprise, to avoid flailing hooves. Harcan dropped onto all four feet again, but continued to stamp and shuffle, tossing his head in obvious agitation.

"Whoa there, Harca... What's the problem?" Hanu spoke calmingly to the horse, but he could not conceal his surprise. He had never once seen Harcan behave like this. Harcan was as unruffled and placid a horse as you could wish for, and Hanu would have sworn that nothing short of an earthquake could disturb him.

Harcan shuddered and exhaled a deep breath, then gave Hanu an apologetic look. Hanu took hold of the reins again and patted Harcan reassuringly. "It's OK," he told the horse, "nothing to get alarmed about. Did something startle you?"

"What's up with Harcan?" Tiski asked, looking equally surprised. "He never does things like that. He's too lazy, for a start. Has he got a stone in his hoof?"

"Don't think so," Hanu said, examining Harcan, who now stood serenely within the traces of the cart as if nothing untoward had happened. "Maybe just the wind made him jump. He seems to be OK now."

With some gentle encouragement Hanu persuaded the gelding to turn the cart around. He led Harcan forward to the main gate at the end of the courtyard, letting him get the feel of the cart before he and Tiski climbed aboard as well. Experience had taught him that Harcan would be more co-operative if he was started off gradually. He didn't want to give the gelding anything else to get skittish about.

The main gate of the courtyard was made of wood, with a crossbar at the top under which the cart had to pass. Hanu glanced up and saw that nailed to the crossbar was a metal semi-circle, in the shape of a horse's hoof-print.

"There's something that's changed for the better," he said, pointing up at the metal loop. "We don't use those anymore."

The object was a horseshoe. A circlet of iron that men had nailed to a horse's hoof in order to prevent wear and damage to the foot. To Hanu, this represented everything that was wrong about men. Instead of taking care of their horses properly, or working them less, their solution had been to nail crude lumps of iron to their feet. Gimrah horses had been bred with hooves and legs that were stronger and more able to resist damage, and careful tending of them with healing energy ensured that they did not need such crude protection.

"They were supposed to bring good luck," Sofia told him

"Not very lucky for the horses who had them nailed to their feet!" Hanu said forcefully.

Sofia looked up at the horseshoe over the gate. One of the nails holding it to the wood had fallen out, and it now hung only by one side, the open part pointing downwards.

"But if they were upside down, then all the luck would run out." She laughed. "An old superstition. Take care, Hanu. You too, Tiski. We'll see you again soon."

Hanu and Tiski climbed up onto the front of the cart and with a light touch on the reins Harcan began to walk forward, albeit rather reluctantly. As they passed beneath the crossbar, Hanu looked up at the upside-down iron shoe, and an involuntary shudder passed through his body.

It must be the wind, he thought. *I'm as bad as Harcan.*

And indeed the wind was now getting up quite noticeably, sending the grey clouds scudding across the sky, and bending the branches of the trees, making the ends of them whip and sing. A couple of fat drops of rain landed on Hanu's head, and he cursed himself for not bringing his heavy outer coat, but the weather had been so pleasant when they'd left Scatterstones he hadn't thought he'd need its protection.

Across the greyness of the sky, two black birds flew, cawing noisily. Hanu wondered how it must feel to be a bird on days when the wind blew strongly, and no matter what direction you wanted to fly in, you could only go the one way. Perhaps the birds thought the same of hara, moved, as they often were, by events in their lives outwith their control.

The Gimrah believed the crows to be birds of omen, their presence signifying a time of change to come. It was the changing of the seasons, echoed in miniature in the changing of the day. A small portent of the future.

Hanu thought about the human race, men and women, and their time of change. Had they known it would come? Had they had any inkling, any premonition or foreboding? Had they woken from dreams of their own destruction and dismissed them as an illusion before returning to their sleep? Had they not listened to the warnings of the crows?

He watched as the two crows circled overhead, still cawing noisily. An uneasy feeling that they were trying to tell him something began to take root in his mind. He tried to dismiss it, but it would not go. *Were* they warning him of something? If so, what? And why him, of all hara? Perhaps they were merely taunting him for their own amusement – you could never tell with crows – but the feeling of dread would not leave him, and he turned to Tiski to see if he was experiencing it too. As ever, though, Tiski appeared entirely unconcerned.

"Do you think," he said slowly to Tiski, "that Wraeththu could ever suffer the same fate as humankind?"

"...huh? What?" Tiski, who had been distracted by his own reveries, or possibly just enjoying the scenery, turned to look at him in confusion. "What are you talking about, Hanu?"

"I was just thinking..."

"Never a wise move."

"...about what happened to the humans, and how they've ended up. Do you think that might happen to us some day?"

"No! I don't know! Probably not. Why should it? What are you talking about? You do come out with the most peculiar things at times, Hanu!"

"I suppose that's what they thought too. That it could never happen. Until it did. Until their luck ran out, and none of their gods or superstitions could help them."

"Are you trying to tell me that they should have nailed their horseshoe the right way up? Is that what you're saying?"

Hanu attempted to deliver a swift kick in the ankle to Tiski, but Tiski had been expecting this and neatly avoided it, sticking his tongue out at Hanu in reply.

"No," said Hanu weakly, somewhat at loss to explain what he

meant. "I mean... yes... sort of. There were things they could have done... better."

"Nirzhen says they alienated themselves from the Goddess and the spirits of the natural world, and that is why the Devastation happened," Tiski said, rather smugly.

"That won't happen to us," said Hanu, with certainty, "because the Goddess, the Dehara and the Aghama are always with us, to protect us and guide us."

"Are they?" Tiski looked at him guilelessly.

Hanu scowled. "Of course they are. They are in every har. And every horse."

"But not horseshoes?"

"No! Not horseshoes! That's just a silly superstition!"

Tiski tried to maintain a straight face at Hanu's outrage but failed ignominiously and dissolved into laughter.

"Oh Hanu! You're so *earnest* at times, I just can't help myself!"

Hanu simply sighed and shook his head. He picked up the reins and gave them a shake to encourage Harcan to get a move on. Surprisingly, the gelding was almost eager to break into a trot. Hanu could feel from him the twin emotions of disgruntlement at being required to go all the way out to Spinnersholm and then all the way back again for no apparent reason, coupled with his desire to get back to his warm stable before the rain started to fall.

"Not far now, Harca," he said soothingly, and one of the gelding's ears flicked back in acknowledgement.

As they approached Scatterstones, the grass gave way to a road, at first merely dirt worn down by countless horses' hooves, then paved with flat stone on which the cart ran easily. As they turned a corner toward the stables, Hanu saw a har run out towards them, his black clothes flapping in the wind like the crows' wings, his arms waving for them to stop. For a moment, he felt an unaccountable sense of foreboding, but he dismissed this when he saw that it was Nirzhen. No doubt he would berate them for spending too much time at Spinnersholm and returning too late to complete their chores.

He reined Harcan to a stop and Nirzhen slowed to meet them, taking hold of Harcan's bridle as he did so, stroking the horse's nose in an instinctual action. Despite this gesture, Hanu could tell from Nirzhen's expression that he was not happy.

"I'm sorry we're late," he began, "but we'll start on the stalls just as soon as we've unloaded this stuff, won't we Tiski?"

Nirzhen waved his hand dismissively, his expression still grave. "Never mind that," he said. "Get Harcan stabled and come up to the Eithak immediately"

"What for?" asked Hanu, feeling a niggle of anxiety return

Nirzhen looked him directly in the eye "It's the Tirtha," he said.

For a moment, Hanu wondered exactly what he had done that was so heinous that the Tirtha himself wished to see him. Surely an eskev being a little late back from a trip to Spinnersholm was not something the Tirtha would concern himself with.

"Is he... angry with me?" he asked apprehensively

"No," said Nirzhen flatly, "He's dead."

Chapter 5
The Funeral

Hanu had never attended a funeral before. This was because, being still young, he did not know any hara who had died, apart from the son of a friend of his hostling who had drowned three summers ago, but he had been given a private ceremony attended only by his close family.

In any case, the funeral of a Tirtha was nothing like the funeral of an ordinary har. And Merac had been no ordinary Tirtha – he had been known and respected by a great number of the leaders and important hara of other tribes in Jaddayoth, and many of these had now come to Scatterstones to pay their last respects.

Hanu could still not bring himself to believe that Merac was really dead. It seemed impossible that a har as vital and alive as Merac had been could be just gone. On that terrible day of dark omens, he had listened in disbelief as Nirzhen had grimly explained to him the circumstances of Merac's death. Apparently the Tirtha had gone over to the marshlands to the west of Scatterstones to help look for a young horse which had managed to get itself lost. The ground was wet and slippery, and Pilar, Merac's horse had lost his footing, fallen and rolled on top of the Tirtha, crushing him and killing him instantly.

Merac's body had lain in the Eithak for three days since that fateful afternoon when Hanu and Tiski had returned from Spinnersholm, while preparations were made for his funeral rites. All of Scatterstones seemed to hold its breath and stand still, even in the midst of this strange activity, even as the tasks of daily life continued on, as they must – the feeding and grooming of the horses, the cleaning of the stables, the harvesting of the crops in the fields. Nature cared nothing for the passing from this life of a har, even one as notable as Merac.

Now his funeral pyre had been built in the fallow fields, and the hienama had come from Ardith, the largest settlement of Gimrah, on the northern coast of the Sea of Shadows. He would officiate at the ceremony and perform the necessary sacraments and rituals, for Scatterstones, like most estembles, did not have its own priests or shamans. Among the Gimrah it was accepted that a har could communicate directly with whichever spiritual guide or being he felt was appropriate and needed no other to intercede on his behalf. It was only for events such as this that the assistance of an experienced hienama would be sought.

The funeral rites are necessary, Nirzhen had told Hanu, *not only for the deceased, but also for the living.*

Hanu wasn't entirely sure what he meant by this. It was clear to him that nothing the hienama or any other har did could bring Merac back or repair the hole in the fabric of their community that his death had caused. Nevertheless, he knew that he had a responsibility to participate in the funeral ceremony, as did every other har from the estemble, in order to honour Merac's life and achievements, and all the things he had done for every har and horse in Scatterstones.

And so, like every other har, he had dressed himself that day in red, the colour of mourning among the Gimrah. The colour of blood and the colour of death. He wore a red tunic, made from some of the finest fabric woven by the women of Spinnersholm and dyed with roots of a particular plant, and a stiff red woollen coat, for the day was chilly. He felt awkward in these clothes, wishing for the comfort and anonymity of his usual well-worn riding leathers, but accepted the discomfort as the small price he was required to pay.

Tiski was also dressed in red, but his garments were of a finer fabric than even the women of Spinnersholm could weave, for they were of silk made by the tribes who inhabited the lands beyond even the farthest eastern reaches of Jaddayoth. He had let down his hair as a mark of respect, and its bright lengths when unbound fell past his waist, shining as softly as the red silk on which it lay. A single red feather was caught into a narrow braid on one side of his head.

Nirzhen, practically and sensibly dressed as always, whatever the colour, examined them both with a critical eye.

"You both look good." he said approvingly, and this was high praise coming from Nirzhen.

"I don't want to do this!" Tiski sniffed, wiping his nose rather indelicately with the back of his hand. "This is awful! Why is this happening? Why did Merac have to die, Nirzhen?"

Seeing Tiski's distress, Nirzhen put an arm around him, rather awkwardly.

"Tiski… even hara do not live for ever," he said, clearly searching for the right words of comfort. "Eventually, all lives come to a conclusion and the soul moves on. It is the way of things. Merac will return to this realm in another form. He is not lost to Wraeththu forever."

"But I saw him that very morning!" Tiski wailed, oblivious to Nirzhen's consolations, "before we left for Spinnersholm, at the stables."

"It's just… Things happen, that's all. There are events in life over which we have no control. We have to accept that we are all at the mercy of fate, even the Tirtha." Nirzhen seemed at a loss as to how to deal with Tiski, who had buried his face in the anskev's scarlet jacket, sobbing noisily and leaving a rather obvious damp patch. Nirzhen patted his back clumsily and looked round in the hope of spotting some sort of escape route.

"It was no way for a Gimrah har to die!" Tiski said, with feeling.

"The horse cannot be blamed," Nirzhen said. "It was an accident."

"Nolath says that just before Pilar fell, he saw some birds fluttering around Pilar's head." Tiski made it clear that he considered this significant information.

"Did he now?" Nirzhen refused to be drawn, and his tone indicated that this was not a topic to be pursued, but Hanu felt his interest rise.

"What sort of birds?" he asked

"Those black and white ones."

"Not crows?"

"Well, they *are* crows. Sort of. Different crows."

"That's enough," Nirzhen told them.

Tiski appeared to recover himself a little, and he finally let go of Nirzhen, who dabbed rather ineffectually at the damp stain on his jacket with a red handkerchief.

"Come along, now," he said, urging both Tiski and Hanu toward the door rather in the way he might herd a group of unschooled foals. "It is time."

Together they left the stables and took the back path down to the fallow field at the southern boundary of Scatterstones, where Merac's funeral pyre had been built.

It was a cold day, summer's brief coda of three days ago now as dead as Merac himself. The wind had blown strongly since, stripping the leaves from the trees and depositing them in captured piles in the corners of the buildings and fencing. The naked branches were starkly visible against the grey sky, offering no concealment for the birds that perched upon them. Hanu thought he could smell winter on the wind; the mountains to the north would have their first covering of snow by Smoketide and, soon afterwards, the lowlands would lie beneath snow too.

Down at the fallow field, the entire population of Scatterstones had gathered, their numbers swelled by many visitors from other tribes. In the centre of the field a great mound of wood had been constructed, atop which lay Merac's body, draped in scarlet. Nearby was a raised platform where the important guests, dignitaries and members of Merac's immediate family stood.

In the centre of the group stood Ren. With the death of his hostling, Ren would now become Tirtha of Scatterstones, even though he was scarcely older than Hanu himself. To Hanu's eyes, Ren did not have the appearance of a leader. He had none of Merac's calm strength or natural authority. He simply looked small and uncomfortable in the formal setting. His dark hair was braided into a single long rope and around his neck he wore a gleaming metal circlet that had belonged to his hostling. It seemed too big for him.

Hanu wondered how it must feel to have the responsibility for the entire estemble suddenly thrust upon you. Of course, it was a great honour to become Tirtha, but Ren did not look as if he particularly wanted it, and Hanu could not blame him. His life would change from now on, with many restrictions and impositions along with the new status accorded to him. Ren had known, almost from the day he was hatched, that this moment would come, but like everyhar else, he had not expected it so soon or so suddenly, and he seemed more like a vulnerable harling who had lost his hostling rather than a new leader in the making

At his side stood Gavax, his hand on the younger har's arm, as if to give him support. To an outsider's view, it would have appeared that Gavax was the highest ranking har – he had an air of command about him that Ren lacked, and it was obvious that he was used to participating in formal ceremonial occasions in a way that Ren was not.

As Hanu watched, the Gelaming turned to Ren and whispered

something in his ear. Ren's face remained impassive. He did not turn his head or reply to his companion, his eyes remaining fixed on the red-covered body of Merac atop his funeral pyre.

On Ren's other side was another har Hanu did not recognise. Unlike every other har present, he was dressed completely in white. He stood out shockingly amidst the sea of red, drawing the eye in the way a single drop of blood on fresh snow would. Hanu knew he must be the hienama from Ardith.

As if by some unseen command, the crowd of hara surrounding the pyre parted like receding waters and through the division between them a solemn har led a large chestnut stallion, fully saddled and bridled but riderless. It was Pilar, Merac's own mount, saddled for the last time, for nohar would ever ride him again after this day.

The horse was led to the very edge of the wooden pyre, and both he and his handler stood there, silent and still in respect. Pilar's head was lowered, as if he realised that his friend and companion of many years would never come to him again or travel with him on pleasant journeys around the fields of Scatterstones and the wild places beyond.

The hienama took up a small metal bowl in his hands and raised it up before the assembled crowd. He spoke some words that Hanu could not quite catch from where he was standing. A thin curl of greenish vapour rose from the vessel, dissipating into the air above it almost immediately. The crowd murmured something in response, and it sounded to Hanu like the low moan of distress a horse gives before it dies.

At his right side, he felt a nudge, and he turned to find Nirzhen passing him another bowl, wooden, with tiny carvings of galloping horses around the rim, containing murky white liquid. He took it, sniffed the contents, then raised it to his lips and took a mouthful, trying not to taste the sour, fermented mare's milk as he swallowed it. He passed the bowl to Tiski on his left, who had been uncharacteristically quiet since arriving at the field, but Tiski simply shook his head, and so Hanu passed the bowl on to the har next in line.

He noticed that Tiski's lips were slightly blue, and he was shivering. This was hardly surprising, given the cold wind and the impractical light silken garments he was wearing. Hanu resisted the urge to admonish Tiski for his choice of clothing – now was hardly the occasion for that. Instead, he slipped off his own heavy woollen jacket and draped it over Tiski's shoulders. Tiski smiled at him gratefully, which Hanu found was ample reward for the discomfort of the chill he was now experiencing.

The hienama continued his liturgy, but the wind took his words away. All Hanu could make out was Merac's name echoed by the occasional caw of a crow flying overhead. He wondered if they'd known, the crows, three days ago, and were trying to warn him. Even Nirzhen, so hard-headed and practical in every other way, respected the crows and their wisdom, and had not mocked Hanu when he had told him of the ride back from Spinnersholm

Finally, the hienama finished his invocations. He stepped down from the platform and made his way to the edge of the funeral pyre. As he reached it, he was handed a flaming torch, which he held aloft for a few seconds before plunging it deep into the base of the pyre, among the kindling of straw and twigs and horsehair.

For a moment, nothing seemed to happen. The flames from the torch vanished into the pyre. Then a small plume of smoke arose, followed by a few bright tongues of fire, which spread rapidly through the base of the pyre, encouraged by the wind. The main wooden structure soon began to burn as well, and the smoke from the fire blew in ever-changing directions throughout the crowd.

Hanu watched in a sort of morbid fascination as the flames licked swiftly upwards, towards the covered body of Merac. Cremation, either horse or har, was not a common method of disposing of the dead amongst the Gimrah – the grassy plains around Scatterstones did not support enough trees to make it entirely practical, and during the summer months bodies could be buried in the ground, or as was often favoured, taken to some remote place to be devoured by wild beasts and birds. It was a last gift to the Goddess, to nurture other living creatures with one's own flesh, once it was no longer required.

However, for the funeral of a har as important as Merac, the fire had a more ceremonial and symbolic aspect; one of light and energy, and of cleansing and purification. But Hanu found that he could only think of the body roasting in the flames, as meat was roasted in an oven; the thought made him feel somewhat nauseous. He watched warily as the wind blew the smoke in their direction, hoping not to catch the smell of burning flesh.

He noticed that many of the hara closest to the pyre were starting to move away now, driven back by the heat of the flames, which Hanu could feel even from his more distant position. He thought now might be a good time to make his exit.

He nudged Tiski with his elbow. "Come on, let's go now. Nothing else we can do here."

Tiski nodded, and the two of them began to make their way back towards the top end of the field and the stables beyond. As they reached the boundary of the field, Hanu turned for a last look and saw a pall of smoke rising up from the funeral pyre. Merac's body, mixed with wood smoke and ash, blown away on the wind as if he had never existed.

"We're going to have to get used to it all being different now, aren't we?" said Tiski in a small, sad voice.

"No, of course not," said Hanu, more confidently than he felt. "Ren will take over. He will become Tirtha, and everything will continue on just as it has done. It'll be the same as before, you'll see."

"The same," said Tiski, "but different."

Hanu didn't even try to argue with this logic.

"I want to go and see Flor," said Tiski suddenly. "She'll be missing me. I haven't seen her all day."

"OK, then, let's do that," said Hanu, doubting that Flor would be pining away after being deprived of Tiski's presence for half a day, but glad of something to do to take his mind off what the future might hold.

They made their way to the stables and entered gratefully into their dim and musky interior. It was warm compared with outside, the harsh wind kept at bay and the inside made pleasant by the heat from the horses' bodies.

Tiski turned to Hanu and smiled shyly. "Thank you for giving me your coat," he said. "I shouldn't have worn this..." He plucked at his silken robe dismissively. "It's completely unsuitable. I don't know what I was thinking."

Hanu blushed slightly. "That's OK," he said. "I was too hot. I didn't need it anyway."

This was a lie. Hanu knew it was a lie and Tiski knew it was a lie, but they smiled at each other in mutually agreed deception.

"Come on," said Hanu, "Flor is desperate to see you, I can tell."

The young horses and foals had all been brought in from the fields and were now gathered together in a large communal area at the far end of the stables, where they would spend a large part of the winter. The arrival of the cold weather and their subsequent relocation to the stables had proved a shock to the young foals, who had known nothing else in their short lives but the warmth of the sun and the sweet fields of grass, and had expected that life would continue in the same way indefinitely. Flor, however, was quite used to this environment, having experienced her first months of life indoors, and her lack of concern about this strange turn of events was reassuring to the foals in the next pen

As usual, Tezuk was standing slightly apart from the main herd. Every time Hanu came to visit him he hoped that Tezuk would be in the centre of the group, half-hidden by the others. Every time he was disappointed.

Tiski leaned on the fence and called to Flor. Immediately, the filly trotted over and nickered her pleasure at Tiski's presence. Tiski stroked her soft nose and scratched under her chin. Hanu spoke to Tezuk, in as encouraging a voice as he could manage, but as usual the colt ignored him.

Tiski laughed at this, then, noticing Hanu's disappointment, patted the back of his hand sympathetically. "Don't worry, he'll learn to come to you soon enough."

"Do you think so?" Hanu asked, morosely. "He doesn't seem terribly interested at the moment. Flor always comes when you call her."

"Flor is older than Tezuk," Tiski reminded him. He turned his attention away from Flor, much to the filly's disgust, and looked at Hanu deliberately.

"All horses are different. Just like hara. It's not right to compare one with another. Every horse – and every har – has things they're good at, and things they're not so good at."

"Perhaps I'm not good at being an eskev." Hanu sighed. "Perhaps it's my fault Tezuk isn't fulfilling his potential."

Tiski laughed. "What an odd thing to say! *Fulfilling his potential.* He's a horse, Hanu, not a Nahir-Nuri! And you *are* a good eskev – Nirzhen wouldn't have taken you on if he thought otherwise."

Hanu said nothing.

"Anyway," Tiski continued, pointing at Tezuk who was standing motionless on the far side of the enclosure, "Just look at him! How can you say he's not *fulfilling his potential?* I'm quite sure there isn't another colt in the whole of Gimrah who looks so magnificent!" Tiski stared at Tezuk thoughtfully for a moment. "He looks like the statue. In the Eithak. Have you noticed that?"

"Do you think so?" said Hanu urgently

"Yes, he's the spitting image! His head, his chest, his legs..."

"... and his hoof." Hanu felt something tightening in his chest. "His back left hoof."

Tiski craned his neck for a better look. "Oh yes. I hadn't noticed that before. How strange."

"They say the Aghama sometimes appears to ordinary hara in the form of a horse," Hanu said, attempting to sound off-hand.

"Why wouldn't he?" Tiski said, grinning. "If you could be anything that you wanted to be, wouldn't you want to be a horse? Especially one as magnificent as Tezuk." He was silent for a moment. "Do you think Merac will be reincarnated as a horse?" he asked Hanu, in all seriousness.

Hanu blinked at him in confusion. "I don't know," he said. "You'd have to ask the hienama about that. I'm sure he'd know."

"That's what I'd like," Tiski said with a wistful sigh. "When I die, I'd like to come back as a horse, and spend all day just galloping over the fields with the wind in my mane, and maybe a har on my back. I would let some nice har ride me, because I would be big and strong and able to carry him and not even notice."

Hanu laughed. "Well you're not going to die any time soon, so there's no point in getting too attached to the idea."

"Oh well," said Tiski, "in that case, perhaps I'll just have to let some nice har ride me in this life." He looked up at Hanu artfully.

At first, Hanu did not understand what he meant, and when he did, he felt a blush spreading from his face, down the rest of his body and taking up residence around his mid-section.

"Did you...er... by any chance leave those cushions in the hayloft above Ishin's stall?" Tiski asked, still all innocence.

"Yes," said Hanu, barely able to get the word out. "They're still up there. Perhaps we should...? I mean, perhaps we could...?"

"Oh, I'm sure we could!" Tiski said, a broad, conspiratorial grin spreading across his face. He beckoned to Hanu to follow him, and Hanu found himself unable to resist.

Tiski climbed up the ladder which led to the hayloft above

Ishin's stall, and Hanu followed behind him. When they reached it, it was dark and full of the scent of hay. In the corner lay the pile of cushions Hanu had slept upon when Ishin had been due to foal.

The ceiling in the hayloft was low, so they were obliged to crawl over to the pile of cushions. There, they kneeled facing each other. Even in the gloom Hanu could see Tiski's pale hair clearly, falling down over his shoulders.

Tiski ran his fingers down his silken robe. In the dim light, its vivid colour looked almost black.

"When I said I didn't know what I was thinking when I chose to wear this," he said, his voice low and husky, "I was wrong. I *did* know. I was thinking that it made me look beautiful. Do you think it makes me look beautiful, Hanu?"

"Yes," Hanu told him, taking a fistful of the soft silk, and feeling its cool, smooth texture between his fingers, "But you would look even more beautiful without it."

And he knew that this was exactly the right thing to say, and even though he could hardly see Tiski's face in the dark, he knew that the other har was smiling as he lifted the robe over his head and uncovered his nakedness.

Hanu laid Tiski gently back on the cushions and ran his hands over the other har's body. His skin was so soft and smooth it made the silk feel like sack cloth in comparison, but it was warm to the touch. He ran his hands up Tiski's belly, feeling him shudder slightly, and his hips rise impatiently.

"You are one with the Goddess," he told Tiski solemnly, in recognition of the fact that Tiski had assumed the soume role.

Tiski giggled. "That sounds like something Nirzhen would say. Just get on with it, Hanu."

"That definitely isn't something Nirzhen would say," Hanu muttered, his hand slipping down between Tiski's thighs and feeling the wetness there.

"Nirzhen takes aruna *very* seriously," Tiski agreed, his voice hitching a little as Hanu's fingers found their target and his hips wiggling to indicate his approval.

"How do you know?" Hanu asked, a little querulously, even as he continued to probe.

"Oh, don't be jealous, Hanu! Anyway, haven't you ever...?"

"... with Nirzhen? No!"

"You're not missing much. It's all Goddess this and Goddess that, and incense and candles and prayers."

"I'm sorry all I can offer you is a cold hayloft."

"Oh Hanu, stop being so negative! Aruna is more than just rituals. It has to *mean* something. You have to *feel* it. Yes, like that!" He giggled again in response to Hanu's assertive entry into his body, and Hanu felt the small tremble vibrate through his own flesh, exiting somewhere around the base of his spine.

"So what do *you* think aruna should be like, if not the sacred worship of the Goddess?"

"Well..." Tiski's words were now coming a little faster, rhythmically synchronised with Hanu's movements, and Hanu could feel his warm breath on his cheek, as intoxicating as any incense.

"...it's like you're riding in the Grand Jaddayoth Challenge Race. You and your horse. And you've just jumped the last fence clear, ahead of every other har. And the rest of them are all behind you – you can hear the thunder of their hoof beats on the grass, but you know they won't catch you now because you can see the winning post coming up, and you're up in the saddle urging your horse on – *come on! come ON!* – and the crowd are all on their feet cheering and screaming and waving and shouting, and it's the Best. Day. Of. Your. Life. Ever. And... Oh."

And after that Tiski was silent for a while, as was Hanu, who offered a little prayer to the Goddess, the Aghama and any other dehar who was listening that he might have given Tiski the Best Day Of His Life. Ever. And by the way Tiski sighed as he laid his head in the crook of Hanu's arm, Hanu thought that he may just have done so.

Chapter 6
Change

In the weeks following Merac's funeral, life at Scatterstones proceeded just as before, and yet with small and subtle changes. A new routine here, a new order there, a new way of stacking hay bales, of repairing harnesses, of cleaning stables. Hanu found it disconcerting, but he could not say why. He began to wonder who it was, exactly, who was responsible for the changes wrought upon Scatterstones' routine. Ren did not look like a har who had the confidence to change his own mind, never mind change the running of the estemble. He grudgingly admitted that some of the innovations were actually improvements on the old ways, but he found himself resenting them anyway, simply because of what they represented. Change.

Hanu had never liked change. Even as a harling, he had preferred the comfort of the familiar, rejecting the new clothes his parents would insist he wore in favour of his worn but cherished older garments. When it was decided that extra windows were to be added to the stables to improve the interior lighting, he felt the same pang within him that he had felt when he had once returned home to find that Kam had thrown away a pair of his favourite old shoes, full of holes and too small for him anyway, and replaced them with shiny new ones, which he had refused to wear for a week until necessity forced them upon his reluctant feet.

The new windows were an improvement – anyhar could see that – but Hanu missed the dark corners of the stables where it used to be cosy and welcoming, and somehow he felt that he missed a part of his life that he hadn't fully appreciated until it had gone.

If Nirzhen disapproved of any of these new arrangements, then he gave no hint of it. He continued to perform his tasks without complaint or comment, for which Hanu found himself oddly grateful. It felt as if Nirzhen was at least one thing in his life he could rely upon to remain absolutely unaltered. In a way, he envied the anskev's ability to accept the new regime without resistance; to simply be borne along by unfolding events, rather as a twig is carried downstream by a river. Hanu felt more like a boulder stuck mid-stream, with the waters crashing to either side of him, unable to move or avoid the oncoming flood. He remembered the woman Sofia's pragmatism in the face of much greater change than he would ever experience, and resolved to try to be more like her, although as the weeks progressed, he was forced to acknowledge his lack of success in this respect.

He felt that the transition would have been made much easier if the new Tirtha had been blessed with the same of sort of leadership qualities as his late hostling, but it was very soon apparent to everyhar that Ren was not the har his hostling had been. Hanu knew from his experience with horses that desirable traits did not always pass from one generation to another, no matter how carefully things were planned, so there was no reason to expect that the same would not hold true for hara. Yet somehow he felt disappointed, although by whom he was not sure. By Ren himself, for simply being who he was? By Merac, for not having a better heir? By the dehara, for not intervening to ensure that Merac's finer qualities were transmitted to his son, or for letting Merac die in the first place? It seemed unfair, and doubly so for having no-one upon whom the blame could be satisfactorily laid.

And there was yet another factor which contributed to Hanu's continued discomfiture. It was announced that Gavax would be staying at Scatterstones for the foreseeable future in order to assist with the transition to the new leadership, and to guide Ren in his new role. Who had actually decided this seemed unclear – whether it was Ren himself, or Gavax, or the Gelaming administration in Immanion. Hanu was not privy to the finer details, as it was not his place, after all, to know or be informed about such things. But along with many of the rest of the estemble, gathered together in the Eithak, he listened as Gavax expressed his wish that the close relationship he had developed during Merac's reign as Tirtha should continue, and his declaration that he would be happy to provide guidance and instruction to Ren for as long as was needed.

In theory, this was a great honour, and a much-needed help to both the young Tirtha and his hara.

As one of Almagabra's closer neighbours, Gimrah maintained a better relationship with the Gelaming that many of the more distant tribes, and this suited both Gimrah and Gelaming, but despite the Gelaming rulers' vague efforts to maintain the convenient fiction that this was an association of equals, there was a power imbalance that everyhar, both Gimrah and Gelaming, were aware of. Thus, if a high-ranking Gelaming official were to graciously offer to mentor a young and inexperienced Gimranish Tirtha, a polite "no thank-you" was not an option to be entertained.

Merac had been an astute politician when it came to dealing with the Gelaming, earning their respect and trust while at the same time maintaining a healthy autonomy from them. Since Merac's death, Hanu had heard grumblings among the hara of the estemble that the Gelaming were now taking advantage of their new Tirtha's lack of experience to exert a greater, and possibly malign, influence among the Gimrah. Others, Hanu's father among them, insisted that closer ties with the Gelaming could only be of benefit.

"Do you want us to end up like some of those lawless tribes on the outer edges of Jaddayoth?" he had barked at Hanu when the issue had arisen at the last family dinner. "Like the Garridan? Or the *Mojag*?"

The last word had been almost spat out, and Hanu had found himself with no adequate response. While the Gelaming might not be as perfect as they claimed to be, it was true that there were far worse things a har might encounter in life.

Compared with some tribes, the Gelaming, for all their political machinations, seemed by far the most benign option, and the Gimrah were pragmatic enough to live with any minor disadvantages in return for the greater advantages afforded by an alliance with Wraeththu's most powerful tribe, and the practical assistance provided to an inexperienced leader.

Nevertheless, it was one thing to be allied at a distance with the Gelaming, it was another to have one of them living right amongst them. And Gavax har Gelaming did not exactly walk unnoticed among the hara of Scatterstones. Gimranish hara were generally well-muscled but of slight build, the better not to burden their mounts with unnecessary weight, and often nut-brown or dun coloured in hair and skin. Gavax har Gelaming was more than a head taller than most of the hara of Scatterstones and his pale skin almost seemed to glow in the early winter sunlight. His clothing was embellished with tiny iridescent pearls, treasures of sea-creatures from the far-off shores of Almagabra, lapped by the waves of an ocean which girdled half the world and touched land again on distant Megalithica. Or, at least, that's what Nirzhen said. (Although how he knew this was unclear, since he had never been to either place, but Hanu knew the futility of arguing with him).

As with most Gimranish hara, Hanu's clothing was designed with ease of movement and comfort in the saddle in mind, although this did not mean that the Gimrah eschewed ornament or decoration. Hanu wore a necklace made from braided horsehair and polished nuggets of coloured stone, given to him by Kam on the occasion of his feybraiha, and his ears were pierced to allow metal hoops to dangle from them, drawing attention (he hoped) to his slender neck. On festive occasions and, indeed, any occasion when he felt like it, Tiski enjoyed wearing streamers of colourful ribbons woven into his hair, but no matter how magnificently they decked themselves out, in the presence of the tall Gelaming, both felt scruffy and inelegant.

Privately, Hanu consoled himself with the thought that the Gelaming's clothing was somewhat impractical, especially for a Gimranish winter. Nirzhen said that the winters in Almagabra were much kinder than in Jaddayoth, with snow and ice unknown to them. Hanu found himself hoping that this winter would be a particularly hard one in Gimrah, and send the effete Gelaming scurrying back to his own temperate climate, or at least force him to don a heavy woollen cloak over his wispy silks. But Gavax seemed impervious to the cold, and continued to float around Scatterstones as if he carried with him his own personal Almagabran summer. Which, being Gelaming, he probably did.

Although he had become an all-too-familiar figure in and around the stables and dwelling houses of Scatterstones, the Gelaming was rarely encountered alone, for he was always in the presence of Ren, the new Tirtha. Or perhaps that was the other way around, for it seemed that the Gelaming was always in the lead, with the Tirtha following a few paces behind. Hanu found this even more infuriating than the Gelaming's fashion choices – no-har would ever have dreamed of behaving like this with Merac – not even the imperious Gavax. Anyhar who did not know better would think that it was the Gelaming who was the Tirtha, and not Ren.

These thoughts distracted Hanu as he went about his daily work in the stables, and he muttered crossly to himself as he broke open some bundles of hay for distribution, jabbing the innocent bales with his pitchfork with more ferocity than they deserved. At least he had the horses to console himself with. On fine mornings, such as this, he would take the geldings and mares who were not in foal out for a gallop across the grasslands for exercise. Some were keen, some less so. He'd given up with Harcan, who only slowed the whole troupe down, so the big gelding was left in his stall until later, when a few circuits of the paddock at a lazy trot could be reluctantly persuaded from him.

Hanu raised himself up in the saddle of the lead mare, Miran – as swift as the flowing river she was named for – aware of her powerful hindquarters moving rhythmically beneath him. His fears and anxieties began to melt away, until he was absorbed entirely by the drumbeat of Miran's hooves across the grass, the wind in his hair and the hot, snorting breath of the other horses behind him as they vied with each other to catch the fleet-footed Miran.

He felt that if he could only ride on and on for ever his life would be perfect and nothing else would trouble him again, but eventually he had to rein back and pull up the indomitable Miran. He walked her gently and easily back to the stables, with the steam rising from her into the chilly air, and sweat forming white, foaming curds across her dark flanks. He rubbed her and the other horses down until they were dry and set about doling out their morning rations of hay.

Breaking open the last bale, he noticed that the hayloft had not been kept properly replenished and was almost empty. He muttered to himself in annoyance, knowing that if Nirzhen saw this there would be trouble, so after giving Miran one last pat on her soft nose, he set off in the direction of the main barn to fetch some more. But as he left the stables he saw Tiski making his way along the main thoroughfare, and he stopped, pressing himself into the side of the nearest building, unsure of whether to continue.

Normally, he would have been pleased to see Tiski – they could have had a long conversation full of complaints about the new regime, boasts about the abilities of their horses and gossip about the luckless Nirzhen, but Tiski was not alone. He was accompanied by a new har, as he often was these days. The new har was Nicu. In a previous life he had been Nicolai, the son of Sofia the spinner woman, but at Smoketide he had been incepted and become har. Hanu had to admit that he made a very attractive har, with his smooth, pale skin, slim hips and glossy mane of hair. Tiski obviously thought so too and had been spending a lot of time with him. Time that he would previously have spent with Hanu.

Hanu sighed. It was perfectly normal for a newly-incepted har to wish to gain experience of aruna with an older har. It was perfectly normal for a har such as Tiski to wish to take aruna with an attractive har such as Nicu. Just because Tiski had taken aruna with Hanu on several occasions did not mean that he was obliged to do so again, or that he should forswear taking aruna with other hara. In fact, that would be downright odd, if not positively weird.

Hanu told himself these things several times. But it did not make him feel any better. He waited until Tiski and Nicu were out of sight, then plodded wearily over to the main barn. Here, he loaded up a hand cart with hay and trundled it back to the stables, keeping his head down all the time in case anyhar should attempt to get his attention or speak to him.

He stowed the bales in the hayloft, stacking it, in a burst of defiance, in the way it used to be done rather than in the configuration demanded by the new Tirtha or his mentor. When he was finished, he slipped quietly out the back and crossed the yard to the rear stable block where Tezuk and the younger horses were kept.

As usual, Tezuk was standing apart from the main group, and showed no sign of recognition when Hanu approached him, but Hanu was grateful to see his friend all the same. He stroked his nose, and Tezuk at least did not shy or pull away, but allowed him to run his fingers down his velvet muzzle and feel the warmth of his skin underneath the finest of hairs. He noticed that a few of the hairs were now white, which had not been the case when Tezuk had been a foal, and in spite of himself, he felt a tight knot of excitement form in his chest. Was Tezuk destined to be one of those horses who changed from black to white? The Great Ledger said no, for neither Ishin nor Tezuk's sire, Torem had Changed, and it was necessary for a horse to receive this gift from at least one parent. And yet... Did the Aghama not change from black to white? From the dark horse of summer, to the white horse of the lean winter months? Perhaps there were greater forces at work in the world than mere genetics.

He rubbed Tezuk's nose again and was gratified when the horse nuzzled his hand briefly, even if he suspected that he was just looking for a treat. Hanu conceded defeat and produced a delicacy for Tezuk, who snatched it away instantly. Hanu was so preoccupied watching the horse's fascinating jaw movements that he did not hear Nirzhen enter the stables and was startled when a voice suddenly spoke quietly in his left ear.

"You shouldn't worry about it; it's only a passing fancy. Tiski is a flighty har, but he is faithful to his friends."

Hanu jumped at this unexpected interruption to his daydreams and pretended he did not know what Nirzhen was talking about. "What? What do you mean? I don't..."

But Nirzhen merely smiled knowingly and handed Hanu a broom, indicating an area of spilled grain on the floor as he walked away.

Hanu scowled at Nirzhen's retreating back, feeling in some way outmanoeuvred. How did hara *know* these things, when he hadn't said anything at all! It wasn't fair. Nirzhen was obviously using some sort of mental trick available to him as a higher magical-caste har!

He pushed the broom at the spilled grain grumpily, then looked up as the door opened again, letting daylight into the stables, and silhouetting the shadow of two hara as they came inside.

Immediately Hanu straightened his posture and made more purposeful movements with his broom. The tall har with the floaty clothing and his smaller companion just behind him were instantly recognisable as Gavax har Gelaming and Ren, the Tirtha. Hanu felt within himself a small premonition of something unpleasant to come but tried to dismiss it. It was unusual for the Gelaming and the Tirtha to visit these stables, but not unheard of.

Nirzhen, too, became noticeably more businesslike when he saw Gavax and Ren, and strode over to them immediately, making a formal greeting to both. Hanu watched out of the corner of his eye. The group of hara stood for a while, discussing something, although he could not make out what from where he was standing. Then his heart sank as all three walked towards him and the stall containing Tezuk and the other three-year olds.

To his relief, they completely ignored him. Nirzhen began pointing out all the horses in the pen, naming them and their sires and dams, and proudly telling of each horse's achievements and abilities. Gavax and Ren nodded silently and intently, as if nothing could be of greater interest to them.

Nirzhen pointed out a white filly. "...and this is Ked, named for the soft snow on the plains. Her dam is Aral and her sire is Bazim. She can jump the height of a fully grown har and has the stamina of a horse twice her age."

The filly, in apparent recognition of this celebration of her magnificence, trotted over to the front of the stall and bowed her head graciously. Her long white forelock fell over her eyes, and she tossed her head back immediately, performing a skittish dance on her dainty hooves as she did so. Hanu could not help but smile to himself. Ked was a bit of a drama queen, but good-natured and inquisitive. Her white coat marked her out as extraordinary, and she was the sort of horse the Gelaming would pay handsomely for, once she was schooled and ready.

Gavax's eyes strayed over the rest of the small herd. "What about that one?" he asked, pointing at Tezuk.

Hanu felt his heart skip a beat.

"That is Tezuk," Nirzhen said. "He's named for his strength. His dam is Ishin, and his sire is Torem. As you can see, he's a magnificent specimen. His conformation is perfect."

"Can you bring him out so I can get a better look at him?" Gavax asked.

Nirzhen stiffened almost imperceptibly, and Hanu grasped the handle of his broom tightly, holding his breath.

"The three-year olds are not yet accustomed to handling in the way that the older horses are," Nirzhen said. "Although some are further along in their training than others. Now, Darun here..." He pointed out a handsome bay colt. Darun pricked up his ears upon hearing his name and ambled forward to greet Nirzhen.

Gavax dismissed him rather impatiently. "No, I really want to see that one. You Gimrah are famous for your horse-handling abilities. I'm sure you can manage him."

Nirzhen looked at Ren, who had apparently decided that was a good moment to study his feet. With a sigh, Nirzhen opened the gate of the pen carefully and reached out his hand slowly towards Tezuk, who regarded him warily, but did not back off.

"Come, Tezuk." Nirzhen spoke softly and gently.

Tezuk swished his tail several times but allowed the anskev to put his hand upon his withers and guide him out of the pen into the outer part of the stables.

Hanu held his breath and concentrated hard on his broom.

"That is certainly a magnificent animal," said Gavax, approvingly. "The reputation of the Gimrah for the quality of their horses is well-founded." He reached out a hand towards Tezuk, but the horse snorted, laid back his ears and took a few jittery steps backwards.

"Careful," said Nirzhen. "Tezuk is very highly-strung, and not used to strangers."

"I *am* familiar with horses, Tiahaar, highly strung or otherwise," Gavax informed him. He reached out towards Tezuk again, but this time Tezuk did not retreat. Instead his neck snaked out and his strong teeth closed on the Gelaming's trailing sleeve, pulling at it and tearing away a large piece of the silken material.

Gavax uttered a word not commonly associated with the Gelaming. Startled, Tezuk reared up on his hind legs. Both Nirzhen and Hanu immediately backed off from the horse, as far as they could get within the confines of the stables, both knowing that this was the safest option. Gavax did not move at first, but when he saw both Hanu and Nirzhen retreat, he looked for an escape route. He moved away from Tezuk, but not quite in time as the horse turned and lashed out with his back legs.

It was fortunate for Gavax that he only caught a glancing blow, for a well-placed kick from a horse can kill a har instantly. As it was, he only ended up on the stable floor, face down in the spilled grain and soiled straw that Hanu had not yet swept up.

Nirzhen helped the Gelaming to his feet, while Hanu, heedless of his own safety, approached Tezuk with calming words and slow movements. Tezuk eyed him warily but allowed him to approach. Hanu could see Tezuk's muscles trembling beneath his skin, although the horse was standing stock still. Hanu did not attempt to touch him but continued to utter soft words in a sing-song fashion, projecting calm and stillness into the horse's mind.

Gavax stood up and brushed the straw and debris from his clothes. He appeared unhurt, with only his dignity somewhat ruffled. Both Ren and Nirzhen made a great show of enquiring after his wellbeing, which he fended off with tight-lipped assurances that he was quite unharmed.

Tezuk twitched a bit, but Hanu continued to sing to him, and he did not rear again. Gavax, however, was in no mood to appreciate Hanu's skill in handling the nervous horse.

"Tiahaara, in my opinion this horse is dangerous," he said, examining his ruined sleeve. "That was not normal behaviour. It's not the sort of thing I would expect from a Gimranish horse." Gavax spoke in his usual dispassionate manner, but a small muscle at the corner of his mouth twitched.

"He's young, he's only a three-year old." Nirzhen spoke apologetically, trying to appease Gavax in the same way Hanu had calmed Tezuk.

Unfortunately, Gavax proved not as receptive as Tezuk. "Then I have to say, Tiahaar, I'm concerned as to what he will be like when he's fully grown. Horses are large and potentially very dangerous animals, I don't have to tell you that, and there is, unfortunately, no place for aggressive ones within harish society. I would be the last person to offer advice to hara as experienced with horses as yourselves, but if this particular horse is not responding to training, then it may be better to have it destroyed than to endanger those around it."

Hanu stifled a cry, but fortunately the three other hara were too intent upon the current situation to notice him.

Nirzhen's face hardened. "We do not kill our horses, *Tiahaar*."

"The decision is not for an anskev to make, I think." Gavax said mildly. "Our new Tirtha assumes the responsibility for such things. Perhaps we should hear what he has to say." He turned to look expectantly at Ren, who had remained silent and in the background throughout the whole episode.

"The horse… is known to have a questionable temperament," said Ren, uncertainly, looking at Nirzhen as if he expected the anskev to magically rescue him from this difficult situation.

Nirzhen's jaw muscles clenched, but he said nothing.

Unable to bear it any longer, Hanu thrust himself squarely in front of Tezuk, and confronted the trio, who, suddenly noticing his presence, all turned to look at him simultaneously. "You can't kill him!" Hanu felt like running away and hiding underneath a pile of manure, but he stood his ground.

"You can't kill him," he repeated, defensively.

"And why not?" asked Gavax, in his customary reasonable tone. "I don't think it's up to you, either."

"Because… He is the Aghama!"

A stunned silence greeted this announcement. All three stared at him as if he had suddenly grown hooves and a tail.

"He is... what...?" Gavax asked him, incredulously.

"He is the Aghama," Hanu repeated stubbornly

"Hanu..." Nirzhen simply shook his head, lost for words.

"And how do you come to that conclusion, my young friend?" asked Gavax

"Because he is like the statue in the Eithak. He has the hoof and everything. And because..."

Hanu had a million other things he wanted to say that proved Tezuk was the Aghama, but he was aware of how ridiculous they would appear if spoken out loud, so he lapsed into frustrated silence.

"Don't be so absurd," Gavax said, as if patiently explaining something very obvious to a slow harling. "The Aghama does not turn himself into a horse!"

At these words, there was a sharp but barely audible sound of indrawn breath from both Nirzhen and Ren, who looked at each other meaningfully for a few seconds.

"Well... actually... Tiahaar..." Ren stuttered nervously. "He... I mean... It is... He does..."

"What the Tirtha is trying to say," Nirzhen said slowly, "is that the Gimrah believe the Aghama *does* appear in the form of a horse. It is his gift to us as the Horse Hara, and it is why we worship him as the statue in the Eithak. No doubt our Tirtha will have explained to you how important this belief is to our tribe." He looked again with deliberation at Ren, who straightened himself up and addressed Gavax more regally.

"It's true, Tiahaar. We are blessed by the Aghama when he appears to us in the form of a horse. I'm sure you meant no disrespect. However, it would be unwise of you to dismiss this devotion of ours as mere superstition. If good relations are to be maintained between Almagabra and Scatterstones, that is."

If Ren could not quite make this last comment sound like the threat he intended it to be, then at least it demonstrated to Gavax that there were limits to the Tirtha's complaisance.

"Of course," Gavax said, with an unconvincing attempt at a conciliatory tone. "The Gelaming respect all tribes' beliefs and customs. No disrespect was meant."

Nirzhen stifled a small sound, which could have been a cough.

"Perhaps you should show our honoured guest some of the horses in the east stables." He addressed Ren with the due degree of deference, which implied a suggestion rather than a directive, and Ren took the opportunity gratefully.

"Yes, I think that would be a good idea. If you would be so kind as to accompany me, Tiahaar..." He motioned with his hand toward the exit, and Gavax swept through it without a backward glance, his silken robes floating behind him.

Hanu gently encouraged the now-quiet Tezuk back into the stall and closed the gate after him. He picked up his broom, which was resting against the bars of the fence, but if he thought he would be allowed to slip back into the anonymity of sweeping, he was disappointed.

"Why...?" Nirzhen asked, shaking his head in exasperation. He didn't even sound angry, which made Hanu feel even worse.

"Because he wanted to kill Tezuk!" Hanu cried defensively.

"But... The *Aghama*? Hanu, really..."

"He's different from other horses. You know that. You can see it. Everyhar can see it!"

"Hanu..." Nirzhen sighed deeply, searching for the right words. He paused for a moment, then continued. "Horses... haven't always been the way they are now. They haven't always been biddable animals that can be ridden and put to work. Once they were wild creatures. Some still are. There are herds of wild horses to the north that have never known saddle or bridle, and never will. But humankind took the ancestors of all the horses here in Scatterstones, and bred them carefully, just as we still do today, to mould them into the creatures we live with in harmony. But the wild horse... it's still there, inside all of them. Still a part of them, deep down. And sometimes, despite all our care, despite all our grand Ledgers, it comes out. Do you understand what I'm saying?"

"Yes," said Hanu sulkily.

Nirzhen nodded and turned to leave.

But Hanu refused to let it go and addressed Nirzhen's back desperately. "But the Aghama *does* appear to us as a horse – you said so yourself! He comes among us to protect us in times of need, and to save us!"

Nirzhen turned round once more. "To protect us from what, Hanu? To save us from what?"

"I don't know, but... You'll see! You will! He's here for a reason, I know it. Can you be so sure that he's *not* The Aghama? Can you?"

Hanu was aware he was speaking out of turn, and showing disrespect to the anskev, but he felt an overpowering compulsion to make Nirzhen see the truth. To his surprise, Nirzhen didn't instantly issue him with a week on manure turning duties in punishment, but instead stood looking at him strangely for a few moments before picking up a sack of oats from the outside of the pen.

"Get on with your work," was all he said, before lugging the oats to the far end of the stables.

Hanu found himself shaking all over, as Tezuk had when Gavax had approached him so carelessly. Normally, he would never argue with an anskev, but this was too important a matter to let his own cowardice prevent him from doing the right thing.

He thought about what Nirzhen had said, about the wild ancestors of the horses of Scatterstones. He could not believe that Tezuk could be a throwback to those distant creatures and would all his life remain too wild and untameable to be ridden. All Tezuk needed was the right handler. The right har, who knew him and his moods. Why, far from being an untameable throwback, Tezuk already would come when called by name, most of the time, and would stand quietly, on occasion, for Hanu to brush him down with the stiff-bristled dandy brush in the mornings, making his dark coat gleam like satin. Those were not the actions of a wild horse. It might take Tezuk a little longer to learn the things that the other three-year olds were already picking up swiftly, but he would, in the end. It just took time, and patience, and the right har.

Very quietly Hanu unlatched the gate of the pen, and slipped inside, making sure to close it behind him. The cluster of horses at the far end took no notice of him, used, as they were, to his presence. Tezuk spotted him immediately and eyed him warily.

"Tezuk..." Hanu spoke soothingly, and the horse's ears flicked back, nervously rather than angrily. He allowed Hanu to come near, standing stock still, his legs four immoveable pillars. Hanu approached him from the side, which is the best way to approach a horse, so that they can see you coming. He reached out and patted Tezuk's neck gently. A muscle twitched underneath the gleaming coat, but Tezuk still did not move.

Hanu entwined his finger in the coarse hair of Tezuk's mane. He laid his head against the horse's broad chest. He could feel the great heart beating within, slowly, steadily, just waiting for the opportunity to pump the huge quantities of blood required to sustain the horse at a gallop. Tezuk was magnificent – every part of him was a perfect running machine, from his long neck, wide chest, broad back and strong legs designed to carry him effortlessly over the vast grasslands around Scatterstones. It was a crime against nature for a horse like this to be kept penned up in a stable.

Hanu tightened his grip on Tezuk's mane, then with a fluid movement born of long practice, leapt up onto the horse's back.

For a moment, Tezuk did not react. Hanu wondered if the horse even noticed him sitting upon him. Hanu was small and insignificant compared to the size of Tezuk, who, at three-years old was already as big as many a full-grown horse. But the wild horse within him knew that enemies and predators would leap on him in this way. A horse has no fangs or claws to fight them off, but those wild ancestors of his had given him a different weapon.

He reared and bucked, twisting his spine and kicking out with his hindquarters. Hanu held on to his mane for all he was worth, but without the aid of saddle or stirrups it was an impossible task, and he felt himself flying through the air for what seemed an eternity before he landed with a painful thump on the stable floor.

He could feel the great bulk of Tezuk rearing above him, feel the heat from his body, and the fear and anger within his mind. He curled himself up as tightly as he could, for he knew if just one of those hooves came down upon him with the force that he knew Tezuk was capable of then he would be killed instantly. Tezuk bucked and twisted a few more times, then, apparently satisfied that the predator had been dislodged from his back, quietened and danced skittishly for a few moments.

Hanu still did not move. If Tezuk was still in self-defence mode, any movement from him could set him off again, risking injury from both his stamping hooves and his strong teeth. He felt something brush past his face, and he curled tighter, expecting the worst, but all was silent, and all he felt was the velvet softness of Tezuk's nose against his face and his hot breath as he nuzzled Hanu curiously.

Hanu sat up very carefully and risked a gentle finger or two across Tezuk's nose. Satisfied that the predator had been vanquished and his eskev had also survived the encounter, Tezuk wandered off unconcernedly towards the hay manger at the side of the stall. He ripped mouthfuls of hay from it and chewed them casually, as usual ignoring both Hanu and the other horses.

Hanu breathed a sigh of relief, and got to his feet, mentally tallying the bruises he would have tomorrow. It had been a stupid thing to do, he realised that. Tezuk had not yet been broken to the saddle, far less learned to tolerate a har upon his back. He had simply been too impatient, and besides Tezuk had still been unsettled after his encounter with the Gelaming, which was enough to make anyone – har or horse – irritable.

He withdrew from the stall, carefully fastening the gate behind him, and resumed his sweeping. In due course, he would begin Tezuk's training, when he was ready. But not today.

Chapter 7
Journey

Winter came and went. During one particularly fierce blizzard, the snow reached almost to the top of the Eithak, and the hara of Scatterstones had to dig their way out of their dwellings. Half a herd of sheep were lost in the lower field and the lone tree on the eastern edge of the estemble came down under the weight of snow on its branches. Older hara said this was unremarkable and told tales from their youth when the snow had been twice as deep and the winds three times as strong.

Hanu celebrated Natalia with his family, as he always did, and received from his parents a pair of earrings set with faceted coloured stones, which danced and sparkled in the light when he turned his head.

The elderly cat belonging to his hostling finally gave up the struggle for existence and departed from its life, as it had been threatening to do for as long as Hanu could remember. Privately, Hanu thought this was a blessing, but Kam was upset, so he said nothing, but merely eulogised the cat's finer qualities, which took some doing as they were limited in number.

Shortly after Natalia, Nirzhen announced that he was with pearl, which came as a shock to Hanu as he had difficulty imagining that Nirzhen had any form of personal life outwith the stables, and he was not entirely sure that he approved. He knew that Nirzhen was blood-bonded with a har named Zanutha who crafted beautiful and intricately tooled leather goods, but he spent all his time working in his studio, and was not greatly sociable, so the eskevi rarely saw him. Hanu wondered how this development would affect the running of the stables, and whether Nirzhen would be less involved with the horses once he had a harling to consider. It seemed unlikely to Hanu – Nirzhen was as much a part of the fabric of life in the stables as the wood and stone from which they were built, but it was yet another change, to which Hanu looked forward with trepidation.

Hanu did not see much of Tiski during the time of Natalia as Tiski was instructing Nicu in the traditions of the estemble –

mostly, it seemed, the ones to do with the drinking of ales and imported wines. However, when the light began to return and the horses stamped their feet and jerked their heads excitedly as if they could smell the grass even before it started growing again, Tiski presented Hanu with a jar of pickled vegetables, which he claimed to have made himself, and said he was sorry for not seeing Hanu at Natalia.

Hanu knew that Tiski had not made the pickled vegetables himself, but had bought them from Ofian, a har who managed a small provisions market in the estemble. He did not much like pickled vegetables, anyway, but accepted the gift in the spirit in which it was offered.

Gavax har Gelaming did not return to Almagabra for the winter, as Hanu had hoped, but he noticed, not without a certain amount of spiteful pleasure, that the Gelaming had taken to wearing a heavy woollen overcoat over his diaphanous garments, and sturdy leather boots instead of his elegant sandals, which quickly became covered in mud as the snow began to melt.

In the spring, Nirzhen was successfully delivered of a pearl, and Hanu attended the harling's hatching ceremony along with Tiski and the other eskevi under Nirzhen's charge, plus members of Nirzhen's extended family, which seemed to comprise at least half the estemble. The Tirtha did not attend, which elicited some gossip amongst hara of a less enlightened nature.

A good number of foals were also born in the spring, and when the warm and lingering days of early summer finally arrived, the four-year olds – grown foals of springs past – were prepared for sale at the Cuttingtide Fair at Ardith.

There were many horse fairs held throughout Gimrah during the year. Some were small, local events confined to one or two estembles, others were grander affairs attracting hara from all over Gimrah and beyond. Of these, the great fair at Ardith, held every year at Cuttingtide, was by far the largest and most important. Every estemble wished to be represented, and would send their very best horses, not only for sale, but also to display their expertise in horse-breeding to the rest of the world.

Hanu had in the past attended some of the small, local fairs which, while a welcome diversion from his daily chores and generally a pleasant day out, were low-key affairs compared with the Cuttingtide Fair at Ardith. Hanu had, in fact, never been to this fair. His lowly status did not accord him all the privileges that more experienced hara might accrue, and a trip to the Cuttingtide Fair was a much sought-after opportunity. However, this year it had been decided that Nirzhen would not attend, because of having to care for his young harling, and that both Hanu and Tiski would be allowed to go in his place, it being right and necessary that an anskev of Nirzhen's experience would need two less experienced eskevi to replace him.

Hanu was delighted with this decision. He ignored the comments of certain hara who suggested that it might be deemed an insult to be considered only half of Nirzhen's worth. He told himself, and Tiski, that these remarks were prompted merely by envy, and in that he was almost certainly correct.

For several weeks leading up to the Cuttingtide Fair, Hanu worked hard on preparing the horses who were to be offered for sale, feeding them the correct diet to bring them into optimum condition, exercising and grooming them so that they would be in peak form. It was not only his own standing as an eskev which depended upon these horses looking their best, but the reputation of Scatterstones itself, and it was a responsibility which Hanu took very seriously.

Finally, the day came for their departure, and Hanu was up before dawn. He'd barely been able to sleep the night before due to his excitement. Ardith was some two days' ride from Scatterstones, west of the Steppelands and situated on the northern shores of the Sea of Shadows, so it was no small undertaking to transport the horses and everything required for their well-being there.

Hanu had packed a minimal amount of clothing and personal effects for himself, but he was generous with the amount of accessories he included for the horses under his charge – not only combs and brushes and oil for their hooves and scented soap for their manes and tails, but ribbons and bells and feathers and other decorations, (which none of the horses had ever worn before, and probably never would again), not to mention spare harnesses and blankets and nose-bags and treats of apples and sweet parsnips in case such things could not be found in Ardith.

At the appointed time, he met up with Tiski in the top field, where all the hara who were going to the fair and their horses were milling around in a buzz of excitement. Tiski, being an excitable har at the best of times, was hardly able to contain his agitation. He jumped up and down on the spot, causing his high tail of hair to flick up and down at the same time.

"I'm. So. Excited!" he told Hanu, breathlessly.

Hanu tried to appear more casual, as if it was nothing to him to be travelling for the first time to the biggest horse festival in all Gimrah, as if it were the sort of thing he did every day, but the knot of excitement in his stomach made a lie of his pretence at a cool exterior. He grinned at Tiski. "We should be going soon. Are you sure you've got everything?"

Tiski nodded. "All packed and ready. And I've got an oilskin in case it rains!"

Hanu looked up at the cloudless sky, pearlescent in pinks and blues in the pre-dawn light. "I don't think that's going to be much of a problem," he said

"You never know," Tiski told him primly. "Oh look!" He pointed to the far end of the field where a har on a beautiful white horse had just appeared, "There's Ren. We must be about ready to go."

Hanu followed Tiski's pointing finger. There indeed was Ren, mounted upon the Faraldienne Ishfar, accompanied, as always, by Gavax on his own weird mount. They looked both magnificent and otherworldly in the early light – ethereal creatures that might vanish as swiftly as the morning mist once the sun rose. In contrast to the herd of young horses milling around them excitedly, both were as still and calm as the eye of a storm. A slight wind lifted the mane from Ishfar's neck, and he raised his head and sniffed the air in anticipation, smelling the day to come, and all its as-yet-unfolded happenings.

At some signal which Hanu did not see, both Ren and Gavax urged their mounts into motion, and the crowd of horses around them fell away. A ripple of anticipation spread through the group, and slowly the company of hara and horses began to drift out of the field, somewhat haphazardly at first, but then with more organisation and purpose.

As well as the horses who were to be offered for sale, there were others acting as pack horses, laden with all the accoutrements which would be required for their stay in Ardith, and riding animals to carry hara like Hanu and Tiski.

Gradually the company formed itself into a long, chaotic

caravan and set out from Scatterstones along the trail that led out over the grassy Steppelands and towards Ardith.

It was a beautiful morning for a ride. When you are a Gimranish har, it is *always* a beautiful morning for a ride (or so Nirzhen would tell his eskevi, on days when the rain was at its heaviest), but this morning was particularly lovely: the sun just barely risen, the air still cool and clear, and the great, rolling plains of grass sprinkled with jewel-like wildflowers stretching to the far horizon. Hanu gave thanks to the Goddess that She had chosen to fashion this world with such breath-taking beauty, and that She had allowed him to be alive and to live in it.

There was only one thing that could have made this morning more perfect, and he tried to put that out of his mind as he rode up alongside Tiski, hoping the other har would notice him.

Tiski did indeed notice his approach and smiled. He was riding Flor, and Hanu had to admit she was looking particularly fetching that morning, with her mane and tail lifting gently in the soft breeze and her golden coat shining like satin in the sunshine.

Flor was not going to be sold. There had never been any possibility of that, from the moment she was conceived. Her lineage was compromised and her configuration imperfect, and while that might not matter overmuch to other hara, it mattered greatly to the Gimrah. It was a matter of pride to each estemble that they only sold the very best of their horses.

And yet, despite her short legs, narrow chest and inelegant gait, Flor had her virtues. She had taken easily to harness and saddle, being more amused than alarmed by this new development. If there was an ancestral fear of predators leaping upon their backs buried deep within most horses, it appeared to have passed Flor by. The mare seemed undisturbed that her harish friend now wished to ride upon her back rather than walk at her side, regarding it as quite the amusing game.

Tezuk, in contrast, had yet to learn to accept saddle and bridle. Hanu was keen to point out to anyhar who would listen that this skill came later to some horses than others. All horses were individuals, just as all hara were, and rigid conformity was neither expected nor desired in either. Tezuk, therefore, would not have been going to the Cuttingtide Fair anyhow, but he was currently confined to a pen alone after breaking down the stable door and smashing it into a thousand splinters with his iron-hard hooves, after one of the other eskevi had unwisely slapped his haunches too vigorously.

Hanu wished that he could have been riding Tezuk. He could imagine all the other eskevi at Ardith looking at him with admiration and envy for having such a beautiful horse, whispering amongst themselves about Tezuk's magnificence, and wishing that they, too, could have such a mount. But it was not to be. Not this year, anyway.

Hanu was therefore riding Miran, the mare who led his unruly troupe for morning exercise, and who could outrun them all. This was nothing to be ashamed of. Miran was as beautiful as she was swift, her chestnut coat the colour of fiery autumn leaves, her mind bright and enquiring. Hanu could feel the mare's mood as easily as he could feel her rhythmic movements beneath him. He could feel her pleasure at the warm sun on her back, her eagerness to stretch out her legs in a gallop across the wide, green grasslands and her pride at the newly-conceived foal inside her, a result of a successful mating with a favoured stallion just a few weeks ago.

Hanu decided to try and forget his disappointment at not being able to ride Tezuk to the fair and simply enjoy the ride. He gave Miran a small prick of encouragement and the mare responded instantly by breaking into a brisk trot, her ears pointing forward eagerly, showing that she was keen to pick up the pace. He heard Tiski's squeal of frustration behind him and Flor's slightly awkward gait and snort of breath as she drew level with Miran.

"Hey, not so fast – what's the rush?" Tiski laughed, trying to steady Flor, who looked a bit surprised at this unexpected turn of speed.

"Miran wants to get moving,"

"Does she now? Well, she'll have plenty of opportunity for that. Don't wear her out – it's two days' ride to Ardith."

"I know, but it's a lovely morning for a ride!"

Tiski laughed. "What do you think we'll do in Ardith?" he asked, leaning over Flor's neck and straightening a few wayward strands of her mane.

"I'm going to get Miran and the others stabled, fed and watered. Then I'm going to wander round and look at the horses from all the other estembles."

"Yes, but after that…?"

"What do you mean?"

"I mean, Ardith is a big place. And it will be full of hara there for the fair."

"I'm sure it will. Your point being?"

"Oh, nothing." Tiski affected an air of nonchalance, which Hanu pointedly ignored.

"We'll be very busy trying to sell the horses," Hanu told him.

"That's Ren's job, surely, as Tirtha."

"He'll need help."

"He's got Gavax to help him," Tiski said, looking over at the Gelaming.

Hanu pulled a face.

"You don't like him, do you?" said Tiski

"No. Do you?"

Tiski shrugged. "He's Gelaming."

"What's that supposed to mean?"

"It means we're supposed to respect him."

"Why?"

"Because they're enlightened or something. They're the most advanced Wraeththu tribe. I don't know! They're Gelaming. That's all there is to it!"

There was silence for a moment or two.

"Nirzhen says that if it wasn't for the Gelaming uniting all hara under the Confederation of Tribes then we'd be overrun by Mojags and the Maudrah. And possibly even the Garridan. And who would want that?"

Hanu was having none of it. "Nirzhen says! Why do we always have to do and think what Nirzhen says? Why can't we think for ourselves?"

Tiski rolled his eyes dramatically. "If you're going to be like that, it's going to be a long ride to Ardith!"

There was another pointed silence, broken only by the regular clopping of Flor and Miran's hooves.

Hanu sighed, recognising that it was now his turn to be the peacemaker. "So, what are *you* going to do when we get to Ardith?"

Tiski turned to him, smiling winningly, as if their spat had never happened. "I hear there are many places that sell the finest food and drink from all over Jaddayoth. I might try a few of those. And I might try a few of the hara, too. There are many different types of aruna practiced by different tribes. A har should always try to broaden his education in that respect, don't you think?"

Hanu knew that Tiski was being deliberately provocative, and that he should not allow the other har the satisfaction of seeing him needled, but his face gave him away.

Tiski roared with laughter. "Oh Hanu, how can you be so *prudish*? You're har. You're supposed to enjoy aruna, as we all are!"

"Yes, I know. How is Nicu, anyway?" he asked waspishly, feeling – somewhat unworthily – that he had equalled the score with this jibe, but Tiski was unabashed.

"He's well. He's a very fine har. I like him." He leaned over in the saddle and patted Hanu's arm. "Don't worry, I like you too. We're hara – it's OK to *like* more than one har at a time!"

Hanu said nothing. He knew he shouldn't hold a grudge against Nicu because of Tiski. Nirzhen said (*Nirzhen said!*) that such feelings only hurt those who harboured them, never those who were the object of them, and that all hara should strive to be above such things, to gain inner peace. Hanu tried to think positive thoughts about Nicu. He was the son of Sofia, the spinner woman, after all, and he liked Sofia. He was sure that Sofia would be pleased if her son were to make friends with other hara now that he was a har himself.

Nicu had taken employment as apprentice to Mizahal, a clothes-maker who sewed some of the finest garments in Scatterstones. This was a sensible move, in view of his background. Clothes were a necessity for every har, so it was a useful profession. Nicu was not, however, a horse-har. He would never be a horse-har. Hanu was a horse-har. Nicu was not. Hanu was not sure Nirzhen would approve, but he felt his inner peace blossoming whenever he reminded himself of this fact.

"Has Nicu been back to see Sofia and the other women since he became har?" he asked Tiski.

"I don't think so. Why do you ask?"

Hanu shrugged. "No reason."

"I think you have a bit of a crush on Nicu," Tiski said, glancing slyly at Hanu

"What? No, I don't! What a stupid thing to say!"

"Don't worry, I won't tell anyone!"

"Tiski!"

Tiski laughed. "I think what you need is to find a nice har in Ardith and take aruna with him. Get it out of your system."

"I haven't got anything to get out of my system, thank you."

"It'll do you good. Nirzhen says.... Oh, look out, Berun is wandering off again. Over there. He really is an idiot! Where does he think he's going to go? You stay here with the rest. I'll fetch him back."

Tiski gave Flor an encouraging poke with his heels. The mare broke into a clumsy canter and set off in pursuit of a large bay, who had decided to trot off in entirely the opposite direction from the rest of the caravan. By and large, horses were not difficult to keep together. Their natural instinct told them to stay with the herd, but Berun had an inquisitive nature, and was easily distracted by the slightest thing. Privately, Hanu thought Berun was not altogether the smartest horse he had ever met, but he would make a good mount for some har who enjoyed visiting unexpected places.

Hanu watched as Tiski made contact with Berun and began herding him back towards the main group. As they passed Ren and Gavax, Hanu noticed that both Flor and Berun seemed to avoid getting too close to the Gelaming and his *sedu*. They knew the *sedu* wasn't a horse, too – Hanu could see it in their body language – the stiffening of their muscles, the twitch of their ears, the flick of their tails. He wondered exactly what sort of creature the *sedu* really was, in reality. It would be pointless to ask Gavax, even if he could work up the courage to do so. The Gelaming would never tell him the truth, he was sure.

Instead, he focussed on the forthcoming events in Ardith. He had been so busy contemplating the fair and the horses, that it hadn't even crossed his mind there might be other adventures to be had in Ardith. Now that Tiski had brought the subject up, though, he felt intrigued. His thoughts seemed to transmit themselves to Miran. The mare quickened her pace, as if she, too, was eager to reach their destination. They rode on, as the sun rose higher and the breeze gained strength, each lost in their own thoughts of what lay at the end of the ride.

Chapter 8
The Fair

Compared with other Wraeththu cities, Ardith was an unexceptional place. It boasted none of Immanion's soaring towers and palaces, none of Jael's airy castles, not even the magnificent, elegant and half-built rose-and-cream turrets and minarets of Kalamah cities. Instead, its buildings were low and modest, built from stone and wood, and its streets cobbled with a horse's hooves in mind rather than the sweep of an expensive gown.

Nevertheless, it was still the biggest place Hanu had ever seen.

Ardith lay on the coast, by a wide bay on the north western shores of the Sea of Shadows. Once there had been human settlements here, but they had been abandoned many years ago and what remained of the buildings had been dismantled and reworked into dwellings and premises more pleasing to the Wraeththu inhabitants who came after.

The town occupied a strategic position, being accessible by sea from all the tribal lands bordering the Sea of Shadows, from Maudrah, Emunah and Kalamah to the east and south, to Ferike in the west. It provided a good staging point for travellers voyaging both west towards Almagabra and Thaine and those heading north and eastwards to the remote corners of Natawni, Garridan and Roselane.

It had the added advantage that the Gimrah remained studiously neutral in respect of many of the inter-tribal feuds which made travel through, and obtaining accommodation in, an opposing tribe's lands problematic for many hara. It was widely accepted by all tribes that Ardith was somewhere a har was considerably less likely to be stabbed, beaten, cursed, poisoned, kidnapped or murdered than in most other places in Jaddayoth, and Ardith prospered accordingly.

The bay formed a natural harbour. Ships came and went on a regular basis, their coloured sails and flags creating a constantly moving mosaic on the water. Wide, golden beaches bordered the bay, where hara would daily bring their favourite mounts to ride across the firm sands at low tide, leaving their hoof-prints as an impermanent record of their passage, to be washed away by the incoming wind and waves.

Clustered around the harbour, and strung out along the shore, were a profusion of inns and taverns and restaurants dedicated to relieving weary travellers of their money. The owners of these establishments were kept busy year-round, but never more so than at the Cuttingtide Fair, an event which the whole of Ardith looked forward to with great anticipation.

When Hanu and the rest of the hara from Scatterstones arrived in the town early that morning, the place was already crowded and buzzing, full of hara looking for places to stay, places to eat, places to do business and places for other activities not necessarily related to the buying and selling of horses.

Avoiding the crowds, the group proceeded to an area on the eastern edge of the town that was designated for the fair. Here, another new, temporary town was in the process of coming to life. Tents and pavilions to provide sleeping quarters for all the hara who could not be accommodated in the main town, stables and pens for the animals, shops and stalls selling food, clothing and a multitude of other goods – all these and more were springing up like lush grass after the rains.

Hanu had never seen anything like it. Compared to the staid day-to-day life in Scatterstones, this was a wonderland of the impossible. That exactly the same thing happened in the same place every year only served to increase the marvel of it.

Naturally, before any thought could be given to their own comfort, the horses had to be taken care of. Hanu, Tiski and the other eskevi were directed to a stable in one corner of the field. Here they settled their charges in, ensuring that each horse, whether it was to be offered for sale or not, had adequate food and water and rest after the long ride from Scatterstones. In truth, none of the animals had been overtaxed by the journey – a Gimranish horse had the stamina for many weeks of travel, which was why they were so sought-after throughout the Wraeththu world, and why so many hara were congregating eagerly here in Ardith. Hanu thought that perhaps Flor looked a little weary, but he did not mention it to Tiski. The mare had borne up well, considering that this was her first long ride and she did not have the stature of the other horses.

Hara from other areas had travelled with their horses much greater distances. From Lemarath in the far north, and Kapre to the south, all the estembles of Gimrah had sent representatives to this, the most important fair of the year. All the Tirthas would be here to participate in the traditional meeting. The Gimrah had no overall leader, like the Tigron of the Gelaming or the Archon of Maudrah. Instead, all the Tirthas would meet six times a year to discuss matters of tribal importance. Due to the large number of Tirthas involved, very little was ever actually decided upon, unless it was a matter of such grave importance that a consensus of opinion was inevitable. This was generally held to be a good thing by the ordinary Gimranish har, who had more important things to do with his time (mostly involving horses) than to keep up with tribal politics. The Tirthas maintained the tradition, however, insisting that it was important for the good governance of the tribe, although there were some hara who said that the good food and drink served at these occasions was the greater incentive.

Having finished tending to the horses, Hanu was able to indulge his curiosity regarding the rest of the newcomers. Next to his stables, he was pleased to discover, were the hara and horses of Tail-and-Tether, an estemble which was only a day's ride north east of Scatterstones. Hanu had met some of the hara from this estemble, and he hoped that they would be here at the Cuttingtide Fair in Ardith. He was not disappointed. Looking over the fence towards the other estemble's stables, he spotted Sable, a har he knew.

Truthfully, he didn't recognise Sable himself instantly at that distance, but beside him, standing idly in the warm sun and flicking his tail to discourage the omnipresent flies, was a horse who could be mistaken for no other. It was Bihan.

Sable said that Bihan was the biggest horse in the world, and while there was no way of actually proving this beyond doubt, Hanu felt it unlikely that anyhar would dispute Sable's claim. Bihan was taller than a full grown har at the shoulder – even the lofty Gavax would not reach his withers – and his neck was thick and arched. He was jet black all over, except for his legs from the knees down, where snowy white feathers, combed and teased to their maximum volume by the attentive Sable, flowed down over his fetlocks.

He was huge and muscled – the type of horse bred for sheer

strength and power and the ability to pull massive loads. When he broke into a trot, the tremors in the earth could be felt by those standing close by. When he galloped, the whole world shook.

It was the custom among the Gimrah for each of the estembles to breed a particular sort of horse, and Tail-and-Tether specialised in producing the great dray horses of which Bihan was such a spectacular example. Bihan and Sable travelled around to many of the smaller horse fairs throughout Gimrah, as a kind of living advertisement for Tail-and-Tether's horses, and Hanu had met them both several times before. Bihan was not for sale. Bihan would never be for sale, but others of his breed were available to be bought here at the fair, some sired by Bihan himself. Hanu found the thought of Bihan and a mare of equal size in the act of mating simultaneously droll and a little alarming.

Perhaps because they found it amusing, Tail-and-Tether also kept a small herd of the sturdy little ponies much sought after by harish parents as first mounts for their harlings. Despite their small size, they were tough and hardy little beasts, strong enough to pull carts and do other labour, if you could persuade them to do so, for they were also notoriously lazy. Bihan had formed an attachment to one of these ponies, called Rok, who travelled around with him to the fairs. Despite the disparity in their sizes, it seemed to Hanu that Rok always had the casting vote when it came to making decisions about where the pair should go, and it was a common sight to see the small pony leading his enormous friend in search of food or a pleasant spot in the sun.

Currently Rok was not interested in going anywhere, as a small contingent of admirers were stroking his rough mane and offering him treats, which met entirely with his approval. Beside him, Bihan was as still and immoveable as if carved from solid rock, apparently entirely oblivious to the three young hara sitting astride his back, clutching each other fearfully as they contemplated the worrying distance from the ground. A ladder to the side indicated how the threesome had reached their lofty perch, the traditional mounting block being of no use when it came to mounting Bihan.

Hanu knew that Sable had no need of either mounting block or ladder if he wanted to ride Bihan. At one gesture from Sable, Bihan would lift one of his front legs – those great feathered columns with their massive hooves the size of a har's head – and Sable would climb up easily onto the horse's back. If Bihan had a saddle which fitted him, Hanu had never seen it, for Sable rode him bareback when he did at all. All hara of the Gimrah could ride a horse as easily without a saddle as with one, but all their horses were trained to accept saddle and bridle to accommodate the majority of other Wraeththu tribes who were not so adept.

Other estembles bred horses whose sole purpose was to race one another, this being a sport popular with hara throughout the entire Wraeththu world. These creatures were delicate and highly-strung, bred for speed alone, and to watch them fly across the ground as if wind-borne was a marvel. The racehorses did not make the journey to Ardith on foot but arrived there in covered boxes to save their precious legs. The boxes, Hanu was amused to note, were drawn by horses bred by other estembles, including some from Scatterstones.

Along with the trading and bartering, which was the main focus of the Fair, there would also be races and competitions to decide which horses could run the fastest, jump the highest and pull the greatest weight. Few of the horses from Scatterstones would enter these competitions, but Hanu did not feel that this in any way reflected badly upon his estemble. A har might go his entire life without needing a racehorse, or a heavy draft animal, or even a harling-sized pony, but few indeed were the hara who would never need the services of a good riding horse. While travelling, Hanu sometimes recognised some of his old charges, and, to his quiet pleasure, the horses recognised him, flicking their ears forward and nickering a happy greeting to him.

Sable noticed Hanu as he approached and waved him over enthusiastically. "Hanu! I thought it was you I saw earlier! I didn't know you were coming to Ardith this year! What have you been up to? How is everyhar at Scatterstones? Where are you staying?"

"Not much. Good. Here, in this pavilion next to yours." Hanu grinned as Sable grabbed him by the arm and pulled him close for a clumsy hug and a brief sharing of breath. Sable was a demonstrative har, occasionally lacking in social graces, but possessed of the sort of distracting beauty which allowed him to escape admonishment.

"And how are *you*?" Hanu asked, addressing the giant bulk that was Bihan. Sable would not think it strange that Hanu enquired after the horse's well-being before his own – he was Gimrah, after all.

Bihan lowered his great head, allowing Hanu to stroke his

nose, feeling the softness of his nostrils and admiring the ribbons braided into his mane in a complex pattern which must have taken Sable many hours.

"I do believe you look more magnificent every time I see you," he told Bihan, who accepted this compliment graciously and exhaled a hot breath through flared nostrils into Hanu's face. Hanu could feel the horse's thoughts, not clear and sharp, like a har's in mind-touch, but softer and rounder and slower, like a water-colour painting where the colours had run together. He remembered Hanu; he was pleased to see him. The sun was warm on his back, the grass was good. He feared nothing. His backside itched.

"He does, doesn't he?" said Sable proudly. "We were up at Long Ride together at Bloomtide, and they all said they had never seen a horse like him! We had a good time there. Have you seen Pasharath? He said he was going to be here, both him and Vinda, but I haven't seen either of them."

"No, but then I don't know half as many hara as you do!"

Sable laughed. "Well, you'll never get a better chance to fix that than here at the Cuttingtide Fair! It's not all about selling horses, you know!"

Hanu wrinkled his nose. "So I've been told."

"Really? By who?"

"Tiski. He takes great pleasure in tormenting me."

Sable grinned broadly. "Ah yes, your gorgeous friend Tiski. I'm sure he knows a thing or two about getting to know hara. I take it he's here too?"

"Of course. We've both been allowed to come because Nirzhen dropped a pearl last Rosatide and doesn't want to be away from his harling."

"A harling!" Sable squealed, his voice rising half an octave. "Oh, I love harlings! I'd love to have one. Or two. Or three. They're so delightful! Like foals, only more... harish!"

Hanu stifled a laugh. "According to Nirzhen, it's hard work looking after one. Even more than looking after a foal."

"What! Couldn't possibly be as hard as that! Anyway, doesn't the harling have a father who could look after it?"

"I'm told even two parents are no match for one small harling. If you want to have your own herd, you might need extra help."

"They would have their very first ride on Rok, before they

were a year old," Sable continued dreamily, obviously unwilling to surrender his fantasy to mere practicalities. Rok, hearing his name, swung around and approached Sable from the rear, and bit him firmly on the back of his thigh.

"Ow! What…? Rok! I've told you before not to do that!" Sable chastised the pony, and tugged on his ear to reinforce the lesson, but Rok ignored him and started chewing the loose end of his leather belt, which bore evidence of having received this treatment on previous occasions.

"Are you sure Rok would be the best mount for a harling?" asked Hanu dubiously. It seemed to him that the little pony had rather a wicked glint in its eye.

"Oh, he's alright, he's just a bit… feisty… at times. You know how some horses can be."

Hanu sighed. "Yes, I know."

"Mmmm. And… er… how is Tezuk?" Sable asked cautiously.

"He is strong and beautiful."

"Is he with you at the fair?"

"No. But Flor is here with Tiski."

"Well that's good! Tell Tiski I'll try to come over and see him and Flor at some point, when it's not so busy. It's going to be a madhouse today!"

"Yes, I suppose I'd better get back and start earning my keep, or the rest of the eskevi will *not* be happy with me."

"See you later, then!"

Sable gave Hanu a parting hug, and, taking care to avoid Rok's inquisitive teeth, Hanu then set off back to the Scatterstones enclosure. He found Tiski already stacking hay bales, perspiring a little in the hot morning sun.

"There you are! Nolath has been looking for you. You're supposed to be over at the end pen. There are some wealthy-looking hara from Maudrah who are taking an interest in some of our stock. You need to go and persuade them they're the finest horses in Ardith. Which they are, of course. Where have you been, anyway?"

"Talking to Sable and Bihan, over there. Sable sends his regards and says he'll come and see you later if he isn't too busy."

"Mmmm… Sable… He's gorgeous, isn't he?" Tiski wiggled his bottom suggestively and grinned at Hanu, waiting for the inevitable blush from the other har.

"I suppose so," said Hanu, trying not to rise to the bait.

Tiski refused to be put off. "I'd like to take aruna with him and Roan from Wind's Edge, at the same time. That would be very interesting, don't you think? Roan is quite adventurous in that respect. I like a har with a spirit of adventure. I haven't seen him here yet – he told me at last year's Shadetide Fair that he'd be here. Perhaps he'll get here later. You *will* let me know if you see him, won't you?"

"Naturally," said Hanu, making a mental note to avoid contact with the adventurous Roan if he saw him.

"Anyway, you best get off. It's going to be a busy day. And an even busier night!" Tiski winked and wiggled again.

Hanu shook his head and made his way to the end pen, where a group of well-dressed hara were examining the horses inside. Hanu could tell that they were important and high-caste Maudrah from their style of dress – ordinary Maudrah would never be allowed to wear such fine fabrics in such bright colours, nor adorn themselves with the jewels that this lot were decked out in from head to foot. Maudrah was Gimrah's closest neighbour to the east, and yet the two tribes could not be more different. Life in Maudrah was strictly controlled by their priestly caste, the Niz, every aspect of daily life subject to scrutiny, control, and a list of incomprehensible rules.

Hanu could not understand why any har would choose to live like this when he could spend his days galloping across the plains on horseback with the wind in his hair. Even shovelling horse droppings seemed preferable to life as a low caste Maudrah, but Nirzhen had explained to him that every har was free to choose his own destiny, even if it did not appear a particularly desirable one to outsiders. When Hanu had pointed out that the Maudrah did not seem particularly free to choose anything, let alone their destiny, he was told to go and shovel some more horse droppings.

Maudrah was not particularly popular with its other neighbours, the Hadassah and Natawni to the north, and the Emunah and Mojag to the south, but as the largest tribe of Jaddayoth, and a close ally of the Gelaming, they needed to be treated with respect, albeit grudgingly.

These particular Maudrah obviously considered themselves to be above the common herd of hara, not only of their own tribe, but of all the other tribes too. They would doubtless feel very superior to a lowly Gimranish eskev. Hanu was not bothered by that – he had encountered this type before – hara who would examine the horses with assumed expertise, ask questions which were supposed to display their knowledge, but only revealed their ignorance, look at the horses' teeth, (everyhar knows you're supposed to look at a horse's teeth before you buy it), complain about some imaginary defect and then demand a commensurate reduction in price.

Hanu was unmoved by any of this posturing. He was constantly amazed by how little the average non-Gimranish har knew about horses, and how far they were prepared to go to cover up this embarrassing lack of knowledge. Hanu knew the quality and worth of the estemble's horses, and no amateur horse-trader would be able to outwit him when it came to bargaining for a fair price. Of course, the final decision lay with the Tirtha, but Hanu did not think that Ren would be inclined to overturn the hard-won agreements of his eskevi and anskevi and recommence haggling himself. Therefore, Hanu approached the Maudrah in his most business-like manner and opened negotiations with confidence.

"Good morning, Tiahaara. I see you have a good eye for horses. Congratulations, you have already spotted the very finest stock for sale here in Ardith. These are Scatterstones horses. I'm sure that name is familiar to you – many tribe leaders and high-ranking hara own the finest animals bred on our estemble. It's a sign of great prestige. I can see that hara such as yourselves deserve that status too."

The Maudrah affected to look stern and important, while preening a little at Hanu's obvious flattery. One of them looked Hanu up and down, as if Hanu himself were an animal for sale, then took a step backwards with a pained expression on his face, as if smelling something unpleasant. Hanu mentally added a percentage to the sale price.

Another of the Maudrah indicated one of the horses in the pen. "This seems an acceptable animal. A little weak in the hindquarters, of course, but that is to be expected. I am told that these are four years old, but to my eye they look somewhat older. Perhaps you would be so good as to let us examine their teeth?"

Hanu suppressed a smirk. This was going to be even easier than he had thought.

"Of course, Tiahaara. Please allow me..."

Many hours later, having dispatched not only the Maudrah but several other buyers off to the Tirtha to complete the deals, Hanu was feeling very pleased with himself. Of course, along with his satisfaction at having helped sell some of their stock, there was also the sadness that these horses, whom he had known ever since they were born, were now going off to new places, new homes, and he would probably never see them again. Because of this inevitable conclusion, it did not do to become *too* attached to every horse that was ever foaled at Scatterstones, but it was impossible for a har not to have his favourites. For once, Hanu was actually grateful for Tezuk's unusual temperament. Tezuk would never be sold on. What exactly Tezuk's future *did* hold, he did not dwell upon too deeply. Surely the Aghama had a plan, or else why had he chosen to take this form at all?

As the last of the buyers and spectators began to drift away, and the sun sank low on the horizon, Tiski arrived from one of the other pens, stretching his arms above his head and groaning. "Oh, Aru's armpits, what a day!"

"Tiski!"

"What? Don't be such a prude. We're allowed to blaspheme after the day we've had. Have they all been sold?"

"Not yet. Myan and Bou are still here, but Ren has a couple of Ferike coming to look at them in the morning."

"That means we'll be free to watch the Grand Challenge Race tomorrow afternoon." Tiski held up a finger even as Hanu's mouth was opening. "Do not even *think* about saying anything, Hanuhathan har Gimrah. About anything! Not one word!"

"I wouldn't dream of it," Hanu said, grinning, enjoying Tiski's discomfiture.

"Anyway," said Tiski, "I don't know about you, but I'm starving. And exhausted. But mostly starving. Let's go and get something to eat."

"There are still some places serving food here," Hanu suggested, indicating some of the remaining stalls, many of whom were packing up for the evening.

Tiski sniffed. "I was thinking we could go into Ardith itself and eat in one of the taverns. And have a look around the place. We haven't seen all that much of it; we've been so busy."

Hanu poured cold water on his agenda before it could blossom. "I think we're expected to put in an appearance at the main pavilion this evening. Ren is hosting a dinner for our esteemed and wealthy clients. If we're lucky we'll get some food, but be prepared for some dish-washing duties as well."

"How unfair," Tiski grumbled, "We've been working hard all day, we should get the evening off at least. I had *plans*, you know!"

Hanu wasn't sure he wanted to know what Tiski's *plans* were, exactly, but he was sure dish-washing would be a lot less likely to land him in trouble.

"That's not what we're here for," he chided. "We've got a job to do and networking with our clients is part of it."

Tiski gave a small squawk of disbelief. "Hanu! Listen to yourself! You sound like Nirzhen! Or possibly even Gavax." A frown creased his face as he mulled over what he'd just said, then he dismissed the idea with a shake of his shoulders.

"Well, if we must, we must." he conceded. "But don't think you've heard the last of this, Hanu. There's still tomorrow night."

Hanu thought of all the things that might happen between now and tomorrow night, up to and including the entire town of Ardith being wiped off the map by a freak hurricane, but he had a feeling even that wouldn't make a dent in Tiski's *plans*.

"Come on," he said, "let's go and grab some food while we can. Once we've eaten, there'll be speeches to enjoy. I mean, listen to. Hopefully they'll put everyhar to sleep and we can all have an early night. I could do with one, I'm shattered."

Tiski rolled his eyes dramatically, but followed Hanu to the main pavilion where the guests were already gathering. Hanu spotted the two Maudrah from earlier, but if they recognised him at all they gave no sign, for which he was not entirely ungrateful.

He felt that he would far rather spend the evening collecting plates, fetching drinks and washing dishes than attempting to make small talk, and fortunately for him, that was exactly how things transpired. At one point, he saw Tiski deep in conversation with a striking Elhmen har, and he could only hope that the conversation was about horses, although the way Tiski was twisting a strand of his own hair around one finger made that seem unlikely.

Finally the last plate was cleared away and the last guest sent off into the cool of the night with the praises of Scatterstones horses ringing in his ears, and Hanu could retire to the peace of his own small cot, whereupon he fell fast asleep immediately and knew nothing until the next morning.

Chapter 9
Seth

The second day at the Fair dawned just as bright and lovely as the first, and Hanu rolled out of his cot at sunrise, refreshed and eager to begin anew. It seemed to him that the atmosphere was more relaxed than it had been the previous day, with hara lounging about outside their tents and pavilions, chatting and sharing gossip. The whole encampment had somehow take on an air of permanence, despite it only having been in existence for two days.

By mid-day, the very last of the Scatterstones horses had been sold, and this was a cause for celebration all round. Once all their chores were finished, in the afternoon, Hanu and Tiski were permitted to go and watch the Grand Jaddayoth Challenge race, which was held on a special course in a field next to the main encampment.

This race was for the title of the very swiftest horse in all Jaddayoth, and was fiercely contested by the estembles which specialised in breeding racing horses. The racetrack was tightly packed with crowds of hara, which Hanu and Tiski had to fight their way through. They did not have a very good view from where they ended up standing, but that did not matter in the slightest. The excitement from the crowd spread like a fever as the horses competing for the title thundered around the track leaving a cloud of dust in their wake.

Hanu had been persuaded by Tiski to place a modest bet on one of the runners, and to his delight, the horse he had chosen – a splendid bay stallion named Shebesh – came in first, despite not being the overall favourite. To his amazement, Hanu found himself in possession of a larger sum of money than he had originally started with. This, according to his father, who disapproved strongly of wagering, was an impossibility, and Hanu could not help but feel slightly guilty about the easy way he had come by this money, but he reasoned that if Nalle never found out about it then it could not upset him. He resolved to keep this particular aspect of his trip to Ardith to himself at the next family dinner when recounting his adventures.

Tiski's horse came in second last much to his disgust, but he soon cheered up when he learned of Hanu's fortune, and celebrated along with him.

"You won!" he cried, slapping Hanu on the back in congratulations. "See, I told you he was a good horse to bet on!"

Hanu refrained from asking Tiski why *he* hadn't bet on Shebesh in that case. Life was too short for the sort of conversation that would ensue if he went down that route.

"What are we going to do with our winnings?" Tiski asked as they elbowed their way through the throngs of hara leaving the race course, some looking very pleased and clutching bulging wallets, others whose faces told their own story.

"...*our*...?" Hanu knew he shouldn't have been surprised by this development, but Tiski never seemed to lose the ability to ambush him.

"I know – we can go into Ardith tonight for dinner. We've got the night off. All the horses are sold, there's nothing else on at the encampment, and everyhar will be out tonight celebrating. It's going to be *fun!*"

Hanu felt in his bones that the crowded, heaving taverns of Ardith would not in any way correspond to his idea of *fun*, but he also knew that this was one of those all-too-frequent occasions on which his considered opinion would not be taken into account, and so he gave in gracefully, or possibly simply due to tiredness.

"Alright," he said, with resignation. "I suppose so."

Tiski brightened immediately. "Marvellous! Let's go and get changed – we can hardly go out looking for adventure and romance dressed in our work clothes, can we?" He plucked at his stained work shirt disdainfully and wrinkled his pert nose.

Before Hanu could protest that he was not looking for either romance or adventure, just dinner, Tiski had bundled him off towards their pavilion, full of excited chatter about the delights which would be available to them in Ardith that evening.

Like many port cities, Ardith was a melting pot of hara from all over Jaddayoth and beyond. A busy place at the best of times, the Cuttingtide Fair swelled its population to such an extent it seemed every street and alley thronged with groups of hara, every tavern and hostel was filled to bursting point and every open door and window gave a tantalising glimpse into myriad different lives.

As they walked along the road leading from the fair enclosure into the centre of the town, Hanu tried hard to appear casual and nonchalant, not wishing to be taken for an unsophisticated har with no experience of life in the city, a projection somewhat undermined by his total lack of experience of city life.

Tiski apparently suffered from no such reservations and was quite happy to gawp wide-eyed at the exotic-looking hara they encountered at every turn, pointing out to Hanu those who, in his opinion, were the most attractive.

Hanu spotted what he thought at first were two human women, but on closer, somewhat furtive, inspection he realised that they were Kamagrian. He tried not to stare. The Kamagrian were a strange, secretive tribe about whom the rest of Jaddayoth's inhabitants knew little. It was unusual for them to be found so far from their tribal lands in the eastern realms of Roselane, but even strange and secretive tribes needed horses.

A nudge from Tiski drew his attention to another har walking alone by himself. This har was a creature of such preternaturally feline mien that Hanu had to check twice to be sure that he did not possess a tail!

"Kalamah!" hissed Tiski, unsubtly.

Hanu was sure the Kalamah har could hear them, but he did not appear to care. The har plainly did not object to being stared at – he was dressed, with outrageous magnificence, in brightly-coloured silks and satins shot through with golden threads and embroidered with pearls and precious stones. Hanu tried hard not to think about what such garments must have cost, or what the har was doing parading such finery through the streets of Ardith, when he looked as if he would be more at home in Zaltana, or even Immanion.

The har's long, slender legs were elongated further by the vertiginous spiked heels of his golden sandals. He strode along confidently, with a train of gauzy silk billowing behind him, floating above his mysteriously absent tail as he twitched his equally non-existent whiskers and ears to catch the breeze that might bring news of intriguing happenings in the bustling town ahead.

Confronted with this vision, Hanu felt woefully underdressed. He had exchanged his work clothes for his best trousers of soft, black leather, and a white overshirt made from Sofia's finest cloth, and was also wearing his horsehair necklace, and his favourite earrings, the ones his parents had given him at Natalia. He felt both comfortable and attractive in these clothes, but worried now that they might be a little too austere for the nightlife of Ardith. Tiski was wearing a sky-blue tunic decorated with a pattern of tiny, flying birds, and had ribbons in the same shade braided into his hair, an outfit which Hanu had thought ostentatious until the encounter with the Kalamah.

Since they were almost at the centre of the town, it was too late to do anything about it now, so he resolved to forget about his clothing, and simply concentrate on finding somewhere to eat. Then he could return to the pavilion and his bed, which was becoming more appealing in his mind by the minute.

They passed numerous taverns, inns and restaurants, none of which were able to accommodate them. Everywhere seemed to be bursting at the seams with hara eating and drinking and talking and laughing, After being turned away for the fourth time, (the frazzled-looking pot-har shaking his head and muttering something about it being the Cuttingtide Fair, and what did they expect?), Hanu was ready to give up and go to bed hungry, but eventually they found an establishment which agreed to serve them. They were directed to a small table in a tiny corner, where they squeezed themselves into the tight space, breathing in to avoid the elbows and knees and precariously perched drinking vessels of other hara at the tables next to them.

"You're lucky to get a table," the pot-har told them. "It's the..."

"...Cuttingtide Fair. Yes, we know."

The pot-har shrugged. "What would you like to order?"

"What have you got?" asked Hanu, looking around at what his neighbours were eating. Large piles of ugly-looking crustaceans and other sea-creatures were being devoured greedily on all sides, but Hanu felt a bit intimidated by the thought of ordering these. Scatterstones was some distance from the sea, and such things were not commonly on the menu at home. He had no idea how you were supposed to actually extract the edible flesh from these monsters, although the collection of terrifying looking instruments of torture with which his dining companions were supplied gave a clue.

"Seafood is finished," said the pot-har, scratching his nose.

"Is it? Oh dear, what a shame. What else is there?"

"Grilled meats."

"Grilled meats sounds fine. I'll have the grilled meats. What about you, Tiski?"

Tiski gave a wistful glance at the pile of dismembered crustaceans and molluscs on the adjoining table. "Grilled meats for me too."

The pot-har nodded. "Wine?"

"No thanks," said Hanu

"Yes please," said Tiski. "Two glasses of red wine."

Hanu scowled at him but received only a beatific smile in reply.

While they were waiting for their meal, Hanu looked round the crowded tavern. The heart of it was an old building, obviously human-built originally, but it had been extended and converted and remodelled and reworked until it now bore no resemblance to the original design, but instead seemed to have grown organically into its surroundings. All the doors and windows were open, as it was a warm evening and the packed bodies inside added to the stifling atmosphere. Hara had spilled out into the gardens at the rear, and the courtyard in the middle. By the road at the front, even more customers were sitting on upturned barrels and boxes, and on the grass and on the occasional chair which had been liberated from inside.

In the corner of the main room, tucked awkwardly into a huge inglenook fireplace which was, fortunately, not in use for its intended purpose at the moment, a har was playing a stringed instrument unfamiliar to Hanu. In plangent tones, he sang a song of romantic misadventure and lost love. At his feet lay a hat with a fairly substantial collection of coins inside, a testament to his musical skills.

Hanu was just considering adding a little to the har's takings when the pot har returned with their food, balancing two plates on one arm, and two very large glasses of dark, purplish red wine.

"Kalamah wine," the pot-har told them, giving them a meaningful look. "Enjoy your dinner."

Hanu looked at his plate. The meats, unspecified, had been cut into pieces, coated in a spice paste and threaded onto wooden sticks before being grilled. They were charred at the edges, and smelt strange, but Hanu was ravenously hungry by this point, and wasted no time in biting off a chunk from one of the sticks. He was rewarded by an explosion of flavour on his tongue, and also a burning of his mouth, since the meat was not long off the grill.

"Oh… ummgh… whoa… Tha's good!" he informed Tiski, gasping a little as he tried to cool his burning tongue. He grabbed the glass of wine next to him and took a large gulp. His eyes widened. "Oh. That's good, too!"

Hanu had drunk wine before. Or, rather, the barley-wine produced at Scatterstones, which was the favourite alcoholic beverage of the estemble. He had also drunk *Sprutt*, the fermented mare's milk which was used on ceremonial occasions, and would not feel that his life was incomplete if he never drank it again.

This, however – this Kalamah wine – was a revelation. Unlike the rustic barley-wine, which was a bitter, earthy brew, the Kalamah wine smelled of fruits and flowers and berries, and tasted like the distilled essence of summer itself. Kalamah occupied the south-eastern shores of the Sea of Shadows, where the climate was right for the growing of vines, and where the hara had the time and the inclination to dedicate themselves to producing luxurious goods such as perfumes, jewellery, carpets – and wine.

Hanu took another large gulp of the wine. It was like angels dancing on his tongue. "I'm beginning to like the Kalamah," he said, happily.

"They will kill you as soon as look at you," Tiski informed him primly, taking a cautious sip from his own glass. "They'll disembowel you with your own shoelaces. You don't even notice it's happening. You're right, it's quite delicious, isn't it?"

"I don't think that's even possible," said Hanu, lovingly cradling his glass between his hands before raising it to his lips again. The dark liquid flowed down his throat and into his belly, leaving a burning trail of angelic footsteps as it went.

"If there's a way for it to be done, I'm sure the Kalamah can do it. Don't drink so fast, Hanu. This stuff is potent, you know. Finish your dinner. You shouldn't be drinking on an empty stomach."

Hanu belatedly returned to his grilled meats, which, mercifully, had cooled to a temperature where he could eat without suffering injury. He drained the last drops from his glass of wine and signalled to the pot-har to bring him another.

In the corner, the musician had finished his ballad of heartbreak and sorrow and was now strumming a furious rhythm on his instrument. A number of hara were clapping along, and a few had been moved to get out of their seats and start dancing, in the very limited space available, which made for some awkward encounters.

There were three Mojags there, dancing to the music, if their jerky and uncoordinated movements could be dignified with that term. Mojag hara were distinguished by their tall, muscular build, and their clothing, which could only be described as functional. As a tribe, they were belligerent and warlike, and often found an outlet for their aggressive nature by working as mercenaries for other tribes. Even the fastidious Gelaming were not above employing the Mojag to do things they considered beneath them. But it was unlikely their presence here in Ardith was of a business nature in that respect. Like all the other tribes, they were here to enjoy the fair, and could probably be considered as off-duty as a Mojag ever is.

One of them caught Hanu's eye. Mojags were not known for being overly concerned with their appearance, and personal hygiene issues were not uncommon either, but this one had been looked upon with favour by the dehara when it came to physical attractiveness. He had hair the colour of the golden sand that fringed the coastline around Ardith which, either by accident or an attention to his personal grooming that was uncommon among his tribe, had been cut into a flattering style, short underneath with a floppy forelock dangling rakishly over one side of his face.

Hanu studied that face with interest and, try as he might, he could find no flaw in it.

The pot-har brought Hanu a second glass of wine, and Hanu flashed him his most dazzling smile, which the pot-har ignored. Finishing off the last of his dinner, which he thought had been the best thing he had ever eaten, Hanu concentrated his attention on the wine once more, marvelling at its ability to taste of so many different things at once. He peered over the rim of the glass, through the mellow haze which suffused the room, watching the sand-haired Mojag and his two companions. As if sensing that he was being observed, the Mojag turned and looked at Hanu, a slightly puzzled expression on his faultless features.

There was a mirror over the fireplace, and Hanu could see his own reflection in it from where he was sitting. He regarded himself surreptitiously, turning his head a little, the better to display his profile, and his long, slender neck.

"You're doing that thing again," Tiski said, still nibbling on his own food daintily

"What thing?" Hanu returned his attention again to Tiski, rather crossly

"That thing where you look in the mirror and turn your head."

"No, I'm not! Don't be stupid! What are you talking about? It's not a *thing*. I'm just admiring my earrings."

"If you say so. But you've been doing it a lot longer than you've had those earrings, though."

"No, I haven't!"

Tiski sighed and shook his head. Hanu ignored him, took another swig of wine and turned again to watch what was going on over in the corner by the fireplace, pointedly ignoring Tiski. The musician had finished his up-tempo number and the dancers had collapsed happily onto chairs, or window ledges, or whatever was available for seating.

"He is *so* beautiful," Hanu said, dreamily.

"Who is?" Tiski sounded a little more peevish than normal, but Hanu failed to notice.

"That har over there."

"Which one?"

"The Mojag. The pretty one."

"The *Mojag*?"

"Yes. Look at him. Have you ever seen such a gorgeous har?"

"Hanu, you're drunk."

"No, I'm not. And even if I was, that wouldn't make any difference. He's still objectively lovely, regardless of my state of inebriation."

Hanu's struggle to pronounce this last word clearly convinced Tiski that his assessment of his friend's condition had been correct, and, scowling, he shepherded his belongings together and dug in his satchel for some money to pay the pot-har "Come on, I think we should get you back to the camp and to bed."

Hanu dismissed this suggestion with a snort. "Don't be a grump. We only just got here. I don't want to go back yet. I think I'll buy that har a drink."

"Hanu! Are you mad?"

"What's wrong with that? It's what hara do in drinking houses, isn't it? To introduce themselves."

"You don't want to introduce yourself to that har!"

"Why not?"

"He's a *Mojag*! He'll murder you horribly. You'll wake up dead, with your giblets tied in a bow around your neck and your kidneys served up devilled and grilled on skewers and sold to the highest bidder."

"He'll have to wait until the Kalamah har has finished disembowelling me with my shoelaces, then," said Hanu, impressed by his own wit.

Tiski was not amused. "Fine," he snapped. "You go right ahead. Get yourself murdered, see if I care. I'm going back to the camp. I'll see you there later. If you're not dead, of course!"

With one last flourish, Tiski stood up, threw some coins onto the table, and marched out of the tavern, his dramatic exit somewhat spoiled by having to fight his way through the tightly-packed bodies between their table and the door.

Hanu poked his tongue out at Tiski's receding back, then turned his attention back to the Mojag. Draining the last dregs from his glass, he left his seat and squeezed his way through the crush, avoiding flailing arms and outstretched legs, until he came to the open window near the fireplace where the three Mojag were standing.

Up close, the sand-haired Mojag was even more appealing. He was wearing a sleeveless shirt which had possibly at one time it its life been of a colour other than its present shade of dried mud, and which showed off his arms, which were tanned golden brown and muscular, and slightly sweaty from his exertions on the dance floor. Hanu stared longingly at those arms and felt his soume-lam pout in anticipation.

"Hello," he said, tearing his eyes away from the upper limbs of distraction.

The Mojag scrutinised Hanu carefully, as if he were a new specimen of night-insect that had flown in through the open windows to join the others dancing in joyous clouds around the lights.

"Do I know you?" he asked, in a manner suggesting uncertainty rather than a challenge.

"Not yet," Hanu said, smirking. "I was watching you from over there…" He pointed in the direction of the table he'd shared with Tiski, which was already repopulated with fresh customers.

"I know. Staring can be considered to be a threat. It's a psychological trick."

"I was only admiring your beauty," said Hanu, pleased with his reply, which he thought clever.

The Mojag's brows creased, as he thought about this for a few moments. "Well, I suppose that's alright, then. You have to check these things."

"Of course. Could I... get you a drink?"

"I don't know. It's crowded in here. You could try, I suppose."

At that moment, the harassed pot-har elbowed his way past Hanu, and Hanu was able to grab him before he vanished into the crowd again.

"Excuse me, I'd like another glass of that excellent wine, and my friend here will have...?"

He looked expectantly at the Mojag, whose face brightened at the prospect of refreshment. "Some of that sour milk stuff. *Sprutt.*"

"Are you sure?" asked Hanu, puzzled. "It can be a bit... surprising... if you've never tasted it before."

"Oh, I've had it before," said the Mojag, "It's good!"

The pot-har and Hanu looked at each other and shrugged, then the pot-har started the fight back through the crowd to get their drinks, leaving Hanu with the Mojag. There was an awkward silence.

"My name is Hanuhathan," Hanu said with a coy smile.

The Mojag's brows creased again. "Ha... "

"But you can call me Hanu. Everyhar does."

The Mojag gave a relieved smile. "Right. That's a strange name."

There was another expectant pause.

"... and your name is...?" Hanu prompted eventually.

"Geth."

"Hello Geth. Are you here for the Cuttingtide Fair?"

"No," said Geth. "Me and my commanders are here because we were tracking a Garridan. Oh, don't worry..." he said, seeing Hanu's expression of alarm, "we found out he was already dead before we got here – one of his own tribe poisoned him. Anyway, they said we wouldn't be allowed into Ardith if we were going to kill anyhar, so we promised not to."

"That's very commendable of you," said Hanu, trying not to

laugh, although it was hardly a laughing matter.

"Commander Athak wanted to come here because you can usually get a drink without worrying that some Garridan har has put poison in it, or the Elhmen have put a hex on it. It's a big problem in other places in Jaddayoth. Have you ever been to Fallsend?"

"No, I haven't."

"Don't go there. Don't go to Oomadrah, either. Or Nightshade. Or Shilalama. You wouldn't believe what goes on in those places. Awful things. Terrible things."

"You've travelled about quite a bit, then?" said Hanu, hoping to avoid revealing that Ardith was the furthest he had ever been.

"Yes. I just go wherever I get sent. I don't really have much say in the matter."

Hanu tried to concentrate on the conversation, but he was finding Geth's physical appearance very distracting. Below the floppy, sand-gold fringe, his eyes were the strange opaque green of the sea after it had been stirred up by a storm, and his teeth were impossibly white and straight. He was much taller than Hanu, taller even than Gavax, and had a far more muscular physique. Hanu followed the contours of the hardened muscles on Geth's arms with his eyes, traced a route up to his broad shoulders and from there down over his chest, and then further down over his flat stomach, imagining every step of the way what lay beneath those unbecoming clothes. He could feel the sticky wetness from his soume-lam between his legs, and it fluttered eagerly, like a mare straining to leave her stall and gallop freely. He had never felt more like Worshipping the Goddess in his life.

"… with a two-handed sword and a pointed stick."

Geth finished speaking and looked at him expectantly.

Hanu tried to pretend he had been listening to his tale of martial adventures. "Erm… yes. Quite. I can imagine. Listen, Geth, are you staying in Ardith tonight?"

Geth nodded, and smiled, showing his astonishingly white teeth. "Yes, here at this tavern."

"Even better. Umm… Perhaps I could… stay in your room for the night?"

Geth looked concerned. "Don't you have anywhere to sleep for the night?"

"Yes, I do, but…"

When he was young, Hanu had possessed a small wooden puzzle where the separate pieces could be moved and slid around until they formed a complete picture. Hanu watched the pieces fall one by one into place in Geth's head and the picture at last becoming clear to the Mojag. "Oh, you want to..."

"Yes, let's go."

It turned out that Geth did not actually have a room at the tavern. Like everywhere else in Ardith, it was full, and what he had secured for himself was a lumpy straw mattress up on the flat roof terrace of the building. There was no cover from the elements, other than a low wall running around the area, but it was a warm night, and in many ways it was preferable to spending the night within the tavern's stifling, crowded interior. In truth, Hanu would not have cared if it had been the bottom of a pit filled with snakes.

Geth removed his clothing without a hint of self-consciousness and stood naked in front of Hanu. Hanu could not help but stare. If the Ferike sculptor who had created the statue of the Aghama in the Eithak at Scatterstones had wished to create a similar tribute to perfection in harish form, then he need have looked no further for inspiration. Like all of his tribe, Geth was unashamedly masculine in his presentation, which at this particular moment suited Hanu very well indeed.

Hanu disrobed too and stood there feeling the warm night air on his naked skin. Down in the street below, he could hear drunken voices, the words vanishing into the night. He shivered a little, not because it was cold, but from the sense of forbidden pleasure. Here he was, naked, out of sight, yet so very close to the mundane world of commerce and small-talk and rules and conventions that he had been part of only minutes before. It was as if he had entered an entirely new realm, secret and dangerous. He no longer felt intoxicated from the wine, but with something else, something far headier and more thrilling.

He pressed himself against Geth, feeling the warmth of his body, skin against skin, feeling Geth's hands run down his back and grasp his naked buttocks firmly. With a swift movement, Geth lifted him up, and Hanu clasped his legs around Geth's waist, giggling a little. Geth carried him over to the mattress and set him down carefully, then lay down beside him. Hanu squirmed a little to find a comfortable spot on the lumpy mattress, found there was none, and solved the problem by climbing on top of Geth and straddling him like a horse. Geth appeared to have no objections to this, in fact if the hardness of his ouana-lim between Hanu's legs was any indicator, he was quite pleased about this development.

Hanu performed some gentle rocking motions, and Geth grunted in what he hoped was appreciation.

"You are so pretty," Hanu murmured. This possibly wasn't the right word to describe Geth's body, hard and masculine as it was, but seemed entirely appropriate as he gazed at Geth's delicate features, his hair now slightly messed and falling across his face.

"So are you," said Geth, smiling. He touched Hanu's face. "You're Gimranish, aren't you?"

"Yes."

"I can tell. You smell of horse."

"What? No, I don't! Anyway, what's wrong with the smell of horse?"

Geth's grin broadened. "Nothing. I like horses. I've got a horse. We Mojags, though, we have a good sense of smell…" He tapped his nose. "…good for tracking. Other hara don't smell as good as us."

"I'm sure they don't," said Hanu, stifling a giggle at the unintended double meaning. He felt himself relax a little.

He let his hands wander over Geth's body, exploring its contours, marvelling at its otherness.

There was a large scar on Geth's right leg, running down his thigh to below the knee. Pink and puckered, still new. Hanu prodded it curiously with his finger.

"Ow!"

"Does it hurt?"

"Of course it hurts."

"Sorry. How did you come by that?"

"We were patrolling the southern mountains, my company and I, this Bloomtide past, and we'd captured two Maudrah spies. We'd disarmed them, of course, but one of them attempted to escape. Naturally, I prevented him from doing so, but he had a hidden dagger and attacked me with it. It could have been worse. His aim wasn't very good. Maudrah have very poor fighting skills. They are a degenerate tribe. He should have gone for the heart, or the throat."

"It's a good thing he didn't!" said Hanu, suppressing a shudder.

Geth patted his shoulder consolingly. "Mojags are very difficult to kill," he said, "but it did put me out of action for a couple of weeks. I missed the selection for the mission up north I was hoping for, and that's why I'm here in Ardith."

"Perhaps it wasn't so unlucky after all, then," Hanu mused. "Sometimes misfortune can be fortune in disguise." He leaned forward and pressed his lips against Geth's mouth, sharing his breath in the wordless Wraeththu fashion, and preventing Geth from recounting any more tales of bloodshed and fighting.

Geth responded enthusiastically. Hanu could feel the other har's ouana-lim stir beneath him, eager to move on to more pressing things. He reached down and grasped it with his hand, feeling a small trickle of pleasure as he discovered that his fingers did not meet around its girth. He pulled on it gently, marvelling at the velvet softness of the skin, and the hardness beneath. Geth's breathing became noticeably heavier, and his back arched a little, thrusting into Hanu's hand. Hanu released his grip, teasing him. In response, Geth arched his back again, hopefully.

Instead of repeating the performance, Hanu walked his fingers around and behind, where he could feel both the damp folds of Geth's soume-lam and the tight-closed sphincter behind it.

"Put your finger in me," Geth whispered.

"Which place?" Hanu asked, teasing again.

"Any one."

That was a surprise. He investigated the area a bit more, and found another scar, this one hard and long-healed, running all the way between both orifices, ragged and lumpy. Being a quick learner, he did not prod but instead traced its length lightly. An unpleasant thought occurred to him, making him feel slightly queasy.

"Was this the Maudrah and his dagger too?"

"No, that would be gross! Even for a Maudrah. The pearl I delivered was bigger than normal and tore me on the way out."

As he processed this information, Hanu found himself feeling if anything slightly more squeamish than before.

Geth must have noticed the look on his face because he laughed. "What? You don't know where harlings come from? Did you think they were found under a thorn-bush?"

"Of course not," Hanu told him, slightly embarrassed at being thought so ignorant. He mentally revised down the number of harlings in any future family.

"My son was big and strong when he emerged from the pearl, though," Geth told him proudly.

"That must have made it all worth it."

"Oh yes," Geth agreed, apparently failing to hear the sarcasm in Hanu's tone. Hanu had the distinct impression that such nuances of conversation were not Geth's strong point.

Hanu decided that there had been enough talking. He lifted himself up, grasped Geth's ouana-lim in his hand and positioned it underneath his soume-lam, just long enough for Geth to feel his readiness, then he lowered himself down on it, slow and deliberate, all the way down, till their bodies were in contact again and Geth was fully inside him. He was still for a moment, all his attention focused on the sensation of fullness, and the pleasure that came from it.

He tightened his muscles, squeezing in a rhythmic pulse, slowly and gently at first, then with more force.

Geth opened his eyes and looked at him in surprise. "You are strong," he said.

Hanu experienced a moment of surprise, too. Then pride. It was true that he did not have Geth's muscular physique, but a lifetime spent on horseback, riding day in and day out, had strengthened his inner core muscles. He was strong where it couldn't be seen. Inside. He squeezed again, harder.

Geth tried to pull away a little, but was unable to, imprisoned firmly inside Hanu's body. "Don't hurt me."

Hanu relaxed immediately. "Of course not," he said. He rocked gently, and Geth followed his lead. At first, they were clumsy and uncoordinated, but gradually they began to move in harmony one with the other, amplifying like a wave form and becoming more than the sum of their parts, like the melding of a horse and its rider.

Hanu was acutely aware of the world around him, in a way that he had never felt before. He could feel the night air on his skin, smell the jasmine blossom from the street below and hear the high bats' squeaks from above, as the creatures flitted about in the black sky, invisible and industrious. If he closed his eyes, he could feel the ground beneath the street, still warm from the heat of the day, and the rocks below that, steady and eternal, and the sea beyond the shore, rising and falling, moving and breathing, filled with a profusion of life-forms, from the tiniest diatoms to the vast, singing cetaceans.

He opened his eyes. All around him and Geth, a ghostly blue light shimmered, illuminating the dark with its pale radiance. Hanu felt his hair rising and crackling, filled with static electricity. He tilted his neck back, raising his head to the blackened sky.

"I am the Goddess."

His ride with Geth stretched on further, not a race, but a journey. He rode him for what seemed days, weeks, years, out to where the horizon ended, where the earth and the sky met, and when the ride ended it was with Geth's cries ringing in his ears, mixed with his own, so that he could not tell which was which.

Afterwards, he lay back on the mattress, which had either been cured of its uneven contours by their exertions, or Hanu just did not care any more, and looked up at the stars. They were not the hard, bright stars of winter; they were the twinkling stars of summer, their light bent and refracted by the dense air rising from the warm earth. They were joined in their nightly performance by a fat yellow moon, just past full, which was starting its progress across the sky. Lunil. The dehar of the moon. Hanu thought that if he had a viewing-scope he could point it at the moon and see a blue-skinned har dancing on its surface, clothed in veils of light.

Instead, Hanu felt a hot fluid leaking out of him, the combined essences of his and Geth's bodies. He looked down and saw it stain the mattress, glowing with iridescence, like the wake of a boat at night, and he felt curiously pleased with himself at this transgression. Had it been Tiski lying beside him, he would have been required to rise and purge himself and make sure everything was clean. That Geth did not seem to care about such things made Hanu feel somehow more worldly-wise and sophisticated than he had been yesterday. He stretched his body languidly, enjoying being naked in the warm night.

Geth touched him lightly on the shoulder.

"Are you still the Goddess?" he asked.

Hanu laughed softly. "No, I'm just Hanu."

Who is the Goddess? Is he one of the dehara?"

Hanu shook his head. "No. The Goddess is..." He paused for a moment, struggling. "The Goddess is All and Everything. She has always been, and will always be. She is the Great Mare of Creation. She is not part of Wraeththu, as the dehara are. She cannot be prayed to, or invoked, or bargained with, or asked favours of. She gives life, but only on her own terms."

Hanu felt strange, trying to explain something which he had known all his life to a har who appeared to have no knowledge of such a fundamental truth. Nirzhen had told him that other tribes worshipped the universal life force in their own way, but he found it almost painful to think that they knew nothing of the Goddess. The Great Mare.

Geth digested this information in silence for a few minutes. "Does this mean I will turn into a horse at the next full moon?" he said at last.

"What??"

"I have heard tell," Geth said solemnly, "that if anyhar takes aruna with a har of the Gimrah tribe, they will turn into a horse at the time of the full moon."

"Er... no! That doesn't happen!"

"Are you sure?"

"I am quite sure!"

Geth seemed almost disappointed at this. "There are also tales told of the Kalamah, who are known as the cat people..."

"I can see where this is going."

"... although that might be because they leave the broken bodies of their enemies on your doorstep as gifts..."

"That might actually be true, now I come to think of it. But you don't turn into a cat at the full moon, if you take aruna with a Kalamah. I'm pretty sure about that."

"That's a pity," sighed Geth. "I think I'd quite like to be a cat. Cats are excellent animals. And so are horses," he added, hastily. "I have a horse. He is a fine pedigree racehorse. His name is Pink."

Hanu felt he was on more solid ground here. "Ah yes. That pinkish colour is called strawberry roan, it's caused by a mixture of red and white hairs in the horse's coat."

"He's brown."

Hanu closed his eyes. "Then why do you call him Pink?" he asked.

"Pink is my favourite colour."

Hanu started giggling and found he could not stop. Geth was

possibly not the most intellectually gifted har he had ever encountered, but he was good-natured and sympathetic, which were rarer traits in a har than might reasonably be expected.

"Tell me about life in Mojag," he said. "What is it like? Where do you live?"

"I live in Shuppurak," Geth told him. "There are many cities, but Shuppurak is the biggest. It is where the Wursm has his Citadel, which is carved from the living rock of the mountains. The Wursm is the leader of the Mojag. He's a mighty ruler, much feared by other tribes."

"What does he look like?" asked Hanu, interested.

"I don't know. I've never seen him. He spends all his time in the Citadel."

"Why?"

"So no-har can kill him. That's how you get to be Wursm – you kill the previous Wursm. This Wursm killed the last Wursm many years ago, so he has been cunning to survive this long. I never got to see the last Wursm either, but I was only a harling at the time of his reign."

"But if you never get to see the leader of your tribe, how do you learn about your tribal customs? Our Tirtha walks among us every day. He teaches us horse-lore and the ways of the Gimrah tribe." As he said this, Hanu realised with a pang that he was thinking of Merac, not Ren, who seemed to have had nothing of value to impart to the hara of Scatterstones since his ascendency to the position of Tirtha.

"Who teaches you the skills of your tribe, such as... er... tracking and killing hara?" he asked Geth.

"We have hara who specialise in such arts," Geth said firmly. "But we do not kill for fun. Well, most of us don't. Some of us, anyway."

"No?"

"No, we only kill if we get paid for it."

"I'm not sure the har getting killed would appreciate the difference. I know I wouldn't."

"I wouldn't kill a Gimrah," said Geth, patting his hand reassuringly. "The Gimrah are the least threatening of all the tribes. Nohar's interested in paying to have them killed."

"Thanks. I think."

"Now Maudrah or Garridan, they will each pay well to kill the other. We Mojag merely act as intermediaries."

"And how much would you get paid for killing a Gelaming?"

Geth looked alarmed. "Don't even joke about that!"

Hanu hadn't been joking, but he wisely changed the subject. "So the Mojag are well-disposed towards the Gimrah?" he asked.

"We dislike them less than some. Although it is said that the Gimrah participate in unnatural relations with humans."

"We allow human women to live among us, if that's what you mean."

"That is unnatural."

"No, it isn't. They spin cloth. We make clothes out of the cloth. There's nothing unnatural about that."

"I suppose not. You don't perform Grissecon ceremonies with them in which you turn into humans and fight to the death with jewel-handled ceremonial swords forged from the remains of human war-machines?"

"No, we don't."

"Just clothes, then?"

"Just clothes. Nice ones. Like my shirt, there. They come in pink as well."

Geth looked rather enviously at Hanu's fine linen shirt, lying discarded by the side of the mattress.

"I will tell the Wursm about this, if I ever get to meet him."

"Thank you."

"I've never taken aruna with a har of a different tribe before," Geth said shyly, giving Hanu a sideways glance to see how he would react to this piece of information.

"Neither have I," Hanu replied. In the light of Geth's confession, he felt no need to hide his own inadequacy on that front, and it was a liberating feeling.

"It's been my ambition to take aruna with a har from each of the twelve tribes. I thought I would start with the Gimrah, as there was less chance of me getting killed that way. I am very pleased that it was you, Hanu. I like you a lot."

"I like you too, Geth."

Hanu rested his head on Geth's chest, feeling the other har's heart beating beneath the skin, slow and steady. Above them, Lunil danced his nightly dance and the stars played hide and seek. The last of the revellers departed from the street below, and sleep came to Ardith, and to the two hara on the roof.

Chapter 10
Missing

Hanu was awakened the next day by the early morning light and the sound of Geth pissing into a metal bucket. At some point during the night, a coarse woollen blanket had been thrown over him, so Hanu was not cold, but he was stiff from lying on the straw mattress, which seemed to have regained all its previous lumps and developed a few more, out of spite.

The air was cooler now, but the cloudless sky promised another glorious day ahead. Hanu ran his tongue around his teeth. They felt peculiarly furry, and his mouth was dry. He looked around to see if there was anything to drink, but there was nothing else on the roof except Geth and the bucket, so he contented himself with admiring the view of Geth from the back, which had a lot to commend it.

When Geth had finished, he began performing some exercises, a series of squats and stretches and other vigorous movements, the regular execution of which probably accounted for his impressive physique. Hanu had a brief thought that, were he to do the same, he too could look like Geth, but then he remembered that he was too lazy even to arrange his hair in the morning and dismissed this notion as entirely fanciful.

"Good morning," he said to Geth, once the Mojag had finished his callisthenics.

Geth looked surprised to see him awake. "Good morning also. It's early, the sun isn't up yet."

"I know."

"Did I wake you?"

"No," Hanu lied. "I could do with a drink, I'm thirsty."

Geth nodded. "You had quite a lot of wine last night."

"No, I didn't. Well, maybe I did, but that's got nothing to do with it."

Geth laughed. "I've heard many hara say that," he said, amused.

Hanu scowled. "Nirzhen says that Wraeththu don't suffer ill effects from the consumption of alcohol, due to the nature of our

132

harish bodies, which purge themselves of poisons and intoxicants."

"Try telling that to the Garridan," Geth said. "Who is Nirzhen?"

"Nirzhen is my anskev. He is in charge of me and some other eskevi."

"Like my Commander?"

"Something like that, yes. He isn't here at the fair this year because he has a harling. It only hatched back at Bloomtide, so it's still quite young."

Geth nodded slowly but said nothing.

Noises from the tavern below indicated that its owners were stirring too. The smell of cooking food wafted its way up from downstairs, teasing Hanu's nostrils and causing his stomach to announce grumpily that it hadn't been fed for a while. Hanu remembered the delicious dinner he had eaten last night and decided that it would be worth his while investigating breakfast in this establishment. "I think I'd like to get something to eat. And drink. Fancy getting some breakfast here?"

Geth shook his head. "I have my own provisions. We Mojag do not eat food not prepared by ourselves when in strange lands. It eliminates the risk of poisoning."

Privately, Hanu considered that the risk of poisoning from a well-run kitchen in Ardith was remote, and one that he himself was more than willing to take, but he felt he ought to respect Geth's tribal customs. "As you wish. Would you hand me my clothes? They're all in that pile there, just at the end of the mattress."

Geth passed Hanu his garments, fingering the fine cloth of his shirt a little wistfully, it seemed to Hanu, and handing it over with some reluctance. He donned his own clothes – the mud-coloured shirt, and trousers of a similar hue made from some sort of coarse material stitched together unevenly.

They descended the narrow staircase from the roof terrace, Geth in front and Hanu following behind. When they reached the bottom, Geth turned to Hanu and gave him an oddly formal little bow.

"Farewell, then, Hanu har Gimrah. I had a most pleasant evening with you, and I will always remember you fondly. Now I have to go and collect Pink from the stables and meet up with

Commander Athak and Sergeant Kare. They are staying at a different inn, with beds."

Hanu returned the bow, with a broad smile. "Farewell to you, too, Geth har Mojag. I also enjoyed our time together. Perhaps our paths will cross again one day."

"That would be nice."

With a last wave of his hand, Geth turned and headed for the stables. Hanu turned in the opposite direction, towards the inside of the tavern, where the sounds of voices talking, and of plates and cutlery clinking, and above all the smell of food, drew him like a magnet.

There was a different pot-har from the previous evening, who sat Hanu down at a table by the window and took his order. The tavern was much less crowded than last night, and the morning sun, which had just risen, was streaming in through the glass, illuminating the wall opposite with its golden glow.

Hanu's breakfast was brought to him. As he ate, he watched a tall har ride out from the stables, mounted on a large, handsome brown mare, whose family tree obviously contained a sizeable contribution from Bihan's bloodline. He grinned, and shook his head, and raised his glass of fruit cordial in salute as Geth disappeared down the street.

Once Hanu had finished eating and paid for his meal, he set off back along the road to the fair encampment. It was still early, but he knew that business would be getting underway in preparation for the return trip to Scatterstones. His presence would be missed if he was late.

He hoped Tiski was not still angry with him. Or worrying that he had been murdered in his bed by a ferocious Mojag. In his now sober state, he realised that his actions the night before had been reckless, and he knew that Tiski's anger had in part been motivated by concern. Merac's consort Nithevan, the father of Ren and hostling of Velisan, had been killed by a Mojag mercenary some years ago on a journey through Natawni to deliver some horses. It was unclear whether the Mojag had mistaken him for somehar else, or had merely killed him for sport, as Mojags were reputed to do, but the event had left nohar in Scatterstones in any doubt as to the murderous nature of that tribe.

Hanu felt slightly guilty now about his dalliance with Geth, but he reassured himself with the thought that Geth was obviously different from other Mojags. He smiled to himself as he imagined Tiski first berating him, then welcoming his safe return with dramatic hugs and tears. Then he would tell him about his night with Geth, describing the Mojag's arunic performance in glowing terms, just to annoy Tiski and make him jealous. And then they would laugh together about the turning into a horse thing, and about the ceremonial swords with jewelled handles, and all would be right between them again.

Despite his urgency to get back to the encampment as soon as possible, Hanu stopped at a small artisanal shop along the way and bought an expensive scarf for Tiski with the rest of the money he had won at the race yesterday, as a peace offering. It was made of a silky material so sheer that it was almost transparent. Fine, silver threads laced their way at intervals through the fabric, catching the light from different angles. It was a vibrant pink, the colour of autumn-flowering cyclamens, and a shade that Hanu was sure Geth would approve of. He folded it carefully and put it in his pocket, then continued on his way.

When he arrived back at the encampment there was already a flurry of activity with pens, stables and stalls being disassembled and animals prepared for moving out. Hanu hurried over to the pavilion, hoping to catch Tiski there, but it was empty, Tiski's bed already made and his personal belongings gone. Hanu shrugged, and made his way over to the stables, feeling sure he would find Tiski there with Flor. Flor was there, indeed, but again no sign of Tiski.

Flor whinnied and stamped her feet, pleased to see him. He stroked the mare's nose, and she searched in his hand for any titbits he might have brought. He realised that she hadn't been fed this morning, and that struck him as very strange, but there was a lot going on in the camp, and Tiski may not have had time yet. Not wishing to allow Flor to go hungry, he broke open a bale of fresh hay, and forked it into the mare's feeding trough, from where she immediately started ripping large mouthfuls with her strong teeth.

Just then, Nolath, one of the anskevi, entered the stable and immediately collared Hanu.

"Hanu, isn't it? Can you get yourself over to pen number 5?

They're having trouble persuading Berun to leave – you'd almost think he didn't want a new life as a mount for one of Ferike's most pampered consorts. Get along and give them a hand – you're known to be good with the awkward ones."

Hanu barely had time to wonder if this was a compliment or not before he was shooed out of the stables by the frazzled Nolath. He traipsed obediently over to the pen, hoping that Tiski, too, might have been sent to deal with the situation, but all he found was a group of Nolath's eskevi trying to persuade the recalcitrant Berun to exit the stall along with his new owner. Berun, however, appeared to think that there was a way out of the stall at the very obviously barred back corner and was convinced that if he trotted hopefully up to it enough times, the obstruction would magically disappear.

Eventually the combined efforts of everyhar was enough to get Berun moving in the right direction, and his new owner led him away, obviously wondering what he'd let himself in for.

Hanu found he was perspiring from his exertions, and from the increasing heat of the morning as the sun rose higher in the sky. He searched in his pockets for a handkerchief to mop his face, but all he found was the silken scarf. *Better not use that*, he thought. Tiski would not appreciate a sweat-stained gift!

Before the other eskevi moved on with their duties, he quizzed them as to whether they had seen Tiski that morning, but none had. Puzzled, Hanu took his frustrations out on the floor of the now-empty pen, sweeping up the soiled straw and droppings fiercely. It was just like Tiski to sulk and hide from him! Obviously, he had not been forgiven for last night's events, and this was his punishment.

By midday, when he returned to the stables and found the forlorn Flor still munching sadly on what was left of the hay, he was becoming worried. Risking the wrath of Nolath and the other anskevi, he slipped away from the pens and began searching the rest of the surrounding field.

Many hara and their estembles had already left or were in the process of leaving. The busy, humming village of yesterday was slowly becoming empty and bare, before vanishing in its entirety, leaving only patches of flattened grass, straw, and the occasional lost item to indicate that it had ever been there. Hanu talked to as many of the hara who were still there as he could, describing Tiski to them in detail, but none had seen him. As he was returning, he came across Sable, who was putting the final touches to Bihan's harness, preparing him to be hitched to an oversized cart filled with an assortment of heavy items.

Sable gave him a friendly wave. "Nice seeing you again, Hanu," he said, tightening the patient Bihan's girth strap. "I hope you'll be at the meet at Kapre come Smoketide. We'll be there, won't we?" He turned to Bihan and gave him a cheerful slap on the rump. Bihan stood patient and resigned, humouring his harish companion's fidgeting.

"Uh, yeah, maybe. Listen, Sable, have you seen Tiski?"

"No, he didn't come round. Give him my best when you see him."

"I'd like to, but I can't find him."

"You can't *find* him?"

"No, I haven't seen him since I got back from Ardith this morning. Nohar else from our estemble has seen him either. All his clothes are still here – and Flor is still in the stables. She hadn't even been fed this morning!"

Sable frowned. "That's very odd," he said. "Did he... er... meet anyhar last night? Who he might have spent the night with and become *distracted* by?"

"No, I don't think so," said Hanu, guiltily recalling his own activities the previous night. "He went back to the camp alone, after we'd had dinner." He blushed, realising that he might have given away more than he intended with this remark, but if Sable noticed anything, he didn't say.

"Well, I'm afraid I haven't seen him either, but if he does show up, I'll let him know you're looking for him."

"Thank you."

Sable paused awkwardly for a moment, fiddling with a few more of Bihan's straps and shining brass ornaments. "Listen, Hanu... I don't know if this is relevant or not, but I've heard that some other hara have... not been where they're supposed to be."

"What do you mean by that?"

"Well, just that we were expecting them to be here, and they're not, and nohar seems to know why. But it might be nothing – maybe they just decided not to come, or just got swallowed up in the crowds – you know how frantic and busy it's been these past couple of days."

Hanu nodded, not sure if he felt reassured by this or not.

"I expect that's the reason," he said, trying to sound convincing. "Anyway, you know Tiski – he'll probably be there when I get back after I've spent all afternoon looking for him, and I'll be in trouble with Nolath for nothing."

Sable smiled sympathetically. "I'm sure that'll turn out to be the case."

Hanu wandered wearily back to his own enclosure, by now almost totally disassembled, hoping against hope to see Tiski's tail of hair bobbing conspicuously among the crowd. At one point, he thought he saw him, and experienced a brief moment of relief and elation but it turned out to be another har entirely, and his heart sank again.

He paused for a moment, sighed deeply and then reluctantly made his way over to where Ren's tent was still standing. He did not really want to talk to the Tirtha, but he felt he had no option. The tent's flaps were closed, and he did not feel he should simply walk in, so he stood outside and announced his presence.

"Excuse me, Tiahaar Ren," he said, in a loud voice, "may I enter? I wish to discuss something with you."

"You may enter," said a voice from within, and Hanu's heart sank even further, because it was not Ren's voice. He pulled aside the flaps and entered to find Gavax relaxing on Ren's silk-cushioned bed, languidly, as if he owned both it and the tent.

Hanu bowed stiffly. "Good afternoon, Tiahaar. I'm looking for the Tirtha. Is he here?"

Unless Ren was hiding under a footstool, it was obvious that he was not in the tent, but Hanu felt any straw was worth grasping at.

"No," said Gavax, "but you may present whatever issue you have to me, and I will pass along your comments."

Hanu sighed, but he was not in a position to argue, so he decided to make the best of the situation. "My friend Tiski appears to be missing," he said.

Gavax's left eyebrow rose fractionally. "*Appears?*" he drawled. "Is he missing, or not?"

"I can't find him anywhere. He wasn't here when I arrived back from Ardith this morning, and I've been all round the encampment and no-one has seen him."

"Perhaps your search has not been as thorough as you

imagine. I expect he's around somewhere, possibly keeping a low profile while there's work to be done." Gavax gave the impression of already being thoroughly bored with the conversation, but Hanu ploughed on regardless.

"He hasn't been to the stables to take care of Flor all day!"

Gavax looked a little displeased at Hanu's strident tone. He rose gracefully from the bed, cat-like in his movements, and stood in front of Hanu, looking down at him from his superior height. "Remind me again," he said. "Who is Tiski?"

"He is one of the eskevi. He has long, flaxen hair that he usually wears in a tail. He talks a lot. He's my friend."

Gavax folded his hands together and made a show of thinking hard. "Ah yes," he said at last, "I remember now. That particular eskev has gone to work at Long Ride Home, an estemble up near Lemarath."

"What?"

"He was made an offer of employment elsewhere, and he took it," Gavax explained in an exasperated tone.

"But... that's nonsense! He wouldn't! Why would he...?" Hanu stood there, his mouth opening and closing like a fish, doing little to dispel Gavax's impression of him.

"I believe that he was offered quite attractive pay and conditions. It's a good career move for him. You should be pleased for him."

"But he doesn't know anyhar there! All his friends and family live at Scatterstones."

Gavax gestured airily with one hand. "Oh, don't worry about him. He'll make plenty of new friends quickly, I'm sure. Young hara are very adaptable, and it's good for them to broaden their horizons and meet new faces." His tone was reassuring, but Hanu refused to be put off.

"But he left Flor! He wouldn't leave Flor! Not ever! He just wouldn't!"

Gavax sighed impatiently. "They have plenty of horses at Long Ride. He'll easily find another mount there."

Hanu just stared at Gavax. In his mind, a tumult of thoughts and ideas vied with each other to communicate themselves to the Gelaming. All sorts of things about being a Gimrah har, about the bond between har and horse, about how one horse could never be simply replaced by another. But it was obvious to him that Gavax did not understand this. Gavax would never understand any of it, because he was not Gimrah. Hanu could only stand there, silent and shaking his head in disbelief, unable to find the right words to explain to Gavax just how *wrong* he was about everything, that Tiski would never leave either his estemble or his horse for something as unimportant as money or position. *The horse belongs to the har, the har belongs to the horse.* Tiski would never have left Flor. Never.

Gavax stared at Hanu expectantly, indicating that the audience was over. Hanu tried to think of something – anything – else to say but he knew in his heart that it was hopeless. Swallowing his anger, he turned and left the tent, almost ripping the entrance flaps on the way out and stomping off furiously.

Hanu knew that Gavax was lying. But the Gelaming did not lie. The Gelaming were Superior. Righteous. *Enlightened.* If it came to a choice between the words of a Gelaming, and of a low-ranking horse-har, he knew who would be believed. He kicked at an innocent stone lying on the ground in his frustration, gaining nothing but a bruised toe for his trouble.

When he got back to his pavilion, he found that it had been dismantled, and there was nothing left but Tiski's belongings lying in a neat pile on the ground. He gathered them up and put them in his own satchel, then walked over to the stables to retrieve Flor.

Chapter II
Evidence

The ride back to Scatterstones was a silent affair. Even if he had wanted to talk to any of the other eskevi, they all seemed mysteriously to be avoiding him. That suited Hanu. He wasn't in the mood for talking. He sat astride Flor in the silent space left by the absence of Tiski's constant chatter. The mare sensed his mood, and was uncharacteristically quiet, picking her way lifelessly through the grass and summer wildflowers, her head down. An east wind had picked up, and drove at them from behind, as if to hurry them away from Ardith, back to the safety of Scatterstones.

When they reached the estemble on the second day, Hanu took Flor to the stables and gave her some hay and fresh water. She seemed glad to be back in familiar surroundings, although still puzzled and saddened by the absence of Tiski. When he was sure that she was settled, he went to Tezuk, three stalls down.

The stables seemed unnaturally quiet now that most of the four-year olds had gone. It was only temporary – soon the younger horses would occupy the empty stalls – but for the moment, a melancholy air hung over the place.

Hanu was immensely relieved to be reunited with Tezuk. This was the first time they had been apart since he had been foaled. He entered the stall, and ran his hands soothingly over Tezuk's back, checking that the eskev responsible for Tezuk's care in his absence had looked after him properly. His dark coat gleamed dully, like satin, in the dim light from the window at the back of the stall. Hanu laid his head on Tezuk's flank. He could hear the horse's great heart beating, slow and steady, within his chest. He found the sound both calming and reassuring.

"Did you miss me?" he asked, searching within the horse's mind for feelings of happiness or satisfaction at the return of his friend. There was nothing. Not even the baseline hum of contentment, curiosity and hunger that most horses projected throughout their day. Hanu sighed. It was wrong of him to hope for such things. It was wrong of him to expect Tezuk to be like other horses. If the spirit of the Aghama truly resided within

141

Tezuk, his concerns would not be those of an ordinary horse. He would not reveal his thoughts to a lowly eskev.

"I'm sorry," he said. "I have no right."

But I missed you, he thought, hoping that the emotion which could not be felt in one direction would be perceived in the opposite.

"Tiski is missing," he said, talking to the horse's flanks, aware that no-har was listening, but needing to articulate his loss. "He just… vanished. Into thin air. Gavax says he went to another estemble, but I don't believe him."

This heresy hung in the air for a moment. A thunderbolt did not strike Hanu dead.

"Do you know where he is?" he whispered.

Silence.

What should I do?

The muscles in Tezuk's flanks twitched, and the horse stamped his back hooves a little. He did not kick out at Hanu, as he did at other hara who got too close. Hanu took this as a sign, although he was not entirely sure of what.

He decided that he should speak to Nirzhen. Nirzhen would know what to do. Nirzhen always knew what to do. If there was ever a crisis or an emergency at the stables, Nirzhen immediately took charge and sorted everything out, and everything was well thereafter. Nirzhen would be able to deal with this current situation. Tiski would be found, Gavax would be dismissed in shame, and everything would be back to normal.

Cheered by this thought, Hanu made his way over to Nirzhen's quarters. Unlike the eskevi, who lived a sort of communal life in residences close to the stables, sharing meals and living quarters, the anskevi had their own dwellings, where they lived singly, or with other hara with whom they had formed close relationships. Sometimes Hanu envied this privacy, but deep inside he knew that he would miss the company, security and friendship of living with the other eskevi.

Nirzhen was at home, as he was quite often these days, taking care of his harling. Harlings were only reliant on their parents for a few short years; by seven or eight, they had reached feybraiha and adulthood. It was not considered unusual among the Gimrah for a hostling to wish to spend time with his offspring during its formative years. The harling's father would also be closely involved with its upbringing, although in Nirzhen's case he did not actually live with Zanutha, the father of his harling, who resided in his own dwelling close by.

Nirzhen seemed unsurprised to see Hanu at his door. He ushered him into the house and led him through to the kitchen at the back. A small creature with Nirzhen's eyes ran out and gazed at him warily. He hid behind Nirzhen's legs, occasionally peeping out to see what Hanu was doing. Hanu smiled at him, and after giving it some consideration, the harling smiled back, making his soft features look even more angelic.

"Have you heard about Tiski?" Hanu asked, breathlessly, sitting himself down carefully on the wooden chair indicated by Nirzhen for this purpose.

"He's gone to Long Ride Home, or so I hear," Nirzhen said, sitting down opposite him.

"No, he hasn't!"

"And you know this, how?" Nirzhen asked, watching him curiously.

"Because... he wouldn't!" Hanu spluttered, feeling his frustration rise again. He searched for the right words. "He never mentioned any such plan to me. We went out for dinner and he left before me. We were going home to Scatterstones the next day, but when I got back that morning, he was just – gone. He left everything behind. *He left Flor!*"

Nirzhen nodded slowly. The harling looked up at his hostling anxiously, and Nirzhen ruffled its hair in reassurance. "Gavax har Gelaming and Tirtha Ren say that he received a job offer from Long Ride and went with them when they departed early that morning."

"And they're lying!" Hanu exploded. "You know they're lying as well as I do! You have to do something!"

Nirzhen gave a deep sigh. "Hanu," he said, "I wasn't there. I don't know what happened. *You* don't know what happened, since by your own admission you also were not there at the time. If Gavax said that he left of his own free will then..." He paused, choosing his words carefully. "It doesn't do to accuse a high-ranking har of lying. He is Gelaming. You're aware of what that means."

"It means we have to pretend he's not lying?"

"Hanu... sometimes we have to consider all the options and

make the best choice available to us in the circumstances. Or, if there is no best choice, make the least bad choice. The Gimrah are not a powerful tribe, unlike some others. You know who I mean. We need to cultivate our allies. An alliance with the Gelaming is the best way to protect ourselves. To protect our future, and the future of our tribe." He looked down at the harling fondly.

"The Aghama will protect our tribe," Hanu said stubbornly. "He will help us if we ask him."

"In my experience," said Nirzhen caustically, "the Aghama helps those who help themselves." He thought for a moment. "Why don't you go and see Ren? He might be able to suggest something."

Hanu snorted. "Ren is a useless idiot," he said, aware that this was a shocking thing for an eskev to say about the Tirtha but feeling that he had already burned his bridges with regard to expressing his feelings about his betters.

Nirzhen did not entirely manage to suppress his smile. "That may be so, but he is still the Tirtha. Go to his office. About this time of day would be a good time, knowing his routine. You may find out something to your advantage. I'll ask around. I have friends who are anskevi at other estembles. Perhaps they might know something."

Hanu stared at Nirzhen, puzzled, but he did not elaborate. The harling made a small squawking noise. Nirzhen bent down and scooped him up in his arms, holding him tightly. "Are you hungry, Issie? Why don't we get you something nice to eat? Would you like that?"

The harling giggled and clapped his hands together. He pointed at Hanu and made a querying sound.

"No, Hanu is just going. Say goodbye."

The harling laughed, gazing at Hanu with innocent, trusting eyes. For the first time in his life, Hanu understood why hara were so sentimental about harlings, and why they said it was a shame they had to grow up. This little creature knew nothing of the heartaches of adult life that lay ahead, but one day he would, and on that day the gates to his childhood world of innocence and laughter would be irretrievably slammed shut. It was not a particularly happy thought, and as Hanu left Nirzhen's lodgings, he pondered why the har had chosen to bring a new life into the world, with all the trade-offs and compromises that entailed, but he could find no good answer.

On the way over to Ren's office, Hanu passed through the Eithak, and went to greet the statue of the Aghama, since he had not paid his respects for several days. To his dismay, it had been moved from its original position in the centre of the Eithak to an alcove on one side, making it difficult to reach the back hoof, but by snaking his arm around he was able to do so. The metal felt cold and smooth to his fingers. The golden hoof seemed less bright than before, but perhaps that was just a trick of the light. Hanu could not help but notice how much the statue resembled Tezuk these days; the dark, burnished metal echoing the gleaming coat of the living horse. The outline of bone and muscle beneath was so life-like Hanu could easily believe the statue would leap forward at any minute and gallop off.

A wordless request for assistance formed in his head, although he was unable to express exactly what form this should take. Sometimes, Hanu thought, it was easy to ask for the things that were less important, but when it came to the really vital things in life there were no straightforward solutions. He hoped that his intention was recognised, nonetheless.

The Tirtha's office was adjacent to the Eithak, and by tradition, the door was always open so that anyhar might seek an audience with the Tirtha at any time he chose. Hanu pushed on the door nervously, found it unlocked as expected, and entered the outer chamber. He had been here twice before – once, on the occasion of his feybraiha, supported by his family and friends, dressed in all his finery, and the other time on the occasion of his inauguration as an eskev. If anything, he had been more nervous the second time.

The chamber was as he remembered it – a circular room echoing the design of the Eithak, although on a smaller scale. The walls were of dark honey-coloured wood, hung with paintings of celebrated horses, both recent and long gone. Hanu recognised the one of Vittoras, the founding sire of the Scatterstones herd, brought from Immanion when the Gimrah left Almagabra to form their own tribe. The painting showed a magnificent dark bay stallion with strong legs, a high, arched neck and an imperious expression, although any of these features could have been down to artistic licence, since Vittoras had been long dead when the painting had been commissioned. It was widely agreed, though, that the quality of the horses of Scatterstones was such that their progenitor must have been an exceptional animal indeed, and therefore the painting was an accurate reflection of this.

At the far side of the entrance salon was the door to the Tirtha's inner chamber. This too was ajar, and there was no sound from within. Hanu crept cautiously towards it, feeling strangely guilty, although he had every right to be in this place. The door was open just enough for him to peer round. He saw that the room beyond was empty. Pushing the door further, he stepped into the Tirtha's inner sanctum. It was not so different from the outer chamber, the same honey-coloured wood and horse paintings on the walls. Other artefacts were displayed about the room, and with a pang Hanu recognised many of these as having belonged to Merac; his ceremonial saddle and bridle; a drinking vessel presented to him by the tribe, a golden necklace, its links fashioned from prancing horses strung together. These items felt so familiar to him – he had seen Merac using them on so many occasions, and now here they were as museum pieces, cloistered away from the hustle and bustle of real life, preserved and useless.

It occurred to him that every such reverently kept article had once had a real owner, with a real life, and had taken part in all the activities of his day to day existence. He wondered what it must feel like, to be suddenly deprived of your entire purpose in life and to spend the rest of eternity as an object merely to be looked at and not used. Then he told himself not to be ridiculous as inanimate objects didn't have feelings.

On a high shelf at the far side of the room, above the solid oakwood desk on which Ren's personal papers lay scattered, was an object which would never be consigned to mere decoration. It was the Great Ledger. The book in which the pedigrees of all the horses of Scatterstones were written. It was a large, heavy tome, bound in leather so well-thumbed that the original colour had long since darkened to black, and the intricate tooling on its surface was worn almost smooth.

Every Tirtha since Scatterstones' beginning had written in that book, and on the very first page was Vittoras' name, and the names of the six founding mares – Eloga, Forada, Aditsa, Shalin, Samari and Zan. Every horse born in Scatterstones could trace its lineage back to these individuals. Every horse's name was entered in the book. Hanu knew if he looked back through the preceding pages he would find both Tezuk's and Flor's names written there.

No such care was taken over the hara of Scatterstones; hara were hatched, lived, worked, moved to other estembles and died without any need for their lives to be written in a book. For once, Hanu felt that it might have been a good idea to have a Great Ledger for hara – there would at least then have to be some record of Tiski and some reason for his going.

For convenience's sake, current breeding records were kept in more portable forms on smaller sheafs of paper. Some of these were spread out on Ren's desk, and Hanu ventured a look at them, hoping to spot some interesting information about forthcoming matings. As well as the breeding charts, there were some other documents written in a language he did not comprehend, and a map, with annotations in the same curious script.

Hanu studied the map. He recognised Scatterstones and its location; the mountains to the north west, the grass plains to the north and east, the valleys, rivers and roads all marked. Just beyond was Spinnersholm, easily recognisable by the elongated ridge that ran along the northern edge of its boundary, and behind that, about another couple of hours ride, was a mark indicating a building or settlement that Hanu had never seen before. He was aware there were abandoned human settlements scattered throughout Gimrah, some crumbled to almost nothing, some still looking as if their departed owners might return at any moment and take up the reins of their old existence. Often, these places had been built because they occupied a strategically useful location – next to a river or sea for ease of transport, or in a valley which was protected from the prevailing winds and the winter storms.

This particular place seemed to possess no geographical advantage, other than being hidden behind the ridge. The terrain beyond Spinnersholm was rocky, and unsuitable for either grazing or ploughing, and few hara ever ventured up that way. And yet, on the map, there were many lines leading from Scatterstones to the location of the settlement, drawn in red ink, criss-crossing at various points, but all converging on this one point. Hanu inspected the map carefully but could find no clue as to its purpose.

Just at that moment, he heard voices, and the sound of the

door of the outer chamber being firmly closed. His heart leapt into his mouth because he recognised those voices instantly. It was Gavax and Ren. He froze, wondering what on earth he should do. There was no other way out of the inner chamber, except through the door he had entered. Any second now, Gavax and Ren would come through that door and find him rummaging through Ren's personal papers on his desk. He would have some explaining to do! There was a limit to how far the open-door policy could be taken, and Hanu was sure it did not extend to an eskev poking about in the Tirtha's private office.

In desperation, he tried the door handle of a sideboard behind Ren's desk, and to his relief found it was unlocked and empty. Rashly, almost without thinking, he scrambled inside. For once, he was thankful for his small, wiry frame, as he was able to squat down within the confined space. Trying to control his frantic breath, he attempted to pull the door shut behind him. As there was no handle on the inside, this wasn't possible, and a small crack remained between the door and the frame. Through this, hardly daring to breathe in case they heard him, Hanu was able to see Ren and Gavax enter the room.

Gavax walked over to the desk and sat down on the chair behind it, just in front of Hanu's hiding place. Hanu dared not think about how long he'd have to hide here. He now thought it had been a stupid idea to do so. Hanu prayed to any dehara listening that he would not be discovered. If being found looking at Ren's papers would have meant trouble, he had no idea how he would explain hiding in the sideboard.

Ren stood in front of the desk, hands down on its surface, leaning forward towards Gavax who spread himself expansively in Ren's chair.

"There must be some other way," Ren said. It sounded more like a plaintive question than an order a Tirtha would issue. If Merac had spoken these words, hara would have immediately leapt to do his bidding, and applied themselves to seek whatever Other Way needed finding.

Gavax did not leap. "I've already told you," he said, in a bored voice, "this is how it is. The fact that you're getting cold feet does not alter anything."

"We shouldn't have harvested so close to home," Ren said, beginning to pace up and down the small space in front of the desk.

Hanu wondered what he was talking about. Harvest season was not until Reaptide, a good number of weeks away yet.

"It was convenient." Gavax said, with a shrug.

Ren shook his head fiercely. "But what if Nirzhen finds out? He's been asking awkward questions. Looking at me with that... look of his. As if he *knows*. He's always been devious, you know. Never does what I tell him or, if he does, in a way that I didn't really mean him to do it, just to make me look stupid!"

Gavax sighed heavily. "He can't do anything. You're the Tirtha, remember, he's just an anskev. He's just one har."

"But there are other hara he might tell! He probably has already! And rumours could spread to other estembles. And they might find it. It's too close, you know it is. We shouldn't keep it there. There's too much evidence, if somehar should find the place."

"It is the best place for it," Gavax said calmly, picking up the map from the surface of the desk and smoothing it with his hand. He traced the lines running across it with one finger. "The Otherlanes converge there like nowhere else."

"I don't like travelling through the Otherlanes," Ren grumbled. "And why does that *thing* have to pretend it's a horse? It's not right."

"It's not just about travel, you know that." Gavax's tight-jawed irritation suggested that this was a discussion he had had more than once before and was not pleased to be having again. "The Otherlanes allow for dispersion and distribution of the energies produced. It would be dangerous for it all to remain in the one place."

"Well, even if we can't move *it*, we need to get rid of the hara from Ardith. One of them was from here! From Scatterstones! That eskev with the long tail of hair, the one who talks too much. He's one of Nirzhen's, for Ag's sake! What were you thinking of?"

Concealed within the sideboard, Hanu suddenly felt his heart leap. Tiski! They were talking about Tiski! He strained his ears to hear what Gavax and Ren were saying, wondering if he should risk pushing the sideboard door open just a fraction more.

"I told his friend he'd got a new job at the Long Ride estemble," Gavax said patiently, attempting to calm Ren.

Ren was not put off. "Hanu might be stupid enough to believe that, but Nirzhen isn't. You need to get rid of him. Send him off to Long Ride for real, or something, I don't care."

Gavax made a disgusted sound. "I'm not running a retirement scheme for simple-minded eskevi, Ren. He'll be dealt with in the usual way, we'll just… accelerate the process. And don't look at me like that – did you think your own estemble would be exempt from having to make sacrifices? Because I can assure you it won't." He looked at Ren meaningfully.

Ren looked away, unable to meet the challenge in Gavax's stare.

Hanu barely had time to be outraged at Ren's casual dismissal of his intelligence before the full import of Gavax's statement hit him. He did not know what *sacrifices* the Gelaming had in mind, but it did not sound like anything good.

Gavax stood up and pushed his chair back to within a finger's distance from the sideboard where Hanu was hiding. Hanu held his breath, convinced that the Gelaming would be able to hear his heart hammering within his chest, and he would be discovered.

Instead, Gavax walked around to the front of the desk and picked up the golden necklace of prancing horses displayed there. He examined its gilded links, then weighed it carefully in his hand, nodding approvingly at its quality. "Sometimes, we have to take a difficult course," he told Ren, "and do things that we may find abhorrent at the time, but I have always found that it is best to concentrate on the positive aspects arising from taking a certain course of action rather than dwell on the negative. For example, now that Merac is no longer Tirtha, you are free of the restrictions he placed upon you. You are able to do things in your own way, as you have always wanted. Is that not worth something, even if that thing was the death of your hostling?"

Ren looked at Gavax dubiously. "Merac's death was an accident, though," he said, a hint of doubt creeping into his voice.

Gavax did not reply. He continued to examine the necklace carefully as if searching for flaws. Satisfied there were none, he looked up at Ren, who apparently found himself unable to meet the other har's steady gaze. "If that is what you need to believe in order to continue with our arrangement, then so be it. It changes nothing. But never forget, Ren, you have benefitted from Merac's death, and the anskevi are aware of this. If there were ever to be any suggestion that his death was less than accidental, your motives would be the first to be questioned. It would be unwise for you to start getting cold feet now – the way back is never as simple as you imagine, once you have started along a particular path.

"It *was* an accident!" Ren insisted. "Pilar slipped on the wet ground. I wasn't even there, I…" He searched for words, trying to deny the significance of Gavax's insinuation.

"So many things in life are accidental, Ren," Gavax said with a sigh. "A bird flies directly at a horse's head, for no apparent reason. A normally well-behaved horse rears in alarm. The ground is wetter and slippier than usual that day, and the horse loses its footing. A chain of events occur. In another chain of events, hara find connections and reasons and evidence, and come to their own conclusions. Or perhaps not. You yourself have the power to dictate which way things go. You can have that future you described to me so often, one of being your own har, respected, and in control of his own destiny, or you can have another future. The choice is up to you, Ren. Think carefully about what you really want, then take it."

Ren stared at Gavax in anguish. For all Gavax's talk of choice, it was clear he knew he had none.

"We will go to the Old House of Men tomorrow, then," Gavax said, taking his silence as acquiescence. "Both of us. Through the Otherlanes. And we will deal with the eskev problem. And any others that need attending to. Come." He let the necklace slip through his fingers onto the desk, where it landed with a metallic chinking. He swept out through the door, followed by the submissive Ren.

Hanu heard the door of the outer chamber shut, and for long minutes he did not move. He felt like he had been holding his breath for ever, and when he eventually dared to breathe again, his head swam dizzily.

He couldn't believe what he had heard! Gavax's implication was obvious – Merac had *not* died of natural causes, the Gelaming had… had… He shook his head. He couldn't even bear to think *what* Gavax had done, but he knew without doubt that the Gelaming was responsible for Merac's death, and if he could kill Merac, then there was no doubt in Hanu's mind that Tiski was in grave danger too.

Slowly, he pushed open the sideboard door and crawled out on all fours. Then he got to his feet, stretching his cramped limbs. He looked around cautiously to make sure that Ren and Gavax were really gone. There was no sign of them. Only the tangled heap of Merac's necklace on the desk was there to convince him that he had really heard what he had just heard. He put the necklace back to how it had been displayed before – it seemed disrespectful to Merac to leave it in a mess.

I have to warn Tiski, he thought. *I have to find him and warn him and get him away from Gavax and tell Nirzhen and…*

How he was going to do this, he was not sure. The Old House of Men that Gavax spoke of must be the place marked on the map. Gavax and Ren would travel there at first light tomorrow using the Otherlanes, which meant they could be there in far less time than it would take for a har to travel on horseback. Hanu looked at the map again. Perhaps if he set off now, he could beat them to it. But it was already dusk. It would be dawn before he could reach the place marked on the map. And there was another problem. To get there by dawn, he needed a fast horse, with both speed and stamina, able to gallop for many miles without rest. Scatterstones horses were second to none, but the brood mares were mostly in foal, the stud stallions were older animals, and the best of the young horses had just been sold off. The three-year olds would not have the stamina for such a ride.

He stood there silently for a moment, as the idea took root in his mind. He did not want to think it, yet he couldn't *not* think it. The idea ambushed his alternative plans at every corner. It was impossible, yet it was the only possibility. There *was* a horse who was young and fast and strong enough to get to the Old House of Men by dawn. That he had never been ridden before was a slight problem, but Hanu knew that if he didn't try, he would regret it for the rest of his life. There was only one horse who could help him save Tiski.

Tezuk.

Chapter 12
The Ride

It was dark by the time Hanu reached the stables. He slipped in quietly and, once inside, lit a small lantern. All the horses were asleep, which is to say, in that semi-conscious state that a horse attains during the hours of darkness, still standing up, some part of its brain remaining alert and on the lookout for predators. All the horses Hanu had ever known slept like this, except for one elderly and idiosyncratic animal called Pidj who, in a display of individualism not common among his kind, had taken to sleeping lying down on his side, giving rise each morning to the worry that he had died in the night. When he eventually did expire the fact was not discovered until a day later.

There was some rustling in the stalls as the horses' gossamer slumbers were disturbed by Hanu's arrival, but the light was dim and his smell familiar, so there was no commotion. Hanu passed by Flor's stall, and she eyed him sleepily and blew softly through her velvet nostrils in recognition. Hanu stroked her nose comfortingly. "Soon have him back with you, Flor," he whispered soothingly, projecting an image of Tiski into the mare's drowsy thoughts, and she nickered softly in hopeful anticipation.

Tezuk's stall was at the far end. As he reached it, Hanu lifted the lantern up, and saw one dark eye staring at him, no sign of sleep in its liquid depths.

"Tezuk," he whispered, reaching forward to stroke the horse's nose. Tezuk allowed him to do so, which he considered to be a good sign.

"We're going outside," Hanu said, keeping his voice low, "Just you and me. I know it's late, but there's something important we have to do."

Carefully, he unlatched the stall door and slipped inside. The light from his small lantern barely reached the back of the stall, and in the gloom, the great, dark bulk of Tezuk seemed to fill it entirely. Tezuk did not turn his head, but his eyes watched Hanu warily.

"Come, Tezuk. With me."

With his hand on Tezuk's neck, Hanu led the horse out of the stall. If Tezuk had not wanted to move, there was nothing Hanu could have done to make him, but the horse followed him obediently, the sound of his hooves muffled by the thick layer of straw on the floor of the stall.

Still keeping his lantern aloft, Hanu led Tezuk through the stable, between the stalls full of his dozing stable-mates and out the main door at the other end, into the stable yard beyond. Outside, the dim yellow glow of the lantern was eclipsed by the light of the almost-full moon which altered familiar daytime hues to their night-time colours of silver and black. Hanu extinguished the lantern and set it down at his feet. In the distance, he heard an owl's eerie cry, and all around him the night insects chirped incessantly.

Hanu stood facing Tezuk. A part of him was appalled at what he was about to do, yet he felt he had no choice. His first instinct had been to tell Nirzhen what he had discovered, but he knew even once Nirzhen knew the truth, he would not approve of direct action – he would gather all the other anskevi together, and they would discuss what needed to be done, and they would make sensible, practical decisions, and in the meantime the clock would be ticking and Tiski would still be in danger And he knew that if he told Nirzhen what he intended to do, then Nirzhen would forbid him to do it, and Hanu would have to obey him, because he always obeyed Nirzhen. But if Nirzhen didn't know, then Nirzhen couldn't object. So Hanu had not told Nirzhen; he had come directly to the stables, and now stood there with an untrained and unpredictable horse, thinking the unthinkable and determined to do the un-doable.

Pushing his doubts and fears aside, he bowed his head, and directed his thoughts out to the cosmos, the great, inky blackness above.

Great Aghama, First of Our Race, hear and acknowledge one of your own. I ask for your help. Not for myself, but for my friend who is in danger.

He looked directly at Tezuk as he projected this thought, but the horse simply flicked his ears and stamped his front hooves restlessly. Hanu took several deep breaths to calm himself, then inwardly began to recite the invocation he had learned as a harling from the visiting hienama.

Aghama, lord of time-space,

Brightest star that shines above and within me,
Take me to the heart of the universe,
Open me to the secrets of time-space
Of imagination that turns into reality.

He couldn't remember how the rest of it went. He wished he'd paid more attention now.

Tezuk showed signs of becoming agitated and rolled his eyes, the whites showing brightly in the darkness, his ears laid back against his head. Hanu reached out to calm him, but the horse jerked his head back and snorted. Hanu felt a wave of anger and frustration rush through him.

"Why are you like this?" he demanded of Tezuk, through gritted teeth, keeping his voice low so as not to alert anyhar as to his activities. "Why won't you let me come near you? You know me. You've known me since you were a foal. I've never hurt you. I would never do anything to hurt you. Why won't you trust me? Why? I need your help, Tezuk. *Please.* I need you."

His anger gave way to a plaintive whisper. Tezuk became quieter and lowered his head a little. With unbearable caution, Hanu reached out his hand again and touched Tezuk's face. A small tremor ran through the horse's body, but he allowed this contact. Hanu moved his hand onto Tezuk's neck, feeling the warmth beneath the skin. The muscles twitched a little, but Tezuk remained motionless as Hanu slowly ran his hand up towards his mane, and the high point of his withers at the top of his shoulders.

Hanu grasped a large clump of the coarse hair in his hand. He paused for a few moments, his heart beating wildly, then using the mane to assist him, swung himself up onto Tezuk's back and clung on for dear life, sure that he was about to be thrown off at any moment.

To his surprise, Tezuk did not rear or buck or attempt to throw him. Instead, the horse stood stock still, every muscle shaking with tension, but allowing Hanu to remain on his back. Hanu was trembling nearly as much as Tezuk and could not release his death-grip on the horse's mane. He repeated fragments of the invocation under his breath, over and over again, to try and calm himself.

...Brightest star that shines above... Brightest star that shines above... Brightest star that shines above...

He did not dare look up at the stars above, not even the brightest one. With agonising slowness, he began to encourage Tezuk to move forward, using the movements of his own body. Tezuk was unschooled, but Hanu had the Gimranish natural, instinctive ability to communicate with a horse in this manner. Slowly, and with a little reluctance at first, Tezuk walked toward the stable yard exit, and out to the road beyond. He was still tense. Perched on his back, Hanu could feel every muscle in the horse's body as tight as a string on an over-tuned musical instrument, waiting to snap. He did not know how long Tezuk would stay co-operative or allow him to remain on his back – he could tell that it was an effort of will on the part of the horse not to throw him off. A horse in this state had only two responses – fight or flight. Hanu continued to pray to any dehar available that Tezuk would not start to fight him. As they reached the end of the road that led away from Scatterstones and out into the wide, open steppes beyond, he spoke to Tezuk by way of his hands, his thighs, his knees, his heels, and let the horse do what every horse is born to do. With one great leap of his powerful haunches, Tezuk took flight.

Hanu had ridden horses, big and small, all his life. It was second nature to him, and he had no fear of them, but the sheer power of Tezuk beneath him almost took his breath away. Not even swift Miran could gallop so fast and so hard. It was exhilarating, and yet at the same time a little terrifying. Hanu steeled himself and took the small knot of doubt forming within him and carefully packed it away in a separate corner of his mind. He must not let it become fear. *A har must not fear his horse's strength. A har must become one with his horse. The horse's strength is the har's strength. The har's strength is equal to the horse's. The horse is the har and the har is the horse.*

Hanu knew he must be equal to Tezuk if he were to guide him in the direction they needed to go. Using every nerve and sinew of his own body, Hanu directed Tezuk along the northern trail, past the outskirts of the growing fields where the trail disappeared, and into the dense, waving grass which grew over everything as far as they eye could see.

Tezuk continued to gallop, but it was not fear that drove him. It was not even Hanu's urgings that made him gallop. It was every one of his ancestors, every horse since the very beginning of time, every cell in his body imbued with the need and the desire to run. It was what he had waited all his life to do. Hanu felt that need within the horse and connected with it, and to it, and became one with it. The strong legs that pounded the ground and the great heart pumping blood to the muscles which drove them, the lungs filling with air, and the long mane and tail flying behind were both the horse and the har in perfect synchrony.

It was well past dusk now, but on the northern horizon, in the direction they were headed, a faint glow in the sky still lingered. Soon, that too would be gone, and they would only have the moon to light their way. Hanu knew the way to Spinnersholm in daylight, but everything looked different in the dark, and he worried that Tezuk might miss his step or worse, break a leg by tripping in a hidden rabbit hole or burrow, but the grasslands were smooth and flat, and Tezuk's stride was sure. As the distance receded behind them, Hanu felt less fearful.

By the time the very last of the deep blue twilight had gone from the sky they had reached Spinnersholm. Hanu pulled Tezuk up, the horse snorting steam from his nostrils in the cool night air, like some mythical dragon-beast from the tales Kam used to tell him when he was young. Hanu guided Tezuk around the back of Sofia's house where he knew there was a water trough, and here he let the horse drink.

Hanu looked up into the clear night sky. The stars did not twinkle the way they had done that night in Ardith. Out here on the plains, the air was colder at night, with a damp, grassy smell.

There was a rattle at the back door of the house, which opened, allowing a pool of yellow light to spill out into the yard.

"Who's there?" a voice asked. A woman's voice. She didn't sound afraid or concerned, merely curious.

"It's alright Sofia, it's only me."

"Hanu? Is that you?"

Sofia marched briskly over to the water trough, leaving the door ajar. She held her lantern up to get a better view of the horse and rider. Hanu could see that she was wearing a night-robe, pale, with a pattern of twining leaves across it, and soft slippers on her feet. She must have been in bed. He felt guilty for disturbing her.

"Hanu! What are you doing here at this time of night?"

"I... It's complicated, I can't... I need to get somewhere. Do you know of an abandoned human settlement about three hours ride from here? Near a ridge, or a hill, or something?"

"Yes, it's almost directly due north from here. But why would you be going there at this time of night? There's nothing there. It's been empty for many years."

"I just… need to go there. I'll explain some other time. I really haven't got the time at the moment."

Sofia regarded him quizzically, then shrugged, realising she was not going to get any more in the way of explanation from Hanu.

"You keep going along the trail heading north. It gives out after a short distance – no-one really goes up there, so it's not used a lot, but the going is quite level most of the way after that. Keep going directly north. There's a large boulder of rock that looks a bit like a horse's head, and a small stand of cypress trees a bit further on. If you pass these, you know you're on the right track. You come to a stony ridge not long after, and the abandoned settlement is on the other side of that. But I still don't think you should be going there at this time of night!"

"I know," said Hanu, "but thank you. I'll explain later, I really will. If I don't come back… Tell Nirzhen where I've gone. He'll know what to do."

"What do you mean, if you don't get back? Hanu…? Hanu!"

But Hanu had already urged Tezuk into motion, and the pair of them set off at a gallop again, leaving behind them a cloud of dust and a puzzled Sofia, still holding her lamp aloft, peering after them in confusion as they vanished into the dark.

Past Spinnersholm, they were now into unfamiliar territory, although the open plain could have been anywhere in Gimrah. The great, grassy steppes stretched all the way from the mountains that formed the border with Ferike in the west, to Maudrah in the east. These endless grasslands were the reason the Gimrah had adopted this place as their home – other tribes yearned for soaring mountains or deep green forests and saw little beauty in the stark landscape of the steppes. The Gimrah saw lush grazing and smooth ground over which a horse could gallop for days without hindrance. Nirzhen had told Hanu that an ancient tribe of humans had once ridden these plains on horseback, conquering all who stood in their way. Hanu had imagined Sofia's ancestors galloping across the grass, laughing fearlessly, their long hair streaming in the wind behind them, and thought that perhaps those long ago women would have approved of the Gimrah as their successors – another link in the chain of horse history, connecting then with now. It saddened him a little to think that Sofia and the other women no longer rode the steppes as they had so long ago, but they seemed happy with their life at Spinnersholm.

Gradually, the repetitive tattoo of Tezuk's hoof beats and the rhythmic movements beneath Hanu's body lulled him into a sort of trance, where all that he had ever known was this ride in the dark, onward and endless, the horse beneath him seemingly unburdened and unconcerned by the small har on his back. Once, they passed a small herd of deer, grey and ghost-like in the moonlight, but when he looked back, they had gone, leaving him unsure if they had ever really existed. At one point, Hanu looked to the sky, and was confused, because he thought he had seen the light go and the day's end – but now there was a new glow in the sky to mark a new day's beginning. Hanu tried to work out from this sign exactly how long they had been galloping – he should know it – but his mind would not furnish him with the information he required. Nirzhen would know it. But Nirzhen wasn't here. At this point, Hanu did not even know where *here* was.

If Tezuk was daunted by the great distance he had covered, he did not show it. He galloped on, though Hanu felt he was slower now, and he could feel the slick sweat covering his body, his heat, and his breath snorting furiously though his flared nostrils, but his heart and legs stayed strong and carried them on.

By the time they reached the ridge, the stars had dimmed, and the eastern sky was pale with the slow coming of dawn. The ground was rocky here, and Hanu pressed his stiff, cramped limbs into action to indicate Tezuk should slow down. For a moment, he thought the horse would not obey him, and would keep galloping until he dropped, but gradually his speed lessened, to a canter, and then a shaky trot until he came to a halt and stood, limbs trembling, head hanging low and sides heaving.

Hanu nudged Tezuk into a walk. It would not do for the horse to stop moving now – his muscles would get cold and stiffen while his body core would overheat, and besides they were still not at their destination. Hanu knew that he should really be attending to Tezuk's needs after his enormous exertion, giving him water and drying him off, but he could not afford the time now.

They rounded a rocky corner of the ridge, and there, in a shallow depression below lay a collection of buildings. They were obviously of human construction – there was something about their form that marked them indelibly as not harish. Some of them were completely derelict, others were showing signs of having stood sentry through too many blistering summers and freezing winters, but they were still standing.

At the far end, there was a building – a house from its appearance – that appeared to be in better condition than the others. Hanu thought he could see a light burning in one of the windows. He persuaded Tezuk down the rocky slope towards the buildings. The horse's hooves skittered a little on the loose shale, sending a flurry of small stones tumbling down the slope. Hanu was worried that Tezuk might lose his footing and fall, but they made it down the slope without incident. Hanu rode Tezuk around the back of the buildings, so he could approach what appeared to be the main building from the rear.

Up close, the house's state of dilapidation was more apparent. The stone was weathered and crumbling, the mortar dry and loose. Moss grew in crevices, and other, more industrious plant life had taken root in inconvenient places, including one small tree, which had optimistically set up shop on the low eaves. An ancient barn or outbuilding of some sort had been built at the back of the house, leaning onto the end wall and open at the front. Hanu directed Tezuk to go in, but he was obviously wary of this new situation – his ears flattened against his head and a front hoof pawed the ground as he refused to go any further, so Hanu carefully slid down off Tezuk's back. His legs nearly gave way beneath him as he landed. Every fibre of his being was twitching – he could still feel the phantom horse beneath him, the sympathetic memory of Tezuk's movements locked into his own muscles, the rhythm of galloping hooves still played in his head.

With quiet words of reassurance, he encouraged the reluctant horse to enter the barn, walking in front of him to show him that there was nothing to be afraid of, although, in truth, his own heart was pounding. Inside it was dark and musty, ancient timbers covered in years of dust, rusting metal implements abandoned on the floor. However, at the far end there was a pump and a stone trough, which looked in better condition, and Hanu found that when he raised the handle water flowed. He filled the trough so Tezuk could drink. In doing so, he became aware of the dryness in his own mouth and, plunging his hands into the water, he scooped up some of the liquid and drank it greedily. It was cold and fresh, with a slight vegetal taste, probably from some underground stream or well.

Hanu leaned his head against Tezuk's side as the horse drank. "Thank you," he whispered, running his hands over Tezuk's stiff coat. The sweat had dried on him in white curds, giving him a ghostly appearance. The dark horse of summer had become his winter avatar.

"You have to stay here," he told Tezuk, in a whisper. "I'm going into the house to look for Tiski."

He gave Tezuk a last reassuring pat, and the horse snorted, but remained standing beside the trough as the har left his side. Warily, Hanu made his way over to the end of the barn where it joined the house.

There were the remains of a wooden door frame, but the door which had partnered it had long since gone, leaving an unsecured entrance into the back of the house. Hanu peered in cautiously before gathering up his courage and entering into the unknown beyond.

Inside, he found himself in a large room, dimly lit in the pre-dawn by the light from an empty window frame on one wall. Hanu guessed this might have been a utility room of sorts at one time. There were old harnesses and other mouldering artefacts piled in a heap in one corner, and a few broken cupboards still hung on one wall. Everywhere was dusty, but the tiles on the floor beneath his feet were visible, indicating that somehar or something had passed this way recently.

Another doorway, on the opposite side from the window, appeared to lead into the main body of the house. This door was still intact, hanging heavy on its hinges, half open. Padding over as quietly as he could, Hanu pushed it tentatively with one finger. It creaked as if in pain, and Hanu winced at the sound, too loud in the silence all around, but the door barely moved. A quick calculation convinced him that he could squeeze his slender frame through the gap already there without opening the door further, and he did so. Once through, he found himself in a narrow, windowless corridor Although it was getting lighter by the minute outside, here the only illumination was from the half-open door which led back to the utility room.

Hanu felt for the wall, to help guide himself. He shuffled along in the semi-darkness, trusting that the corridor led somewhere.

His foot encountered something on the floor, which was not the ancient floorboards. It felt wet and slippery. He rubbed his foot back and forth on the substance, probing in the dark. Slippery, yet sticky. Not water. He looked down, but in the gloom all he could see was a slightly darker patch on the dark floorboards. He took a step back and crouched down, then dabbed a tentative finger in the liquid. Wet and viscous, it left a dark stain on his skin. He raised the finger closer to his face to examine it more closely and smelt an unmistakeable sweet-salt-metallic scent. Blood.

He started back, and almost fell over. He wiped the finger frantically on his clothing, desperate to be rid of the horror. He scrambled to his feet and clung onto the wall for support, willing himself to continue, even as he entertained very seriously the concept of running back the way he had come, finding Tezuk and galloping back to Scatterstones as fast as possible. He crept along a little further, and now, as his eyes grew accustomed to the gloom, he could see more dark stains on the floor, which he avoided assiduously.

His exploring fingers finally encountered the edge of another door frame in the wall, the door within it shut. He reached for the handle and found that it moved freely. Pausing with his hand on the smooth metal, he was aware of his heart hammering in his chest. On the floor his foot encountered something else – something that was not blood, something solid, yet yielding. He did not look more closely this time, telling himself that it was not what he thought it was. He put from his mind the memory of when he had helped to butcher a pig, and the feeling of its solid, heavy flesh as it was cut into pieces.

Swallowing hard, he turned the handle and pushed the door open. It swung inwards easily, without resistance, suggesting frequent use. Inside was a large room, much larger than the utility room at the back, with windows down one side, still with the glass intact. Through one of these, the first rays of sun streamed in, illuminating the opposite wall in pale dawn colours, but Hanu barely noticed this. What he noticed first was the smell. The memory of the butcher's shop returned even more vividly, overlaid with a recollection of when he'd discovered a long-dead fox beneath the floor of the stables, and had been instructed by Nirzhen to remove the decaying corpse.

Then the flies. They buzzed noisily and drew Hanu's attention to a large object lying on the floor across from the entrance. He had never wanted to do something less in his entire life, but he walked the six paces from the door to the thing on the floor and forced himself to look down.

The watery daylight from the window showed clearly that it was a large, brown mare, her throat slit open, her dead eyes wide and dull. The smell almost made Hanu retch, but there was an even worse shock. He recognised this mare – her large, clumsy hooves and coarse fetlocks, and the single white star on her forehead. It was Pink.

Only the fact that he had not eaten for many hours kept Hanu from ejecting the contents of his stomach, although he felt his innards twist and heave. Shaking, he backed away from the dead horse, knowing without looking that he was leaving bloody footprints in his wake. There was a lot of blood in a horse. He turned away, not wanting to look at the grisly scene any longer, and instantly wished he hadn't as his eyes took in what lay before him at the far end of the room.

A rope had been attached to the high rafters of the ceiling, and from it swung the body of a har, upside down, the rope tied to his ankles. His arms were bound to his sides, and across his throat was a livid red slice from which blood was still dripping, into a wooden bucket below.

Hanu did not even have to see the floppy fringe of sand-coloured hair, now stained with crimson, to know that it was Geth.

He stifled a cry, and tried to run, but his legs refused to obey him – they were trembling now more than when he had dismounted from Tezuk. He took several deep, shaky breaths, trying to compose himself. *What would Nirzhen do?* He wished the anskev was here to tell him what to do. He wished *anyhar* was here to take charge, but there was nohar but him, Hanu. And if there was going to be anything done here, then he would have to be the har to do it.

He looked at Geth hanging from the rafters. He could not

leave him like that; it just wasn't right. There was a chair at the side of the room, so Hanu dragged it over until it was next to the Mojag's suspended body. He moved the bucket of congealed blood away, then climbed onto the chair. Reaching as far as he could, he sawed through the rope with his belt-knife. It took a while – the rope was thick and his knife small and meant for less terrible tasks – but eventually the rope parted and Geth's body fell to the floor with a loud thud.

Hanu knelt down next to Geth and put his head in his hands, his thoughts returning to that night in Ardith three days ago. It seemed like a lifetime ago now. How could things have changed so much in such a short space of time? If he could ask one thing of the dehara now, it would be for them to reverse time and make it still the morning of his departure from Scatterstones to the Cuttingtide Fair, to make him still that har full of excitement and anticipation.

He knew this was one request the dehara never granted, for all that they had been pleaded with by distraught hara throughout the ages. *Just make it so these last few seconds or hours or days have never happened. Just make everything like it was before.* A simple enough request. But one that Hanu suspected even the dehara were incapable of granting. Even the Aghama, Lord of Time-space.

He reached forward and stroked Geth's face with his fingers. His tanned skin was soft. Soft, and still warm. For a moment, the significance of this did not register with Hanu, then his heart gave an enormous leap within his chest. He pressed his fingers firmly into the hollow at the nape of Geth's neck, but it was slick with blood that was still oozing from the gash across his neck and he could feel nothing. He bent forward and placed his cheek close to Geth's parted lips. There was the very faintest suggestion of warm breath on his skin.

Hanu placed both his hands firmly on Geth's chest, palms down. He tried to visualise within himself the concept of agmara, the energy of the universe that could be directed for the purposes of healing. Hanu was not an experienced practitioner of agmara healing. What little experience he had was confined to treating horses, healing the small cuts and abrasion on their legs, or strained muscles. He had no idea if the same principles could be applied to hara, but he tried to remember his teaching, nevertheless. In his head, he heard Nirzhen's voice: *Concentrate, let the energy flow into you and through you. Focus it through your hands.*

He strained to reach the energy source, to no avail. Nirzhen said that it should be effortless, that it should not tire a har or deplete his own energy to channel agmara. Hanu deliberately relaxed himself, from his feet up through the energy centres of his own body. He controlled his ragged breathing, concentrated only on being a conduit, a pathway. He felt his hands on Geth's chest become warmer as energy flowed through them. It wasn't much, but it was enough.

Geth gave an involuntary twitch, and drew a small, sharp gasp of breath into his body. Through the skin and muscle and bone, Hanu could feel the har's heart beating, weakly but steadily, pumping what little blood remained in his veins around his body. Hanu could hardly believe it possible that a har could bleed so much and still live, but truly, Mojags were difficult to kill. He continued to channel the healing energy as best he could until he could no longer maintain the required concentration. Whatever Nirzhen said, it was hard work for an inexperienced har, but it would have to do for the time being.

He wondered what he should do with Geth now. Although he was breathing, the Mojag was still unconscious, and likely to remain so for some time. Hanu did not want to leave him in that place, not with the flies and the smell and the terrible corpse of Pink lying in a pathetic heap at the end of the room. He wondered if he could move the har somewhere more comfortable. He undid the ropes around Geth's arms and took hold of him under his armpits. Geth was a large har, and a dead weight, but Hanu was strong – *the horse's strength is the har's strength. The har's strength is equal to the horse's* – and he succeeded in dragging Geth across the floor, past Pink's body, and out into the corridor beyond.

As he left the room, he was forced to confront the thing which he had avoided on the way in; it was a lump of flesh. An arm. With a hand, and fingers. The incongruity of it, separated from its usual position attached to a harish body, was disturbing, but by now Hanu felt that he was incapable of further shock. He felt numb from the things he had witnessed and done. Gritting his teeth, he concentrated only on dragging Geth's uncooperative body across the corridor.

There was another door directly opposite the one he had just exited, but some instinct told him not to go in there, even though it was the nearest. Instead, he dragged Geth further down the corridor to the point where it opened out into what appeared to be a broad hallway. It was lighter here, with windows, and Hanu could see a number of options for places to put Geth. Close by, there was a furnished room with the door open, so Hanu could see that there was nothing dreadful within.

He dragged Geth in there, gasping a little now from his exertions.

The furnishings within the room were old and musty smelling, but still in a usable state. There was a long couch, upholstered in a rough fabric from which any pattern or colour had long since faded, worn through at one end exposing the ancient stuffing within, but it seemed serviceable enough. With the last of his strength Hanu was able to haul Geth onto it and cover him with a mildewed rug.

Hanu felt that all he wanted to do at this point was to lie down and sleep, but he knew he didn't have much time if he was to find Tiski before Gavax and Ren arrived. He checked that Geth was still breathing steadily, then slunk out of the room, pulling the door closed after him so nohar would see Geth inside. He stood for a minute and thought. He remembered the door across from the room where Pink's body was still lying, and how some inner intuition had told him that something... *not right*... lay behind that door. It was the last place he wanted to go right now, but he told himself that if he were to find Tiski he would have to be brave. There was obviously *something* in that room that needed investigating.

Reluctantly, he returned to the gloomy corridor and crept cautiously towards the door in question. The closer he got, the more his inner senses screamed a warning at him. Hanu had learned to trust his instincts – all hara had enhanced abilities which enabled them to sense danger. It had saved Hanu's life on one occasion, some years before, when a sudden presentiment had made him move away just before a large tree had crashed down onto a spot where he'd been standing moments before.

If Hanu was sure of anything, it was that whatever was behind that door was worse than a falling tree, but he screwed up all his courage, grasped the handle, and opened the door.

Chapter 13
The Room

Once, during the spring following his feybraiha, Hanu had found himself walking alone through the woods on the western boundary of Scatterstones. He was alone in that he had no harish company, but behind him trailed Beyra, the pony he had ridden since he had been a harling. Beyra had a brave heart and stout legs, but his age was beginning to tell on him, and in this last year or so it had seemed that Hanu had grown too big for the pony. There were, of course, other horses available for him to ride, but somehow it seemed to him like a betrayal to abandon Beyra. He could not bear to think of his old friend left alone in his stall, gazing mournfully at him while he saddled up some new horse and rode away without a backward glance.

In the distance, he could hear the other riders. They were taking the designated route along the western trail and out past the grazing fields before swinging back round to return through the low ridings, but Hanu knew a shortcut through the woods that would save Beyra's ageing legs.

He was thinking about a har called Sarian, and how best he could tell him that he no longer wanted to take aruna with him. It had been fun at first, but Sarian had lately talked of nothing but his and Hanu's future together, breeding goats and harlings. Hanu wanted to tell him that this future only existed in Sarian's mind, and that all Hanu's dreams were of becoming a horse-har, in a future which did not include Sarian.

In the silence of the woods he kicked his way disconsolately through the litter of last year's fallen leaves when he spotted something shining. He bent down and picked it up, and found it was a curious device comprising of metal hooks and two circles of glass. It was plainly meant to be worn on the face, the glass lenses in front of the eyes and the hooks around the ears to hold it on. Hanu became excited at his find. It was a seeing-device! Obviously, it was a scrying tool, which would enable the wearer to see visions of future events, or perhaps even look into the depths of his own soul.

Hanu rubbed the dirt from the glass lenses and carefully placed the seeing-device on his face, hoping that it would let him see a solution to his problem. To his disappointment, it merely rendered the surrounding trees and landscape blurry and indistinct.

Later, his high-hostling told him that it was a human device used to correct defective vision, and that such things were not uncommon, as human bodies were often defective. Hanu wondered aloud why the humans did not go to a healer to heal their bodily defects, but his high-hostling just laughed and said it didn't work like that, not with humans.

Slipping the device into his pocket, he led Beyra on to the place where the woods rejoined the official trail back to Scatterstones...

As he walked into the room in the abandoned House of Men, Hanu experienced the same sensation he'd had when he'd placed the old human seeing-device on his face. Everything seemed out of focus and blurred, all the sharpness and clarity smudged away and replaced by a shifting, shimmering blur.

No – that was not quite true. The doorway where he had entered and the area in the immediate vicinity were as clearly visible as one might expect, but in the far corner of the room, the light seemed to bend and waver, and skid off the surface of... something. Hanu had the feeling that if he could just look hard enough, just focus with enough conviction, his eyes would see the thing which all his other senses were screaming was there.

He tried to remember his training, Nirzhen's patient instruction on how to perceive an object's true nature. It was a skill that, in truth, Hanu had never tried very hard to master, but now he summoned all his somewhat limited power of will and directed it at the presence in the corner of the room.

Slowly, the thing swam into focus, although this didn't help Hanu much, as what he perceived before him bore no resemblance to anything he had ever seen in his life. It was a living entity, of that he was sure, it's outline... feathered? Or something else. Limbs. Or perhaps organs for some other purpose. Impossible to know. The only thing he could feel sure of was the collection of jewelled, whirling eyes, looking directly at him, pinning him like a butterfly to a piece of card. This thing, whatever it was, saw him and knew he was there.

Which Wraeththu are you?

The shock of this question delivered to the inside of Hanu's mind almost made him collapse to the floor. He was accustomed to mind-touch, har to har; a warm, intimate feeling. This was cold, hard, angular. It left a metallic taste in his mouth, and his teeth stinging.

"I..." he started to speak aloud, then realised that the creature almost certainly didn't use air vibrations to communicate. Although he recoiled from the prospect, he sent his reply via mind-touch, wincing internally as he made contact with the alien mind.

I am Hanu.

That is not useful to know. You are not Gavax or Ren. Explain your purpose here.

Hanu had absolutely no intention of telling this creature what his purpose here was. He decided that attack was the best form of defence.

No, you explain your purpose here.

The creature's response made Hanu's head ring. He could not decide if it was anger or amusement or something else entirely.

The purpose of life is not known.

Hanu muttered a curse under his breath. This was exactly the sort of cleverness that Nirzhen would respond to with one of his most withering looks.

I wasn't asking about the purpose of life; I was asking about you. Who are you? What are you? And what are you doing here?

I am known to your kind as a sedu.

As the creature imparted this information to him, Hanu suddenly realised why a small piece of his brain had been infused with a nagging sense of familiarity ever since he'd walked into the room. The *otherness* of this creature, it's strange aura – he had encountered it before, and he knew, even as the *sedu* revealed itself, that it was not lying.

You don't usually look like this.

If there was such a thing as a mental shrug, the *sedu* directed one at Hanu. *We may take any form we choose. When not constrained.*

Hanu pondered the implications of this last comment. *You are constrained now?*

The Wraeththu who is Gavax har Gelaming would put a binding on me.

Hanu was confused by this statement. He might have expected

some sort of anger or hostility to accompany it, but he could detect none. He could not tell if this was because the *sedu* was truly unconcerned, or if its alien nature prevented him from interpreting its mental state.

Why? Why would he do that?

The usual reason.

Now there was a definite emotion. A jangle of contemptuous amusement.

What is the usual reason? Hanu felt out of his depth here, but he continued doggedly.

Power.

Power?

Two meanings of it, for which you only have one word. That is irresponsible. Words are dangerous things if used improperly, and they should not be allowed to carelessly alter their meaning on the whim of the user.

In his mind, Hanu found himself both agreeing and disagreeing with this statement, then he berated himself for allowing the *sedu* to distract him with its clever sophistry again. He returned stubbornly to his original questioning. *What power does Gavax har Gelaming want?*

Power in the form of energy. The energy of the universe. Wraeththu can access this energy themselves, poorly, but the sedim are able to draw upon it much more fully.

Like the energy we use for healing? Hanu asked, thinking of Geth.

*Yes, but more. **Much** more.* The faint aroma of condescension accompanied this response, which Hanu ignored.

And what other power does Gavax want?

Even a low-caste Wraeththu such as yourself knows the answer to that question.

Hanu had to admit to himself that this was true. *And what does Gavax intend to do with all this power?*

I neither know nor care. Your petty Wraeththu politics do not concern me.

Hanu shot back an angry thought. *If you are so much more important, and so superior to Wraeththu, how is it that you are bound here by a har, and unable to free yourself? Answer that?*

The *sedu* was unmoved. *At this point in time, I am bound. At other points in time, I may not be. I have been free in the past. I will be free again. All things return to the beginning, all events conspire towards an end. The time may be sooner than we think.*

Hanu was stung by this dismissal of both himself and his entire race, but he decided there was no point in trying to make sense of the *sedu's* pronouncements. The creature seemed minded to answer his direct questions, though, for reasons of its own, so he asked the one at the forefront of his mind, the one that he both did and did not want to hear the answer to. *Why is there blood and... body parts... in the corridor? Why is there a dead horse in the room opposite? Why is there a har with his throat cut and a bucket to catch his blood?*

The *sedu's* eyes glittered like faceted jewels, dark and unknowable, and Hanu felt that his head might explode at any minute. He thought that perhaps he had pushed his luck a little too far, and had caused the *sedu* to become angry, but the creature responded in the same mild manner as before.

Since I am part of this realm of flesh, I require flesh to sustain my flesh.

It took a moment for this to sink in, and when it did, Hanu took an involuntary step backwards away from the *sedu* as a mixture of horror and disgust washed over him.

You mean you are... eating hara? Drinking their blood?

That is what creatures of flesh in this realm must do to survive. It is what you do. It is what I am compelled to do.

No! We don't... I don't... There are other things you can eat! Not hara!

The *sedu* regarded him coldly. *Not if I am to be capable of drawing energy as I am commanded by Gavax har Gelaming. The life force of your kind is more sustaining than that of mere animals. If I do not consume it, I will perish. What would you have me do?*

The *sedu's* thoughts were bland and reasonable, carrying no hint of guilt or remorse. Either the creature had no moral imperative or it was lying, Hanu was unsure which. He did not know what to do. He was filled with revulsion towards the creature before him, and yet, at the same time, a degree of sympathy. The creature was obviously a victim of Gavax's machinations as much as Tiski and Merac had been, although what the purpose of it all was, Hanu had no idea. He did not even know if he could trust anything the *sedu* had said, the whole situation was so bizarre and outwith his limited experience. The only thing he knew was that whatever was going on here had to be stopped.

It's not right you're kept imprisoned here against your will, he told the *sedu*. *I'll see what I can do to free you. There are hara more adept than me who might be able to release you from whatever Gavax has done to you. I'll help you as best I can, but you must promise not to... consume... any more harish flesh.*

171

Why?

Because I won't help you if you won't keep that promise.

In that case I agree to your condition.

Again, it crossed Hanu's mind that the *sedu* might be lying, although it was impossible to determine this from either the creature's mental projections or its body language. There were no tell-tale signs, such as those that might be detected from a har who was being untruthful: no discomfort, no awkward shuffling, no faint flush of embarrassment. Hanu was acquainted with those, because he had been informed, in no uncertain terms, that he displayed all of them himself in abundance when he was lying. He did not trust the *sedu*, and yet there was nothing he could do but accept its assurance at face value.

In the meantime, it was even more imperative that he find Tiski before Gavax turned up and did to Tiski what he had done to Geth, and the unknown ex-owner of the hand in the corridor. Hanu shuddered as he recalled what lay out there.

Hanu felt he had spent enough time in the presence of this disturbing creature. He turned to leave, but before he did so, his curiosity got the better of him, and he put one last question to the *sedu*.

If you may take any form you choose, then why do you choose to take the form of a horse?

If the creature was capable of smirking, then that was what Hanu was convinced it did.

We don't. The choice is yours.

Confused, and with a small shudder both of relief and revulsion, Hanu closed the door on the room, leaving the sedu behind. He made his way back down the corridor to the main hallway, being careful to avoid contact with anything on the floor as he went. He briefly checked on Geth, but the Mojag was lying exactly where Hanu had left him, and there seemed nothing else he could do at present, so he continued his search of the house.

The main hallway offered a number of other options – doors, archways and corridors. It was very confusing. Hanu thought that perhaps it offered an insight into the mentality of those who had built it. The *men* who had built it. No har would design a habitation like this – it was all angular corners, dark tunnels and rooms in difficult places. There seemed to have been no attempt to render it beautiful or congenial to the senses. Of course, it was in a state of disrepair, but even when in its prime, Hanu wouldn't have felt comfortable living in it.

He tried two of the doors, but these both led to empty rooms, one with a large, ornate mirror on the wall opposite, cracked down the middle. When Hanu peered cautiously into the glass, he started at what appeared to be the sight of two strange hara peering back, until he realised it was simply his own reflection, split in two. He had heard that men did not show their reflections in a mirror and had never been sure whether to believe that or not, but the presence of this mirror here appeared to refute the myth. Why have such an ostentatious object in your home if you couldn't make use of it?

The third door Hanu tried was locked, but as he twisted and turned the handle, he heard faint noises beyond it – the sound of scuffling, not made by a rat or a mouse, but by something larger. He tried again, and this time the scuffling was louder, and accompanied by a muffled squeal. His heart began to pound erratically. There could be anything behind that door. Another *sedu*, or something worse.

The squeal had not sounded like a *sedu*. He was pretty sure *sedu* did not squeal. He tapped lightly on the door and whispered hoarsely: "Tiski?"

There was silence behind the door, so he repeated himself, louder this time, feeling utterly conspicuous in the empty silence of the house.

"Tiski! Are you there? It's me, Hanu!"

There was silence again for a moment, then more scuffling, the sound of feet and a thud against the door. Then a voice, muffled through the thick wooden panels of the door, but instantly recognisable. "Hanu! Hanu, is that you?"

Hanu felt an enormous wave of relief pass through him at the sound of Tiski's voice. "Yes, it's me!"

"Hanu! How did you get here? Have they got you too? What's happening? What's going on?"

Hanu could hear other voices in the background, so he knew that Tiski was not alone. "They haven't got me," he said. "I've come to get you out."

"It was Gavax," Tiski said. "He brought me here. Did you wonder where I'd gone? He brought me here. He kidnapped me, Hanu! Kidnapped! Me and the others! You know I'd never leave

Flor. Is Flor alright? And Ren is in on it too. Our Tirtha! That's disgusting! I want to get out, Hanu. Can you get us out of here? I want to go home!"

"Who else is in there with you?" Hanu asked, trying to sound calm and hoping it would transmit to Tiski.

"Vinda and Pasharath from Long Ride, and Lynx from Tail-and-Tether, and Perdix and Sula, they're from East of Heaven. I don't know where that is. Out east, I think. And Ruzhu from Wind's Edge. And Polly, he won't say where's from. I don't think that's his real name, either. He's a bit confused. I think he might have hit his head. They were all kidnapped too! Hanu, what are we going to do?"

"Is there any way for you to get out?" Hanu asked, tugging at the door handle again. It rattled but remained firm.

"No!" Tiski wailed. "The door's locked and the windows are barred. Gavax took the key, I think. What are we going to do, Hanu?"

"Hang on, I'm thinking." Hanu studied the door. It was made of strong hardwood, with a sturdy frame inlaid with thinner panels. At the top he noticed a heavy iron bolt, which had been slid into a thick staple on the wooden door frame. At the bottom there was another bolt. Hanu stretched up, for it was quite a high door, and reached for the top bolt. It slid across easily, revealing that it was in constant use. He reached down and slid the bottom bolt too, which was slightly stiffer, but moved with a sharp tug. He grasped the door handle and pushed. No luck. The door was not just bolted but locked, too.

He pushed a tentative shoulder against the door, considering trying to break the door down, but the thought of the noise this would make persuaded him that it was not a good idea, even if he had the strength to break the frame, which he did not think he did.

He knelt down and examined the lock carefully. He recognised the construction, a simple lever mechanism, but it was old and worn. He knew that if you could push the metal bar inside the keyhole in just the right way then it would unlock. A period during his youth when his desire for the preserved fruit his high-hostling kept locked in a cupboard had overcome his sense of honesty had taught him this trick – but it was a fiddly business, and he had none of the tools to hand required to perform this act.

He whispered through to Tiski, hoarsely, trying simultaneously to keep his voice low, yet be loud enough to be heard through the door.

"Tiski. Have you got any hairpins or anything on you?"

"Hairpins? What? Of course I don't! I never put pins in my hair. Who does that? What do you want with hairpins?" Tiski did not seem to feel the need to reciprocate the whisper and Hanu was sure his voice could be heard throughout the entire house.

"It doesn't have to be a hairpin, just something long and thin that will go through the keyhole of this lock. And keep your voice down a bit."

"No, I haven't got anything like that," Tiski replied, lowering the pitch of his voice, if not the volume. "Hang on, I'll ask the others."

There was a silence, during which Hanu could hear muffled voices from within discussing the options. He rested his head on the side of the door frame and tried to move his cramped legs into a more comfortable position, with little success. His mouth felt dry and he was woozy from lack of sleep. It felt a little like the time he had eaten some narcotic berries given to him by one of the other eskevi.

Finally, Tiski returned and whispered noisily through the door. "I've got a couple of things that might do. There's a brooch from Sula, and a pen from Lynx."

"Push them under the door, then, if they'll go through."

There was a scraping sound at the bottom of the door, and the pen and brooch appeared on Hanu's side. He picked them up and examined them. The pen, with its shaft of polished wood and metal nib, was obviously too thick to go into the keyhole in the lock. The brooch, however, had a long, straight pin at the back that looked as if it would do. Hanu took the brooch and inserted the pin into the lock, feeling for the part of the mechanism inside that needed to be moved.

His heart was thudding wildly, causing his hands to shake and jump with each beat and making fine, co-ordinated movements almost impossible,

He took several deep breaths to steady himself and then twisted the brooch pin inside the lock again, but his hands were still sticky with Geth's blood and he could not get a proper grip on the brooch's smooth surface. It slipped uselessly through his fingers. He rubbed his hands on the floor to try to clean them, leaving dark smears on the rough boards, then he tried again, all the time remaining painfully aware that Gavax and Ren could arrive at any minute and discover him crouching there in the semi-darkness.

It took all of his willpower to concentrate on guiding the pin of the brooch to the exact spot within the lock mechanism and not to turn and look behind him. Once, twice, three times, and then yet again a fourth time he tried to move the lock and each time the brooch pin slid off. On the fifth try, he felt it catch, and with a combination of agonising slowness and maintaining *just* enough pressure he finally, miraculously, felt it move and heard the small *snick* as the lever turned and the lock released.

He turned the handle, and the door opened inwards. On the other side of the room stood Tiski and a group of young hara Hanu did not recognise, huddled together for reassurance. They looked bewildered and apprehensive, uncertain as to what to do next. There was a moment's shocked silence, then Tiski yelled "Hanu!" and rushed forward to entangle himself around Hanu fiercely. The other hara stood back, not sure what to make of this dramatic development.

"It's Hanu!" Tiski cried. "This is Hanu, my friend. He's come to save us!"

The other hara approached cautiously, and one of them reached out to pat Hanu's arm shyly. The others gazed at him with a mixture of admiration and wonder.

"You got the lock open." The har closest to him looked at him with wide-eyed astonishment. "How did you do that? We kept twisting it, but it wouldn't budge."

Hanu felt acutely embarrassed at this attention, and not inclined to reveal the source of his lock-defeating skill, so he simply shrugged and mumbled something about being lucky, to nods of amazement all round.

"Come on," he said to the still-clinging Tiski and his crowd of admirers, "we need to get out of here before Gavax arrives."

"How did you get here?" Tiski asked him.

"On Tezuk."

"*Tezuk?* You *rode* Tezuk?"

"Yes."

Tiski's mouth opened, but no sound came out. Hanu took advantage of this unaccustomed development to hurry the small group out of the room. Once outside, they stood looking around in bewilderment, and once again Hanu had to herd them across the hallway toward the corridor at the far end.

"It was awful!" Tiski told him as Hanu urged the little band along. "I got back from Ardith that night – you remember, we'd gone to that tavern for dinner and you were planning on rooning that over-muscled Mojag..."

"I remember," said Hanu, wondering how he was going to break the news to Tiski about who was in the room opposite the *sedu*.

"...and I was going to go to bed, but then Gavax and Ren arrived. Ren said something about how he had a new position for me, and I got all flustered, because I didn't want a new position. I like being an eskev to Nirzhen, but, you know, he's the *Tirtha* and all, and I was trying to think of something to say when Gavax just... did something. Hexed me. I don't know. A Gelaming thing, I suppose. But I couldn't move. And then they picked me up – can you imagine? – and took me out of the pavilion and then... I was on that *thing* that Gavax rides, the thing that pretends to be a horse, and then I was... I don't know, but it was cold. And dark. And nowhere. And then I was here. But I don't know where here is."

"We're at an abandoned human settlement to the north of Spinnersholm."

"Why? Why has Gavax kidnapped us? He's Gelaming. The Gelaming don't do that sort of thing! Why are we here?"

"It's..." In the space of about three heartbeats, Hanu considered, and equally swiftly dismissed, three separate explanations of their current situation, deciding that each successive one was more likely than the last to make Tiski dissolve into a state of panic, and took the coward's way out.

"...complicated," he finished lamely. "I'll explain later. The important thing right now is to get out of here. There's also... There's somehar else here too. We have to take him as well."

"Who? Where?"

"In this room here."

"What – here?" Tiski put his hand on the handle of the door on the left-hand side.

"No!" Hanu snatched Tiski's hand away and pulled him over to the door on the other side of the corridor, away from the room containing the *sedu*. He opened the door and the little group of hara dutifully trooped in. Geth was still lying on the ancient couch, and still breathing, for which Hanu was profoundly grateful.

One har of the group made a small noise of concern and rushed forward to examine Geth. "Oh! What's happened to him?" He pulled back the filthy rug to reveal the wide gash around Geth's neck. "Did Gavax do this to him?"

"Yes," said Hanu, "Do you have healing skills? I tried my best, but..."

"A little," said the har, placing his hands on each side of Geth's face.

"That's Ruzhu, from Wind's Edge," Tiski told Hanu. "He's a student of their healer. It's a bit like being an eskev, I think." He stepped forward and took a closer look at Geth lying on the couch. "Hanu! Isn't that...?"

"Yes, it is."

"The Mojag from Ardith? What's he doing here?"

"The same as you, I expect."

"A Mojag?" wailed one of the group, a dazed-looking har with long hair dyed in stripes of various hues, "There's a Mojag here? Aghama save us! We're all going to die!"

"Hush, Polly." Tiski put a reassuring arm around the har's shoulders. "He can't do you any harm, and anyway he's a friend of Hanu's.

"I had a friend once," Polly told Tiski seriously. "He was green."

One of the other hara spoke up. "He hasn't been right since he came through the Otherlanes."

Hanu recognised an amulet in the shape of a hoof-print around the har's neck, which was a popular piece of jewellery among the hara from the estemble Tail-and-Tether.

"It affects some hara like that." the har said.

"How are we going to get away from here?" one of the others asked, a tall har with white hair shaved close to his scalp and a gold ring through the side of his nose. "We can't escape through the Otherlanes, and even if we could..." He looked meaningfully at Polly, who was rubbing the ends of his hair between his fingers and singing softly to himself.

"Don't worry," said Tiski, "Hanu has a plan, don't you Hanu?

Hanu's always very organised. He's a good har in a crisis."

This was news to Hanu, and welcome though it was to hear Tiski's glowing estimation of his leadership skills, Hanu had to admit to himself that he really hadn't thought his whole rescue plan through. He certainly hadn't considered the possibility that there might be eight other hara involved, one of them unconscious.

"Well… the first thing we need to do is get Geth out of here." He turned to Ruzhu, who was still kneeling beside the couch, his hands on Geth. "Can we move him?"

"I think so," Ruzhu said, "but he won't be going anywhere under his own steam for a while."

"How *are* we going to move him?" A slender har with eyes that looked too big for his face regarded the unconscious Geth dubiously. "He's quite big."

"I'm sure two of us can lift him," Hanu answered. "I managed to drag him in here and get him on the couch by myself, after all. You, whatever your name is…" He pointed at the tall har with the nose ring.

"Perdix," the har said, straightening his shoulders, which were wide and bony.

"And… me, I suppose."

"Where are we going to take him?" Tiski asked.

"Out the back, I suppose. I left Tezuk out there. Perhaps we can get Tezuk to carry him, or pull him or something… I don't know. I think we should make for the ridge. It's quite steep, but if we can get to the other side, we won't be visible. From there we can head towards Spinnersholm. Once we get there, I'm sure Sofia will lend us horses so we can get back to Scatterstones."

Hanu delivered this speech with a lot more confidence than he felt. He knew Tezuk would never submit to having the dead weight of Geth on his back, and he had no schooling in the harness, so even if there was a cart or trap of some description, there was no way Tezuk would pull it. The steep incline up to the top of the ridge would be all but impossible carrying Geth, and once out on the open grasslands between here and Spinnersholm they could be easily spotted. Even if by some miracle they made it to Spinnersholm, Sofia and the other women could do nothing to protect them against Gavax's superior powers.

It was a terrible plan, but it was all they had. Hanu looked at

Perdix, and the other har gave a curt nod. They lifted Geth from the couch, Perdix with his arms under Geth's shoulders, Hanu grasping his legs, while the others hovered around being distinctly unhelpful.

Together, he and Perdix carried Geth outside, towards the barn at the back of the house. The whole time Hanu prayed fervently that Tezuk would still be there. It was daylight now. The sun had risen, bees and other insects had started their daily routine, buzzing to and fro. In the early morning sun, the old house looked less threatening, its ancient paintwork peeling and cracked, its windows looking out like sightless eyes.

In the barn, much to Hanu's relief, Tezuk was still standing in the corner by the water trough. On hearing the strange voices, he swung around, and his feet stamped nervously, but to Hanu's relief the horse didn't appear frightened or distressed.

Hanu and Perdix laid Geth down on a pile of straw. Hanu felt like collapsing himself – he had not slept in over a day. The adrenalin which had kept him going for the past few hours was now rapidly draining away, but he had to see that Tezuk was alright. He hauled his exhausted body over to the horse, quietly, so as not to alarm him. Tezuk snorted, which Hanu took as a sign of recognition, and allowed Hanu to stroke his nose.

"I'm sorry there's nothing for you to eat here," he whispered, "I know you're hungry. I'll try to get you some fresh grass soon, I promise."

Perdix had wandered over from the main group and approached Tezuk admiringly. "Is that your horse?" he asked Hanu.

"Yes. He... I wouldn't do that..." He fended Perdix's hand off as the har reached out to pat Tezuk, who'd laid his ears back in warning. "He isn't good with strangers," Hanu said, by way of apology.

"Ah. That's OK. Some horses are like that."

"Yes, they are," said Hanu, warming to Perdix. "Where are you from?"

"East of Heaven. It's actually east of Lemarath, near the border with Maudrah, but there you go, you can't have everything I suppose." He gave Hanu a wry smile.

Hanu decided he liked Perdix.

"Sula and I were at the Cuttingtide Fair in Ardith. In the

evening we went to a dance in one of the other pavilions – well, I say *dance*, it was more a sort of drunken roon-fest with added music and shuffling – you know the sort of thing – and your friend Gavax was waiting outside afterwards and… whoosh. One bit of Gelaming witchcraft later and we find ourselves in this charming residence, where there are some very dubious practices indeed going on."

"He's no friend of mine, and yes, there are crimes being committed here."

"What do you know?" asked Perdix, looking at him intently. His eyes were an intense shade of blue.

Hanu decided to trust him. "Gavax is keeping a *sedu* prisoner in the house. He but's using it to draw energy."

"Why would he do that?" Perdix frowned. "What does he want with the energy?"

"I don't know, but in order to keep the *sedu* alive in this realm he's… he's feeding it blood and flesh. *Harish* blood and flesh."

The expression on Perdix's face went through a series of changes, from outrage to horror, and then finally to dawning realisation. "So that's why we were kidnapped. We were intended as snacks for his pet. How lovely! We need to get out of here, Hanu, and, as soon as we can, let all the Tirthas know what's been going on, so they can put a stop to it. How *are* we going to get out of here, by the way? I don't see any more horses."

"Well…" Hanu squirmed a bit, unwilling to admit that he had absolutely no idea what to do next. He'd been hoping that Perdix might have been able to suggest some plan of action – he seemed like a capable har – but before he was able to confess his own shortcomings as a leader, a shadow fell across the open doorway. Hanu looked up to see two darkened figures standing there. His heart seemed to make a bid for freedom up through his throat, because he knew instantly who it had to be.

"Well, here we all are!" said the taller figure. "I was wondering where you'd got to. Is this really the best hiding place you could find? Oh dear. I despair of young hara these days. They have no initiative whatsoever. Now I'm sorry to break up your little party here, but I think you had better all go back into the house – immediately, if you don't mind."

Even if Hanu had not recognised him from his attenuated silhouette, the voice identified him instantly. It was Gavax.

Chapter 14
Magic

Gavax's sudden appearance precipitated a small commotion among the little group of hara in the shed. There was a moment when it appeared that some of them might make a bid for freedom through the open doorway, but none had the courage to be the first. Instead they cowered in the gloom, pressing tightly together in the hope of deriving some safety from the presence of their companions.

Over in the far corner, Hanu's shock at the sudden appearance of both Gavax and Ren was slowly mutating into something quite different; something with which he was not on intimate terms because he encountered it so infrequently. That something was not anger, but it was fuelled by the same nagging internal thoughts that were providing the genesis of anger; that he was responsible. Responsible for the safety of Tiski, and Tezuk, and Geth and Perdix and the others. And in some unspecified way, responsible for the situation they found themselves in now. If only he had gone back to the camp with Tiski that night in Ardith... If he had told somehar with more authority about his disappearance... If he'd left Scatterstones earlier... If he hadn't stopped to talk to the *sedu*... If he'd had a better plan...

All these fragments of *What If* danced in his head and welded together to form a force that was stronger even than his fear of Gavax. That force was not merely anger, but pure incandescent rage. Hanu marched forward from his corner and positioned himself between Gavax and the little group of hara, as if daring the Gelaming to come through him.

"We're not going back to the house," he told a startled Gavax. To his own surprise his voice sounded loud and firm. "I know what's back there. I know what you've been doing, and you're not going to do it to any of us here!" He was aware of the other hara behind him mumbling words of muted agreement.

Gavax stared at him for several long seconds, the way he might look at a fresh deposit of equine excrement obstructing his path. "You're that odd little eskev from Scatterstones, aren't you?" he said at last. "The one with the ill-tempered horse. I'm sure I didn't bring you here. How did you get here? Never mind, it's not important. You've just saved me the trouble, that's all. Now get back to the house," he told Hanu and the others, who were still standing clustered behind Hanu, watching fearfully.

Hanu ignored the implicit threat in this response and stood his ground. "No!" he said, displaying a bravery he did not actually feel, but which he somehow felt compelled to enact for the sake of his companions. They were his responsibility now. He did not know how this had come to be. Nohar had elected him the leader, and yet all around him he could feel their expectation, their faith in him and his ability to save them. He would have given anything for it not to be him in this position, and yet it *was* him, and he would have to do the thing he did not want to do, because there was nohar else to do it.

"What do you mean, *No*?" Gavax asked, irritated. "It was not the preamble to a negotiation. It was not a request that you can either agree to or not. You will return to the house now. If you do not go willingly, then you will go unwillingly."

"You can't make us!" Tiski spoke up, emboldened by Hanu's resistance. Hanu was not so confident.

"Actually, I can."

At that exact moment, Hanu felt a strange buzzing inside his head, not unlike when he had been conversing with the *sedu*, but different in tone, or flavour, or some other quality that he had no word for. He felt the presence of Gavax inside his own mind, an unwelcome intrusion, without his permission. He felt his own will melt and give way as invisible tentacles of intention wound their way around his prefrontal cortex, replacing his thoughts and feelings and desires with Gavax's own.

Hanu struggled to resist, but it was as if his mind was caught in a butterfly net of silken threads spun from something infinitely fine yet unbreakable. He remembered once seeing a bird which had become caught up in a skein of yarn, and how the more it had struggled, the more it entangled itself. He remembered how his hostling and his father had held the bird immobile as they carefully untangled the yarn from between its legs and feathers, and so he tried not to resist Gavax's restraint, but let it lie loose. He did not struggle to pull away from Gavax's mind, even as something inside himself revolted against this enforced intimacy.

He became aware that his was not the only consciousness within Gavax's mind. He could sense flashes – sights, sounds, smells – of other hara. He recognised Tiski – *flax tail red silk ashes regret* – and Perdix and the others, all tangled around each other the way the yarn had been around the bird's feathers, and something else, too – *strange familiar* – something *not-har*, but something he knew and recognised because he had met it before, in the room, across from where the dead horse and the not-dead har lay, the thing imprisoned in the room, not now in the room, but in Gavax's mind. The *sedu*.

Hanu had little expertise in the use of Wraeththu mind powers. A har did not begin life as an adept, it took many years of study and training to achieve mastery. Many hara never progressed beyond raising their magical caste one or two levels, leaving the more esoteric aspects of such things to tribes and individuals who dedicated themselves to the arts. It was apparent to Hanu, if he hadn't already known it, that Gavax was a very high-caste har, probably Nahir-Nuri, a level of ability which was almost beyond Hanu's comprehension, although he knew enough to realise that any struggle between himself and Gavax was going to be so unequal as to be nonsensical.

His only hope would be if he could unite the others to help him. He did not know how he was supposed to do this. He knew that it was possible for hara to combine the power of their minds, but he had never experienced such a thing before, and certainly not within the confines of another har's mind while in the process of being actively coerced into surrendering his own will.

He tried to concentrate – not easy with the humming and buzzing within his brain, and the invisible silken cords of Gavax's will digging ever deeper into his mind – and project a mind-touch like he would do normally, as if this were any other day and he was standing beside Tiski in the stables at Scatterstones, and he wanted to share some unsayable, vulgar comment about Nirzhen's latest admonishment.

Help me.

Some ripples of acknowledgement suggested that the others could hear him, but there was no reciprocal contact. He tried again.

Help me. Help me fight Gavax.

Only confusion in response; the fragmented thoughts of seven consciousnesses struggling to maintain their identity, and underneath it the low, rumbling hum of the *sedu*, patient and persistent, waiting for something.

A part of Hanu knew it was useless, but he threw everything he had at Gavax; every particle of energy contained within his physical body, every ounce of his will. He visualised Gavax crumbling like one of the fences used to train inexperienced horses to jump, which looked solid, but collapsed instantly into a pile of flimsy sticks when struck.

Gavax's attention turned upon Hanu, but he failed noticeably to collapse. He pushed back against Hanu's attack, and it felt to Hanu like the Gelaming was holding him at bay with one contemptuous fingertip, whilst he screamed and flailed and struggled with every fibre of his being, to no avail.

Hanu thought of all the things he had yet to experience; all the things he had planned to do with his life in the future. He thought of his family, his hostling and his father. He thought of Tezuk, and Flor, and Tiski, and Nirzhen, and wondered, if he were to die here, now, would they remember him? Would they miss him, or would their lives simply continue as if he had never existed? Was it worth sacrificing everything he would ever be, in the hope that some others would get to live the life he would not?

His strength failed, and his legs collapsed beneath him, and as he dropped to the floor he felt the iron grasp of Gavax's will crushing his own.

To his surprise, he did not die. Although he was not really surprised at all. He was not *anything*.

He felt nothing at all. He was merely an assembly of flesh and bone and blood which had no will, no soul, no personality of its own. All those things which had seemed so important to him only seconds before were now meaningless. Gavax spoke, but he felt no fear, or despair or even anger at his words.

"That was a pointless exercise," Gavax informed him.

Hanu remained on his knees in front of the Gelaming, on the bare floor, neither acknowledging his words nor offering up any resistance.

"Get up," Gavax commanded, and Hanu's body performed the action smoothly, raising him from the floor until he was standing in front of Gavax, looking him directly in the face. One small bead of sweat had formed upon Gavax's temple. As Hanu watched, it slowly made its way down the Gelaming's face and neck until it vanished beneath the collar of his cloak. His face looked unnaturally still and beautiful, free from any of the little ticks or movements that could turn a waxen idea of beauty into a living, breathing har. His eyes were pale and glassy, not windows to his soul, but silvered mirrors, reflecting back Hanu's own pale face.

"We are all going back to the house now," Gavax told them.

As one, the group of captives began to shuffle slowly towards the barn door. Hanu noticed that they looked strangely passive and concluded that Gavax had control of their minds in the same way that he had control of his, but it did not concern him at all.

He also noticed that the hum in his head was now also in his ears. A dense vibration, which travelled through the bones of his jaw and his skull, at a frequency simultaneously too high and too low to be heard in the conventional sense, but which could be *felt*, like the buzz of a thousand angry bees. Hanu could not be sure that what he was sensing was real, because nothing seemed real to him at that moment, but he could see the long timbers that supported the barn shaking and shedding splinters of old, dry wood. Behind him, he could hear Tezuk stamping and whinnying in fear.

Hanu himself felt no fear, only a sort of detached interest, which made him note that they were leaving behind in the barn both the horse and the unconscious body of Geth. Gavax herded them back through the connecting doorway into the house.

Of the group, only Ren seemed to be displaying any emotion at all, jumpy and nervous, searching around in vain for the source of the vibration. "What's going on?" he cried. "What's that noise? What's happening? Gavax?"

"Nothing. It's not important. It doesn't matter. Just shut the door and keep this lot under control."

Ren stared around, wild-eyed, as if searching for an escape route, but he closed the door as Gavax had instructed, and waved his hands ineffectually at the group to drive them further back. "What are we going to do with them?" he asked.

Gavax's eyes were half closed, and Hanu noticed another bead of sweat running down the Gelaming's face. He also felt a strange sensation in his head, as if he had fallen asleep on part of himself and it had become numb and lacking in feeling, but now was beginning to come back to life with a painful tingling sensation.

He realised that Gavax's control on him was lessening, and it occurred to him that, as strong as Gavax's mind powers were, they were not unlimited, and controlling seven reluctant hara *and* an enigmatic other-worldly creature was probably pushing the very edge of those limits. He struggled again, and felt Gavax's control crumble a bit, like stepping on rotten wood or thin ice.

"You can't do it," Hanu managed to gasp out. "You can't hold us all."

"Doesn't matter," Gavax told him, panting slightly. "It is coming. It is coming for you."

"What is coming?" Hanu asked, fearfully, although he knew the answer, in the humming and vibrating of the air all around. Beside him, Tiski and the other hara were also regaining control of themselves, looking round in confusion.

Gavax pressed his fingers to the side of his head and muttered a few words that Hanu could not understand, but the sound of them unsettled him. The humming seemed to abate slightly, but then resumed almost immediately.

An inexplicable feeling of dread crept up Hanu's spine. It felt oddly like insects marching over his skin. He could not tell if this was caused by the vibrating sound or by the strange words Gavax had uttered. He wanted very badly to flee from both, but the door was now firmly closed and there was no way out.

"Why are you doing this?" he demanded, his voice cracking with desperation. "Why are keeping that *sedu* prisoner in the house?"

"That doesn't concern you," Gavax snapped.

Hanu's laugh had a crazy edge to it. "Oh, but I think it does, Gavax! I'm trapped here in this house with you and I *know* what you've been doing here. I've spoken with the *sedu*. I've seen things here in the house. I know what's going on. I know what you intend to do with us."

"You have really no idea at all." Gavax was icy in his dismissal. "It is for the greater good. I know what I'm doing."

"And do the rest of the enlightened Gelaming know what you're doing?" Hanu shot back. "Do they know that you have enslaved a creature from another realm and are feeding it harish flesh and blood?"

"Gavax's air of detached superiority deserted him briefly,

much to Hanu's satisfaction. "There is no need for them to know. The *sedu* is not being harmed in any way. I am merely using its essential nature to assist me, as you do with your horses."

"It told me you'd put a binding on it."

"As you put harnesses on your horses, which can be removed later."

"This is nothing like that, and you know it. Ren..." Hanu turned to the Tirtha standing by the door. "How can you be part of this? How can you be associated with this har? Because he's a Gelaming? This is not the way Gelaming are supposed to behave. Can't you see that?"

Ren glanced at Gavax nervously. "You told me animal blood would do. You said it would be content with that. I... the goats and the deer...I let you have them..." He shot a quick apologetic glance at Hanu. "....so you wouldn't need anything else."

"Things change," Gavax said, "and we have to adapt to changing circumstances. It accepted animal blood in the beginning, but after a while it became clear this was no longer sufficient."

"And you agreed to give it harish blood instead?" Ren said, recoiling a little even as he spoke the words.

"Yes. What else could I do?"

"You could have said no."

"That was never an option, Ren. You know what's at stake here."

"Yes, but..." Ren's voice trailed off unhappily as he failed to adequately marshal any argument against Gavax.

Hanu, however, decided he had had enough. "What are you talking about, Ren? Tell me what this is about."

Ren swallowed hard. "The tribes of Jaddayoth are repeating humanity's mistakes," he said woodenly, as if reciting a script he had learned. "They fight and feud amongst themselves. They value conquest and expansion, and the possession of others' lands and properties – and hara. They have split into factions, each convinced that they, and they alone, know the true way. That was humanity's downfall, and it must not be allowed to happen again."

"Oh really?" Hanu said, failing to keep the scorn from his voice. "And how, exactly, do you intend to stop it happening again?"

"I am charged by the Hegemony of Immanion with

maintaining the Confederation of Tribes in these parts of Jaddayoth," Gavax interrupted, rescuing the floundering Ren. "It is my responsibility to direct the leaders of the tribes, and all who serve under them, to a path of peacefulness, enlightenment and co-operation. Unfortunately, not all the hara of Jaddayoth are amenable to this – the roots of aggression and ill-will run deep and are not purged easily. In order to eradicate this poison, to alter minds and emotions, energy is required. The *sedu* is providing me with that energy. I am doing what is necessary. It is a difficult decision to make – I understand that there are unfortunate aspects to its implementation. I appreciate that not everyhar will agree with my actions – but they are necessary, nonetheless."

"No, they aren't!" Hanu found himself almost yelling, unable to believe what he had just heard. "You have no right to force the hara of Jaddayoth to live the way you want them to. Even if they are repeating humanity's mistakes. Which they're not."

Gavax's expression hardened imperceptibly. "And what do *you* know about it?" he asked in a tight voice. "You know nothing of what brought you here, what made you. You know nothing of your own history – of the terror and violence in which Wraeththu was born, of the bodies piled high, the blood and the burning cities. And you know even less of the history of those who preceded us, the race of humanity, whose corruption and greed and despoiling of the earth and hatred for their own kind not only caused their own downfall, but nearly destroyed every other living thing on the planet. You know nothing. Not a thing. And you have no conception – *none at all* – how easily it can all be lost, how it can simply slip away, if nohar is prepared to do what is necessary to prevent it. But I *will* do whatever is necessary. Whatever it takes."

Hanu stared at Gavax uneasily. Beneath the veneer of the urbane and sophisticated Gelaming he thought he knew, he could see the light of genuine fanaticism burning, and it disturbed him greatly.

He is actually mad he thought, with sudden clarity, as if the evidence contained within the house had not already led to that obvious conclusion.

He wasn't sure what this epiphany implied for he and his companions' chances of escape, but he could only continue trying desperately to make Gavax see the monstrousness of his actions.

"How can imprisoning a *sedu* and killing hara to feed it change any of that?" he demanded. "That was years ago, in the past. We're better than that now Or at least we're supposed to be. Isn't that what the Gelaming are always telling us?"

"You haven't understood a word of what I've said, have you?" Gavax looked at Hanu pityingly. "Well, it hardly matters. Your tribe's purpose is to breed horses, which you do well enough. The rest of it is beyond your understanding. But you will also be doing your part to help Wraeththu society flourish here in Jaddayoth, so you can console yourselves with that. Ren, you know what you have to do. Bring the knife."

Ren did not move. He merely looked at Gavax strangely. "And am *I* only a horse-breeder too?" he asked, his voice wavering.

"Of course not, Ren." With difficulty, Gavax produced a tight smile to placate Ren, which did nothing to disguise his irritation. "You have been of invaluable assistance to me. Your contribution will be recognised not only by the Gelaming but by all the other tribes of Jaddayoth too. They will no longer speak of Ren as the son of Merac har Gimrah, but of Merac as the hostling of Ren har Gelaming."

At the mention of Merac's name, Ren shook his head, seemingly trying to remove some unwanted thought or image from his mind. "You told me it was an accident," he said "You said Merac's death was accidental. And you said the *sedu* would only take animal blood. You *lied* to me." His voice rose plaintively, making him sound like an aggrieved harling.

Gavax sighed, his patience evaporating. "And you believed it because you wanted to, which is a failing of many hara."

"One which you share, apparently." Hanu could not resist the jab, although an inner voice – and a warning kick on the ankle from Perdix – cautioned him that this was not perhaps the best time to antagonise Gavax, but Hanu was still too angry to care.

"And you…" Hanu turned to Ren, who was still standing at Gavax's side, his face a mute symphony of conflicting emotions. "How can you do this? How can you continue to support this har, after what he's done? You are the Tirtha, Ren. You're supposed to protect your hara. You're supposed to be their leader. You're supposed to look after them, and…" Hanu just shook his head in disgust, unable for a moment to find further words. "What would Merac think of you?" He glared at Ren, who refused to make eye contact with him. "What would he say if he could see you now?"

"You don't understand..." Ren muttered, still avoiding Hanu's contemptuous stare.

"What is there to understand? Your hostling was a good Tirtha and a good har. You may be his son, but you aren't half the har he was."

"Do you think I don't know that?" Ren finally looked up, his face red with sudden anger. "Do you think that I haven't been told that by every har in existence since the day I was hatched? Including Merac? Do you know what it's like to be compared unfavourably with your hostling, every day of your life? To hear those snide comments and judgements? The laughter behind your back? And to know that they are right! And what am I supposed to do? Find some magic that that will make me Merac's equal? That will make hara respect me the way they respected him? At least by helping Gavax unite the tribes I will have done *something* useful."

Hanu could only stare in surprise at this sudden outburst. The unexpectedly raw nature of this revelation almost made Hanu pity Ren, but then the memory of the arm in the corridor, the ugly gash across Geth's neck and Merac's not-so-accidental death resurfaced, and any feelings of sympathy vanished. "You're deluding yourself if you think this will earn you the respect of anyhar." he said, not even trying to conceal his contempt. "You know that as well as I do."

Ren said nothing. He merely hung his head in silence, but Hanu could see his jaw tighten and a small vein in his temple pulse, a testament to his emotional turmoil.

"Enough of this!" Gavax barked, losing patience. "Ren, I know that Merac's death was distressing for you, and if there had been another way I would have taken it. But we must complete our task, otherwise his death will have been in vain. You must not falter now." He took a sudden, sharp intake of breath. "The *sedu* comes," he said. "I can feel it. If we do not supply it with what it wants…it is unpredictable. It is not like the others of its kind. If it were, it would not have agreed to assist us."

"What do you mean *agreed*?" Ren asked. "I thought you had bound it? I thought you controlled it?"

Gavax's eyes closed briefly, as if he were searching inwardly for an explanation. "It is a powerful creature," he said. "I have laid a geas on it, but it does not work in the same way as on a har or any other earthly creature. It has a strong will. But it will do as I ask. It has its reasons."

Hanu found himself somewhat alarmed by what Gavax had just said. He wondered how it was possible that Gavax could maintain his influence over the *sedu* by his own will and mind power alone. Gavax was a powerful har, but the *sedu* was something else entirely. He remembered its lack of concern about the idea of captivity, and its cryptic comment:

At this point in time, I am bound. At other points in time, I may not be. I have been free in the past; I will be free again. All things return to the beginning, all events conspire towards an end. The time may be sooner than we think.

He could only speculate what the exact nature of the relationship between the *sedu* and Gavax was, and which one was truly in charge.

Lynx, the har from Tail-and-Tether, stepped forward. "Please, don't do this." His face was pale, and he was obviously on the verge of tears. "Please just let us go! I don't want to be here. I don't want to die. I don't want to be fed to a *sedu* and WHAT IS THAT NOISE?" He clasped his hands over his ears as if that alone would block the bone-deep, thrumming vibration

"I'm afraid it's not possible for you to leave," Gavax said. "It needs... more." Again, he shuddered, and closed his eyes briefly as if in pain. The vibration grew more intense. "You are what it needs."

With a small cry, Lynx made a dash towards the door, but before he had taken more than two steps, Gavax casually raised his hand and an instant shock wave of energy propelled Lynx backwards, throwing him against the opposite wall with a loud and sickening thud. He fell to the floor, limp like a discarded puppet, and remained unmoving. Hanu's heart was in his mouth for a few moments, but then a wave of relief washed over him as he saw Lynx slowly begin to struggle up from the floor. A crimson flower bloomed on his right temple, its tendrils slowly making their way down his face, but he seemed otherwise unharmed.

"You have value dead as well as alive; it makes no difference to me," Gavax said conversationally, as if he were discussing the weather or the price of oats.

Hanu thought that he had never hated anyhar so much in his

entire life as he hated Gavax now. As if sensing the animus he was projecting towards him, Gavax turned his attention to Hanu. "You are the ringleader, so I think we will start with you. That makes sense. Yes." He nodded, as if agreeing with himself. He looked over at Ren, still standing by the door. "Bleed them," he said. "Do it now."

Colour drained from Ren's face. "Kill them? All of them? Me?"

Gavax glared at Ren with something approaching disgust. "Yes, you."

"I..." Ren stood there transfixed, like a rabbit caught in a snare.

Gavax pulled a knife from his belt. "You can't, can you?" he said contemptuously. "Your hostling was right. You're a coward. I'll do it."

Ren's face twisted in anguish. "No," he said, his voice cracking "I'm not. And you won't."

"Get out of my way."

"No." Ren pulled a peculiar shiny object from his pocket and pointed it with trembling hands at Gavax.

Gavax immediately stopped short, and the expression on his face changed instantly from one of disdain to one of fear.

This seemed a curious reaction to Hanu. The object did not look large enough for Ren to reach Gavax with from where he was standing, or dangerous enough to inflict a serious blow. It was smooth and tubular, with an angled section which fitted neatly into Ren's hand and a small lever around which Ren's forefinger was curled. Hanu realised the device was actually made of metal. It reminded him of something – the metal frame of the seeing-device he had found in the woods. It was a human thing, forged for human use. Perhaps it was capable of exerting mind control. He thought that if he could grab the object from Ren, he could use it to free himself and the others. He began to move towards Ren but was stopped by Perdix grabbing his arm.

"Don't be stupid. He's got a gun."

Hanu thought he had heard the word before, but in his mind it conjured an image of a weapon much larger and more terrible than the small device in Ren's hand. But Perdix's tone was urgent, and he seemed more familiar with the object in question than Hanu. So Hanu held back and watched as Gavax slowly stretched out his hand towards Ren, as if he was trying to approach a nervous horse.

"Just give it to me, Ren," Gavax said slowly.

Ren took a step backwards. "No." he said.

There was a terrible sound – a sudden, sharp report, louder than the droning in Hanu's ears, louder than anything he had ever heard before.

Gavax's hands flew up to his neck, a look of surprise on his face. Hanu watched his mouth move, but no sound came out. Then a red stain began to spread through his fingers, slowly at first, then in a hideous spurt, which Gavax's clutching fingers could not contain.

Time seemed to stop for several heartbeats, freezing this scene in Hanu's vision, then Gavax dropped to his knees, and collapsed onto the floor, his limbs twitching and a horrible wet, gurgling, choking sound issuing from his blood-stained lips.

Ren stared at Gavax in horror, as if he could not believe what he had done. His hand holding the gun was trembling and shaking. Hanu feared that he might invoke its power again accidentally. But Ren walked over to the prostrate form of Gavax still jerking on the floor, pointed the gun directly at his head and fired again and again and again, until the gun clicked uselessly and roared no more, even as Ren continued to pull the trigger repeatedly over and over again.

If Hanu had been in any doubt as to the terrible destructive power of the gun, he was no longer. Nothing in his life had prepared him for the mess that a gun fired at close range into harish flesh and bone could make. There was little left of Gavax's face that was identifiably harish, it was a bloody pulp with fragments of skull and brain and other, mercifully unidentifiable bits of what had only moments before been a living, breathing har. Worse still, linked tenuously as he still was to Gavax's mind, Hanu felt the Gelaming's life-force leave his body, a ghastly sensation akin to feeling all the skin peel away from his flesh, sloughing off like so much dead matter, Behind him, Hanu heard the sound of somehar retching, and he had to exert all his self-control to prevent himself from doing the same.

The blood seeping from the horror that had once been Gavax's head continued to flow, pooling and creeping slowly across the floor towards the horrified Hanu, as if it was still possessed of some unnatural sentience of its own.

As Gavax's spirit was severed from his body, a mighty howl shook the whole house to its foundations. The continuous rumbling sound grew even louder, making Hanu's ears hurt and his whole body tremble in sympathy.

Freed of the geas that Gavax had put upon it, the *sedu* was now at liberty to do whatever it pleased, and Hanu did not think that its intentions were benign. The sound continued to intensify, with the low frequencies insinuating their way into Hanu's flesh, making his diaphragm stiffen and his breathing become irregular. The floor beneath his feet began to undulate, and he feared the ancient floorboards would collapse.

He tried to stifle the feeling of panic, which rose in his throat and threatened to choke him. It felt like *something* was bearing down on him, something nameless and unstoppable, something that would suck the marrow from his bones and the life from his body. He remembered Gavax's warning:

It is coming

He knew what was coming.

The wall in front of him seemed to lose its integrity; it oscillated and shook, waves rippling its surface. Hanu blinked. He seemed at one instant to be able to see right through the wall, and then it was solid again. The wall became the *sedu* and the *sedu* became the wall, and then they became separate and the sedu was there, in the room with them.

Hanu could feel the *sedu*'s hunger. This was a need that was more than physical, a compulsion that had driven everything else from its thoughts, all compassion or love or honesty or goodness. It made Hanu feel sick just to touch the edge of such insanity, and his mind recoiled from the horror of it, but there was no escape.

There was consternation among the little group of hara, stifled cries of alarm and terror. Hanu did not know if they could see the creature's true form – to his own eyes it seemed to shift and change even as he watched it, but there was no mistaking its murderous intent. He tried to touch its thoughts as he had done before, in an attempt to reason with it, even as he flinched from the very idea of linking with it, but it was too far into its madness and too driven by its need for sustenance.

Blood. Hanu thought. *It wants blood. Harish blood and harish flesh.*

A thought occurred to him.

"I know what you want," he shouted, over the vibrating din,

unsure if the creature could actually hear him or not. "Here it is. Take this."

He waved his arms and pointed at the gory remains of Gavax lying on the floor.

"He was a powerful har, his flesh and his blood will nourish you. He's already dead. You don't even have to kill him. I know you want it. Take it. Everything you need is here."

There was murmur of disgust from the group, but Hanu ignored them and continued to wave his arms and point to Gavax's remains. The *sedu* turned its attention towards the corpse but did not approach it as Hanu had hoped. Instead, globules of half-congealed blood began to rise from the floor, drawn by an invisible force towards the *sedu*. They moved lightly through the air, reminding Hanu of the soap-bubbles he had blown as a harling, and he winced internally, knowing he would never be able to witness that innocent pastime in the same way again.

The blood bubbles reached the *sedu* and it licked them greedily from the air, savouring them with a shiver. Hanu found the sight utterly repugnant, but he could not look away. More and more of Gavax's blood made the horrifying journey to the waiting sedu, not only what was spilled on the floor, but from his body too, which became paler and more ghost-like as it was drained. Eventually it resembled the bleached, skeletal husk of a dead starfish left drying on the shore.

Hanu felt himself now beyond any possibility of further revulsion, but he was wrong. When all the blood had finally been drained from Gavax's corpse, the soft grey pulp of his brain tissue, glistening wetly inside what was left of his head, was also sucked into the *sedu's* waiting maw. Hanu had to turn away at this point; he simply could not bear to watch anymore.

Nothing he did, however, could shield him from the creature's mental emanations. Hanu was forced to experience its relief as the hunger which had been gnawing at it continuously ever since it entered the room was sated. The ecstasy which flooded Hanu's mind and body was immense and overwhelming, and for one brief second, he understood what drove it. He knew with a terrible certainty that, were it him, he, too, would do anything – *anything* – to relieve the pain of the Hunger and feel the rapture of deliverance from its grasp.

It was not a piece of self-knowledge he was happy to

experience. He fought fiercely to keep the creature's thoughts and emotions out of his head. Fortunately, the *sedu* now seemed less agitated, and its mental aura became less intense as it sank into a kind of stupor. At the same time, however, the noise and vibration grew even stronger, as if what had fed the *sedu* had also fed whatever energy was shaking the house.

Hanu turned to the others who were cowering in the far side of the room. "We have to get out of here!" he shouted.

At first the group didn't respond, perhaps incapable of thinking or moving. Hanu shot a look at Perdix, who seemed more alert than the others, and with a nod of agreement and understanding they formed a pincer movement together to direct the others towards the door.

In the confusion, though, Hanu had forgotten about Ren. Standing directly in front of the door, his face very calm, Ren stood holding the gun. With great deliberateness, he raised his arm, pointed the gun directly at Hanu, and slowly exerted pressure on the trigger.

Chapter 15
Rescue

"No!" Hanu cried, reflexively raising his hands to protect himself, expecting at any moment to hear the same ear-splitting roar from the gun which had announced Gavax's death. He expected to feel his own throat torn away, to feel himself choking and drowning in his own blood and his life ebbing away to nothing on the dirty floor.

The shot did not come. Instead, Ren stood passively in front of them, seemingly oblivious to the thunderous sound all around them, the gun still pointed at Hanu, his finger still on the trigger.

"Ren, why are you doing this?" It was Tiski who spoke, pushing his way to the front of the group, shouting to make himself heard over the noise, his voice almost tearful. "Please, let us leave. It's not safe in here, that thing is... is... I don't know, but it isn't good. It doesn't sound good. Please, just let go. We won't tell anyone you killed Gavax. We'll say it was an accident, won't we? Please let us out, Ren. I want to go home!"

Ren shook his head. "I can't let you leave." he said, as unemotionally if he were keeping them behind at the stables to do some extra chores in punishment for slacking.

"But why not?" Tiski persisted desperately. His face was contorted from the noise and vibration, the struggle both to hear and to make himself heard.

By contrast, Ren looked unnaturally calm, freed from the inner turmoil he had displayed earlier. "I have to destroy all the evidence," Ren told them, as if it were the most logical thing in the world. "You are evidence."

"Ren, we'll all be killed if we stay here!' Hanu yelled. "*You'll* be killed too! You've seen that thing, and what it does. It's satisfied for the moment, but it won't be for long. We have to go!" Hanu knew it was pointless trying to reason with Ren – his mind had fractured under the accumulation of guilt and horror it had experienced, until now it had constructed its own reality.

"I am evidence too," Ren said, as if he hadn't heard Hanu. "I must be destroyed too. They will blame Scatterstones, and our estemble will be shamed in the eyes of the Gimrah tribe, and of

Wraeththu-kind. The honour of Scatterstones will be tainted forever. My hostling, and my high-hostling, and all the Tirthas that came before will be disgraced and their names stricken from the histories. Our horses will no longer be spoken of with pride. This is the only way to make sure that doesn't happen. I have to do this. You must see that." Ren tightened his grasp on the gun and aimed it directly at Hanu's throat and pulled the trigger. It clicked uselessly, as it had when he had emptied the last of the bullets into Gavax's head. Ren stared at the gun perplexed, looking down into its hollow barrel, trying to determine the reason for its malfunction. Hanu, Tiski and the others stood stock still, unsure of what to do next, unable to move, frozen by indecision and fear.

There was a sudden loud crack, and Hanu winced instinctively, but it was not the gun going off, it was the wooden frame of the door to the outside splintering and cracking. For a moment, Hanu thought that the intense vibrations had finally caused the whole house to give way, but the floor still held firm beneath them. Then the door cracked again, its wooden panels disintegrating. As he watched, small fragments and splinters flew inwards, followed by two black hooves, and then, in one final, furious burst, an entire equine form. A huge horse, dark, sweat-stained, rearing, stamping, snorting, with fire and smoke pouring from his flaring nostrils. At least, Hanu thought so until he realised it was the dust and dirt from the shattered door, and the light streaming in from outside, and the horse was no hellish apparition, but Tezuk!

Tezuk – maddened by the hell-sounds all around, kicking, snorting, destroying everything around him in a frenzy of rage. His instincts had told him to flee from danger, but the unfamiliar surroundings had caused him to panic. He had charged the door blindly, crashing through it, forcing Ren's attention away from his captives. Whatever had drawn the horse to the house, it had now provided them with a means of escape.

"Quick, everybody out!" Hanu shouted. He began to shove the dazed group of hara towards the exit. But Tezuk stood in their way, and Hanu realised he would have to take control of the horse if they were to make it out through the remains of the doorway.

Tezuk reared and screamed, his front hooves thrashing the air. One kick could crush a har's skull, so Hanu would have to be very careful. He pulled himself inwards, shrinking his frame, trying to appear as unthreatening as possible. He approached Tezuk slowly and cautiously, from the side, trying not to alarm the horse any further, all the time fighting through the thunderous tsunami of sound that threatened to overwhelm him at any moment.

"Tezuk!" He had to shout the horse's name to make himself heard, instead of using the quiet, reassuring tone he had employed so often in the past to calm him.

Tezuk's ears flattened against his head, and his eyes rolled. Hanu could see the whites – and see the fear within – the same fear that surged through Hanu's body, forcing itself up through his throat like bile.

He swallowed hard and tried again. "Tezuk!"

Tezuk remained on four feet long enough for Hanu to reach him and place a hand on the horse's back. The skin was hot beneath the stiff coat, as if fuelled by some internal fire. Hanu slapped Tezuk, as he would when he wanted the horse to move. With one last angry snort, Tezuk swung around, leapt through the open doorway and bolted off past the barn and towards the grassy plains beyond.

"Now!" shouted Perdix.

There was a scuffling of feet, pushing, shoving, bits of broken wood scattering, bright light, the noise – *the noise*!

Hanu ran from the house as if pursued by angry demons, his only thought to catch Tezuk and prevent the horse from hurting himself. A har on foot had no chance of outpacing a horse, but by some fortune there was a thicket of bushes and trees just by the house and it was here that Tezuk had run. Finding his way blocked, the horse had stopped, trembling and quivering, uncertain what to do or where to go.

Slowing, Hanu approached him as gently as he could, trying to reach him with his mind, to reassure him that everything would be all right. He grasped a handful of the horse's mane, almost weeping by this time with the effort of fighting Tezuk's will, and his own fear.

The noise had reached a level that seemed impossible for mere sound. Hanu felt his bowels twist under its assault, and his legs turn to jelly. Holding on to Tezuk for support, he turned to look back to see what had become of the others.

What happened next would stay with Hanu for the rest of his life. In his dreams, it would all unfold in slow motion, as if everything had suddenly been slowed to an agonising crawl, and all the players were wading through water or mud. He would turn to see Vinda and Pasha fleeing from the house at a run, Perdix and Sula carrying the unconscious body of Geth from the barn, with Ruzhu hovering beside them, and Lynx hurriedly shepherding the bewildered Polly towards Hanu and his thicket.

And Tiski…

Framed in the broken doorway of the house, Tiski stood motionless. Unmoving, because one of Ren's arms was wrapped tightly around his neck, holding him fast.

Hanu tried to run towards his friend. But the noise had become so intense it was like a physical barrier. His legs would not move, his guts heaved. He felt acid burn his throat as spasms wracked his body. Still he tried to move, one agonisingly slow step at a time. Not fast enough. Not nearly fast enough. Must go faster. Behind him, Tezuk reared and screamed in terror, again and again, the sound somehow piercing through the all-encompassing thunder of solid noise.

With an enormous effort, Hanu took one last step towards the house. He saw Tiski look towards him pleadingly, saw his lips move, saw him mouth the first syllable of his name. And then…

The shock wave was visible. That was the thing that Hanu would remember with surprise. It was a circular, shimmering wave, blasting outwards, followed instantly by an enormous gout of orange flame, shooting upwards into the clear blue sky, for a moment outshining the sun itself in its intensity. Then a shattering bang, a blast of wind, which knocked him to the ground, a wall of intense heat and then…

Silence.

A silence all the more profound for the tumult that had preceded it. Hanu could not be sure if he even retained the power of hearing any more – perhaps he had gone deaf? There was a ringing in his head, but the world seemed devoid of sound. Then he became aware of a distant roaring, which seemed to become less diffuse as he concentrated on it. He hauled himself to his feet, slowly, painfully, and watched without any sensation of emotion as the orange flame consumed what was left of the house and the barn, and whatever had been inside.

After that, he remembered sitting in the grass along with the others and not knowing what to do, and therefore doing nothing. He remembered the strangeness and the incongruity of it all. How peaceful and calm it all seemed, with the warm sun on his back, insects buzzing. High above in the cloudless sky a small bird hovered and twittered, pouring out its heart through its song. He remembered watching Tezuk grazing serenely on the grass as if nothing had happened. And if he kept his back to the house – to the charred remains of what had been the house – and if he looked only towards the ridge on the horizon, then he could tell himself that nothing *had* happened.

After a while – it could have been hours, or days, but probably wasn't – figures appeared on the ridge. Suddenly, Sofia and the other women from Spinnersholm were there, with horses and carts, and water and food and blankets, and the world speeded up again, and the Time of Doing Nothing was past. There was a flurry of activity, and a lot of Doing of Things – helping hara onto the backs of patient horses, or into the cart, lifting the inert body of Geth. Checking that everyhar was accounted for. Explaining those who were not.

Hanu stood beside Tezuk watching the proceedings, but not feeling a part of it in any way.

Sofia noticed him and stopped what she was doing. She approached him cautiously. "Hanu? Are you OK? What happened here?"

Hanu looked over to where the house had stood, then looked away quickly. "I don't know. Gavax and Ren. Tiski..."

"Yes. That other har – Perdix – told me."

There was silence. Sofia put a comforting arm around his shoulders.

"How did you...?" Hanu asked

Sofia shrugged. "When you turned up in the middle of the night like that, I knew there must be something amiss. This place... it has a reputation. Bad things happen here. I didn't like the thought of you out here all by yourself, so I woke some of the others up and we decided to come out to see if you needed help."

"Good thing you did," Hanu said, with a watery smile. "I didn't really have a plan for getting back. I didn't really have much of a plan for anything, as it turns out. Perhaps if I had..."

"Hanu," Sofia's voice was firm, "you did everything you could. It wasn't your fault. You saved all these hara. They'd be dead if it wasn't for you." She wrapped her arms around him in a comforting hug, pulling him close.

Hanu breathed in the scent of her body, which was nothing

like a har's.

"I'm so sorry about Tiski," she whispered.

Hanu could only nod voicelessly in reply.

"Come on," she said, releasing him, "We need to get you all back to Spinnersholm. Do you want to ride with me? Fila can easily carry two."

Hanu shook his head firmly. "No, I'll ride Tezuk." He said this with more confidence than he felt. He did not know if Tezuk would consent to be ridden again after all he had been through, but he grasped Tezuk's mane and swung himself up without incident other than a snort and a shuffle of hooves. It seemed that Tezuk was less fearful of Hanu's presence on his back now.

He guided Tezuk over to where the women and the other hara were preparing for the journey back to Spinnersholm.

Lynx pointed at them. "It was the horse who saved us. Hanu's horse. Tezuk."

The others mumbled in agreement, and Hanu rubbed Tezuk's neck with pride. It felt as though he had been waiting a very long time for this – for other hara to recognise Tezuk's greatness and to see that he was a true Scatterstones horse, and not a misfit or a reject. "He carried me all the way here, at the speed of the wind," Hanu said solemnly. "He broke down the door and allowed us to escape. No other horse could have done what he did. He deserves every praise he receives."

Again, there was a rumble of agreement.

Sofia smiled at him. "He is a fine horse, Hanu, and he has an equally fine har."

Hanu felt tears prick behind his eyes. In no way did he feel worthy of Tezuk. Tezuk had been destined for great things from the moment he was foaled, and it was only fate, or chance, that had made Hanu a part of that. Perhaps now that the world knew the truth about Tezuk, Hanu would no longer be part of his story, and would fade into the background. Hanu wished he could be unselfish enough to let Tezuk go, but he knew that if he were to lose Tezuk, a part of himself would be ripped away, and he had lost too much already today to endure any more.

It was a long ride back to Spinnersholm, in contrast with Hanu's precipitous flight the previous night. Hanu was exhausted from lack of sleep and proper food and from the events at the old house. By the time they reached Spinnersholm it was only pride which kept him upright on Tezuk's back.

As they reached the community, other women rushed out to assist them. A woman Hanu did not recognise reached up to help him down, and he fell off in an ungainly slide rather than dismounting in the standard fashion. But strong arms were there to catch him and help him into the main dwelling. In his mind, he knew that he should be seeing to Tezuk – a good har always put his horse's needs before his own – but his body refused to cooperate. He agreed with himself that just this one time he would let the women take care of Tezuk. He trusted them – they were as knowledgeable about horses as any Gimranish har. He knew Tezuk would be in good hands. He mumbled some advice, and some warnings, about the best way to handle the horse, but the women just patted his hands and smiled and told him everything would be fine.

Sofia led him and the others into the rambling kitchens where there was food waiting for them. Hanu did not think he would be able to eat, he was so tired, but as soon as he smelt the delicious aromas, and put a forkful in his mouth, he realised he was ravenously hungry. He ate as if there was a good chance he would never see food again. The other hara sat around the table with him and did the same, as if by the simple and ordinary ritual of sharing a meal they could wipe away the horrors of the past few days. At one point, Hanu caught Perdix's eye over the table, and they looked at each other in silence for a second or two but said nothing. There was nothing that needed to be said.

With a full stomach, Hanu sat back in the chair and enjoyed the luxury of not caring about anything, just for the moment. His eyelids began to droop, and small gaps smuggled their way into his consciousness making time seem to jump forward in random little hops rather than flowing smoothly as it ought to. He could hear Sofia and the other women discussing something in the background, but their voices were indistinct, and he only caught a few words – Scatterstones, Tirtha, Gelaming – and once, his own name, but it all seemed very distant and unimportant.

At some point Sofia must have led him off to bed, because his only recollection after that point was of crisp linen sheets smelling of new-mown hay, a soft, downy quilt and a deep, much-longed for oblivion in which visions of orange flame, and blood, and guns, were mercifully absent.

Chapter 16
Going Home

Hanu awoke the next day to the late morning sunshine poking its way through a gap in the curtains and trickling across his face. For a moment he couldn't remember where he was, or anything of the previous day's events. When, seconds later, it all came crashing back into his mind again, like a huge wave breaking on a rock, he wished for that innocence to return more devoutly than he had wished for anything in his life before. But there was no way to put the thing back in the box and nail down the lid to keep it from troubling him ever again. So, he lay in the bed and wondered if it was worth his while getting up, now, or at any point today, or for the rest of his life.

He stayed in bed, engulfed by its softness, and studied the curtains drawn closed across the window. They were dyed a subdued shade of yellow and patterned with an embroidered trellis of leaves and intertwining flowers, matching exactly the cover of the quilt lying over him. The fabrics were luxurious and beautiful, and of a quality that many a har would be pleased to display upon himself in public in order to impress others, and yet here they were, in a room where their only function was to delight the solitary occupant in private.

He also noticed that there were clothes hung in a closet, some coarse workaday garments and some made from fabrics whose finery put the quilt and curtains to shame. He recognised the work clothes, and it dawned on him that this was Sofia's room, and Sofia's bed. The guilt that came with this revelation, and the realisation that she had given it up for him, was enough to force him to sit up, then roll awkwardly out of the bed. He searched for his clothes, which he found in a sad and crumpled pile by the side of the bed, next to a neat stack of clean items, miraculously in his size and of that distinctive Spinnersholm design.

He dressed himself in the strange clothes, taking time to admire the skill that had gone into them, then pulled back the heavy, embroidered curtains and looked out of the window and down into the main yard below. Women were bustling about the place, to-ing and fro-ing, carrying bolts of fabric or skeins of yarn or buckets of water or other necessities of daily life. The domestic ordinariness of the scene reminded Hanu of the stables at Scatterstones first thing in the morning, and he felt a pang of homesickness, even though he had only been gone for just over a day. It felt like a lifetime.

Somewhat reluctantly, he left the bedroom and made his way downstairs, creeping quietly, trying not to make a noise in case anyone was still sleeping. The house seemed to be empty – all the women were out working, presumably. He investigated a couple of rooms, but found no-one, only the ghosts of breakfasts and lively conversations past. The main door was open, so he stepped outside and took a deep breath of the fresh morning air. He could smell grass and soap and horse dung and flowers. He could hear sounds of wood-chopping in the distance, and women's voices, talking and laughing.

He hurried over to the stables, and found it, too, empty, except for the one stall which housed a dark horse. Tezuk. Hanu breathed a sigh of relief, although he did not know why he had been anxious. He knew the women would have taken good care of him. He approached the stall and noted with professional satisfaction that the horse had been fed and watered, and also groomed to remove all the previous day's sweat-stains, leaving his coat gleaming and soft.

He opened the door of the stall and entered. Tezuk snorted and stamped, and Hanu smiled wryly to himself. If he had thought that yesterday's ride had tamed Tezuk's wild spirit, then the horse was keen to show him that he remained as indomitable as ever, and that Hanu would have to work for his approval in the same way he always had.

"Tezuk," he said, softly. "You did well, friend. Thank you for letting me ride you. Thank you for carrying me such a great distance. You are the best horse in the whole world. There is no other like you. You saved me and the others. It wasn't your fault we couldn't save Tiski." His voice broke a little, and he hugged the horse's neck. Tezuk stamped a little in agitation but allowed the contact.

Hanu experienced a niggle of concern that Tezuk might have suffered some damage or injury when he kicked the door of the old house down, so he carefully examined his legs and hooves, but found them intact and flawless, the hooves shiny and black, apart from the brown one. He polished that one particularly carefully with a handful of straw, even though it didn't need it. It felt almost like touching the golden hoof of the statue in the Eithak for luck. The statue had not brought him luck, but the living horse had given him something better – not luck, or chance, but something real.

"We'll be going back home today," he told Tezuk, as he carefully smoothed away some non-existent blemishes in the horse's immaculate coat. "Back to Scatterstones. I'll have to tell them all what happened. I'll have to tell Nirzhen. I'm not looking forward to that. I don't suppose he'll be very pleased with me. Perhaps I'll have to leave the Tirtha's stables, in disgrace. I can't leave you, Tezuk. I *won't* leave you. We don't even have a Tirtha now. What's going to happen? Who will be in charge of the estemble now? What are we going to do?"

His questions hung in the air unanswered. He sighed and patted Tezuk's neck, and laced his fingers through the luxurious mane, feeling its coarse texture, so unlike the long, silky hair of a har.

"I'd better go and see what's happening with the others," he told the horse. "But I'll be back soon."

He pulled a handful of hay from the manger and offered this to Tezuk, who refused it. Hanu shook his head, and left the stable, stepping out into bright sunshine and a warm breeze.

He made his way to the main workshop where he hoped he might find Sofia. This was a large courtyard surrounded on all sides by a covered area constructed from wood that could be opened up in the summer to let in light and air, while being closed in the winter to provide protection from the elements. In the courtyard at the centre were piles of the raw materials – flax and wool and other goods. Inside, it was a hive of activity with women stirring great vats of steaming dye, working away furiously at clacking looms, and participating in the industrious operation of other strange-looking machines which Hanu could not identify.

Hanu found Sofia over at one of the dyeing tubs, supervising the addition of some shredded stems and roots into the seething cauldron of dark red liquid. There was a small wood fire built underneath the vessel to keep it boiling, and the smell of the woodsmoke mingled pleasingly with the herbal scent of the dye plants.

Sofia looked up from the cauldron as he approached and gave him a smile. "Hanu! You're up!" She scrutinised him carefully. "How are you feeling this morning?"

Hanu shrugged. "OK," he said. It wasn't true, but he didn't know what else to say.

Sofia nodded, not fooled by his pretence, but willing to go along with it, for which Hanu was grateful. At the moment, he did not think he could cope with any great outpouring of sympathy. He found Sofia's matter-of-fact attitude and her solid ability to get on with life, no matter what the circumstances, far more comforting. "We've been in contact with Scatterstones," she told him. "They know what's happened. They'll be sending some hara and horses out to take you all back there today. They'll be arriving some time early this afternoon, I should think."

Hanu nodded, relieved that arrangements were being handled by others now. He'd had enough of making decisions and taking action and was more than happy to leave everything in Sofia's very capable hands. "I've just been to see Tezuk," he said. "Thank you for taking care of him. And thank you for the clothes as well." He tugged at the sleeve of his shirt, noticing for the first time the fine woven pattern.

Sofia eyed him approvingly. "They suit you," she said. "You can keep them if you like. They belonged to Nicolai... Nicu, but he didn't want to take them with him."

"Thank you," said Hanu, wondering if Nicu would object to him wearing his old clothes, and wondering why on earth he would have discarded them in the first place.

"Have you had any breakfast yet?" Sofia asked.

"No."

"Oh well, there's food in the kitchen – look in the pantry. Just help yourself to what you want. The bread should still be OK, it was only baked yesterday. If you want to wait for a fresh loaf, there should be some quite soon. Eva was just putting it in the oven, the last I saw."

"That sounds like a good plan." Hanu paused for a moment, thinking. "Where are the rest?" he asked. "I mean, the hara who came back with me last night?"

"We spread them out throughout the houses," Sofia said. "Found spaces for them all. I haven't seen any of them this morning yet; they were still sleeping when I last checked."

Hanu shuffled uncomfortably, then blurted out: "The Mojag – the har who had… his throat… is he…?"

Sofia looked at him with narrowed eyes. "We took him to Sasha's house. She's a healer. While she might not have the same abilities that your people do, she has plenty of knowledge and experience. Would you like to see him, your Mojag friend?"

Hanu nodded, wordlessly relieved that Sofia had not delivered the news he had been dreading.

"Come with me, then." Sofia wiped her hands on the stained apron she was wearing, then took it off and laid it over a nearby chair.

"Remember to use more salt this time," she told the woman stirring the cauldron, who nodded in acknowledgement.

Sofia led Hanu across the main yard and down a gentle, grassy slope towards a small house, which stood on the edge of the marshy area around Spinnersholm, where reeds poked up through the wet ground. In the distance argumentative waterfowl could be heard honking and flapping.

"Perdix told me that you carried him all by yourself," she said, referring to Geth. "That must have taken some doing."

"Oh well," Hanu managed an embarrassed shrug. "It was only for a short distance, you know."

Sofia shook her head in mock despair. "Don't put yourself down, Hanu. What you did was quite remarkable. Very few people, or hara, would have done what you did."

They arrived at the house, which was small and low-roofed, built of ancient, weathered stone. Sofia knocked on the wooden door, alerting the occupant to their arrival.

"Sasha!" she called "Are you there? I've brought Hanu to see his friend."

There was a brief pause and then the door opened and another woman that Hanu did not recognise appeared. She was even older than Sofia, to judge by her face and her stooped posture, but when she spoke her voice was firm and clear.

"Hello Hanu," she said, briskly. "I'm Sasha. Come on in. Your friend is just in here. He'd lost a lot of blood, but he's a fighter."

"Mojags are very difficult to kill," Hanu told her, and she grinned, showing a missing tooth.

"This one is, that's for sure."

Sasha showed Hanu through to a small back bedroom. The house was, in truth, no more than a small cottage, unlike the rather grander residence inhabited by Sofia and some of the others.

To his surprise, Geth was awake, and immediately pleased to see him.

"Hanu!" he croaked, hauling himself up into a sitting position. The gash around his throat was still red and livid, but held together by a row of black stitches, like tiny insects. His voice sounded a little hoarse, and his appearance was pale, but otherwise he looked quite cheerful, all things considered.

"You're still alive," Hanu said, by way of a heartfelt but unnecessary observation.

"Yes," said Geth proudly. "Mojags are very..."

"... difficult to kill!"

They both laughed, and Hanu sat on the edge of the bed.

"What happened?" he asked. "How did you end up getting captured by Gavax and Ren?"

Geth gave a dramatic sigh and flopped back on the pillows. "I went back to meet up with my Commander that morning – you remember, in Ardith, after the night we..."

"I remember," said Hanu with a slightly embarrassed smile.

"Anyway, apparently Commander Athak and Kare had been gambling the night before and had lost a lot of money – some new game they weren't familiar with, because we Mojags are generally good at gambling, and rarely lose, but anyway... He needed to pay off the debt he had accrued, so he had made a deal with Gavax har Gelaming that he would get money in payment for sending me to meet with Gavax. Whereupon Gavax did that thing the Gelaming can do, where they make you do things you don't want to do, and I ended up at that old farm, somehow, me and Pink."

"Wait a minute..." Hanu's brow creased and he analysed what Geth had just said. "... you mean, your Commander *sold* you to Gavax?"

"Yes," said Geth

"I... Is that *legal*? I mean, of course it isn't, but is it the sort of thing that Mojags do? Is it your tribal custom, or something?"

"Oh no," said Geth, scratching at the stitches on his neck absently. "We Mojags are an honourable tribe. It's the sort of thing the Maudrah would do, no doubt, but that's Maudrah for you. They are very untrustworthy, as tribes go."

"Can't you ask your tribe leader..."

"... The Wursm."

"Yes, him. Can't you ask The Wursm to do something? Punish them? If a Gimrah har did something like that, we'd take our grievance to the Tirtha, and he would see justice done. Probably..." finished Hanu lamely, thinking of Ren's recent ignoble performance as Tirtha.

"Oh no," said Geth "The Wursm doesn't get involved in petty disputes between individual Mojags. We are supposed to deal with it ourselves. The next time I see Commander Athak and Kare, I will have to kill them."

"No, you won't!" said Hanu. The vehemence of his own response caught him unawares. "There's been enough killing, there should be no more! I saved your life. You owe me that, at least!"

Geth looked at him in surprise. He thought about it for a minute, then said: "That sounds fair. I think there's something in Tribal Law about that, when somehar saves your life. I'm sure it counts for hara of different tribes, too. I will honour your *vretch*, Hanu har Gimrah."

Hanu had no idea what a *vretch* was, but he was relieved that he had been able to dissuade Geth from killing his ex-companions. He was beginning to suspect that Geth was not nearly as keen on killing and conquest as members of his tribe were supposed to be.

"So how did you end up at that place?" Geth asked, "Did Gavax bewitch you too?"

"No," said Hanu, "It was my friend, Tiski – he was with me that night in Ardith, I don't know if you remember him. Gavax kidnapped him, and after I overheard him saying that Tiski was at the Old House of Men, I rode out on my horse, Tezuk, to save him. Not that it did any good," he ended bitterly.

"Why not?"

Hanu did not want to say the words, but he had to. "He was killed when the house exploded."

"Oh." Geth frowned. "That's bad."

"Yes, it is."

"They killed Pink as well."

Hanu was glad that Geth already knew about that, because he

didn't want to have to be the one to tell him. "I know," he said.

They sat in silence for a few minutes, which Hanu found strangely comforting. After a while, Geth reached over and touched Hanu's hand, but still neither of them said anything.

There was a rustle at the door, and a cough, and then Sofia's head poked round it.

"We were wondering," she said, "when the hara arrive from Scatterstones, will Geth be able to travel, do you think?"

She looked questioningly at Hanu, but before Hanu could reply, Geth sat up and announced that he was entirely fit to do anything, up to and including taking on the entire Gelaming army.

"I don't think..." Hanu began, doubtfully.

"I am a Mojag!" Geth told him firmly, and that seemed to settle matters, at least in Geth's mind.

Hanu could only shrug hopelessly at Sofia. "He says he is. You can't argue with him. He's a Mojag."

Sofia stifled a laugh. "Right, well, if you, Hanu, want to come back over to the main house with me, we'll round everyone up and get you all fed. And you, Geth, can get yourself over when Sasha is satisfied that you're not going to pass out."

"Who's coming from Scatterstones?" Hanu asked anxiously.

"I don't know. One of the anskevi and a few others, I expect."

Hanu hoped it would not be Nirzhen. He knew he was going to have to face the anskev at some point and tell him the whole story, but he didn't want it to happen so soon.

Hanu and Sofia left Sasha's house and walked back up the grassy slope together. On the way, they passed a woman with two children, and this time it was someone that Hanu did recognise. It was Gina carrying the baby he and Tiski had delivered a birthing-day present to the previous summer. It must be almost a year old now, yet still could not walk or talk. He thought of Nirzhen's harling, hatched that spring, and marvelled at the difference between the two.

Holding on tightly to Gina's other hand was another This one was a girl. Hanu could tell this because she had ribbons in her hair. That was how you told them apart, human children. That and some arcane system of colour coding which he could never quite understand. He was sure there must be some other method, but he was too embarrassed to ask. At any rate, he was pleased that Gina also had a girl-child because it meant that there would, in time, be another adult woman to keep the community going. It troubled him that women had much shorter lifespans than hara. He didn't like to dwell upon the fact that he would outlive all the women currently living and working at Spinnersholm, and that he would, in the turning of time, get to know their daughters and grand-daughters and great-grand-daughters, and outlive them too. Life seemed very unfair to Hanu when he thought about these things, so he tried not to think about them too much.

Back at the house, the other hara were gathering in the kitchen for a late breakfast. They all looked much the better for a good night's sleep, and Hanu wondered gratefully how many women had given up their beds last night for the dispossessed little group of hara. *It's good to have friends who'll do things like that for you*, he thought. He would definitely do the same if any of the women came to Scatterstones needing assistance. He would give up his own bed in a heartbeat for any of the women here.

Perdix rose from his seat and gave Hanu a rib-crushing hug. He was wearing a floral garment that somehow seemed at odds with his personality – obviously a gift from one of the women – but Hanu did not say anything. Clean clothes were clean clothes, and anything that removed the memory of the smell of the old house had to be a good thing.

"There you are," Perdix said. "Lilian here says you were visiting the Mojag. Is he alright?"

"Pretty much," said Hanu, eyeing the food on the table hungrily.

"Sit down, then. Have some of these cake things, they're delicious."

Sula and Lynx shuffled up to make room for Hanu on the wooden bench, and he took a couple of the flat objects Perdix had recommended. They weren't remotely cake-like, but they were hot, and speckled with aromatic seeds, and swimming in butter. He ate them shamelessly and greedily, washed down with a large mug of rather bitter coffee, and then went back for more.

Ruzhu was trying to persuade Polly to eat some of the not-cakes, but he seemed more interested in cutting them into small pieces and arranging the pieces into complex patterns on his plate.

"What are we going to do about him?" asked Perdix, his mouth full of food. He pointed at Polly with his fork. "We don't even know where he comes from."

"We have mind-healers back at Scatterstones who might be able to help him," Hanu said, looking around hopefully to see if another batch of the not-cakes were forthcoming. "If not, perhaps he'll have to be sent to the Gelaming."

Perdix said nothing but rolled his eyes expressively.

"They're not all like Gavax," Hanu said, feeling somehow embarrassed for having to defend Wraeththu's most exalted tribe in this way.

"None of them are supposed to be like Gavax, or so we're led to believe!" sniffed Sula.

It was plain to Hanu that the Gelaming were not entirely well thought of at East of Heaven, and Gavax's recent activities had done nothing to boost their popularity, so he wisely decided to change the subject.

"You will be coming back to Scatterstones with us today?" he asked Sula politely.

"Yes, it's five days' ride home, so we'll need to get some provisions and borrow some horses – if that's alright with your Tirtha."

There was a slightly embarrassed silence.

"What I mean is..." Sula looked mortified.

"No, it's OK. The anskevi will see that you all get everything you need to get back to your home estembles."

At that moment, Sofia appeared, looking somewhat flustered. Have you all finished? Good. The hara from Scatterstones are here – I wasn't expecting them quite so early. If you've anything to collect, go and get it, and meet us back in the yard.

The group quickly dispersed. Hanu retrieved his few belongings from upstairs. Filled with trepidation, he went out to meet the rescue party from Scatterstones.

To his immense relief, Nirzhen wasn't among them. He knew it was only putting off the inevitable, but any reprieve however short-term was welcome. There was Zolta, one of the anskevi, and a couple of other young hara whose services had obviously been deemed dispensable for the day. One of them was Nicu.

Hanu watched with interest as Sofia approached him, rushing quickly to greet him, and then slowing, her body language indicating uncertainty. Nicu did not look comfortable either. Hanu was too far away to hear what they were saying, but it looked like an awkward encounter, so he turned away, meaning to go to the stables and get Tezuk, but one of the women had already brought him out. Zolta was leading him by a thin rope slung loosely around his neck. The horse looked restless and slightly irritated by this, so Hanu ran up to him to reassure him.

"Be calm, Tezuk," he said, stroking his neck. "He doesn't like the rope," Hanu told Zolta. "I can take him."

Zolta looked at him dubiously. "This horse is not to be ridden," he said. "There are… circumstances."

Hanu had no idea what he meant by that. Zolta indicated the horses they had brought from Scatterstones. "There is a mount for you."

Hanu looked and saw that it was his old friend Harcan, and his heart melted. If he could not ride Tezuk, then it would be fitting to ride Harcan home, and no dishonour to either horse.

"You still need to take the rope off him," he said to Zolta. "It's alright – he won't run away. He'll follow us home. He'll always come home."

Zolta hesitated for a moment, then nodded, and slipped the rope over Tezuk's head. Tezuk snorted, and shook his mane irritably, as if to free himself from the stain of the rope.

Sofia came over to them. Hanu thought her expression looked a little more strained than usual, but he may have been imagining it.

"Are you ready?" she asked. "Ruzhu and Geth are going in the cart with Amalla. The others are all mounted."

Hanu indicated Harcan, who was snuffling in one of the women's pockets looking for some hidden treat. "I'm taking Harcan," he said. "Tezuk will follow us."

Sofia smiled at him, and gave him a big hug, which knocked the breath out of him. At this close range, he could see clearly that her hair was changing colour. Hanu had asked her about this, feeling rather more comfortable about that aspect of human biology than some others. She had told him it happened spontaneously without recourse to dyes or potions or alchemy, and that it was a measure of the passage of time. Hanu thought that was quite magical, and it was something that would be quite useful for hara, who tended to forget how old they were after a while.

"Take care of yourself, Hanu," she said. "And come back soon. You know you'll always be welcome here."

"I know," said Hanu.

He swung himself up onto Harcan's back – he had somehow forgotten how easy this was using reins and stirrups and saddle – and they set off down the track in the direction of Scatterstones. As promised, Tezuk followed Hanu, keeping his distance, but always staying with the herd.

Hanu felt at peace sitting on Harcan's broad back. Harcan was a steady mount, reliable and even-tempered, bred for stamina rather than speed. To Hanu, he represented everything that was good about Scatterstones, all its rightness and solidity, and his even-tempered, horsey thoughts were a calming presence. As they rode, Hanu tried to concentrate on the feeling of the sun on his face and the whisper of the wind in the long grass, and the steady, muffled clop of Harcan's hooves. He put from his mind what had happened at the old house. He knew once they reached Scatterstones there would be no running away from the harsh reality – the space that Tiski had occupied in his life would be empty, and would remain so, for ever. But just for this moment, he let the dependable Harcan carry him.

After a while, he noticed Nicu riding beside him. Nicu was on Perian, a staid, older mare often chosen as a mount for less experienced riders. Nicu was a good enough rider, but he had only been har for a short time. He'd not had the same experience of growing up with horses that Hanu and others like him had, and that made a difference, although Hanu could not quite say exactly what it was. He found himself wondering if Nicu resented the implied slight in giving him Perian to ride, or if he even noticed.

He remembered that Nicu and Tiski had been quite close at one point and felt a pang of sympathy for him. It was enough to jolt him out of his own self-absorption, and to realise that he would not be the only har affected by Tiski's death.

Harcan edged towards Perian, giving the mare a friendly snort and a flick of his ears. Perian replied with what could only be considered the equine equivalent of rolling eyes and a heavy sigh, and Hanu found himself smiling in spite of himself.

Nicu gave Harcan a wary look, and tried to pull Perian away, but Hanu reassured him.

"It's alright. Harcan doesn't mean any harm. He's very friendly. Perian's just putting him in his place. She isn't worried by him at all."

Nicu looked slightly dubious but allowed Perian to remain close to Harcan. The mare continued to ignore Harcan, but Harcan appeared oblivious and trotted alongside her happily.

"He likes company," Hanu explained, "and he's always had a bit of a crush on Perian."

Nicu scowled at him. "He's a gelding," he said, as if that was a fact unknown to Hanu.

Hanu laughed softly. "Yes, but that doesn't... I mean..."

The words tailed off. What it was he meant, he wasn't entirely sure. "They have their own preferences," he said, shrugging. "Just as hara do."

"Oh."

"You must have noticed."

"I suppose so."

Hanu got the feeling that Nicu was not particularly keen on having this conversation, and he wondered if he had done something to offend him. Apart from, of course, being responsible for Tiski's death. He wondered how many other hara would blame him for that. He was also acutely aware he was wearing some of Nicu's discarded clothing and wondered if the har was angry with him about *that*, too.

"I was surprised to see you come out to Spinnersholm with Zolta," Hanu said, attempting to steer the conversation in what he hoped would be a less contentious direction.

"Nirzhen said I was to go."

"I see."

"I told him I didn't want to, but he said that was all the more reason for me to go."

"That sounds like Nirzhen, all right."

A brief smile passed between them, dissipating the tension somewhat.

"Why didn't you want to go?" Hanu asked.

Nicu kept his gaze firmly on the back of Perian's neck, as if he found the small, random movements of her mane the most fascinating thing in the world. "You were born a har, weren't you?" he said, more of a statement than a question. "Hatched. Whatever."

"That's right."

"It's different for me."

"What is?"

"Everything. I used to be one thing, and now I'm another, and I can't go back to what I was, can't relate to people the same way I used to."

"By 'people', I assume you mean Sofia."

"My mother."

The word sounded strange to Hanu. Archaic. It was a word that was rarely spoken these days, having been rendered obsolete by events.

"Things change," Nicu said, suddenly sounding much younger, "And they can't be un-changed. They only go in one direction. Does that make sense?"

It made all too much sense to Hanu, and he could only nod mutely. "Would you still choose to become har?" Hanu asked, "Knowing what you know now?"

"Of course!" said Nicu, looking at him as if he were mad. "You know what the alternative for me would have been!"

There was nothing Hanu could say to that. Once, he had believed there were good choices in life, and bad choices, and that it was easy to tell the difference, but now he knew that Nirzhen had been right – that sometimes there were only bad choices and less-bad choices, and that in order to gain something, sometimes you had to give up something else.

The sun was high in the sky now, and Hanu squinted into the distance to see if he could catch a glimpse of the rooftops of Scatterstones, but they were still too far away. Ahead of him, Perdix and Sula were riding next to each other, sharing some unheard exchange, while Zolta led the group onwards. He looked behind him, at the others following in single file, and Tezuk hovering close by, not close enough to be part of the formation, but not so far away that he was separate from the main group.

Nicu noticed him watching Tezuk. "Your horse is the talk of Scatterstones," he said.

Hanu turned to him in surprise. "What?" he asked, taken aback.

"They are saying he saved you from Ren and Gavax."

"That's true. He did."

"They are saying that the spirit of the Aghama was in him."

"That... may be true."

"Apparently the Aghama can take the form of a horse."

"Yes. He can." Hanu's brow furrowed as he thought about

this. "How do they know all this?" he asked, wondering if he would be spared the ordeal of relating the events at the Old House again.

"Vika rode out before daybreak this morning, before you were awake apparently, in order to fetch assistance. She told the anskevi what had happened, and, naturally, it went round the estemble faster than a Faraldienne promised a bag of oats. You and your horse are famous."

"Oh." Hanu didn't know what to say to this. He didn't want to be famous. And if he was going to be famous, he would rather not be famous for this particular reason.

"Nirzhen and Zolta organised the rescue mission," Nicu continued, sounding rather over-dramatic, in Hanu's opinion, "And Vika sent a bird back to let Spinnersholm know we were coming."

Hanu nodded. Using birds was an elegant work-around for a species which had no way of communicating telepathically, either over long or short distances. Although it had to be the right type of bird. – the little fat grey pigeons, who seemed happy to do what was required of them. It didn't work with crows, who refused to cooperate."

Uncooperative crows were a feature of life in Scatterstones in general, as the regular occurrence of uprooted crop seedlings would testify. The system gave Hanu at once an increased respect for the women and their ingenuity in the face of their handicaps, and a twinge of pity that there was so much they missed out on in life. He said as much to Nicu, who pulled a face in response.

"You don't miss what you've never had," he said, "But there are some skills which Wraeththu possess that women do envy. Sasha is a skilful healer when it comes to wounds of the body, but she cannot mend him…" He nodded towards Polly, who was riding along in a state of blissful vagueness, looking up at the sky.

"The mind-healers will help him remember who he is," Hanu said, all the time wondering if Polly would actually thank them for that.

There was a shout from Zolta up ahead. He was pointing to where, on the horizon, Hanu could see the outlines of the rooftops of Scatterstones, lumpy and undulating, the fat bump of the Eithak instantly recognisable in the middle. Horses and riders perked up at the sight, and the pace quickened noticeably. It wasn't long before they reached the outskirts where the grassy steppes thinned and gave way to well-worn tracks and roadways.

Some hara were standing at the side of the road, and others came out to join them as they passed, confirming Nicu's story of Hanu's unasked-for celebrity status. A part of Hanu was not looking forward to what had to come next. But for all that he dreaded the inevitable questions, and the answers he didn't want to give, inside his heart rose and his spirits lifted as they rode through the houses and farms, through the curious onlookers, towards the stables. Despite the ominous events still to come, it was good to be home!

Chapter 17
Scatterstones

A Gimrah har spends his life learning about horses, and not everything he learns about them has a rational explanation. For example, it happens that sometimes a horse will refuse to go down a path it has happily taken its entire life. It will shy at a certain tree that it has passed every previous day without incident. It will refuse to enter its own, familiar stall for no apparent reason. It is as if the horse believes that its whole world, and everything in it, has been taken away and replaced by something which looks identical, but is in some subtle and inexplicable way different.

Hanu thought that he now had an insight into what this felt like. Scatterstones was his home. He had lived his whole life here, and everything about it was exactly the same as it had been a few days ago – and yet, somehow on his arrival back from Spinnersholm, it was changed. He could feel it in the way that other hara ceased their casual conversations as he walked past and turned to look at him with a mixture of pity and curiosity. How everyhar was suddenly kind, yet distant. He was acutely aware of an enveloping silence around him that had once been filled with the sound of high-spirited chatter.

For once, he could find no comfort in Tezuk either, for the horse, too had changed. Or, rather, the estemble's relationship with the horse had changed. No longer was he an unwanted reject. Word had gone around the estemble of Tezuk's act of rescue. Whispers and rumours had spread that the horse was, indeed, the manifestation of the Aghama, for how else could he have performed such a feat that no ordinary horse could have been capable of? Tezuk had not been returned to his old stall at the far end of the stables. Instead he was garlanded with summer flowers and led reverently to the handsome and spacious private stable reserved for the Tirtha's own mounts.

Hanu wanted to protest against this, as he knew that Tezuk did not like change – no horse did, but Tezuk even more than most – but he could see that it would do no good. The hara of the estemble were determined to honour their newfound champion, and he felt helpless in the face of their earnest adoration. Besides, he felt as if all the energy he had ever possessed had been used up – as if he'd crammed several years' worth of his life into a few short days, and he would now have to wait until the rest of him caught up before he could ever do anything again.

Hanu woke early the next morning, images from his dreams still echoing in his head. He tried, without success, to dismiss them from his mind as he got ready for work, concentrating on washing, brushing his hair, dressing in familiar clothes and gathering up his small collection of personal tools and equipment. He felt that if he could just follow his daily routine as he had done so many times before, then the rest of his life would automatically fall into place too. It didn't seem to work that way.

Inside the east stables, there was still work to do, still other horses to attend to, but Tezuk's stall, empty and silent, reminded him only too well of the empty room next to his own in the lodgings. He tried not to look at it as he set about his work, scrubbing viciously at a harness to remove a particularly difficult stain. He was so intent upon his task that he didn't notice Nirzhen's stealthy arrival and jumped at the sound of his name, almost dropping the harness onto the floor.

"Hanu," Nirzhen said, "What are you doing here?"

The question baffled Hanu. This was where he worked. This was where he belonged. Where else should he be? "The harnesses needed cleaning," he explained, offering the one he had been working on for Nirzhen's inspection.

Nirzhen did not look at it. "You don't have to be here, you know," he said gently.

"But there's work to be done," Hanu insisted stubbornly, "The horses need feeding and watering."

"The other eskevi can do that. You don't need to do it. Not today, anyway. Why don't you go back to the lodgings for a bit?"

"I don't..." Hanu swallowed hard, trying to find a way to explain to Nirzhen that he could not go back to the lodgings, could not sit in his own, small room in silence, nor could he find the courage to enter the empty room next door where the small pile of belongings he had brought back from Ardith still lay on the neatly-made bed, but the words would not come, so instead he said, "The horses need me. They know me. I can't let them down."

Nirzhen eyed him silently for a while. "Is this about what the horses need, Hanu?" he asked at last. "Or is it what *you* need?"

Hanu felt his hard-won composure crumble. "Everything is different," he wailed. "Hara look at me as if I'm a freak. The horses are nervous around me. Even you treat me differently – don't deny it! Why is that, Nirzhen?"

Nirzhen sighed and sat down next to Hanu. "Hanu," he began, "You've been through an incredible ordeal. You can't just pretend it didn't happen. Scatterstones is still the same as it always was – but *you* have changed."

"No, I haven't!" Hanu insisted. "I'm just the same as I was before, so why do hara stop whatever they're doing and look embarrassed every time I appear? What's that about?"

"They just need time to come to terms with what happened. The same as you do..." Nirzhen held up his hand to deflect Hanu's protest before it could begin. "Now, I think it would be better if you took the morning off – your mind is not going to be on your work, and that cannot be good for the stables, the horses or the rest of the eskevi – but I can see that you need some order and stability in your life at this moment. So, I may be prepared to turn a blind eye if a certain eskev manages to keep himself occupied doing a few non-essential tasks around the stables – as long as he does not get in anyhar else's way." Nirzhen's tone softened and he looked at Hanu with something resembling pity.

"There'll be a meeting in the Eithak this afternoon that you'll be required to attend," he said. "Perhaps it's best that you distract yourself in the meantime. It's a formality, but you'll have to give a detailed account of everything that happened at the Old House. All the anskevi will be there. And the relatives."

Hanu nodded. He didn't have to ask which relatives. He wished Nirzhen hadn't reminded him of it, but he was grateful at least for the permission to busy himself in the stables until then.

He would still have felt happier if Nirzhen had shouted at him to get on with his work, thrust a broom into his hand, shaken his head in disappointment, pursed his lips, anything – anything at all but this unnatural solicitousness.

When Nirzhen had gone, Hanu walked past the empty stall at the far end without once looking into it and instead turned his attention to the stall on the opposite side where Harcan was dozing contentedly, hoping that nohar would ask him to do anything energetic that day. When he saw Hanu enter his stall, he opened one eye suspiciously, then closed it again immediately, pretending to be asleep in the hope of being left alone. Hanu was not fooled and slapped his haunches teasingly.

"Don't worry, Harca," he told the gelding, "I haven't come here to ruin your morning by making you work. How would you like a bit of beauty treatment?"

Harcan opened his eyes again, this time with more interest, and Hanu spent the next couple of hours braiding his mane and tail into an intricate pattern and oiling his hooves until they shone, all of which attention Harcan accepted with his usual obliging camaraderie.

Shortly after midday, Nirzhen came to fetch Hanu. The anskev had a look on his face that told Hanu it was time to face the gathering in the Eithak and tell his story. Nirzhen stood patiently as Hanu washed his hands and face, slowly and carefully, then dried them with even more attention to detail, but finally Hanu could put off the moment no longer. The two of them walked together in silence from the stables, across the cobbled thoroughfare that ran through the centre of Scatterstones and entered the Eithak.

It was quieter inside than usual. All the anskevi were there, seated in a semi-circle, with other hara of the estemble who had chosen to attend sitting in front of them to either side. Tiski's family were there, too. His hostling, his father, his brothers, his high-hostling, two of his hura. They sat to the right of Hanu in the Eithak, and Hanu did not dare turn his head or make eye contact.

On his left were members of Ren's family, including his brother Velisan, and Hanu felt he might have been able to be less concerned about them except for the fact that he could not put it out of his mind that they were Merac's family, too, and that whatever Ren had done, he still had kin who cared for him, in the same way Tiski did.

Directly in front of the anskevi was a single chair which Hanu, rightly, assumed was for him. Nirzhen indicated for him to sit, then went to take his own seat, completing the semi-circle.

Hanu felt very alone, naked, and vulnerable sitting in front of these esteemed hara. He knew them all, of course, he worked with them on a daily basis. They were his superiors, and yet he had never felt intimidated by them the way he did now. It was not a pleasant feeling.

Nirzhen leaned forward and spoke. In the absence of the Tirtha, it seemed that he would be responsible for guiding the proceedings. "Please try to relax, Hanu," he said. "I know this is an uncomfortable situation for you to be in, but you're not on trial for anything. We only wish to establish the facts, and as you were the one most closely involved it's important that we hear first-hand from you what happened."

Hanu nodded, his mouth too dry to speak. Part of him knew this to be true, but another, more primitive, part of his brain could not help but feel threatened by the attention fixed firmly on him. He felt like a rabbit surrounded by a group of wolves, and once that unfortunate image was in his head, he found it impossible to dismiss.

"Please just tell us, in your own words, everything that happened," Nirzhen said.

Hanu nodded again, licked his dry lips, cleared his throat and began. His voice sounded odd to his ears, thin and strained, and it threatened to give out at any minute, but he reminded himself that he had already done far more terrifying things than this, and that merely recounting them would be nothing in comparison. Somehow that thought gave him the strength to continue speaking.

He began with his return to the camp from Ardith that morning and his discovery that Tiski was missing. He did not mention what he had been doing in Ardith the night before, although he knew that he would have to explain later how it was that he already knew Geth. But he put that out of his mind for the present and concentrated on relating how Gavax had told him that Tiski had accepted a job at Long Ride. He explained how he'd not believed this, owing to the fact that Tiski would never have abandoned Flor. He described how he had gone to Nirzhen on his return to Scatterstones, and also how he had hidden in the cupboard in the Tirtha's chamber, while Gavax and Ren had discussed their plans. And he spoke of his decision to ride out to the Old House to find Tiski before Ren and Gavax could get there.

On hearing this part of his story, there was some murmuring among the anskevi. One of them interrupted him as he was speaking.

"But why didn't you go and tell somehar about this?" he asked.

"Nirzhen, or one of the other anskevi?"

Hanu squirmed, struggling for words. *Because you would have forbidden me to go,* he thought, but of course, he could not say that. "I didn't think there was time," he offered weakly.

The anskev nodded and wrote something down in a small notebook.

Hanu continued his tale, trying his best to give as truthful an account as he could, but he realised even as he spoke that there were some things he could never say or admit to, for reasons which had nothing to do with the business with Gavax and Ren, but which made the whole situation he was in now even more complicated. The best he could do was try to negotiate his way through the different versions of truth available to him and find one that would satisfy his inquisitors without causing more harm somewhere else.

He was surprised that nohar questioned his miraculous ride on Tezuk, the horse that had never been ridden before. But it seemed they were all willing to accept that the spirit of The Aghama had aided him, and Hanu found himself grateful that he wasn't pushed for further explanation, because he was not sure he could give one.

Finally, he came to the part that he did not want to tell. He shook as the image of Gavax's bloody, ruined face once more rose before him like a nightmare apparition, His tone was flat as he described both the murder and the ultimate fate of the remains. Perhaps the anskevi thought him callous, but he could not trust himself to maintain his composure if he thought about it too hard. So he recited the details of Gavax's demise as if he were merely reading a list of jobs needing done in the stables.

"But why did you not make your escape when you saw that Ren had run out of bullets?" asked Zolta.

"Hanu had no knowledge of guns or how they operate," Nirzhen said briskly. "For all he knew, the gun could have been fired again at any moment."

Hanu shot him a grateful look, relieved that an answer had been provided to the very question he had been asking himself. It seemed obvious now, but at the time, with fear clouding his thoughts and paralysing his actions, it had all been very different. He could not explain himself to this group of calm, rational hara sitting here in the safety of the Eithak because they had not been there, and they did not know what it had been like.

"Please continue, Hanu," Nirzhen said. "Tell us what happened next."

Hanu closed his eyes, as if to blot out the memory, but he knew there was nothing he could say or do that would ever erase it from his mind. It was burned indelibly into his brain. Burned there by the orange flames that had consumed the house, and the remains of Gavax, and the two hara standing in the doorway, one with his arm around the other's neck...

"I don't know what happened," he said. "There was all this noise – I can't even begin to describe it. And then – an explosion. Or something. Tiski was still in the house. Ren... he had hold of him – and wouldn't let go. They didn't get out. There was fire and flames, great orange flames, and everything burned. Everything."

He bowed his head, unable to continue. Behind him, he was aware of the presence of Tiski's family. He didn't turn to look at them, but he could feel them, and hear them, hear the small, dry sobs from Tavim, Tiski's father, as he described the house going up in flames with Tiski still inside, hating himself for having to say the words, wishing that he could just lie, and make the lie be truth.

"And you're quite sure...?" one of the anskevi began tentatively.

"Yes, I'm sure!" Hanu retorted angrily. "Go and have a look, if you don't believe me. You know where it is. Go and check that I'm telling the truth!"

"Nohar doubts you, Hanu," Nirzhen said gently. "We only want to know what happened."

"Well, now you know!" Hanu nursed his brief spasm of anger jealously, because bad as it was, it replaced the pain, at least for a short while.

Nirzhen nodded. "Are there any other questions?" he asked the anskevi.

A few of them requested Hanu to clarify some of the things he had related before, some writing down notes in response to his answers, others merely nodding gravely as he spoke. He wondered if they thought he might change his story if they asked him often enough, but, of course, it was always the same – the house, the sedu, the gun, the noise, the orange flame. Nothing would ever change that.

Eventually they all seemed satisfied. Everyhar rose and began to depart from the Eithak. Hanu watched as Tiski's family departed, wondering if he ought to say something, but he could not find the courage to do so. Perhaps at a later time, but not now.

Just at that moment, he felt a hand on his shoulder. It was Nirzhen.

"That was very brave of you, Hanu."

Hanu did not know if the anskev was referring to the events at the house, or to the interview that had just taken place, so he just nodded.

"Before you go," Nirzhen said, "There are two hara who would like to speak with you." He turned and pointed at two individuals who had just entered the Eithak. For a moment Hanu's blood seemed to freeze in his veins, because their clothes, their bearing and their overall demeanour marked them instantly as Gelaming.

Nirzhen noticed his reaction. "Don't worry," he said, "They are not here to cause trouble. They would actually like a chance to explain some things to you, which might help you make sense of what happened. If you agree, of course."

Hanu thought for a moment. The last thing in the world he wanted was to speak to these Gelaming hara, but he knew that if he did not, he would always be left wondering. There were things he needed to know, if he was to be able to move on with his life, and so, reluctantly, he signalled his agreement to Nirzhen, who nodded in approval and immediately steered him over towards the visitors.

"Tiahaara, this is Hanu," he addressed the Gelaming. "I believe you wish to speak with him. Hanu, this is Perael har Gelaming and Sehireb Beh har Gelaming. They have come here from Immanion."

Both Gelaming inclined their heads slightly in a gracious sweep. Hanu wondered if he should do the same, but decided that since they were in Gimrah, then Gimranish customs should prevail, so he straightened his shoulders and replied with the traditional formal Gimranish greeting. "You have ridden far," he said. "Your horses are welcome in our stables."

Nirzhen smiled to himself. "I will leave you hara to discuss things," he said. "I have work to do."

Hanu would much rather that Nirzhen had stayed, but if the

anskev thought that Hanu could handle two Gelaming on his own, then he wasn't about to disappoint him.

Sehireb Beh inclined a small, stiff bow to the departing Nirzhen, then addressed Hanu directly. "Thank you for your courteous welcome, Hanuhathan har Gimrah. We are pleased to make your acquaintance. Your mentor speaks well of you." He smiled, but Hanu remained stony face and suspicious. He was not about to be taken in by Gelaming flattery.

"Perhaps you would like us to explain why we are here?" Sehireb Beh's companion ventured.

The reply that Hanu formulated in his mind involved sarcasm, invective, and a scathing review of Gelaming foreign policy in Jaddayoth, and while it sounded both witty and trenchant in his head, he had enough sense to make sure it stayed there. "Please go ahead, Tiahaara," he said, and awarded himself a small measure of congratulation on his own restraint.

Sehireb Beh clasped his hands together tightly. "We must offer our deepest and most sincere apologies for the actions of Gavax har Gelaming," he said. "Please be assured that none of it was at the behest of the Hegemony of Immanion. He acted on his own volition. We are greatly distressed by the harm he has caused."

Not as distressed as some, Hanu thought bitterly. His restraint failed him. "Why didn't you stop him?" he demanded. "You could have stopped him, surely? You're the Gelaming. You can do anything."

Sehireb Beh's hands twisted even more tightly, and he shifted uncomfortably. "Tiahaar, had we only known, we would have taken action, of course. But he deceived us. And we had no cause to suspect. He is... He *was* a har of good character who had worked for many years for the betterment of Wraeththukind."

"Then why would this perfect and virtuous har suddenly become a killer? It doesn't make sense." Hanu was insistent in his rejection of Sehireb Beh's explanation. It sounded like an excuse to him, and not one he was willing to accept.

Perael sighed and shook his head. "Gavax was not perfect. Nohar is. Perhaps one day Wraeththu will finally overcome the worst parts of their nature – anger, resentment, fear – and become the faultless beings we strive to be, but that is not yet our condition. We are flawed. Cracked. Damaged by the life we live and the experiences we endure. And sometimes those cracks can widen and deepen, or become a breech in our defences which lets the evil in."

He looked at Hanu directly. His eyes were very large and slanted, giving him a strangely alien appearance. "Hanu, the origins of our species, and the times immediately preceding that, were violent and turbulent. Gavax knew those times and carried from them a determination that such horrors should never happen again. This was his strength, but in the end also his weakness. A weakness that the *sedu* was able to exploit."

Hanu frowned. "Gavax captured the *sedu* and held it prisoner," he said. "That's what it told me."

Perael shook his head. "No. It lied to you. It lied to Gavax also. Gavax was a powerful har, but even he could not bind a creature of pure energy such as the *sedim* are. When he cast his binding geas upon it, all it did was disguise the *sedu's* presence from others of its kind who would have prevented it from doing what it was doing."

"Then why was the *sedu* drinking blood and consuming flesh if it wasn't because it was imprisoned?" Hanu asked, feeling more confused than ever.

"That is a story of another weakness." Perael produced a wan smile and gazed out through the high arched window at the far end of the Eithak. "Look at your world, Hanu, look closely. Look at its beauties and marvels. We see them every day, and we take them for granted. But there are other realms where all these wonders that surround us do not exist. Neither the beauty of the external world, nor the joy that we feel in our experience of it."

"Imagine, then, Hanu, how our world appears to other beings. See it and feel it through their eyes. Not only its infinite pleasures, but its equally limitless pains. All these experiences, unique as they are to our world, can exert a dangerous power. The *sedu* tasted the forbidden, and it wanted – and then *needed* – to taste it again. A craving grew within it, which could only be satisfied by consuming more of what had caused it."

"I felt it," Hanu said, his eyes half-closed, seeing neither the two Gelaming nor the familiar surroundings of the Eithak around him, but reliving once again the mind touch of the *sedu* and its all-consuming hunger. "I felt its need. So strong. So powerful." He shuddered and with an effort pulled himself away from the memory of the malignant force that had driven the sedu to commit its unspeakable acts.

"You understand, then," Perael said solemnly.

"I understand," Hanu replied, "but I do not forgive."

"Forgiveness can be hard." Perael said.

Hanu was not sure whether this was an acknowledgement or a judgement. "What happened to the *sedu* when the house exploded?" he asked. "Was it killed? Did it die? *Can* it die?"

Perael shook his head. "No," he said. "Without Gavax's binding geas to assist it, it could no longer conceal itself, or the energy it had accumulated from... ingesting... blood and flesh. The energy was released, resulting in the explosion that destroyed the house, and the *sedu* returned to its own realm, where its own kind will deal with it as they see fit."

"Will it be punished?"

"I don't know. It is not given to us to know the minds of the *sedim* and how they view such transgressions."

"Oh." Hanu was surprised to hear a Gelaming admit that they didn't know everything. He mentally added this to his collection of things he had experienced for the first time recently.

"It will not return to this realm, of that I am sure."

"But other *sedim* will?" Hanu asked.

"Yes, they will." Perael said, "But you need have no fear of them. Not all *sedim* are as the one you encountered, just as not all Gelaming are like Gavax. We are all of us, *sedu*, Gelaming or Gimrah..." he smiled with genuine warmth at Hanu, "...unique and uncommon individuals."

"Will it be safe for you to use the Otherlanes?" Hanu asked, thinking about how this particular ability was a vital part of the Gelaming's authority and ability to control the Wraeththu world.

"Oh yes," Perael reassured him, before his thoughts could gain any momentum. "Just not in *certain* areas... for a time."

"The site where that old house stood is a rare and unusual place," Sehireb Beh said. "Its properties have been known about for a very long time – even humans realised there was something strange and dangerous about it. They had many tales and legends about the place. It was variously attributed to its being haunted, or possessed, but in actual fact it's a nexus – a crossroads, if you like – where many other dimensions meet. Many of the Otherlanes through which the Gelaming travel meet or cross at that particular point."

"The site will be quarantined now," Perael continued. "We'll construct wards around it so that nohar will be able to enter it, or even see it. To all intents and purposes, it will disappear. It will also be isolated from the rest of the Otherlanes, even if this causes some inconvenience for those of us who use them."

"So that's it, then. Everything taken care of." Hanu felt that he should have known that the Gelaming would manage an effective damage limitation exercise and return everything to how it was before, as if nothing had happened.

Perael smiled sadly. "Not quite," he said. "I have other duties to perform."

"What duties?" Hanu asked.

"I must discover the identities of all the hara Gavax kidnapped and killed. Then I must seek out their tribes and their families and let them know what has become of their loved ones, make what amends I can, offer what apologies I can, on behalf of myself and the Gelaming."

"Why you?" asked Hanu. "You were not to blame. Why are they making *you* do it?"

Perael blinked slowly. "Hanu, we are *all* to blame," he said. "And if not me, then who? It has to be somehar. I can only hope that they will forgive me."

Hanu remembered the sound of Tiski's father's sobs in the Eithak, and the feeling in his chest when he could not turn and face them. He thought of all the hara who had died in the Old House – how many? He had no idea. He thought of Perael having to bring the terrible news to families, not once, but many times. Having to be the vessel for their grief, for the grief that they had no place else to put. And he felt sorry for him.

"Forgiveness can be hard," he said, wondering at his newfound understanding.

Perael and Sehireb Beh bowed their heads formally, and Hanu did the same. The two Gelaming took their leave, walking from the Eithak in a cloud of pale, silken garments and vanishing like mist as they turned the corner out of Hanu's vision.

He watched for a while, even after they had disappeared. He wondered if he should go back to his room in the lodgings now. That was what Nirzhen would tell him to do, but he did not feel ready for it. Not yet.

Instead, he left the Eithak and headed for the private stables of the Tirtha. He found Tezuk within, looking somehow smaller and less commanding within the confines of the spacious and luxurious stall he was housed in.

Hanu was quick to check that Tezuk had been properly groomed and exercised and fed, but of course, no horse however humble would ever lack the best of care from the Gimrah, never mind a horse who was now held in such high esteem as Tezuk. Tezuk snorted and laid his ears back when Hanu entered the stall. Hanu gave a weak smile for what felt like the first time in ages. That was Tezuk's way of welcoming him. Had Tezuk not wished to entertain his presence within the stall, teeth and hooves would have been employed, as many of the other hara knew to their cost.

Hanu laid his hand on Tezuk's darkly gleaming coat, scratching gently at the skin beneath as he knew Tezuk enjoyed this. "I'm sorry," he sighed. "It's all my fault you're here. I know you don't like it. Things are going to be different now. I don't know in what way. But I'll still be with you. I'll never leave you. Whatever happens, I'll stay with you."

Tezuk responded to this by depositing a substantial amount of excrement on the pristine straw covering the floor, narrowly missing Hanu's feet. Hanu found himself laughing, and it sounded strange, even to himself. Tezuk obviously did not appreciate this outburst either. He backed up nervously, his one light-coloured hoof landing directly in the pile of his own droppings, which only made Hanu giggle even more, although it hardly warranted that degree of amusement.

"You're a celebrity now," he scolded Tezuk. "You can't do things like that. The Aghama wouldn't stand in his own shit, would he?"

Years of training took over. Hanu took a shovel, scraped up Tezuk's offering and removed it from the stall, replacing the bedding with a pile of fresh, sweet straw from outside. Even this seemed luxurious – the best and softest, mown from the barley crop grown in the low meadows. It smelt of warm summer breezes and aromatic herbs. Hanu suddenly felt incredibly tired, and the straw looked and smelt incredibly inviting, so he flopped down on it. He felts its scratchy, prickly softness beneath his shoulder blades, and inhaled its herbal fragrance mixed with a faint odour of horse dung. The bed was so warm, so comforting and familiar that he was asleep almost instantly, while the dark outline of Tezuk stood as still as a statue next to him, keeping guard.

Hanu awoke to darkness and a scratchy feeling in his left ear where a piece of straw was lodged. He sat up and removed the errant stalk, scratched and stretched, and waited for his thoughts to reassemble themselves. On the other side of the stall he could just make out the shape of Tezuk, unmoving in the dark, probably asleep. Hanu had never been able to understand how horses could sleep standing up without falling over – it was just another of their mysteries that he felt he would never truly comprehend no matter how long he studied them.

He got up quietly and exited the stall, being careful to latch the gate after him. He had no idea what time it was, but from the quietness and lack of activity, he guessed it was either very late or very early. He made his way rather groggily to the Eithak, meeting nohar on the way. The light was dim inside, but a few lamps still burned. The Eithak was never closed – anyhar could enter at any time. It looked different in the lamplight, though. Hanu was accustomed to seeing the bright sunlight stream in through the tall windows. Now they were dark and opaque, like closed eyes.

But it was the quiet, more than anything else, which made it seem like another place entirely. During the day, the Eithak was never empty, with hara coming and going about their business all the time. Now Hanu was the only soul present, and his footsteps, which would never have been noticed during the day, rang oddly loud in his ears.

He noticed with a rush of emotion that the statue of the Aghama had been returned to its rightful place in the centre of the hall. Somehow that act, more than anything else, seemed to signify that Gavax's malign influence was gone for good. He wandered over to it and stroked the shining, golden hoof with affection. It felt warm to his touch, which it shouldn't have, since it was metal, but that seemed to him to be only right. Hanu did not know what type of metal the statue was made of, but obviously nohar would cast a statue of the Aghama himself in anything base or ordinary.

There was a noise behind him, and Hanu turned, startled, to see Nirzhen standing there. He was sure that the anskev had not been there a second ago, but Nirzhen's ability to materialise out of thin air was well known to every eskev. This only seemed to confirm Hanu's sense of a return to normality.

"There you are," said Nirzhen. "I was wondering where you'd got to."

"I went to see Tezuk," Hanu told him. "I... must have lost track of the time."

"Easily done."

This wasn't the rebuke Hanu had expected, but he had the distinct impression that Nirzhen had been treating him differently since his return. He wasn't sure if he liked that or not. On the one hand, it was a relief to escape the rough edge of his tongue. On the other hand, he wondered if this was simply the calm before the storm, and any minute now a slew of extra duties and impossible demands would descend upon him. He decided to make the most of it while it lasted.

"You did very well at the hearing today," Nirzhen told him.

Hanu felt a warm rush of pride, in spite of himself. Praise from Nirzhen was still rare enough that it had the power to affect him like that.

"Did the two Gelaming explain to you about Gavax and the *sedu*? And what would happen now?" Nirzhen asked.

Hanu nodded. "Yes," he said "They're going to fix everything. Or at least, as much as they can."

"Some things can't be fixed, though, can they?" Nirzhen said sympathetically.

"No," said Hanu. He thought of his life, and the lives of all the other hara affected. Cracked. Broken. Perael would mend those cracks, using all the skills at the Gelaming's disposal. Fill the holes and smooth the surface. But the marks would remain, always. Perhaps that was for the best.

He was silent for a while, as Nirzhen stood patiently waiting for him to speak, then the unpleasant thought he had been harbouring ever since his confrontation with Gavax in the old house could not be contained any longer and burst out of him

"But, Nirzhen, what if Gavax was right? What if Wraeththu *will* destroy themselves, just as humans did, by splitting up into opposing tribes and fighting amongst themselves?"

Nirzhen leaned forward a little and looked directly at Hanu, his expression serious. "Then, Hanu, it is up to us to make sure that he is not. We all have the ability to affect how the future unfolds. It's not written in stone. Every action we take in the present bends the shape of the future. There are hara alive today who, in a different timeline, would not be, and that is entirely down to what you did these few days past. Everything is connected. Everything has consequences. Never forget that."

"I won't," Hanu said. He felt somewhat humbled by this unusually impassioned speech from the normally reserved Nirzhen.

"Anyway," said Nirzhen, resuming his business-like demeanour in order to cover his embarrassment, "I have some other news to relate which may be more welcome. We have a new Tirtha! It will be Velisan. It has been unanimously agreed by all the anskevi that, as Merac was his father, he is the next in line of succession."

"Velisan? But he's hardly any older than Ren! He has no experience of leadership." Hanu's brow furrowed as he digested this information. "We need somehar who knows what he's doing! I think *you* should be Tirtha!"

"Me?" Now it was Nirzhen's turn to be surprised. "Don't be ridiculous, Hanu. You know the position of Tirtha remains within the same family."

"Well, why should it?" Hanu asked stubbornly, refusing to be dissuaded. "You never know what sort of har you're going to get if you do that. I mean, sometimes you might get a good Tirtha, like Merac, and sometimes you might get somehar like Ren! If we actually chose the best har rather than just accepting who is next in line it would be a lot better."

"Well, perhaps it would," said Nirzhen, his impatience showing. "However, since I don't want to be Tirtha, then the point is entirely moot."

"You don't?"

"Of course not. It's a terrible job. Far too much paperwork involved." He narrowed his eyes at Hanu. "Are you sure you're not just trying to get rid of me so you can become an anskev?" he asked.

Hanu was appalled. "Of course not!" he said. "I don't want to be an anskev! I'm not..."

His jaw worked, but his words failed, and Nirzhen nodded at him with satisfaction. "If it's any consolation," he said, "Velisan does not want to be Tirtha either. But he's accepted the responsibility has fallen to him. Don't worry too much. He's a good har, willing to learn, and with the help of the anskevi, he will be a good Tirtha, in time. And I'm pleased to report that his first act as Tirtha is to announce that you are to be given a reward for your bravery!"

"A... what?" Hanu was stunned by this unexpected news.

"You are to be awarded the Tirtha's Token."

"What... What is that?"

"It's a piece of jewellery. You'll like it, it's quite a pretty thing. You can wear it or hang it on your wall. It's what it represents that's important. It's an acknowledgement from the Tirtha, and by extension, the whole tribe, that you have performed an act of great bravery and been a great credit to the hara and horses of the Gimrah."

"Oh."

Nirzhen raised one eyebrow. "You don't sound exactly thrilled about it."

"Well, of course I am. Who wouldn't be? It's a great honour. An award. For me. From the Tirtha. Himself. Only..."

"Only what?"

"I'm not sure I *have* been a great credit to the hara and horses of the Gimrah. I... I'm not sure I deserve this."

Nirzhen tilted his head in sympathy. "I'm sure that if Tiski were here he would want you to have this award," he said. "You can't always blame yourself for his death."

"No, I..." Hanu squirmed in his seat. "I know. That's not..." He swallowed hard, three times. "Nirzhen, I did not complete the whole course in The Ride. I took a shortcut. Through the woods."

There was silence for the longest three heartbeats of Hanu's life, then he felt Nirzhen's hand on his shoulder, gentle and reassuring.

"I know," he said. There was no hint of anger or recrimination in Nirzhen's voice, only understanding.

"You do?" Hanu looked up cautiously.

"Of course I do. We anskevi know everything."

"I don't deserve an award," Hanu said bitterly. "I'm not even fit to be a horse-har."

"Hanu, there's more to a har than the winning of a race," Nirzhen told him softly. "There's kindness and compassion, and the refusal to abandon an old friend, even though it conflicts with his own interests. You knew Beyra wasn't up to going the distance in that race, so you took him a different way. You put the horse's needs first. *That* is what makes a har fit to be a horse-har."

"You mean I'm not going to be dismissed?"

"Of course not. I've spent precious years of my life training you, Hanu. I'm not about to waste any more training a replacement!"

Hanu felt as if a stone in his shoe had finally become dislodged after years of suffering its constant irritation. He felt as if a poison had been drawn from him. The relief was almost narcotic.

"I..." He hardly knew what to say. "Thank you, Nirzhen." The words tumbled out of him in a rush, as if they had been waiting for this moment for an eternity. "Thank you for *everything* you've done for me. I want you to know I truly appreciate it."

"You are most welcome, Hanu." said Nirzhen, smiling broadly. He stood up, stretching his limbs and stifling a yawn. "I think we've covered everything. Come along now, it'll be starting to get light shortly by the look of things, and we both need to get some sleep – there'll be plenty of work for us in the morning."

Hanu remained silent for a few moments, simply experiencing the heady feeling of release which flowed through every vein in his body. He looked over to the statue, remembering all the times he'd mentally confessed his sins to it, seeking the absolution which never came. The golden hoof glowed bright in the lamplight. He wondered how many other hara's darkest fears and hopes and iniquities were made physically incarnate in that small area of shiny metal.

A thought occurred to him. "Nirzhen, what will happen to Tezuk now?"

"What do you mean?" Nirzhen asked him.

"Will he be allowed to stay here at Scatterstones?"

"I should think so. I can't imagine the good hara of this estemble allowing their divine protector to be whisked away to Almagabra, if that's what you mean."

"Will I still be allowed to care for him?"

Nirzhen put a hand on Hanu's shoulder. "Of course you will. Tezuk still needs an eskev, and I can think of none better."

"It's strange," Hanu mused. "All the hara in Scatterstones think that Tezuk is the manifestation of the Aghama, because he saved us at the old house."

"What's strange about that?" asked Nirzhen. "I remember a young har insisting to all not so long ago that his favourite horse was the Aghama, in spite of the lack of belief from some of the more exalted members of the tribe. Are you telling me you've changed your mind?"

"I don't know. Do you think the Aghama would take the form of a horse in order to help hara in trouble?"

"The Aghama may take many forms in order to protect his children," said Nirzhen, looking at Hanu meaningfully.

"I prayed to him, that night I rode out to the old house," Hanu said. "I prayed to him to help me, because I wanted Tezuk to let me ride him, even though he'd never let me ride him before. And he let me ride him. Was that because the spirit of the Aghama is in him?" Hanu scrutinised the familiar contours of statue fiercely, as if the answer to the puzzle could be found somewhere deep within its metal body.

"Perhaps," Nirzhen replied. Hanu and Sofia left Sasha's house and walked back up the "Perhaps it was divine intervention. Or perhaps it was because you were patient and kind to a horse since the day he was foaled, when others were not, so that he trusted you enough to let you ride him."

"Well, which is it?" demanded Hanu, exasperated. "How do I know? Tell me!"

But Nirzhen merely smiled and walked away, leaving Hanu still staring at the rearing, motionless form of the statue, and still wondering.

Chapter 18
The Bar and the Horse

There are some days, in the great, grassy steppelands of Gimrah, after the summer rains have fallen, when the air smells of wet earth and the grass springs up lush and green, renewed and full of vigour after the listlessness of the summer heat. The birds sing again, as if they have suddenly remembered the songs they did not have the energy for only a few days ago. The sky clears of the darkened clouds, leaving only high streaks of cirrus striping the blue above. The air is clear like water, and the world breathes again. It was just such a day when Hanu stood at the top of the small rise north of Scatterstones and bid farewell to his friends and companions from the Old House. They had been given horses and provisions in order to return to their homes, and had spent the morning packing and fussing and organising and delaying, but eventually they had set off from the stables, in single file, along the cobbled roads and dirt trails leading to the wide open spaces beyond. Hanu accompanied them, both to show them the route, and because, in a way, he was not ready for them to leave yet.

Reaching the crest of the low hill, they stopped and dismounted. Hanu breathed deeply and looked down at the waving grass stretching all the way to the horizon, and beyond, to places he had never been, things he had never seen.

Perdix grabbed him in a fierce hug that almost knocked the wind from him. "You know you'll always be welcome at East of Heaven, don't you?" he said. "I mean, it's a run-down old place, it's freezing cold most of the time and the Tirtha's a mean old sod, but – it's home!"

He grinned, and Hanu could see that he didn't mean a word of it.

"Thank you for everything you have done for us." The har who spoke had multi-coloured hair and until a few days ago Hanu had known him only as Polly, but the mind-healers at Scatterstones had worked their skills on him, and Polly was now once again Nuan-Nuen, a Frodinne dreamer from far away

Roselane. Unusually for members of that tribe, he had been expanding his mind through travel rather than through dreams and had found himself in Ardith at just the wrong time.

Hanu blushed. "I hope you don't think too badly of Gimrah, once you've returned to Roselane," he said. "I know you had a terrible experience here, but there are good things about Gimrah too, and parts of it are really beautiful, and if you should choose to return at some point, I'd be happy to show them to you."

Nuan-Nuen smiled. "Thank you, Hanu, that's very kind of you. However, I think my desire for travel in foreign lands has now been fully sated. I shall continue to explore the world through dreams, and perhaps I will dream of Gimrah one day." His smile faded a little. "I really did think that the whole experience in the Old House was a dream. My mind couldn't conceive it could possibly be reality. But I should have known – nothing I've ever dreamed has been as terrible as that."

"We can't let this one experience frighten us into becoming sad little recluses," Sula declared stoutly. "We need to have something positive come from it, if we're not to remain victims of Gavax for the rest of our lives. I think we should all meet up again next year at the Cuttingtide Fair in Ardith and resolve to have a good time there! You, too, Nuan-Nuen."

There were murmurs of agreement from the others.

"That works for me," Perdix said, grinning. "Share breath with me, Hanu, to seal the pact!"

Before Hanu could even think of objecting, Perdix had pulled him into an embrace, and Hanu felt the other har's mouth press against his own, filling him with his warm breath. He could taste the smell of the east wind blowing down from the great plains of the north, and the thunder of hooves on frozen ground, and the warmth of blazing fires, and naked, languid bodies stretched out in front of them. His head swam and stars appeared before his eyes, and he returned Perdix's offering enthusiastically, only forced to break away, finally, by lack of oxygen.

Their farewells concluded, the group mounted once more and rode slowly down the gentle slope towards the waiting plains, looking back and waving occasionally. Hanu watched, and waved also, until they were too far away to see clearly. He stood for a while, thinking to himself how strange it was that he felt closer to these hara, whom he'd only known for a matter of days, than to some he'd known his whole life. Then, sighing, he swung himself back up onto Miran's back and turned back towards Scatterstones.

"Come on, Miran. Back to work. You know where we're going, don't you? Take it away." He gave the mare the lightest of prods and in a short time they were back at the stables where the daily buzz of activity felt like a warm blanket wrapped around him. He settled Miran in her stall, then walked three stalls along, to the one in the corner, to see Flor.

Flor pricked up her ears when she heard him, but as soon as she saw it was Hanu, her head drooped, and Hanu felt his own brief cheerful mood evaporate.

Sweet, pretty Flor, with her golden coat and silver mane and tail, and her awkward gait and her wistful, hopeful expression every time the stable door opened, and she looked for Tiski, and it was only Hanu. Again. Hanu wished he could explain to the mare why her friend did not come anymore. Wished he could douse that small spark of hope that flared in her thoughts every time the door creaked, knowing that sometimes hope was the cruellest and most painful thing of all, but a horse cannot understand such distinctions. A horse understands life, the scent of the grass, of the wind, the firm ground beneath galloping hooves, the sweet hay and the foals in spring. It does not understand death, and in this one thing, Hanu envied his friends more than anything. He rubbed Flor's ears consolingly and promised her that he would take her out for a gallop soon, and she nuzzled his face by way of acknowledgement.

There was a noise behind him, and he turned to see Geth, the Mojag, standing outside, peering in at him curiously. Geth had made a good recovery from his injuries but was still not deemed to be sufficiently restored to health to leave Scatterstones, and so he had not departed with the others. The only reminder of his ordeal at the Old House was the scar across his throat, now fading daily. Hanu had offered him the pink scarf, the one he had bought in Ardith, to cover it, but Geth had laughed, showing his white teeth, saying that a Mojag did not cover his scars, he displayed them proudly. Nevertheless, he had taken the pink scarf and now wore it wrapped around his head, which he thought made him look bold and piratical. Hanu thought it made him look ever so slightly louche, but he wisely kept this opinion to himself.

"Have they gone?" Geth asked.

Hanu nodded in reply.

"Oh. I was going to go with you, but the horse I was supposed to ride took a dislike to me – Nirzhen said I was too big for him – and by the time I found one willing to let me ride you had gone. That's a pity – I wanted to say goodbye to them all."

"I'm sure you'll see them all again another time," Hanu said, by way of consolation. "Especially…" he gave Geth a crafty smile, "…if you're ever in Ardith for the Cuttingtide Fair."

Geth thought about this for a moment. "I suppose that's a possibility," he conceded.

"I'm going to take Flor out for a ride and go down to the lower meadow. Do you want to come?"

"Yes, that would be pleasant. If you can find a horse that will let me ride him."

"I know just the one," Hanu said. "And he needs some exercise. See that big gelding in the next stall? His name's Harcan. He'll let you ride him. Get him saddled up, I'll do the same with Flor, and I'll meet you outside."

Geth saluted briskly at Hanu's instructions and went to make Harcan's acquaintance. Hanu watched him go with an odd feeling in his chest. He still found himself faintly amazed that Geth had not only survived but had recovered his strength and his handsome looks so quickly. His hair still fell over his face in a very fetching manner – it seemed a little longer now – and his smile was still as dazzling. With his sand-coloured hair and sea-green eyes, he reminded Hanu of Ardith, and the wide, curving beach around the bay there. He wondered if he would ever be able to tell Geth this without feeling foolish.

Once the horses were saddled up, they left the stables and took the back way down to the lower meadow, which bordered on the river. Harcan had no difficulty bearing Geth's weight, and the two seemed to hit it off immediately, which did not surprise Hanu as they were both of a type – open, friendly and obliging. Geth was a good rider, despite not being Gimrah, but Harcan could sense his lack of Gimranish authority and kept edging over to Flor, making hopeful whuffing sounds in the mare's direction. Hanu had picked a number of the small, white flowers that gave Flor her name and fashioned them into a circlet, which he had placed on the mare's head, around her ears. He hoped that it made her feel beautiful. Certainly, Harcan's advances suggested that Flor had other attractions, which rendered her small stature irrelevant.

Hanu was pleased to see Geth forming a new relationship with a horse. He had offered to hold a *Birvega* with Geth for Pink, explaining that this was a ceremony that the Gimrah held to commemorate the passing of a favourite horse. Geth had been touched by this gesture, all the more so when he found out that the *Birvega* involved the consumption of copious quantities of intoxicating liquor.

They reached the lower meadow, disturbing a group of crows that flew up into the clear sky, cawing and throwing insults down at them.

"We offer our apologies for our intrusion, Brothers of the Sky!" Geth shouted up at the crows, touching his pink-scarfed forehead in salute.

Hanu looked at him in surprise. "Why did you say that?" he asked.

"You have to keep on the right side of the crows," Geth explained. "They remember things. And they hold grudges. A crow with a grudge is a dangerous enemy."

"Really?" Hanu was surprised to hear this but made a mental note to treat crows with the utmost of respect from now on. Any creature that a Mojag considered to be a dangerous enemy was obviously not to be trifled with.

The only other occupant of the meadow seemed untroubled by the crows' presence, either on the ground or in the air. It was Tezuk. The Tirtha and the anskevi had decided that as a reward for defeating Gavax and Ren he should be given the freedom of the best pasture in Scatterstones. No-har would ever ride him again – or attempt to ride him. For everyhar except Hanu that was entirely irrelevant, but Hanu was glad. Tezuk had given him the gift of riding him once in his life, and that was enough. He was glad that Tezuk would not have to suffer any other har trying and failing to ride him or trying to put him to work in the fields, or worse, selling him as worthless to another tribe for a pittance. Tezuk would spend the rest of his days being honoured by the hara of Scatterstones, and for that, Hanu felt rewarded in a way that no Tirtha's Token could ever begin to come close to.

Both he and Geth watched as Tezuk galloped furiously down the length of the long pasture, the thunder of his hooves across the ground, tail and mane flying behind him. Outrunning the wind. His coat gleamed, and every muscle and bone and sinew was defined perfectly beneath his skin, like a machine. Or a sculpture. He was flawless. The perfect horse. Except for one thing. Hanu tried to reach him with his mind, but as always, Tezuk was beyond reach.

To the north, far up near the border with Elhmen, lived a tribe of true wild horses. Stocky, dun-coloured creatures with thick necks and short, stubby manes, they roamed free among the grasslands – horses unshaped by the hand of either human or har, horses as nature had made them. He wondered if it was true, what Nirzhen had said, that the wild, atavistic ancestor still existed deep within the soul of every horse. He wondered if Tezuk would be happier with his wild cousins in the north. He did not think so. Tezuk did not belong with the horses of Scatterstones, but neither did he belong with the wild northern herd. He belonged nowhere and to nohar. He belonged only to himself. Sometimes, that was enough.

Geth watched him admiringly till he was almost out of sight at the far end of the meadow. "Yaz the Healer says that this horse is the Aghama," he said. "He says that the Aghama is known to appear in the form of a horse. I told him that he has never appeared in the form of a horse in Mojag, and he said that was because the Mojag are uncultured barbarians, and I said that was a very insulting thing to say and he apologised and offered me a drink."

"That's good," Hanu said, distractedly, staring into the distance after the vanishing Tezuk. "Yaz is a good har. I'm sure he didn't mean to be rude. Also, you're a lot taller than him."

"That's true."

Geth studied Hanu with interest. "Do you think your horse is the Aghama?" he asked.

Hanu shrugged. "Does it matter?" he said. "All the hara here in Scatterstones think he is. It makes them happy to believe it. What happened with Ren and Gavax was a great shock to them. They need something to hold on to, to reassure them that such things couldn't happen again. If the Aghama is among us, they feel protected. And special."

"But what about *you*?" Geth persisted. "What do *you* believe?"

Hanu was silent for a while. "Yaz and the others believe that the Aghama saved us at the old house. But he didn't save *all* of us, did he? I don't believe the Aghama would be so cruel as to save all of us but one, and let that one perish. I don't *want* to believe that we are the children of such an unfair deity. Or that we are so helpless that we need divine entities to step in and protect us at every difficult time in our lives. If we waited for the Aghama to do everything for us, we would never do anything ourselves!"

"There are some hara I have met who would do that," Geth said, "but you're not one of them. You're as brave as you are beautiful, Hanu har Gimrah, and the Aghama must surely be proud to claim you as one of his own."

Hanu blushed furiously at Geth's extravagant compliment, but inside he was secretly thrilled. No-har had ever called him *beautiful* before, not even Tiski. Hanu was not sure if he *was* beautiful – Nirzhen said that *all* hara were beautiful, but it had always seemed to Hanu, unfairly, that all the other hara were more beautiful than he was – but the fact that Geth thought he was beautiful seemed to make up for all the other times he had felt ugly and unwanted. For a brief moment he felt he understood what Nirzhen had meant when he had said that a har may be the most exquisite creature imaginable on the outside, but if he did not believe himself to be as beautiful on the inside then he would never be satisfied with himself.

"Thank you, Geth," he said. "You, too, are beautiful. Your hair is the colour of the golden sands of Ardith, and your eyes like the sea after a storm."

Geth beamed, revealing his astonishing white teeth. "We Mojags are not so often praised for our physical attractiveness as some other tribes," he said. "Hara tend to be so impressed by our fighting skills they overlook that aspect of us."

"You are definitely the exception, Geth," said Hanu, smiling.

"I myself have discovered things about the Gimrah that I was unaware of before my journey here," Geth told him.

"Oh? Really? Such as?"

Geth adopted a serious expression, the better to convey his conclusions. "The Gimrah may be small, but they are fierce," he said. "And it's impossible to win an argument with one. They are definitely my favourite tribe of Jaddayoth, and I'm sure that will not change, even after I have encountered hara from all the other tribes."

"I hope not," Hanu said, surprised to find how much he meant it. "Come on, we need to go and collect some new harnesses from Lathi. He's made one especially for Flor. Maybe it will cheer her up to have something new."

With one last look at the dark horse still cantering gracefully through the meadow, lost in his own world of green grass and open skies, the two hara reined their mounts around and headed back up the hill in the direction of the workshop of Lathi the harness-maker.

"What do you intend to do now?" Hanu asked Geth, somewhat awkwardly. "Will you be going back to Mojag? I mean, you're welcome to stay here in Gimrah, but I suppose you must be eager to get back to your son."

Geth was uncharacteristically silent for a few moments. Then he said: "In Mojag, a harling is brought up by his father. He does not know his hostling. He's taken away shortly after he emerges from the pearl. Hostling and harling do not meet. It's considered the best way to raise harlings, to avoid them becoming too feminised. I haven't seen my son since he was less than a day old. It is the Mojag way."

Geth's voice took on a strained quality that Hanu did not recognise. "There's not a day passes when I don't think of him."

Hanu suddenly felt cold, as if a cloud had passed in front of the sun, although no such thing had occurred. He thought about Nirzhen, and little Issie, and the expression in Nirzhen's eyes when he looked at the harling. He remembered Sofia's words about the children, and about Nicolai, and it was as if a knife, sharper than the one that had cut Geth's throat, had run through his vital organs. He wondered how hara could bear to invest so much of themselves, when it could all be taken away at a moment's notice, or little by little over time, so slowly that you didn't notice it happening until it was gone. It seemed to him that to bring a child into the world was a much braver thing to do than any fight or any ride.

He was suddenly overcome with an almost unbearable sense of loss, which came at him as if from nowhere and manifested as a physical pain deep within his chest, driving the air from his lungs and the blood from his heart. To his horror, he found himself unexpectedly choking out deep, primal sobs, barely recognising the guttural sounds he was making as coming from his own body. He could feel the tears flowing down his cheeks, but he was totally unable to stop them.

Geth watched him, silent and unembarrassed by this display.

After a while, Hanu's sobs grew less intense, then faded gradually until all that was left was a series of squeaky hiccups, incongruous after the emotion that had preceded them. Hanu was aware of Flor's distress, the mare's concern for him mixed with her own sadness and confusion, and he patted her neck reassuringly.

Geth leaned over and performed a similar gesture on Hanu's shoulder. "Are you alright now?" Geth asked.

Hanu nodded, wiping away the residual dampness from his face with his sleeve. Surprisingly, he did feel better, as if the horrors of the past few weeks had somehow washed away with the tears. "Yes," he said, his voice still sounding shaky, but firm. "I'm OK. I just… It's…" He shook his head, unable to finish his sentence, unsure of what he was even trying to say.

"I know," said Geth. "In Mojag, they teach us it is better to accept that death is a natural part of life, and not to become emotional about it. It doesn't work. I have seen the bravest, most battle-hardened Mojag commander weep more bitterly than anyhar over the death of a young recruit. We can't pretend to be something we're not, however hard we try."

Hanu smiled at him. "Thank you," he said.

Geth looked puzzled. "For what?"

"For everything."

"I understand," said Geth, his face giving away his lack of understanding quite hilariously, but Hanu politely said nothing.

"I suppose," said Hanu, with some reluctance, "that you could always go and work for the Gelaming. They are known to employ Mojags as mercenaries."

Geth snorted with indignation. "I might not have much in the way of standards," he huffed, "but I do have *some*."

For some reason Hanu found this incredibly funny and began to laugh, with a slightly hysterical edge. Geth joined in and they giggled furiously until they were both out of breath.

"What are we laughing for?" gasped Geth, when they could continue no longer.

Hanu panted until he regained his breath. "I'll tell you later," he said, grinning, which seemed to satisfy Geth.

They came to a field at the top of the hill where a small group of two-year-old colts were grazing and sunning themselves. As Geth and Hanu approached, the colts pricked up their ears and tails in interest and came galloping over to the fence to see what was happening, full of youthful curiosity.

The two hara pulled their own mounts to a stop at the field's boundary. Harcan whinnied a greeting to the colts, which simply got them more excited, and Flor found herself obliged to act as the grown-up leader of the whole herd, telling them to calm down, a role which Hanu could tell she secretly enjoyed.

One particularly large strawberry roan colt, half a head taller than all the rest, shouldered his way to the front of the group, enquiring thoughts regarding food treats projecting in Hanu and Geth's direction. He trotted up to Geth, nuzzled his face and chewed experimentally on Geth's hair, mistaking it for hay. Geth reached into his pocket and pulled out a rather shrivelled carrot. He offered this to the colt, who accepted it rapidly, munched it down in two bites and licked Geth's face in appreciation.

Geth laughed and patted the colt's nose.

"This is Eper, named for the red-berried plant that grows in the woodlands" Hanu told him. "That unusual coat colour is caused by a mixing of white and red hairs. It is quite a sought-after colouring."

"If he was mine, I would call him Brown." Geth looked at Hanu slyly, and Hanu could only laugh.

Eper nickered with amusement too and stuck his nose into Geth's pocket to see if there were any more carrots.

The horse belongs to the har and the har belongs to the horse.

Perhaps this thought came to him by himself, or perhaps it came from Flor, still standing patiently by the fence, pacifying the colts in a gentle, motherly way.

"In the spring," said Hanu, "these colts will be ready to learn to be ridden." He looked at Geth shyly. "Will you still be here in the spring?"

Geth glanced over at the western horizon, where the strips of clouds were just beginning to take on the golden colour of early evening, before fishing another wrinkled carrot from his pocket and offering it to Eper.

He turned to Hanu and smiled. "Yes," he said, "I think I will still be here."

Glossary of Wraeththu Terms

Aghama (ag-uh-mah): Title of the first Wraeththu. The Aghama eventually became a spiritual symbol, an idea more than a real har. He is now regarded as the prime dehar of Wraeththu. In Gimrah, he is commonly imagined in the form of a divine horse

Agmara: The life-giving energy of the universe, used for healing

Almagabra: Country of the Gelaming

Anskev: An overgroom at a Gimrah estemble (plural: anskevi)

Archon: The title of a tribe leader

Aruna (A-roo-nuh): Sexual communion between hara

Arunic: Pertaining to aruna

Birvega: A Gimranish ceremony to commemorate the passing of a beloved horse

Blood-bond: A ceremonial commitment between hara who are chesna

Bloomtide: the festival associated with the spring equinox

Chesna (chez-nuh): A close, abiding relationship between hara

Chesnari chez-nah-ri) A har in a chesna relationship, a har's life partner

Cuttingtide Fair: A large horsefair held in Gimrah at the summer solstice

Dehar: A Wraeththu deity (plural: dehara)

Devastation, the: One of the terms given to the decline of human civilisation, when it was decimated by war, disease, infertility, pollution and natural catastrophe. The time when Wraeththu arose from the ruins

Eithak: The central meeting hall of the community of Scatterstones

Elhmen (ell-men): A tribe of Jaddayoth, famous for their feylike appearance and tricky ways

Emunah (em-oo-nah): A tribe of Jaddayoth, renowned as traders and merchants

Eskev: An undergroom at a Gimrah estemble (plural: eskevi)

Estemble: The term for a settlement or large farm in Gimrah

Fallsend: A town in Thaine of ill reputation

Faraldienne: A breed of Gelaming horse particularly prized for its grace and beauty

Ferike (fer-i-kuh): A tribe of Jaddayoth, renowned for their artistic talents

Feybraiha (fay-bray-uh): A harish coming of age, and its attendant celebration

Garridan (gah-ree-dan): A tribe of Jaddayoth, founded by Uigenna who fled Megalithica, famed for their poisons and toxins
Gelaming (jel-a-ming): A powerful Wraeththu tribe, originating in Almagabra
Gimrah (gim-rah): A tribe of Jaddayoth, the Horse Hara
Grissecon (griss-uh-con): Sexual communion between hara to raise power; sex magic

Hadassah (had-uh-sah): A tribe of Jaddayoth
Har: Wraeththu individual (pl. hara)
Harling: Young har until feybraiha
Hegemony: Ruling body of the Gelaming
Hienama (hy-en-ah-muh): Wraeththu shaman or priest
High-Hostling: A har who hosted somehar's hostling or father, equivalent of a human grandmother
Horse Hara: Another name for the Gimrah
Hostling: Har who carries a pearl (Wraeththu foetus), who hosts the seed of another
Host (verb): To carry a pearl

Immanion: Capital city of Almagabra
Inception: the process through which humans were mutated into hara

Jaddayoth: A country east of Almagabra, Thaine and Florinada

Kalamah (kal-uh-mah): A tribe of Jaddayoth, the Cat Hara
Kamagrian (ka-mag-ree-an): A mysterious tribe, part of the Roselane, who appear to include human females. Known as great adepts

Maudrah (maw-druh): A tribe of Jaddayoth, known for their ascetic ways
Megalithica: A Western continent taken from the Varrs by the Gelaming
Mojag (mo-hag): A tribe of Jaddayoth, renowned for favouring a prevalently ouanic aspect.

Nahir Nuri: A har adept and well-trained in spiritual and magical matters. A high-ranking hienama within the magical caste system
Natalia: The festival of the winter solstice
Natawni (nat-taw-nee): A tribe of Jaddayoth, famed for their earth magic, known also as the Hara of Bones, or Bone Hara

Otherlanes: The etheric channels between the worlds, or different layers of reality

Ouana (oo-ah-nuh): Masculine principle of hara

Ouana-Lim: Masculine generative organ of hara

Ouanic – Relating to ouana

Pearl: Wraeththu embryo

Rosatide: A festival in the harish calendar corresponding to the old pagan Imbolc, 2nd February

Roselane (roz-uh-larn): A mystical tribe of Jaddayoth, the Dream Hara

Sahale (sarl): A subterranean tribe of Jaddayoth, famed for their fire magic

Sea of Shadows: A Jaddayoth Sea, connected by canal to Florinada. The coastal tribes are Ferike, Gimrah, Maudrah, Emunah and Kalamah

Sedu: A creature that appears in this reality as a horse, that has the ability to traverse the otherlanes, the paths between the worlds. Owned only by Gelaming. (pl. sedim)

Shadetide: The festival held in late autumn, mirroring the old pagan festival of Samhain (Halloween)

Sharing of Breath: A kiss of mutual visualisation

Shuppurak: Capital city of Mojag

Smoketide: The festival associated with the autumn equinox

Soume (soo-me): Feminine principle of hara

Soume-Lam: Feminine generative organ of hara

Soumic: Relating to soume.

Spinner: A coin of Jaddayoth currency

Suri: A cousin

Thaine: Northerly region of Almagabra

Tiahaar: Respectful form of address (plural: Tiahaara)

Tigron (tee-gron): A leader of the Gelaming

Tirtha: phylarch (estemble leader) among the Gimrah

Uigenna: The proto-tribe of Wraeththu, who were renowned for their wild savagery

Wraeththu (ray-thoo): The race of androgynous beings that evolved from humankind

Wursm: Title of the leader of the Mojag tribe

Zaltana: capital city of the Kalamah

Characters of Scatterstones

Scatterstones Estemble

Hara:

Gavax: Gelaming har, associate of Ren
Hanu: An eskev in the Tirtha's breeding stables
Kam: Hanu's hostling
Lathi: A harness maker
Merac: A Tirtha of Scatterstones, Hostling of Ren, father of Velisan
Mizahal: A clothes-maker
Nalleshu: Hanu's father
Nicu: A har incepted from the women's collective at Spinnersholm
Nithevan: Merac's consort
Nirzhen: An anskev in the Tirtha's breeding stables
Nolath: An anskev in the Tirtha's breeding stables
Ofian: A har who runs a provisions shop
Ren: A Tirtha of Scatterstones, son of Merac, younger brother of Velisan
Reska: Hanu's suri (cousin)
Ruta: An eskev in the Tirtha's breeding stables
Tiski: Hanu's friend, an anskev in the Tirtha's breeding stables
Velisan: A Tirtha of Scatterstones, son of Merac, older brother of Ren
Yaz: A healer
Zolta: An anskev in the Tirtha's breeding stables
Zanutha: Nirzhen's chesnari
Polly/Nuan-Nuen: A Roselane har, held hostage in the Old House of Men

Horses:

Aditsa: A founding mare of Scatterstones
Bazim: Sire of Kem
Berun: A young horse sold at Ardith
Beyra: A domestic horse of Scatterstones, Hanu's first mount
Bozim: A gelding of Scatterstones
Bou: A young horse sold at Ardith
Aral: dam of Kem
Dirdun: Flor's sire
Darun: A young colt
Eloga: A founding mare of Scatterstones
Eper: A strawberry-roan colt
Flor: Tiski's horse
Forada: A founding mare of Scatterstones
Harcan: A gelding of Scatterstones

Gorak: A stallion of Scatterstones, Ren's horse
Ishin: Tezuk's dam
Ishfar: Ren's Faraldienne horse
Kavel: A gelding of Scatterstones
Kem: A young filly
Lohish: A chestnut colt
Miran: A breeding mare of Scatterstones
Myan: A young horse sold at Ardith
Perian: A domestic mare
Pilar: A stallion of Scatterstones, Merac's horse
Rashal: Flor's dam
Nuviak: A mare of Scatterstones
Samari: A founding mare of Scatterstones
Shalin: A founding mare of Scatterstones
Tezuk: Hanu's horse
Torem: Tezuk's sire
Vittoras: The founding stallion of Scatterstones
Zan: A founding mare of Scatterstones

Tail-and-Tether Estemble

Hara:
Lynx: Har held hostage at the Old House of Men
Sable: Har of Bihan and Rok

Horses:
Bihan: World's largest horse, Sable's horse
Rok: Small pony, companion of Bihan, Sable's horse

Long Ride Home Estemble

Hara:
Pasharath: Har held hostage at the Old House of Men
Vinda: Har held hostage at the Old House of Men

Wind's Edge Estemble

Hara:
Roan: A friend of Tiski
Ruzhu: Har held hostage at the Old House of Men

Horses:
Shebesh: Winner of the Grand Jaddayoth Challenge race

East of Heaven Estemble

Hara:
Perdix: Har held hostage at the Old House of Men
Sula: Har held hostage at the Old House of Men

Mojag Tribe

Hara:
Athak: Geth's commander
Geth: A har that Hanu meets in Ardith
Kare: Athak's second in command

Horses:
Pink: Geth's horse

Spinnersholm:

Humans:
Amalla: A woman of Spinnersholm
Eva: A baker
Gina: Mother of Max and two other children
Lilian: A cook
Sasha: A healer
Sofia: Leader of the women of Spinnersholm, mother of Nicolai/Nicu
Vika: A woman of Spinnersholm

Horses:
Fila: Sofia's horse

Appendix I
Little-Known Facts About the Gimrah

The Gimrah are a matrilineal (hostlilineal?) society in that inheritance and family succession passes down the Whoever-Hosted-The-Pearl line. The same applies to their horse-breeding records, inasmuch as all the horses can trace their ancestry back to the Founding Mares of each estemble. This really only has any practical application in the inheritance of the title of Tirtha and in the absence of a suitable distaff descendant, a son-of-a-father is quite acceptable. Particularly if the lack of a true descendant of the Tirtha's line means that some unfortunate anskev is going to get landed with the position.

Some forward-thinking Gimrah have questioned the tribe's system of inherited leadership, arguing that election on merit and ability would produce a better quality of leader. The truth is that the position of Tirtha is not a coveted one among the Gimrah, there being an awful lot of paperwork involved (see above: horse-breeding records). The Gimrah do not enjoy desk jobs, and would much rather spend their time outdoors improving their horseharship, and if there was an election for the position of Tirtha, it is unlikely that anyhar would put himself forward, all having simultaneously discovered that there was urgent business an hour's ride away to deal with.

The dedication of Gimrah hara to their horses is a subject of some humour amongst other tribes as illustrated by this joke commonly told in Jaddayoth:

> *"Why does a Gimrah har have two chesnari? So the ouana will think he's with the soume, and the soume will think he's with the ouana, and he can get down to the stables and spend some time with his horse."*

Gimrah harlings learn to ride almost as soon as they have hatched from their pearl. Their first mounts are usually the small domestic ponies that the Gimrah breed for this purpose, and which are experienced animals which generally pass from harling to harling as the young har grows and becomes ready for his first full-sized horse, usually around the time of their feybreiha. A Gimranish har never forgets his first pony, and when the creature finally departs for the great pasture in the sky, it is traditional for all the hara who learnt to ride on him to gather together and tell tales of their own youthful clumsiness, and sing the pony's praises, whilst toasting him with a mugful of *Sprutt*, the sacred fermented mare's milk, and then swiftly moving on to rather more mugfuls of barley wine or beer. These pony-wakes, or *Birvegi* as they are known, are very democratic affairs and may include hara from the lowliest farm-har to the Tirtha himself, all of whose drunken reminiscences of the pony's stellar qualities are listened to with equal respect.

The Gimrah are an agrarian society, and as well as breeding horses they also grow crops and breed other livestock for meat and wool. At Scatterstones, the farming hara maintain small herds of sheep, goats, cows and alpacas. Because who doesn't love alpacas? Horses are bred for domestic use by each family or, in the case of the heavy horses used for farm work, bought from other estembles who specialise in such breeds. The horses for sale are bred in the Tirtha's stable; jobs there are in limited supply and much sought after. It is not uncommon for young hara who have not been able to secure a position in the Tirtha's stable, or even those who just want to see a bit more of the world, to relocate to other estembles, or other tribes. All Wraeththu tribes use horses as their main form of transport, so jobs are easy to find, and any high-ranking hara and tribal leaders who wish to advertise their status to the world must be able to boast of a Gimranish har employed in their stables. This, of course, can work both ways, and the fact that the current Head Groom in the Tigron's stables in Immanion is a member of Merac's extended family is something that never goes unremarked upon by the hara of Scatterstones when discussing such things with hara of other estembles.

Gimranish hara are generally quite small in stature, but due to their hard-working outdoor lifestyle they are very strong for their size compared with other hara, who may or may not spend all day lounging about on silken cushions reading poetry and sighing dramatically. Out in the further reaches of Jaddayoth, should a har ever find himself placing a wager on one of those arm-wrestling competitions which hara who have consumed rather too much of the unusual liquors found there have a habit of engaging in, the smart money would be on the Gimranish har.

Gimranish society is not as strictly regulated as some tribes, and as long as you are prepared to work for your living and respect other hara then you are free to live whatever lifestyle seems appropriate. However, there are a few laws enforced by all the estembles. Horse-stealing, or ill-treating a horse, are considered to be serious crimes and are dealt with accordingly. Punishment usually involves the felon being sentenced to a year or more's indentured labour on one of the estembles or being handed over to the Gelaming for 'Rehabilitation'. Most hara finding themselves in that position are happy to choose the former option.

The Gimranish estembles maintain a symbiotic relationship with satellite communities of human women, who have the necessary skills to process the raw materials that the estembles produce – wool, leather, flax, etc. It is not generally appreciated how much expertise is required to produce yarns and fabrics*, and certainly, in the aftermath of the collapse of human civilisation and the formation of the Wraeththu tribes, knitting socks was fairly low on the list of most hara's priorities. Fortunately, surviving human women were able to keep these skills alive, and they now flourish all over the Wraeththu world, much to the relief of all hara who enjoy wearing nice clothes.

The women of Spinnersholm specialise in spinning, weaving and dyeing flax and linen. These fabrics are sold to the hara of Scatterstones who have them made into clothes by the estemble's tailor and dressmaker, or they can design and create their own clothing and furnishings with them.

There is also a community of women specialising in tanning and processing leather. This community is further to the east, due to the prevailing winds and the smell produced. Good quality leather is essential for the saddles and bridles and harnesses required by the Gimrah, and every other tribe, so this is a prosperous, if rather remote, community.

---

* *Although in many post-apocalyptic and/ or pre-industrial fantasy worlds it is quite common for all the inhabitants to be wearing fine woven, knitted, or embroidered fabrics while eating out of rough wooden bowls and using crude implements and weapons, despite the fact that smelting metal and making ceramics are fairly simple processes compared with growing, spinning, weaving, knitting and sewing fabrics into opulent garments. Or even just decent undies that don't chafe.*

Appendix II
Little-Known Facts about Mojags

Mojags cannot dance, but they can sing very well, and are not reticent about doing so in public. In fact, there is nothing an upstanding Mojag enjoys more after a hard day's looting and pillaging than to get himself down to the local hostelry where recreational singing takes place and join in the vocal fun with a few renditions of his own, usually involving old favourites such as *Stand By Your Har*, *Born To Roon*, and, of course, that sensitive Mojag ballad, *You Broke My Heart So I Fractured Your Jaw*.

This propensity has earned them the undying enmity of the Kalamah. Not because the singing is bad, far from it, but because the Kalamah hara would themselves dearly like to participate too. However they refuse on principle, on the grounds that it would be unthinkable to risk looking foolish in public. No such inhibitions trouble the Mojag, who enjoy the sort of unselfconsciousness that only those who are in possession of a surprisingly large number of empty wine bottles and a body mass noticeably greater than everyhar else present can experience.

It is worth noting that Mojag interpretation of songs tend to be extremely literal, as exemplified by Grukker har Mojag's famous rendition of *Love Will Tear Us Apart* at the Gelaming Tigron's prestigious Natalia Celebration in *ai cara* 39, which is still talked about, for all the wrong reasons.

Mojag reproduction has often been the subject of speculation among other tribes. They appear to make little concession to their feminine side, which would seem to be an obstacle when it comes to taking on the role of hostling, yet their numbers continue to increase. As it happens, Mojags produce harlings in exactly the same way as any other hara, but as soon as the pearl hatches, the harling is given into the care of its father, and never knows the identity of its hostling. If by some terrible social *faux pas* a Mojag finds out the identity of his hostling, he must never acknowledge the relationship. Thus it is that the Mojag way of dealing with the aftermath of an embarrassing sexual encounter is to pretend that it never happened. (and I think we can all relate to that).

As might be expected of such a militaristic society, Mojags are good not only at fighting, but also at taking orders, which was to stand Geth har Mojag in good stead in what was to become a long and fulfilling relationship with Hanu har Gimrah. After many happy years they had a harling together, with Hanu hosting the pearl, as was traditional for a Gimrah anskev, and Geth taking on the role of the harling's primary care-giver. This pleased Hanu because it meant that Geth was finally able to have the experience denied to him with his first son. And it meant Hanu could get down to the stables and spend some time with his horse.

About the Author

Fiona Lane is a wee Scottish wumman who was born near Glasgow and now lives in rural Aberdeenshire. She studied zoology at Aberdeen University, which has so far proven to be of little use in her day-to-day existence, unless you count that whole chicken-keeping thing back in the eighties. She likes hats, gin and going to the pub, and on a good day can combine all three. She has the usual number of children, husbands and cats, a garden that needs weeding, a house that needs tidying, and very little enthusiasm for doing anything constructive about the latter.

On writing Wraeththu Mythos fiction, Fiona says: 'Coming to the end of a book you love is always a bittersweet experience. No matter how slowly you read in order to postpone the inevitable, eventually the last page is reached and all you can do is close the cover, stare at it fiercely, pout, and try to make the story continue by the force of your will alone. This doesn't actually work – I know, I've tried it. 'What *does* work is if you and your fellow stare-and-pouters take matters into your own hands and decide to write the bits of the story which obviously were *there* all the time, but somehow were missed out for some inexplicable reason.

'This doesn't happen with all books. Some lie quietly once they're finished, done and dusted. Some others may leak out at the edges every now and then and require a bit of gentle mopping up. Storm Constantine's Wraeththu series laughed in the face of the law of the Last Page, and tunnelled its way vigorously out through the back cover, allowing the characters contained within to escape into numerous fan fictions, and depositing on the way out, almost as an afterthought, the History of the Twelve Tribes of Jaddayoth.

'These brief descriptions of twelve different tribes contain within each of them the seeds of many more stories, only waiting for a shovelful of writerly manure to get them growing. Into this fertile mix, Storm Constantine herself came along with her Watering Can of Encouragement, sprinkling her advice and wisdom. and thus the Wraeththu Mythos stories blossomed. I, myself, encountered one in the wild not long ago. "Yoo-hoo!" it cried, waving its hooves at me, "Over here! Write me!"

'So I did.'

Wraeththu Mythos Titles

Published by Immanion Press

The Original Wraeththu Books
By Storm Constantine

The Wraeththu Chronicles
The Enchantments of Flesh and Spirit
The Bewitchments of Love and Hate
The Fulfilments of Fate and Desire

The Wraeththu Histories
The Wraiths of Will and Pleasure
The Shades of Time and Memory
The Ghosts of Blood and Innocence

The Alba Sulh Sequence
The Hienama
Student of Kyme
The Moonshawl

Blood, The Phoenix and a Rose
A Raven Bound with Lilies

'Para' Anthologies
Edited by Storm Constantine & Wendy Darling

Paragenesis: Stories of the Dawn of Wraeththu
Para-Imminence: Stories of the Future of Wraeththu
Para Kindred: Enigmas of Wraeththu
Para-Animalia: Creatures of Wraeththu
Para Spectral: Hauntings of Wraeththu

Songs to Earth and Sky: Stories of the Seasons
By Storm Constantine and Others

Other Wraeththu Novels

By popular Mythos writers

Breeding Discontent by Wendy Darling & Bridgette Parker
Terzah's Sons by Victoria Copus
Song of the Sulh by Maria J. Leel
Whispers of the World That Was by E. S. Wynn
Echoes of Light and Static by E. S. Wynn
Voices of the Silicon Beyond by E. S. Wynn

Further details of Wraeththu Mythos and other fiction
can be found on our web site

www.immanion-press.com
info@immanion-press.com

Wraeththu Story Anthologies

The 'Para' series of Wraeththu short story anthologies began with *Paragenesis* in 2010. Four more have followed, and others are planned.

These collections explore different aspects of Wraeththu: their origins, their future, their anomalies, their spiritual affinity with animals, and the ghosts that haunt them. All titles include stories by Storm Constantine & Wendy Darling, as well as contributions from other Mythos writers. Full details on our web site.

www.immanion-press.com

Lightning Source UK Ltd.
Milton Keynes UK
UKHW040946280921
391315UK00001B/266